OUTLAW JUSTICE

A Space Opera Adventure

THE FIRST GUARDIAN: BOOK 1

CHERI BAKER

First edition. September 29, 2023.

978-1-952200-26-7

Designed and produced by Patrick Baker
Cover art by Cheri Baker

230B5BF8B3

When I was a child, my second father taught me that Mars was destined to become the cradle of the universe. He believed our enlightened example would inspire humanity's grand expansion into the stars and bring us into a peaceful, harmonious whole.

Experience taught me he was full of shit.

Humanity is an arrogant species and impossible to control. Any yoke strong enough to bind us together inevitably provokes war.

Journals of the First Guardian
Recovered Fragment. Hellas Detention Center
Selven Beta Historical Society

CHAPTER ONE

Loretta Ryder raised her pulsar to eye level, aiming and firing in one smooth motion. Fifty meters away, through the pink morning haze, a pinpoint of white light appeared at the center of the targeting stone. Three quarters of a second later it exploded in a puff of dust and gravel.

Her trainees snapped to attention as she turned. They were a mixed group, ranging in age from seventeen to seventy-six. Half were still chewing their way through the Diplomatic Corps' foundational curricula while the rest were either looking to maintain their pulsar certification — a requirement for anyone assigned a security rotation — or hard-core shot jocks eager for some range time.

The latter category included Risha Shay. Loretta's former mentor was her oldest trainee by at least two decades, but her enthusiasm dwarfed that of even the greenest recruits. Risha's impish grin flashed through her helmet whenever she caught Loretta's eye.

Could Risha sense her nervousness? Was that why she kept smiling? Either that, or someone had shared the new lesson plans. The Diplomatic Corps was as leaky as an antique hab suit. Everyone knew it. Everyone pretended otherwise.

Either way, it was nice to have an ally in class.

The shooting range was nestled into a low valley sixteen clicks from the capital city's southern gate. The area had been deemed useless by geologists and biologists alike, freeing it up for recreative purposes. Loretta's gaze caught on the jagged line where distant red rock cliffs met the sky's edge. Sol had left a faint blue glow in her wake, a luminous line of contrast that looked like it had been painted across the cliff tops by a child's finger. When it came to waxing poetic about the beauty of Mars, most artists turned their attention to Epiphany's soaring, gold-tinted domes and dramatic blue spires, but to Loretta, no amount of human ingenuity could ever compare to the unspoiled, desolate beauty of the Martian outback.

Every botanist, biologist, and geologist on the planet was dedicated to the vision of a lush Mars, a livable biosphere with a breathable atmosphere and a stable web of organic life. As admirable as that was, Loretta couldn't help but hope the future generations would remember *this* Mars, wild and mountainous, with epic vistas that went further than any eye could see.

Her home. Humanity's first foothold among the stars.

She turned her attention to the class and held her weapon muzzle up. "At ease, everyone. Take a good look. We're working with a standard issue pulsar today. Don't let its simple appearance fool you. Your pulsar is a sophisticated piece of defense technology, designed to protect lives and bring down threats with efficient, rapid, and non-lethal force."

She moved the plastic thumbwheel one click clockwise.

"Knock the wheel to toggle between pulses. You can stun, push, or punish your target as is situationally appropriate." She pivoted her wrist, turning the butt of the handle forward. With her gloved finger, she drew a line beneath the wide muzzle. "The pulsar's guidance system interfaces with your forearm shield for wrist stabilization and trajectory correction. Once you've painted your target, hold the trigger until the pulse releases. Be certain of your shot. You have only a fraction of a second to change your mind."

She looked from student to student, checking for understanding. Mostly she saw eagerness and a certain impatience to get started — always a good sign — but Cadet Tina Brown's mouth was flapping like a windsock in a sandstorm. Tina had set her com to proximity mode, but the stony-faced expression on Cadet Nguyen's face made it clear who she was yammering at. He was plainly annoyed, but Janus was a good egg and not the type to get his teammate into trouble.

"Tina." Loretta clicked her pulsar into safe mode and dropped her hand, letting the weapon dangle. "Do you have a question?"

Tina's mouth moved soundlessly until she remembered to switch her com to wideband. "No questions, Captain. I read the manual, and we all passed the simulator already. I mean, how hard can it be?"

Loretta permitted herself a soft snort over the com. Youthful overconfidence was one thing; ignoring the lecture to blather to your teammate was something else. She holstered her pulsar by placing it against the mag-grip on her thigh. "Let's find out, shall we?" She directed the class toward the first set of targeting stones. "Line up, everyone. Let's see what you've got!"

Before long, a familiar popping sound filled Loretta's ears. Targeting stones were reddish ovals of machined waste rock with a compressed gravel sphere packed into the center. When struck dead-center on *push*, the compacted gravel core exploded in a satisfying burst of kinetic energy. Loretta switched her com from wideband to proximity and went up and down the line, offering suggestions and correcting posture. She loved the way their eyes lit up when they hit a target for the first time.

That moment when knowledge became understanding.

How could an arbiter call themselves a defender of Mars without understanding, in *truth*, the connection between pulling a trigger and hitting a target? Simulations were helpful, to a point, but understanding a pulsar happened at the level of physicality. Until you'd experienced firing in real conditions, you couldn't do more than grasp at the concepts. Loretta felt intimately the bright silver line of mastery that ran from her trigger finger, through her arm, and directly into her heart, the organ that knew what was just and what was unjust. When your aim was true...

Was there anything more satisfying?

Today, she hoped to give her students that same feeling.

When every stone had been burst and the targeting stands stood empty like rows of upright black claws, she switched to wideband. Predictably, her students were looking pretty pleased with themselves. "Any problems so far?"

Most shook their heads. Janus raised his hand. He was tall and wiry with earnest brown eyes and a zig-zag mop of black hair that fell attractively over his forehead. He must have spent a fair amount of time styling the fringe to keep it out of his eyes. Tina looked up at him, fluttering her blue-tinted eyelashes. Her mouth turned sulky when he didn't seem to notice.

Ah, to be seventeen and endlessly horny. I don't miss my time in the cadet wing. At all.

"I keep getting shocks through my forearm shield," Janus said, rubbing his wrist, frowning a little. "It stings."

Tina elbowed him. "That means your aim sucks ass."

And now she's negging him! What a charmer.

Her limited store of patience depleted, Loretta shot Tina a look that invited her to kindly shut the fuck up. Tina dropped her smirk and straightened her shoulders.

That was better.

"If your wrist stings, it means your stabilizer is working overtime. Slow down and steady your aim before you paint the target. That should help." She gave him an encouraging smile. "And don't worry. My first class, I went home with bruises all the way up my arm. You'll be surprised how quickly you improve. Speaking of which, let's try something different."

She directed the trainees to a second set of targets, only these were half as far away. Even without the aid of helmet magnification, Loretta could see shear marks on the stones from where they'd been cut.

Risha shielded her eyes with her hand. "We're working at close range? Why?"

A flutter of excitement sped through Loretta's body as she tapped a command into her teaching console. After many careful arguments and two full rounds of appeal, the education subcommittee had finally given her what she'd asked for. "I'll answer that question in a moment, Ombudswoman. Let's repeat the same drill at half distance. Center fire, straight down the barrel. Remember, I want to see your mark at the center of each stone. We'll do synchronized fire this time. Ready, aim, fire!"

Twelve fingers pulled twelve triggers. Two stones exploded. Another toppled out of its stand, singed black on the outer edge. The rest didn't so much as wobble.

Muttered curses competed with one another through Loretta's helmet speakers.

"Weapons safe! Holster your pulsars. Tell me. What was different this time?"

"I sucked worse than Janus!" Tina moaned.

"My shot went wide," another cadet complained.

A tiny smile played at the corners of Risha's mouth. No doubt she'd figured it out, but she wouldn't deprive the cadets of their chance to shine. "There must have been something wrong with my gun, Captain. I'm normally an excellent shot."

Loretta glanced at two of the veteran arbiters. Darren and Mary had both hit their targets on the first try. "Any theories?"

Darren considered the question for a long moment before answering. "It felt normal to me."

"For me too." Mary shifted her weight from one foot to the other, then back again. She might look like she was fidgeting, but as an old hand, she knew it helped to keep your muscles warm when shooting. Feet should be mobile, always.

"When did you two first complete your pulsar certification?" Loretta asked.

"Twenty-five years ago," Mary said in her soft-spoken, melodious voice.

"Twenty-two for me." Darren shot Mary a tiny smirk. "You know, back when sandworms still roamed the outback."

Loretta chuckled at the reference. Darren was raising two kids with his wife Alicia. No doubt he'd read them *The Sandworms of Cassini Crater* when they were small, just like her parents had read it to her.

She gestured at Risha with an open hand. "Ombudswoman Shay is on the right track. Before this last volley, I turned your guidance systems off. Darren and Mary, congratulations. You are both *very fine* shots."

Risha looked ruefully at her holstered gun. "Apparently I'm slipping."

Loretta grinned. "No worries, Ombusdwoman! We're going to practice until you don't need any stinking guidance system. Only after we've proved to ourselves that we don't need it will we turn it back on."

Janus raised his hand. "I don't get it. Isn't the whole point of tech to make our lives safer and easier?"

"That's an excellent question, and one I encourage you to chew on. Are you taking ethics this quarter?"

He nodded.

"Good! You'll need to come to your own conclusions. But because you asked, I'll share my personal view. When it comes to public safety, I'd argue that we must be, above all, self-sufficient. A smart weapon can aid us in that goal. If you have a concussion from a fall, or if you're sprinting on uneven terrain, you'll want those advanced features. But if we rely on technology, we become dependent upon it. And if technology fails, as it sometimes does, we must be prepared to do our duty without it. It would be foolish to delegate our responsibilities to a machine."

Loretta watched them chew the ideas over. They'd been told this was an easy course, one that would earn them development points to apply toward their first posting. Now she was changing the rules, making the lesson harder, expecting more.

"It feels good to do it on my own," Janus said, breaking the silence. "I don't know why, but it does."

"Do you want to try again?" she asked the class.

Their eager assent was everything she'd hoped for, and she set them loose on the remaining targets. Gradually, their groans of defeat were buried in whoops of celebration. Targeting stones burst into puffs of gravel and dust. With every small explosion, the students cheered one another on.

Tina struggled for longer than most, but after a bit of coaching, she hit her target too. Loretta held out her hand for a high five. "You've got it! Keep going. And don't forget to breathe."

Loretta stood back and watched, her hopes rising like an atmospheric survey balloon. This, more than anything else, was what she loved to see as an instructor. Her students were working hard today, not only because it might result in a better job, or praise, or a better grade. They were learning it was possible to become the best version of themselves.

For too long, the citizens of Epiphany had been treating the corps as a fallback option, or at best, a respectable way to serve when you weren't brilliant enough to join a scientific team. They were dead wrong about that, but the worst part was how that attitude had seeped through the organization itself.

Mars was busy training bureaucrats when it needed true believers, guardians devoted to the ideals that had brought humanity to the stars in the first place.

Janus jogged over, his pulsar holstered safely at his side. "Captain, can we move the targets further out? I want to see if I can hit one at range."

"Why not? You're looking good out there." She sent a ping through her com to grab everyone's attention. "Weapons safe! Cadet Nguyen believes you're ready for more. Do you agree?"

She grinned at their eager cheers. "Let's make it happen. Form a line and reset the stones on firing range alpha. On the double! Move!"

Loretta watched as Risha set her targeting stone into place. The older woman's brow shone with sweat, but she was keeping pace with the others. Loretta tapped Risha's com as she jogged by. "May I have a word, Ombudswoman?"

The rest of the class continued to set up the firing range, their breathing labored. Loretta felt a flutter of amusement at the sight of cadets picking up speed to pass one another, showing off, looking to prove who was at the top of the stack. In contrast, Darren and Mary had settled into a fast walk, carrying a targeting stone in each hand, pacing themselves, getting more done with less effort.

Risha fingered her wrist control, sending a cool jet of air over her face. "I'll feel this tomorrow. Working at a desk, you forget how damn heavy these suits are."

"Well? What do you think?"

Her mentor's breath, warmed by brisk exercise, fogged her face shield, but her suit's environmental controls quickly cleared the moisture. Risha rolled her narrow shoulders back and shook out her legs, one at a time. "You've got the gift. I admit, when Marcus asked me to hand over the reins, I wasn't thrilled when he offered his ward as my replacement. A twenty-year-old, no less! You were a crack shot, but that didn't mean you were ready to be an instructor. Although you proved him right, didn't you? I couldn't be prouder."

Risha's praise warmed her from the inside out. Like every arbiter, her primary duty was to her home district, administering the Martian code and overseeing security for the citizens she was responsible for. Yet these part-time teaching duties had enriched her life in ways she'd never expected. In her five years running this course, her students had taught her as much as she'd taught them. Risha understood that better than most.

"Coming from you, that's high praise indeed." Loretta smiled. "How's life at the university?"

Risha's nose crinkled. "Complicated. They send me the cases no one else wants to touch. Usually, that means brats with well-connected parents who somehow believe they're above the code."

"But the council backs you, right?"

She barked a harsh laugh. "Every damn time! It's not difficult so much as it's repetitive. Have you ever worked with academics?"

"I'm assigned to forty-two beta."

Risha's pale forehead furrowed. "Botany?"

"Food sciences," Loretta said. "We're not at a university proper, but I'm responsible for the safety and security of two thousand PhDs. and their research assistants. They think that because they're experts in pea proteins, or whatever it is they're nerding out over, that they're automatically experts in everything else too. Including my job."

"Welcome to Epiphany." Risha chuckled. "We're here to serve the scientific interest, and don't you think the lab coats will let us forget it. But I assume you didn't invite me over for small talk."

Loretta glanced out at the field. Following Mary and Darren's example, her students had formed a circular route, picking up targeting stones in each hand, speed-walking them to the range, and placing them in the racks with near-mechanical precision.

"What do you think about the new lesson?"

Despite the butterflies having a dance party in her stomach, Loretta kept her expression neutral. Anyone who knew Risha understood not to ask questions unless they were prepared for a complete and honest answer. No matter how bitter or unwelcome the news might taste, she'd give it to you straight.

Thankfully, Risha's smile portended good news.

"I like it. You're right about the need to keep ourselves sharp. Classroom simulations can only approximate reality. But don't forget, we old-timers were thrilled when the pulsars came out. They're idiot proof."

She was right. Anyone could hit a target at fifty meters

using a standard issue pulsar. Once a target was painted with light, aided by the internal guidance system, the energy pulse tracked to that point unless the shooter lifted their finger off the trigger before the safety delay ended. "To avoid mistakes", the training manual claimed.

"I get that," Loretta said. "But what if someone hacked our weapons server? Or what if the guidance system fails during a crucial moment? Would we have the skills to defend our people? Or would every arbiter just stand around with their thumbs up their asses, waiting for a software patch?"

Risha barked a laugh at the imagery. "I hear you. I do! But remember, it's our values that keep us safe, not the strength of our weapons systems."

Loretta bit her lip. "So my superiors keep telling me."

Risha looked pained. "Lore, I want you to be more careful with what you bring to the ombuds. You're ambitious, and that's not a bad thing. But you aren't doing yourself any favors with—"

"Help! We need help!" Panicked voices competed over the com.

"What in the hell was that?"

"Did she just—"

Loretta turned, sweeping her gaze across the field. Her students were clustering near the supply shed. Someone was down. Someone else — Mary? — was waving her arms frantically.

"Captain!" Mary shouted.

Loretta sprinted, pressing hard off her heels, using every bit of momentum to propel herself forward.

The shed door was wide open. Pallets of targeting stones waited inside, and more stones were scattered on the crumbly red soil where they'd been dropped. Her students were staring down at the ground, horrified.

Loretta pushed her way into the crowd. Her stomach collapsed into a black hole when she saw who had fallen.

Janus.

"What happened?" she demanded.

Darren's mouth tightened. "Tina shot him."

Cadet Nguyen was flat on his back, staring up at the hazy pink sky. A spiderweb crack marred his face shield, and there was an ugly black burn on his chest, mere centimeters from his environmental control unit.

After a heart wrenching delay during which only the faint sound of the wind came over the coms, Janus stirred. "What? Did I..." His gloved hand went up to his helmet, but another hand gently grasped it and put it down at his side. Mary was suddenly there, kneeling next to him. Loretta dropped down too, lightly touching Janus's shoulder to still him as Mary pulled data from his suit to hers.

Right. She's medic trained.

Crows' feet crinkled at the corners of Mary's soft brown eyes. "The seals held, thank Sol. MedStar shows a concussion and first-degree burns. We can move him."

That should have been a relief. Somehow, it wasn't. Only a few minutes earlier, Janus had been smiling, learning, even taking the lead. Now, he was frightened and pale, bewildered like a child who'd been slapped by someone he trusted. She watched as he tried to master his emotions, to appear stoic, if only so his team wouldn't worry.

Fury flowed through Loretta's body like waste heat from a reactor. Tina could have killed him. Out here, in the outback, the difference between life and death was a few millimeters of high-tech fabric and the life support system that powered it.

Loretta blinked the sting out of her eyes. Her chest smoldered. Fists knotted. Her voice felt strangely thick as she said, "I'm *so* sorry, Cadet. This never should have happened. That's on me."

That stupid little idiot had hurt *Janus*, the sweet kid who'd been eager to push himself, to learn! Would he do the same thing next time?

Trauma left a mark as real as any physical wound.

She squeezed his hand. "Be still. You're going to be okay."

Darren had Tina's pulsar in his hand. He held it up, showing the position of the thumb wheel, his mouth set in a grim line. "She had it set to punish, Captain. If she'd hit his control unit..."

Loretta forced a smile and pressed gently on Janus's unwounded shoulder. "Does anything hurt? Wiggle your fingers and toes for me."

He did so. "My head stings."

She glanced at Mary.

"Neuro looks good."

Loretta struggled to keep her voice even. "Excellent. Let's get Cadet Nguyen to the hospital. Risha, grab a patch kit. I don't want to take any chances with that helmet. Mary, choose two helpers and move Janus to trover number one. Everyone else, pack up. We're going home."

Risha was at Loretta's side. She held out a hand, palm down. "Yes, but—"

Loretta brushed past. She'd make sure this never, *ever* happened again. Not on her watch, nor on anyone else's. "I'll be right back."

"Captain Ryder!"

Risha's voice sounded very far away. Tina had been standing apart from the group, looking sorry for herself. Now, she backed into the supply shed, bumping into the black corrugated wall. "I'm sorry! I didn't mean to—"

Loretta's hand caught Tina's shoulder and sent her flying sideways onto the hardscrabble ground. With one quick drop of her knee, she pinned her. "What in the ever-loving *fuck* were you thinking?"

"You're hurting me!"

"No. I'm restraining you. But I wouldn't expect someone as reckless, as arrogant, as profoundly *stupid* as you are to understand the difference." Loretta clamped one hand on Tina's shoulder. "I suggest you explain yourself, right now, because I have half a mind to pack up the class and let you walk back."

Tina squirmed. "You can't do that! I'd die!"

Loretta shrugged. "Oh, I'm sure there's a spare oxygen pack around here somewhere." She shifted her kneecap to the left and put pressure on the relay bus that fed data to Tina's helmet display. The readouts inside blinked red. Alarms sounded. Harmless error messages, but Tina didn't know that.

I'd expect this kind of reckless, asshat behavior from one of those Free Mars activists. But here? In the corps? I wish sandworms were real! Would they bother to eat her, though? This level of stupidity might be catching.

"I didn't mean to hurt him!" Tina's breaths came faster. "The training manual said our suits protect against pulsar blasts. It was a joke! I figured I'd just knock him down or something."

Loretta released her. She stood and brushed the dust off her legs, letting every bit of disgust she felt flow into her voice. "Safety gear can fail. You know this. Working in atmo is doubly dangerous. You know that too. Yet you chose the highest, most dangerous setting and took aim at your teammate. You put his life in danger, for laughs. The correct response to seeing a friend in safety gear is *not* to shoot them point blank in the chest for shits and giggles."

"I didn't know! The manual—"

"Bullshit. Contrary to what you might think, the work of the Diplomatic Corps is not a game, safety is *not* a joke, and our organization is not open to people like you."

Tina scrambled to a sitting position. "But I—"

"Zip it. You're done." Loretta turned and headed for the trover, where the others were working together to load Janus safely inside.

She forced a deep breath to calm her pounding heart. With effort, she loosened her fists and unknotted her shoulders. In all her years teaching, she'd seen a certain amount of arrogance and plenty of beginner mistakes. But this?

It was unforgivable.

Tina's footsteps chased her from behind. "I'm sorry! I'll take remedial classes. I'll pay the fine. I'll apologize!"

Loretta wheeled to face her. "You're not hearing me. You are *done*. Go home, pack up your things, turn in your uniform, and if you happen to see me walking up the corridor, I suggest you turn around and find another route."

Angry tears streamed down Tina's face. "You can't eject me. You don't have the right."

Loretta raised an eyebrow and recited the words that every recruit learned on their first day in the Diplomatic Corps.

"Justice has been provided in line with the Martian code. You have the right to file an appeal. Should you do so, arbitration services will be provided by your home office."

CHAPTER TWO

Travis Wells rubbed his damp, dark hair with a towel and tossed it overhand at the open wall hamper. The metallic hatch slid closed with a tiny burp.

"Pardon me!" Loretta's HomeBot said.

He ignored the joke. HomeBots came installed with three standard voice profiles, all equally pleasant and familiar, yet somehow, Loretta had made hers sound faintly embarrassed. And just a few minutes earlier, her shower had whistled appreciatively at him while he'd soaped up.

Was everything a joke to her? Sometimes, it felt like it.

He grabbed his gray-blue uniform slacks off the back of the sofa. Loretta was in the kitchen, rummaging in a drawer. "Those janky off-market mods will brick your system," he cautioned. "And I'm serious about today's hearing. I don't understand how you can be so blasé. How do you know you're not walking into an ambush? You can't keep doing whatever you want and assuming it will all work out."

Loretta stepped around the kitchen counter and into the living room. She shoved a breakfast bar at him. "Try it. It's a new strawberry-date hybrid the geeks are working on. They say it tastes better than the last batch." She nibbled hers cautiously, then nodded. "Not bad! And anyway, I'm not blasé. I'm prepared. There's a difference." She swept her long reddish-brown hair back, separating it into three plaits by feel, then braiding it with nimble fingers. "Put on your shirt, why don't you? I need to finish getting ready, and that cute bod of yours is distracting me."

Travis reached for his undershirt and slipped it on. Loretta hated accepting help, even from him. Hinting hadn't worked, so it was best to handle things like she would, head on, taking no prisoners.

Loretta was going to be Loretta. Still, he had to try.

He plucked a hair elastic off the coffee table and handed it to her. "Tina Brown is Councilor Sapari's granddaughter. She's well connected, and that's why I'm worried. Aren't you? I mean — what happened to your whole 'I want to be the youngest councilor in Martian history' thing?"

She glanced over, apparently caught off guard.

Yeah, I thought that might get your attention.

"I've been kicking ass and taking names since the moment I was commissioned. And I'll continue to do so. Although," she shot him a rather sweet smile. "I hope you'll give me a run for my money. Remember how much fun it was when we were in the cadet wing? You pushed me, and I pushed you. You're only a few thousand advancement points behind me, and—"

He shook his head. "You know I don't care about things like that. It's just..."

Her forehead furrowed. "What is it? You can tell me."

Well, she asked for it.

"It's just that for someone who wants political appointment, you have a shockingly naïve take on the power structure. You can't eject whoever you want and strut around like the cock of the walk, assuming you'll win because you were right."

For a second, he thought she might actually listen. He could see her thinking it through, trying to see his side. But just as quickly as the moment arrived, it slipped away.

"You're cute when you lecture," she teased. "Did you know that? When the time comes, you should take up a position at a university." She held out her hands like she was highlighting a marquee. "Travis explains politics."

Looking away to hide his disappointment, he glanced out the habitat's big, oval window. It faced the city center, showcasing Epiphany's iconic blue-onyx spires, representing the centers of science, commerce, and government. The narrow buildings shot straight up, topped with curved, blade-like shapes that scraped the pinkish gray sky. Morning sunlight cast golden highlights on hundreds of domes and habitat towers. They spread outward from the city center, almost as far as the eye could see.

His gaze landed on her desk, piled with junk at the back of the room. Board games, toys, and a random smattering of sports equipment that looked ready to topple. He'd hung her uniform over the back of the chair while she was showering. "I pressed your clothes. You'll want to look your best today."

Loretta raised a sardonic eyebrow. "Would you like to brush my teeth, too?"

Loretta regretted her quip as soon as it escaped her throat. Without meaning to, she'd hurt his feelings. Again.

Travis Wells was a man of a thousand small routines. Each decision he made fit neatly into the next like a nested programmatic statement. Like the way he'd laid out his clothing the night before, checking each item for imperfections and placing the garments in reverse order, underpants on top, outerwear on the bottom. Sometimes, she messed with him just to interrupt his flow. As much as she adored him, and she did — especially that diligent, careful mind of his — it was hard not to toss a little whimsy into his day.

Sometimes, she missed the mark.

She and Travis had surprised almost everyone by becoming lovers. Themselves, too. During their time in the cadet wing, she'd accused him of having a stick up his ass the size of Venus. He'd shot back that her ego was massive enough to consume not only Venus, but every planet in the known system. Yet in competing for the top slot in their graduating class (they'd tied) they'd developed a grudging respect for each other, and in the years that followed, their slow-blossoming friendship had become something else.

Opposites might attract, but Loretta knew it was their commonalities that kept them together. On the surface, Travis Wells was everything she wasn't. Fastidious. Patient. Irritatingly humble, even when any sane person would have seized their moment in the spotlight. He drove her crazy, insisting on seeing every problem from all angles, withholding judgment until the last possible moment. But at the same time...

He was hard-working, intelligent, and sincere. And if he challenged her sometimes, well, she could give as good as she took. She hoped in time they'd find their balance, exchanging strengths and bolstering each other's weaknesses.

Even when sheltered from harsh elements, everything seemed to grow slowly in Martian soil. Breakthroughs took time. And perhaps that was as true for human hearts as it was for scientific discovery.

I'll be patient with him, she thought.

Even though he was only trying to help, it was hard not to feel... parented whenever Travis stayed overnight. She'd been on her own since she was thirteen, and she wasn't looking to be told how to live.

No matter how much she loved him.

She reached for his hand. "I'm sorry. What I should have said was *thank you*." She activated the big viewscreen in front of the sofa and pulled up her notes with a gesture. Text flowed down it at a comfortable reading rate.

When he didn't respond, she paused the scroll.

"Look. Tina's appeal is standard stuff, and the code's on my side. That's what matters, right? Not who a person's parents are. Isn't that what we teach?"

"Of course! But—"

"Well, are we teaching lies?" She raised an eyebrow and met his gaze evenly. "Is it all just bullshit?"

Most people would look away, Travis thought, basking in the harsh light of Loretta's sharp-eyed gaze. Her trademark intensity had a way of making people uncomfortable. Not just their peers, but their teachers too. He'd never felt that way, not even when they'd been at odds with one another. What some saw as arrogant bluster, he knew to be something rare and beautiful.

Loretta was the only person he'd ever met who lived in full alignment with her values. She had a good heart, and sometimes her powerful sense of right and wrong overrode everything else.

Even when it got her into trouble, he couldn't help but love her for it. Who was he to dampen her spark? It was what made her... her.

"No," he said, smiling now, relishing the way her confidence ignited his own. "We don't lie. We teach to our highest aspirations, and then we seek to fulfill them. Sometimes, we fuck up. But we keep on reaching."

She leaned in for a soft kiss that tasted like strawberries. "Exactly. *In Mars I trust.* That's why I have no reason to fear doing the right thing. Still," she lowered her voice to a confessional tone, "I like it when you worry about me. It makes a woman feel special."

You are, he thought. Knowing such a tender expression might spook her, he held it inside, where it would keep.

"You and Dad are two peas in a pod," he teased, reaching for the uneaten half of his breakfast. "I must have been absent from class the day they handed out endless optimism."

Her freckled nose crinkled. "Can you not call him 'Dad' when we're together? It makes this thing we have seem..."

"Kinky?" he suggested hopefully.

She laughed! "I was going to say creepy. But sure. Let your freak flag fly, Trav."

"Apologies." He raised his hands in surrender. "I dropped a pronoun. You and *my* dad are two peas in a pod. That's probably why he thinks you hang the moons. I, on the other hand, still have a lot of growing up to do."

She curled her fingers inside his hand.

"I love Marcus. And I'll forever be grateful that he spoke for me after my parents died. But I'm glad I never lived under the same roof as you two when I was a kid."

"Because that would make us..." he waggled his eyebrows. "Kinky-creepy?"

"No!" She shook her head. "Because there's nothing like living with someone you admire to shatter all your illusions."

"So I should take the burping hamper as a warning?"

For once, she didn't respond to his teasing with more of the same. "Of course it's easier for your dad and I to get along. He doesn't have to deal with my nonsense on a daily basis, and I don't have to live up to his lofty expectations. I'm just a wild orphan child, remember? You're his only son. He puts all his hopes for the future into you. It's not fair."

"Why not?"

"Because they aren't your hopes! They're his. And having kids doesn't give you a two-fer."

"He only wants what's best for me." He smiled when she leaned close for another kiss. Her breath smelled like industrial food paste, fruity with hints of bitter vitamin, so he crinkled his nose. "Thanks for the sleepover, Lore. And about your hearing—"

Her finger touched his lips before he could finish the thought. "You're right. About everything. And I should finish getting ready. Aren't you due for your shift soon?"

He took the hint and stood, collecting the rest of his belongings. "Okay then. We'll connect later. Who's representing you today?"

Loretta's attention was back on her screen. She waved him off. "I'll tell you the whole story at dinner. Promise."

CHAPTER THREE

Loretta stood at the front of the hearing room and waited for the proceedings to begin. Compared to the modest facilities of forty-two beta, this space had been designed to impress. The room itself was shaped like a white half-bubble and a soft glow illuminated the walls. A colorful stone mosaic depicting Sol's system covered the floor, with the path of each elliptical orbit spun out in long brass threads. The three senior arbiters sat at a high, arc-shaped table before the petitioners. In the gallery at the back of the room, a dozen individuals waited their turn to speak, sitting at long, high-backed benches that curved along the wall.

Ombudswoman Anis Gregory had taken the center chair. Her glossy black hair was piled high in a triple bun atop her elegant head, bound with metallic bands reminiscent of the artwork on the floor. Her pale gray robes, the traditional uniform of arbiters administering justice, flowed gracefully from her narrow shoulders. She flicked through the evidence on her tablet with the practiced ease of someone who'd been through this song and dance a million times before. Her peers, granite-faced Tom Oberlin and the soft-spoken, ageless Michaela Sanchez, sat quietly on either side of her.

"Are you ready to begin, Captain Ryder?" Gregory asked.

"I am."

"And you, Captain Hamid?"

Tina's representative stood alone, looking dapper in his uniform and well-trimmed black beard. Tina hadn't bothered to show. Probably she wasn't keen on being publicly humiliated. Either that or she had a busy schedule of fucking things up and making excuses.

Janus Nguyen had suffered greenstick fractures on two ribs. The burns weren't life threatening, but despite his attempts to be bad-ass, Loretta could tell he was still in pain when she'd stopped by the med center. And how many times had Tina Brown come to visit her "friend"?

Zero. Not a single visit logged at the desk.

Loretta accepted the ombuds' scrutiny serenely. These three were the cream of the crop of the Diplomatic Corps, chosen to administer the code at the appellate level. They were well along the path she was traveling, and as such, they represented her future.

Aspiring arbiters spent three years in the cadet wing, learning the code, studying philosophy and law, preparing their minds and bodies for the challenges ahead. Epiphany was divided into ten quadrants, each with a presiding trio of ombuds, and quadrants were split further into districts, each one assisted by a small team of arbiters and their captain.

And because not all matters could be resolved locally, the ombuds chose from their ranks their seven most honorable to serve on the Martian council, six leaders dedicated to governing in line with Martian values, plus their chief, authorized to break ties.

At twenty-four, Loretta had been the youngest arbiter promoted to captain in the history of the corps, and she was only getting started. Someday, she'd leave her mark on Martian history just as surely as any good scientist did. Marcus Wells himself had been elected to the council in his early forties.

She'd beat his record.

More than that, she'd make him proud. All of them, really. In the wake of her parents' deaths, Epiphany had scooped her up and given her a home, an education, and a purpose worth striving for. She'd spend the rest of her life repaying that gift.

Mars is just, she reminded herself, steadying her nerves as Ombudswoman Gregory's sharp gaze landed on her. *Good luck getting that anywhere else in the universe.*

"Let the record show we are here today for administrative review of case number 239064. Captain Ryder, you say you're ready to begin, but I don't see your representative."

"I'm representing myself today."

Gregory's mouth pinched. "Are you certain that's wise?"

Ombudsman Oberlin tapped his tablet with a meaty finger. He was a heavyset man with unruly gray hair that he'd unsuccessfully tried to tame with pomade. "In the absence of appropriate representation, I recommend we table today's hearing until representation can be secured."

Something scraped behind Loretta. The sound of a woman clearing her throat followed. She caught a flash of surprise on the ombuds' faces.

Shit. What could surprise those three?

Councilor Tamatha Clarke made a soft *tsk-tsk* noise as she advanced slowly through the waiting area. The audience had hardly been paying attention earlier. Now, they sat up straighter. One woman leaned close to her companion to whisper.

"Captain Ryder is no cadet, Tom. She's well appraised of her rights under the code. Given the gravity of the situation, I recommend we proceed without delay." Clarke inclined her head, then took her seat in the front row of the gallery.

Loretta blinked. Twice. Council members weren't in the habit of bursting into mid-level hearing rooms. If anything, they were practically silent on matters of everyday law. Still, she wasn't about to look this gift horse in the mouth.

"Thank you, Councilor," she said.

Ombudswoman Gregory didn't seem to like this, but when no one else spoke, she nodded. With a flick of her finger, she sent a section of text from her tablet onto the wall closest to Loretta.

"During a live fire exercise, Cadet Tina Brown fired a pulsar blast at her teammate, Janus Nguyen, resulting in moderate injuries. Arbiter Darren McManus secured the cadet's weapon. Captain Ryder, after attending to the emergent medical needs of the injured cadet, ejected Cadet Tina Brown from the corps. Is this substantively correct?"

"It is." Loretta said.

"Accepted without argument," Tina's rep responded.

Ombudswoman Gregory made a notation in her file. "What is the basis of Ms. Brown's appeal, Captain Hamid?"

"This wasn't an act of violence, Ombudswoman. It was an honest mistake arising from a misunderstanding. According to the training manual used in Captain Ryder's class, Cadet Brown had no reason to believe her teammate would be injured. Was this a disciplinary matter? Certainly. But we don't eject promising young leaders from the—" He paused. "Captain Ryder. I'm sorry. Did you have something you need to say at this time?"

Loretta froze. Had she snorted? Out loud? It was hardly her fault. The notion of Tina Brown as a "future leader" of Mars was laughable, to say the least.

Lock it down, Lore.

"No, representative. Please continue."

"As I was saying, we don't eject promising cadets for making mistakes. We appeal this decision on the basis that Captain Ryder overstepped her authority."

He'd chosen *that* defense? Out of all his options, it was the simplest to refute.

"Your response, Captain Ryder?"

"The code is clear in these matters. Any commanding officer who determines a cadet has willfully endangered the life of a Martian citizen is authorized to eject them from the program. On that day, and on that field, I was Ms. Brown's commanding officer."

Hamid frowned. "This was not willful endangerment. To meet that criteria, Cadet Brown would have—"

Loretta barked a laugh. "She shot him point blank in the chest, my dude. How much more evidence do you require? Would she have needed to crack open his helmet with a screwdriver?"

Hamid shot a pleading look at the ombuds. "If the captain could refrain from calling me 'my dude'? A young woman's career is at stake. I hold that—"

"Hold whatever you like. It won't change the facts. The *former* cadet proved herself a danger to her team. To all of us. These decisions are painful, I agree, but we're not depriving Ms. Brown of anything she's earned. She's free to pursue other employment. Cadet Nguyen is on the mend, and to his credit, he hasn't requested criminal charges. He's ready to put this unfortunate incident behind him." She shot Hamid a more respectful smile this time. "My advice? Tell your client to take the win. She wouldn't have been happy with us, anyway."

"Why not?" he asked.

"The corps doesn't reward stupidity."

"Captain Ryder—"

Loretta put a finger to her chin and tilted her head.

"Maybe she should get a job at the AR-cade? They'll let you shoot anyone you want in the combat simulator. I hear they give you a free meal each shift." She looked around the room with a smirk. "I mean — Who among us would say no to a free cheeseburger after a long day of poor-ass decision making?"

"Ombudswoman," Hamid blurted. "I *must* insist—"

"Enough." Gregory raised her hand. "Captain Ryder, rein in the verbiage. Let's let Captain Hamid finish his sentences, shall we?"

"If I may." Councilor Clarke's dry voice held a note of amusement. "I wonder if both our captains are missing the bigger concern at play."

The ombuds exchanged worried glances. There was nothing that prevented them from accepting comments from observers in the gallery. It was just that it rarely happened.

Loretta turned, curious. Clarke looked faintly embarrassed, a strange expression for someone known for her quiet dignity and grace under pressure. "Apologies, captains. I'm afraid I've spoken out of turn. I won't interrupt again."

"No objection here." Loretta shot Hamid a look that dared him to complain. When he didn't, Clarke spoke again.

"What about mitigating factors? Have you considered them, Captain Ryder?"

"She *shot* her teammate."

"Yes. That much is clear. And I share your alarm. But why did she do so?"

"Does it matter?" Loretta asked, taking a more deferential tone. "If someone shoots me, on purpose, it seems clear that they're a danger not only to me, but to everyone else too. It would be negligent to put Ms. Brown in a position of authority after this."

"Her emotions got the better of her," Clarke said.

"That's a generous interpretation. But I'll concede the point. I saw no evidence Ms. Brown was hateful or malicious."

"I'm curious to what extent your emotions played a role in this situation, Captain."

Loretta's face prickled with heat. "If you're asking if I was angry, the answer is yes. I'm protective of my trainees. But—"

Clarke held up a hand. "Take a moment if you need to calm yourself, dear. We're not in a hurry. Truth is a patient thing."

Perhaps Travis had been right. Councilor Sapari knew he couldn't sail into his granddaughter's hearing to throw shade, and he might have sent a colleague to do it for him. Still, Tamatha Clarke's presence made little sense, even in that context. Council members were nothing if not discreet. Why risk the damage to her reputation?

Hamid's forehead furrowed as he read something on his tablet. "Ombuds, Cadet Brown decided to test the hab suit's defenses only *after* Captain Ryder deactivated the safety system on the pulsars." He glanced at Loretta, confident now. "You set an example, Captain. Your recruit followed it."

"That's a foolish justification," Loretta replied. "It's also deceptive. Ms. Brown told me she shot Cadet Nguyen as a joke."

"Oh, I'm sure she didn't do that," Hamid scoffed, shooting a disbelieving look at the ombuds.

Of course Tina hadn't shown him her helmet footage. She knew how bad it would make her look.

"I was there," Loretta snapped. "You weren't. Are you calling me a liar?"

Hamid's eyes widened. "That's hardly fair."

"May I assume Ms. Brown neglected to show you her record of these events?"

"Her hab suit suffered a malfunction."

"How convenient." Loretta felt a tiny surge of triumph. She'd noted the disgust on the ombuds' faces at the notion that the shooting had been "just a joke". Now she had her closing argument.

She opened her encrypted files and searched for the relevant clip. Flicking it to the wall screen with one finger, she left the image frozen on Tina's defiant expression.

"I haven't reviewed this footage," Hamid protested.

Gregory raised an eyebrow. "Captain Ryder—"

Satisfied that the screencap had served its purpose, she snatched it back. "Acknowledged. If Captain Hamid would like a recess to verify my account of these events, I have no objection."

He'd be wise to accept that offer. During recess, he could negotiate a face-saving resignation for Tina Brown. Without the expulsion on her record, she could move forward without embarrassment.

No doubt he'd understood the subtext. So why did Hamid look so eager?

Loretta's gut sent up a warning flare.

Hamid folded his hands in front of his body. "Given that Captain Ryder has generously introduced video footage into evidence, I propose that we watch a full accounting of the events of that day. She wishes to share my client's statements. I don't object. However, we must view that information in context."

"I do not consent," Loretta said shortly. "Via section fifteen—"

"We all know the code, Captain." Hamid interrupted, his tone bland. "No one forced you to share your personal data today. Yet the ombuds retain the authority to expand the scope of testamentary evidence when it's entered into the record during a live proceeding."

Fuck. He was right about that.

"I'm not offering unlimited access." She glared, silently demanding he back down. "Would you?"

"I'm not the one who opened this particular Pandora's box. Is there a reason you're hesitant to share footage of your class? Is there something you don't want us to see?"

"I've given an account of my actions that day." Loretta's face burned. She felt it, but she couldn't control it, and the ombuds were watching closely. She'd accurately described what happened, but she'd done so in writing, using the fact-based, unemotional style of a standard incident report. Given the way Tina had behaved, she knew the former cadet wouldn't be in any hurry to share her video feed, either.

Seeing it would hit differently.

He played me. Baited me! And I walked right into the trap.

Suddenly, the notion of having her own representative at the hearing didn't seem so bad.

But it was too late for that.

Ombudswoman Gregory responded as Loretta expected her to. It's what she would have done if their positions were reversed. Words were one thing, but cameras caught what text never could. Why miss the opportunity?

Anis Gregory met Loretta's eye. "Show us."

About an hour later, after a recess that took far longer than any recess should, Loretta stood, ready to receive judgment.

Mortifyingly, the gallery was now full. Word had been spreading, and no doubt the images of Tina Brown's frightened, tear-streaked face would travel far and wide. It didn't matter that she'd needed some sense knocked into her. Nor did it matter that she'd almost killed a man, or that she'd left the shooting range unscathed, other than a few hits to her ego.

Loretta's heart sank. Marcus would never forgive her for screwing up this badly. And why should he?

Ombudswoman Gregory spoke in a clear voice that carried easily through the space. "Here are our findings. We fully agree that Cadet Brown showed an egregious lapse in judgment on the shooting range. She may be unsuited for service in our organization. But we must take a wholistic view of this unfortunate situation. Captain Ryder, who is responsible for safety during weapons training?"

"I am."

"And what were you doing at the precise moment when this incident occurred?"

"I was speaking with another student."

"If you'd been watching your students more closely, might you have seen Cadet Brown unholster her weapon in time to deactivate her pulsar?"

"Possibly. But teaching requires that I—"

"Were you teaching, in that moment?" Gregory was relentless, parrying truth from justification with ease, setting matters straight. Even under the circumstances, it was impossible not to admire her.

Loretta squared her shoulders. "No. I was discussing the lesson plan with Ombudswoman Shay."

Her answer earned her a small nod of approval. "Our ruling is this. Cadet Tina Brown's expulsion is overturned. *However*, her status is probationary. At the end of her training period, the disciplinary committee will assess her readiness for service before she applies for a commission. We also assign her to two thousand hours of remedial service and fine her for medical services rendered to Cadet Nguyen."

Hamid seemed pleased. "We accept. Cadet Brown and I thank you for your wisdom in this matter."

"Regarding your own conduct," Gregory said, locking eyes with Loretta, "while your frustration was understandable, we were frankly shocked to see you threaten a student under your care. Your written report failed to adequately describe the extent to which you worked to frighten and intimidate Cadet Brown. This abuse of your position will *not* go unanswered."

"Ombudswoman, if you'll—"

"I'm not finished. A portion of the blame also rests with us. Why are we allowing our own safety protocols to be undermined? An independent review of the pulsar system has confirmed that if the guidance system had not been turned off, firing at another student would have been rendered impossible by the software. We never should have permitted that risk be taken. That's on us."

Her peers nodded solemnly.

Loretta's eyes burned. Her chest felt strangely hollow. If they needed to punish her, so be it! But they were talking about undermining everything she'd been working toward.

"Our work can be dangerous," she countered, lifting her chin defiantly. "We *must* hone our skills. Please, don't put lives at risk because I lost my temper."

Until now, Michaela Sanchez had hardly said a word. Now she leaned forward and spoke in a soft voice. "I've read your file, Loretta, and I can see your passion. More than that, we remember that same passion from the first day you stood before the council after the tragic loss of your parents." She shot Loretta a sympathetic smile. "None of us doubt your good intentions. But I must ask the question we've been dancing around today. Who exactly are you preparing your students to fight?"

It was hard to grasp what she was driving at. Ombudswoman Sanchez knew the purpose of the corps as well as anyone.

"I've looked through your appeals history," Sanchez continued. "There's a concerning trend there. You find our security practices lacking, and you're a constant presence on the docket. You use whatever scrap of influence you have to push us toward a defensive posture. So I'll ask again. Who are we supposed to be fighting?"

"It's not about fighting..." Loretta stammered, trying to put what was obvious into words that wouldn't offend. "Security isn't about preparing for a specific threat. It's about protecting our citizens from all threats. Known and unknown."

"Yet Mars is a peaceful community," Ombudsman Tom Oberlin said. "A beacon to all of humanity."

Loretta bit her lip. They were going to punish her for losing her temper. That much she knew. What she couldn't stand was being treated like a child. Did they still see her as that thirteen-year-old girl who'd made an emotional appeal to keep her family home?

If they wanted data, she'd give them some.

"The outpost at Selven Beta A believed they were safe until the uprisings began. Small ones, at first. Then, the destruction of the biodome. Thirteen of our scientists died there."

"Mars isn't Selven Beta," Councilwoman Sanchez countered. "Mars isn't Earth. Watchfulness is one thing, but I'm concerned about your desire to militarize our practices. We're mediators, first. We resolve conflict. We're not here to inflame it."

"And you don't think I agree? Of course I do! Unfortunately, our high-minded ideals can't always keep us safe. You want threats? I can give you dozens. Smuggling, for example. We accept deliveries every day from Earth. We have visitors. Some arrive with forged identities, but we never seem to figure it out until they're long gone. And then there's the Free Mars movement. Most people are reasonable, peaceful, yes. But if even one of them—"

"We've had no murders in seventy years." Arbiter Gregory said. "No criminal incidents more significant than petty theft or assault in more than ten."

"Just one year ago we found unsecured explosives along with anti-charter propaganda. We're still looking for the source. Or have you forgotten?"

"No one is suggesting we lower our guard," Councilwoman Gregory said calmly. "But it's time we take a step back. Are we making prudent, evidence-based decisions, or are we jumping at shadows? Fear can be dangerous too. I suggest we avoid stoking it in the classroom. We each bear some responsibility for what happened to Cadet Nguyen. Mistakes must come with consequences, but those consequences should give us opportunities to learn and grow. Wouldn't you agree?"

Loretta's shoulders sank. "I do."

"Good. Because on the matter of *your* conduct, we've made the following determination..."

CHAPTER FOUR

Loretta tucked her tablet beneath her armpit and hurried. Her tight hamstrings stretched as she lengthened her stride. It felt good to move, to burn off some of the tension left over from a long night tossing and turning. She stayed within the reflective yellow lines marking the pedestrian path. To her right, a two-lane road ran along the full length of the docklands, to be used by trovers and other ground transport. She glanced up at the massive gray superstructure, not minding how insignificant she felt beneath it, like a lowly aphid crawling in the shade beneath a potato seedling. Perhaps those feelings were right, given the mess she'd made. In just one afternoon, she'd struck a fatal blow to her career while spitting in the face of everyone who had ever trusted her.

The problem wasn't that she'd scared Cadet Brown. Well, yes, that had been a mistake, but her fuck-up in the hearing room had been far worse.

Epiphany's centennial celebration was only ten days away. Along with the parties, wine, and way too many speeches, there would also be a vote. It was time to renew the Martian charter, either that or discard it in favor of writing an entirely new constitution.

No reasonable person wanted to blow up what was

already working. Unfortunately, Free Mars activists weren't above using lies and propaganda to achieve their aims. They were adamant that the Diplomatic Corps and its system of justice be dismantled in favor of something "more democratic."

Now, at a crucial moment, she'd handed those hyperbolic asses the world's best recruiting video.

She gritted her teeth, sending a flare of pain from jaw to temple. How was it possible that one person could screw up this badly? And why hadn't she seen this coming?

She looked up again, squinting. Even with helmet magnification, the roof was far enough away she'd need a distance scope to see the weld marks holding the building together. Some of these docks were older than Epiphany itself, yet they'd endured.

So would she.

Years ago, as a cadet working guard shifts here, she'd admired the massive delivery shuttles with their colorful murals. Visitors had arrived in small groups, members of scientific or government delegations, mostly, but sometimes they brought their families with them. Children would inevitably jump and bounce, eager for real-world data on the new balance of forces exerted on their bodies. Adults were more circumspect, walking down the shuttle platforms carefully, their hands anxiously checking the seals of their hab suits.

Even amid the well-oiled rhythms of interplanetary commerce, there had been surprises from time to time. One morning, a specialized transport had delivered a live elephant! She'd delighted at the sight of its delicate trunk probing at the glass of the carrier, proving that curiosity didn't belong to humanity alone.

Maybe this wouldn't be so bad.

Mountains of white steam billowed from overhead vents

and faded into the chilly air like phantoms. To her left, the massive slablike doors of shuttle bay twelve stood open; the bay was empty save for a work crew preparing for the next delivery. Their hab suits were a rusty orange, just like hers, only they'd opaqued their helmets. Most remedials preferred anonymity. Why give strangers any ammunition against you? If you were lucky, you could fit in your service hours around the edges of your normal life, and no one need be the wiser. Employers were prohibited from terminating a work contract simply because remedial service hours were due, thus there was no incentive to shame a person for making a mistake.

Well, not usually.

Loretta stubbornly kept her face shield clear, making eye contact with anyone who came into view. If that made people uncomfortable, well, that was their problem.

Everyone saw me fall. They may as well see me pick myself back up.

Three thousand hours of remedial service, plus the loss of her rank and all accumulated advancement points. Those would be her punishments for roughing up Tina Brown. Her dream of becoming the youngest councilor in Martian history was irretrievably dead. She'd felt it slip through her fingers the moment judgment was rendered.

She'd been furious. Speechless. Glowing with an incandescent rage she'd been wise enough not to express.

However, in the cool light of a new day, after tossing aside sheets damp with sweat, she'd found herself face to face with truth.

What was done was done.

Anger had a logic to it. Most emotions did, when you dropped your ego and thought things through. Anger arose from being treated poorly. From being betrayed or lied to. Or, worst of all, from losing someone you cared about. She'd felt that kind of anger before, but this was different.

Slow down, Marcus was always telling her. *You can't just come out swinging; you need to think more than one or two moves ahead.*

He'd been right. And the ombuds? They'd performed their duties to perfection. If she'd come clean from the beginning, if she'd gone to them apologetic for how she'd reacted in class, her punishment would have been less severe.

They wouldn't have needed to make an example out of her.

A trover sped past, wheels whirring. Three long cargo segments followed the engine. Yellow markings on the crates showed they were headed to twenty-one alpha, near the university where Risha worked.

Her mentor hadn't been in touch. Not yet. Not that Loretta blamed her for keeping a distance. News of her behavior had spread far and wide, and already the corps was distancing itself. Their statement had been as scathing as it was bland.

We are deeply disappointed by the actions of one of our officers during a training exercise. Their behavior was unacceptable. To avoid similar incidents in the future, a committee has been convened to review pulsar safety protocols, and all captains are remanded to de-escalation training immediately.

Loretta stifled an eye roll. *Sure. Sending everyone else to school because I fucked up is an excellent use of our time.*

Not only had she pissed everyone off, she'd erased six years of hard work in one afternoon. That had to be some kind of record. Not the kind of mark she'd hoped to make on history, granted, but a footnote nonetheless.

Her tablet sounded a warning and she picked up her pace, not quite running. The spot where her pulsar should have been felt oddly light, and her new hab suit was loose and floppy, sized generously to fit a wide range of bodies.

An arbiter needs to look respectable so people will listen to them. All a remedial needs to do is blend in, shut up, and not die.

Up ahead, a shuttle bay door was open. Remedials were lining up inside, standing on orange dots painted on the floor. There were about fifty so far, with more arriving by the minute. Loretta took an empty spot in the front row. She stood with her spine straight, feet shoulder width apart, hands interlocked at the small of her back.

At the appointed time, a dark-haired woman in her late forties stepped to the front of the group. She tapped her com panel and spoke in a clear and courteous tone, leaving her face shield clear. Her pale brown eyes moved from person to person as she spoke, perhaps counting off attendance.

"Welcome to remedial work crew number four. My name is Avery. I have two goals. First, to keep you all safe. There's a lot of heavy equipment here, so keep your coms active and follow instructions. I don't want anyone losing an arm because they weren't paying attention. Second, let's stay on task so I can verify your hours for the disciplinary committee. Show up on time, do a good job, keep your drama at home with your mama," her mouth quirked up on one side, "and we'll get along just fine. If those terms don't work for you, I hear work crew number two is digging trenches in the outback for the geologic survey. Any volunteers for that?"

When no one raised their hands, she looked pleased. "Okay then. Returners, you'll find your assignments on your tablets. New people, hold tight and we'll get you sorted."

She made her way down the line. As she approached, Loretta held up the ID code on her wrist to be scanned.

Avery nodded. "Your file says you're an arbiter. Good! I need a solid communicator to track down signatures from the delivery crews. They're usually in a rush, and they like to blow us off, so I need someone who can be persuasive without starting an interplanetary incident. Are you fit? It's a lot of running back and forth and I can't spare you a trover."

Three thousand hours, Loretta thought ruefully. *But tomorrow, fewer.*

She nodded once. "You can count on me. Just tell me what you need."

Early that evening, after a scalding hot shower and a dose of anti-inflammatory meds, Loretta headed to the Wells habitat. Her finger hesitated at the call button. The lump in her throat was too big to swallow.

Marcus must have been checking his camera, because a moment later the door slid open. Marcus Wells had the same good looks as his son, albeit he was more weathered around the eyes. A distinguished hint of silver touched his temples and deep laugh lines framed his mouth. Like Travis, he was of middle height and rangy, with the body of a runner.

Loretta's tongue felt like it was coated in sand. An apology hardly seemed adequate. Hell, she wouldn't blame him if he sent her away until things had blown over. Certainly it couldn't do the chief of the Martian council any favors to be hanging out with Loretta Ryder, social pariah and planetary embarrassment.

"Marcus, I—"

He swept her into a hug. "I've been worried about you, kid. Trav said you haven't been returning his messages."

Relief flowed over her. After a restful moment, she pulled back. "I told him I was fine. I just needed..." She broke off the sentence. Was there anything she could say that wouldn't sound selfish?

"I get it," Marcus said. "You needed to regroup."

"Travis. Is he—"

She was going to ask if he was upset with her, but that was a stupid question. Travis had warned her. He'd practically begged her to be more careful. And she'd blown him off.

"He's in his room. Come on in. Tell him dinner will be ready in a few minutes."

Travis was at his desk, engrossed in the newsfeeds when she opened his bedroom door. It looked like a storm had blown through, scattering clothing and snack wrappers across the floor. He'd flung his uniform haphazardly on the bed, and his hair was a messy tangle.

Guilt flashed uselessly in her belly.

"Hey," she said lightly, bending down to pick up the trash. "Look at this mess. Who are you? And where did you put my boyfriend?"

Travis quickly blacked his screen and spun around in his chair. He crossed the room to meet her. "Where have you been? I've been losing my mind! You didn't answer your door last night, and your tracker was off. How was I supposed to know you were okay?"

"I'm sorry." Her gut twisted like a dirty rag. "After what happened... I wasn't ready to face anyone."

He wrapped his arms around her. She buried her face in his neck, enjoying the minty scent of his shampoo and the softness of his sweater. The way he held her close without confining her. His essential Travis-ness.

"You were right," she said. "About everything. I'm so sorry."

His voice was low in her ear. "Is that why you didn't answer your door? Were you worried I'd be on your back, saying 'I told you so'? Because that wasn't why I came."

"I know." She stepped back but kept her hands linked with his. "But one of us needs to say it, so it may as well be me. If I hadn't been so full of myself..."

He waved off her apology and reached for a black-rimmed tablet on his desk. "Check this out. I've been working on your appeal. I know I can't represent you, but there's this guy in my district, super-smart, and I've come up with an argument that will—"

"I'm not going to appeal."

"But they were too harsh! No one in their right mind would believe your penalty is fair. You need to ask for a modification, at least."

She gently extracted his tablet from his hands and set it back on his desk. "It's not the end of the world. They didn't kick me out of the corps, and they could have. I'm getting a second chance! This time, I won't take it for granted."

"But your plan..."

She turned away so he wouldn't see the mishmash of emotions on her face. There was a difference between knowing what was right and being happy about it. Couldn't he understand this wasn't easy? "There's no way I'll rank up fast enough to beat Marcus's record. Besides, what is it your dad's always saying? A wise person focuses on what they can control."

Travis seemed skeptical. "It's not like you to turn away from a fight."

"Exactly. And look at what that got me." His hurt expression pricked her heart. "Thanks for working on my appeal. It means a lot that you're willing to stand up for me."

Finally, she'd earned a smile. It smoothed out the worry lines on his forehead.

"Well, I *am* a pretty great boyfriend."

She pulled him in close for a kiss. "No argument from me."

At dinner, Marcus dished a second helping of vegetables onto Loretta's plate without asking. He often invited guests to these dinners; friends, visiting dignitaries, or people he deemed interesting enough for a few hours of conversation, but tonight he'd set one end of the long table for just the three of them, with his good china and an electric candle for ambiance. "So, I understand you started your service hours already."

She shrugged. "I figured I may as well hit the ground running."

He slipped into his high-backed chair and poured a smidge of wine from a dark bottle into his glass. Martian wine from Martian grapes; the liquid had a pretty, pinkish hue. "No one expected that. You could have taken a few weeks to wrap up your open cases." He raised an eyebrow. "Some might accuse you of hiding from your critics."

She accepted the bottle from him. "May I know the names of my detractors? Or is this an exercise in hypotheticals?"

Marcus raised his glass with a tiny smirk. "Okay then. What if I said it? What if *I* said you were hiding at the docks today?"

"Then I'd say you're wrong." There was no point in concealing her irritation. Marcus's bullshit detector was as finely tuned as the most sensitive geological equipment. He was trying to prepare her for the challenges she'd inevitably face — she appreciated that — but would it have killed him to give it a rest for one night?

Exhaustion tugged at her like a heavy anchor. Yes, it would have been easier to ball up in her hab for a few days of leave, eating ice cream and killing monsters in an augmented reality game. She'd tried to take the high road, to do the right thing. Yet here Marcus was, demanding she stand up for herself. He expected her to prove her mettle, to herself and to everyone else.

To him too, maybe.

No cowards in this house.

She sat up straighter and met his gaze. "When Ombud Sanchez pinned Captain Nancy's insignia this morning, I was there. I'm not hiding from anyone."

"But..." Marcus prompted.

"But, I can't have everyone looking at *me* every time Nancy makes a decision they don't like. Nancy's leading forty-two beta now. I'm not. She deserves space to find her footing."

"I see." Marcus's tone was bland. Not quite disbelieving, but mild enough to convey her answer hadn't impressed him.

"You don't believe me? The lab suits don't care that Nancy's qualified. All they care about is working with the person they know, and they'll go right around her so long as I'm in view."

"And that was your only reason for reporting early?"

"No." Loretta's face felt hot. "I'm well aware that I'm all over the feeds this week. I figured it's better that people see me taking responsibility. They expect me to lurk in my district, glowering at people, looking all butthurt."

Marcus lifted an eyebrow. "And are you?"

She reached for the basket of rolls next to the seasoning rack. "Yes. My butt hurts. So does my back and everything else. I spent all morning running up and down the docks. And apparently I was overzealous, because I ran out of work by lunch and the supe had me shifting boxes until my shift ended." She shrugged. "At least it kept me too busy to feel sorry for myself."

Marcus sipped his wine with a too innocent expression. "And did you see any... smugglers down there? Dastardly criminals with fake papers? Severe threats the council should be aware of?"

Travis, who had been watching the exchange like it was a tennis match, choked on his wine. Loretta aimed her vilest glare right at Marcus's smug face, giving him what she knew he wanted. She pointed at his hawkish nose with her index finger. "Listen, you sonofabitch..."

Laughter exploded from Marcus. Glorious, contagious cackling. Before long, Loretta succumbed. The "high and mighty" Councilor Wells looked downright goofy when he was guffawing like an idiot. She wiped her stinging eyes.

It felt good to laugh.

"You two need better material," Travis said, shaking his head, smiling a little.

Loretta didn't disagree, but she knew Marcus never tired of the joke. She'd been thirteen when her district's ombuds had tried to evict her from her hab. Marcus had been serving that day, and after he'd struck a nerve by questioning her maturity, she'd shoved her finger at him and spat:

Listen, you sonofabitch, my parents are dead. I'm not letting you take my home too. Living in some home for troubled teens won't make me any safer. And don't you dare say you're doing this for me, because you're not! I'm not troubled. I've never been in trouble. Not once! And you want to throw me out? You people are so busy pushing words around that you can't see me, standing right here, begging for mercy.

That's when she'd burst into tears.

She'd been mortified. Small children might cry in public, but she'd sworn to herself she'd be an adult. Observers in the gallery had been horrified by her sudden and blatant disrespect for her elders. The other two ombuds, well, she'd embarrassed them by calling them out, although they were trying hard not to show it. Marcus, after smothering a sudden smile, had offered a compromise. She could stay in her home with him as her legal guardian, if she satisfied certain conditions. Getting good marks in school. Attending therapy. Submitting to unannounced visits. Eating evening meals with him and Travis. There'd been a big, long list.

That 'sonofabitch' had done for her what no other adult in the room had been willing to do. He'd listened. He'd treated her like a human being with a brain instead of a stupid kid to be shunted off to one side. And even after the safety committee had ruled her parents' death an industrial accident, he'd backed her request for an independent review of the evidence.

Marcus had been there for her then, and he was here for her now. Despite her screw ups. Despite everything. But that didn't mean he was going to let her off the hook easily.

I may as well take my lumps.

"How many times did you watch the hearing?" Loretta asked, wincing.

Marcus touched his chin. "Ten? No, twelve times."

Loretta lowered her face into her hands. It was easier than looking at him.

"My favorite part was when you'd *thought* you'd won. You puffed up like a cartoon dog who'd caught the burglar. You were so proud. Do you want to see it? I saved the clip."

"Dad..." Travis sounded pained.

Loretta forced herself upright and brushed her hair back. "Ugh! And then Hamid just wiped the floor with me. It wasn't even close. I mean, by the time I saw what was coming, it was too late." She held out a hand, as if shielding her eyes. "Oh look! The consequences of my own actions! Who could have guessed?"

That earned her a laugh from Travis. She shot him a tiny smile.

"You've been working so hard to prepare for the charter renewal. Meanwhile, those Free Mars idiots keep lying about us, pretending like we're part of some grand conspiracy to keep them from being free."

"They mean well," Marcus said, wiping his mouth with a napkin. "We shouldn't demonize them for seeing things differently than we do."

Loretta scoffed. "Like we aren't free? Have you seen Earth? They've been in a downward spiral for centuries. Crisis after crisis with no real hope of resolution because every idiot they elect is more interested in pushing their pet causes than in serving the people. Those Free Mars bozos want to bring that style of government, here? That's bad enough! And now, with the vote on our doorstep, here comes Loretta, screwing things up for everyone." She stabbed a green vegetable with her fork. "The ombuds should have kicked me out. At least then Free Mars couldn't use that video against us."

"You have more support than you think," Marcus said. "You aren't the only one who has concerns about how permeable Epiphany has become. And there are those on Earth who'd love to see our charter replaced with a new constitution for the simple reason that it makes their governments appear less inept if we follow their lead." He paused for a moment. "Make no mistake, Free Mars would use that vid against us whether we kicked you out or not.

"Why fall on your sword to please people who already hate everything you stand for? If Anis had kicked you out, we would have lost one of the best arbiters in the corps."

"Loretta doesn't want to appeal, Dad." Travis looked expectantly at Marcus. "If she *tried*, at least—"

His father's bland smile cut off Travis's words as cleanly as scissors slice through paper. "Loretta's accountable, Trav. She's owning her mistakes. That's what leaders do."

Travis glanced down at his plate.

"Can we talk about something else?" Loretta asked. "Anything else?"

"Yes," Marcus said. "But first, I have something I want to show you both." He went into his bedroom, then came back holding an older model data tablet. He unlocked it, selected a file, and handed the tablet to Loretta.

She scooted her chair closer to Travis so he could read along. It was an incident report, although the format was years out of date. A photo in the upper right corner showed a much younger Marcus. His right eye was swollen and bruised. Triangular sutures ran across his nose like tiny white flags.

Travis inhaled sharply after skimming the top of the page. "Holy shit, Dad! You served time in Hellas? For assault?"

Loretta was having a similar reaction. It was difficult to believe what she was seeing. Marcus could be every bit as stubborn as she was, and he was a formidable opponent across a bargaining table, but it was impossible to imagine him losing his temper. Not like that.

Marcus took the tablet back. "It's no big secret. Plenty of people remember those days. Well, people closer to my age. You two were still in diapers at the time."

"It had to be self-defense," Loretta said. "You were standing up for yourself, right?"

Marcus chuckled. "It's sweet that you kids are so surprised. No, I was at fault. I was out walking the gardens that night, having had a few too many drinks, and Greg Qual saw me vomit on a rare flowering cactus."

Loretta remembered Qual. The former Chief Councilor had passed away just two years prior. He and Marcus had been as close as brothers.

"Greg pulled me aside that night. I figured he'd ticket me for public intoxication, and I didn't much care, but instead he started laying into me about my attitude. I'd been in a downward spiral, and apparently everyone could see it but me." He glanced at Loretta. "Your father had already tried talking to me, by the way. I told him to mind his own damn business." Marcus frowned at the memory. "My wife was dead, and I was furious at the council for letting her go to Earth. I'd been lashing out, getting into arguments, practically begging for an ass kicking. The only problem? No one would give me one. And I was so damn sick of everyone's kindness. Empathy wouldn't put my family back together. No number of kind words would bring my wife back. I resented the way everyone expected me to move on."

Loretta squeezed Travis's hand beneath the table. He'd shown her old vids of his mother. Bianca had left her son with her laugh, and her calm brown eyes, flecked with gold.

"Greg implied that I was being a shit father — which was fair, by the way — and I took a swing at him. I was halfway to Phobos and feeling no pain, and he was pretty fit for an older guy. The next thing I knew, we were whaling on each other in the hallway. I lost that fight. Later, Greg came to visit me in lockup. During my remedial service, he suited up orange and worked alongside me for weeks. He said he was going to stay right by my side until I'd decided not to kill myself."

Travis stiffened. "You never told me—"

Marcus held up a hand. "It wasn't conscious on my part. What he said shocked me, even as angry as I was. But he was right. I was looking for a way out. After Bianca died, I saw no reason to go on."

Travis glanced away.

"You were in pain," Loretta said to Marcus. "Not thinking clearly."

"Yes. But it was more than that. When I say I understand where Free Mars is coming from, I mean it because Bianca and I used to be a part of the movement ourselves."

Travis's eyes went wide.

"Seriously?" Loretta's voice was almost a squeak.

"Oh, the group didn't have a name back then. It was more like a loose association of friends-turned-political activists. We believed, as some still do, that the charter is too limiting. That it concentrates too much power among the elites. In a different era, I suppose you might have called us hippies. Free love and self-determination." He smirked. "Sticking it to the man."

Travis seemed to be thinking hard. "Is that why Mom and Aunt Fae went to Earth?"

Marcus's smile wasn't a smile at all. "They wanted to make a difference. Mars has no poverty because we don't allow unlimited reproduction. We respect the constraints of our environment because we have no choice, otherwise we'd be dead. And we refuse to let dangerous movements grow unchecked, no matter how well-intentioned those involved may be. Earth was in crisis then, much as it is now. After medical school, Bianca and Fae wanted to volunteer for half a year, to do good where their skills were needed most."

Loretta rested her hands in her lap. Travis had told her the story of how his mother died, but she'd never asked Marcus about those days. Tonight, for some reason, the wall of privacy he'd erected around his personal pain was absent.

"And they were killed," she said quietly.

"By a mob," Marcus said, "religious extremists who didn't like women practicing skills they believed their God had allocated to men." He rubbed his eyes. "The thing is, I'd been every bit as idealistic as your mom, Trav. I celebrated their decision to go to Earth, and I was damn proud of them. Why *not* contribute to the greater good? Why not put power in the hands of the people? I was on board with that right up until the point where reality fucked us. After they died, it was as if the ground beneath my feet had been snatched away. I kept thinking: why care about anyone? Why stick your neck out? Caring about other people only gets you killed."

Travis and Loretta exchanged glances.

Marcus smiled at their worry. "Of course, I was entirely wrong about that. Long story short, Greg worked hard to become my friend, and after I completed my remedial service, he recruited me to the corps. More importantly, he showed me that I took the wrong lesson away from your mother's death." He rested a hand on Loretta's shoulder. "Getting thrown in detention wasn't the end of my career, kiddo. It was the beginning."

He gave them a moment to digest that, then stood. "Now, who wants dessert?"

CHAPTER FIVE

"Well fuck me dry and grill me up a waffle! Lore, is that really you?"

Kacey Holt's girly laugh spiraled out in front of her as she flew through the shuttle bay doors with her arms out. Her glittery silver hab suit was missing its helmet, and her bubblegum-pink mohawk flopped loosely over one ear as she ran.

They collided in a hug that would have toppled Loretta over if she hadn't outweighed her friend by a good ten kilos. She clapped Kacey lightly on the back, happiness bubbling inside her from a source she couldn't quite name.

Kacey's elfin smirk was well-complemented by her dramatic black eyeliner and pink-fringed eyelashes. As usual, she smelled like spun sugar and engine solvent, and while it looked like a strong wind could blow her over, Loretta knew better.

"I missed you too, Kace. How was the milk run?"

"A total shit show, as usual. Some dweeb over in thirty-eight alpha decided it would be "fun" to transport live cattle to test new radiation shielding." She snorted. "And of course my boss said yes, because she's a capitalist pig with no sense of proportion. Have you ever spent three weeks in an airtight space with a herd of cows?" She pinched her nose and pantomimed gagging.

"An entire herd?" That seemed unlikely.

"Five, anyway. We kept them isolated in the research pod, but their minders ate with us, and let me just say..." She stuck her tongue out as far as it would go. "Yuck."

"So a literal shit show."

Kacey barked a laugh. She was equal parts girly-girl and scrapper, and on any given day, it was hard to tell if she'd insist on painting your nails for you or threaten to bust your face for looking at her funny. Today, she was all sunshine and roses, which probably meant she was flush with cash.

"I thought you weren't due back till next week." Loretta grabbed the helmet mount on Kacey's hab suit and shook it lightly. "And where in the hell is your safety gear? If the bay blows atmo—"

Kacey snorted like a teacup pig. Her head tilted quizzically. "Well, she looks like Lore. And she *sounds* like Lore. But she's dressed like a miscreant." She flung up her hands. "Wait! Don't tell me. Your boy Trav had you cloned so one of you can work while the other one services him sexually. You found out, and you strangled him to death with a hair scrunchy." Her eyes narrowed. "Or are *you* the clone? That must be it! Because the Loretta I know would never break the rules." She gestured at the dark orange hab suit. "Nor would she wear a fucking trash bag to work. Where's your self-respect?"

Loretta grabbed Kacey by the hand and dragged her bodily into the shuttle bay. "Will you *please* wear your helmet? You're giving me anxiety."

Predictably, the rest of Kacey's gear was resting atop a giant mound of pink luggage. Behind it, the *Poppy Moon* stood gracefully in the launch bay, her soft curves and white hull making the shuttle seem more diminutive than she actually was. Just inside the shuttle bay doors, an impressively muscled blond guy stacked cargo crates without the assistance of a lifter. Normally that would be a recipe for a hospital visit, but he moved the crates around like they weighed little more than air. His biceps had to be the size of her thighs! He gave Loretta a shy smile and a tiny wave when he caught her looking.

She waved back.

Kacey had picked up her helmet and tucked it beneath her skinny arm like a glassy basketball. "You realize it would take whole minutes to lose consciousness in here, right? Your pressurization tech is amaze. Stop avoiding my question."

"I'm not a clone. And I didn't kill anyone."

Kacey cupped her hands around her mouth and shouted one word at a time. "Then. Why. Are. You. Wearing. That. Shit. Outfit?"

If it had been anyone else talking to her this way, Loretta might have been annoyed. Kacey might be a brat, but she made most people seem positively dull in comparison. "I take it you haven't read the local feeds?"

Kacey made a show of inspecting her short, multicolored fingernails. "Nah. Pro-charter propaganda doesn't really do it for me these days. I mean, if I *wanted* to read about an unstoppable power structure fucking everyone within reach, I'd dip my nose into that space whale erotica making the rounds."

"Please don't tell me more."

Kacey's grin was pure evil. "Hey! It's a long flight from San Diego. Sometimes we work through all our media before we hit the turn and burn and we're stuck trading files with the tourists. So, what did you do? Did you mouth off to an admiral or something?"

Kacey knew very well that the corps didn't have admirals. She'd done a brief stint as a cadet before declaring the entire organization 'a conglomeration of dicks' and sweet-talking her way into a pilot training program instead. Now, she ran cargo on behalf of one of the few corporates authorized to transit between Mars and Earth.

Kacey was, in some ways, the same smart-assed girl Loretta had met in court-mandated group therapy when they were teens. Brilliant. Funny. With zero respect for anything resembling authority.

She had her reasons. A salvage team had found Kacey inside an abandoned transport vessel at the tender age of eight. Although perhaps the word 'tender' wasn't an apt description. Her rescuer had needed stitches after Kacey bit him, right through his hab suit.

They'd bonded over a mutual hatred of their court-assigned therapist. Shared trauma had a way of papering over superficial differences, and their friendship had held even as their lives had diverged.

Kacey huffed out her breath. "Fine. You're going to make me guess? Let's see... You were *so* awesome that they arrested you to give someone else a chance at scooping up all those gold stars."

With a quiet sigh, Loretta opened her tablet and sent Kacey the video file. Kacey watched it, fast-forwarding through the gaps in the action. Her eyes widened at the sight of Janus lying dazed on the reddish soil.

"She shot him. That little bitch actually shot him!" Her voice spiraled up to a high point. "She's lucky she didn't try that up there." Kacey pointed skyward without looking. "We don't tolerate that shit in *my* house."

Loretta felt her mouth twitch. Kacey loved to talk like she was a spacefaring badass, as if every cargo run were a wild and crazy adventure full of danger and narrow escapes. Maybe it made her work seem more exciting? That, or her wildly exaggerated stories kept people from getting too close to her.

Kacey wasn't what you'd call a people person.

"Right," Loretta said with mock seriousness. "You throw people out into space if they cross you."

Kacey seemed to sigh with her whole body, never satisfied with mere words when a full dramatic performance would do. "We're not *monsters*, Lore. We pump whatever room they're in full of gas, wait for them to hit carpet, and truss them up, safe and secure. *Then* we steal their shit and space them." Her smile was angelic.

"No you don't. They'd be missing off the manifests. You'd have to turn them into the authorities here, or risk arrest."

Kacey fluttered her eyelashes. "Sorry, sweetie. Mars has exceeded its quotient of assholes already. You're *completely*, totally full!"

Loretta laughed! It felt good to let loose. To remember that there were people in her life that didn't expect her to be perfect, a shining example of Martian excellence. Kacey didn't give a shit how successful Loretta was, or what anyone else thought of her.

With Kacey, once you were loved, you were loved forever.

"How bad is it?" Kacey's smile faded. "I mean, are you okay?"

Loretta's boot scraped the hard ground as she shifted position. "They busted me down to zero."

"They did *not*. Lore! You've been kissing ass for years. You wear their stupid, itchy uniform and—"

"It's perfectly comfortable."

"you walk around like a rule-worshipping douche—"

"Harsh."

"and you're even banging Wells' uptight kid because—"

"Travis is my boyfriend. You *know* this."

"All I'm saying is," Kacey's expression softened, "these people suck. They don't deserve you." She stomped her foot. "Screw Mars! And screw the council. Come work with me instead. We've got a two year tour coming up." She smiled at the sight of Loretta's crinkled nose. "No cows this time! One of the big Earth telcos hired us to drop com beacons for the interstellar network. I'm talking about *wide open* space! We're leaving Sol's sandbox. Can you believe it?" She bounced up and down on her thick-soled boots. "Think about it. There are thousands of worlds out there. Maybe even alien life! Shouldn't we see it now, while we can? Before..."

"Before what?"

Kacey bit her lip. "I was nuts to ask. You'd rather be right here."

"Among the douches," Loretta shot back a tiny smile. "Two whole Earth years? That's—"

"About seven hundred sols."

"I wouldn't want to be away from Travis for that long. And you know he'd never leave Mars."

"*He* wasn't invited."

She ignored the barb. "Want to have dinner tonight? Just you and me? It'll be like the old days, except you won't need to sneak out of your room, and no one is going to come busting into my hab to check on us. Also, we can eat all the sugar we can stand."

Kacey's smile lit up the entire shuttle bay. "I wouldn't miss it."

A short time later, Loretta was back at work, standing on a safety platform alongside a delivery shuttle with outdated paperwork. The *Steady as She Goes* loomed overhead like a birdlike monster, angular and dark, her ancillary engines purring low with pre-flight checks. Sloped 'wings' spread out below her beak-like protuberance up top. Overhead lights reflected off the cockpit window below the bay's upper doors. The *Steady's* mural depicted a snowy Earth mountain rising majestically above a fringe of evergreen trees. Sol hung in the sky above it, ridiculously large and blurry as seen through the lens of Earth's atmosphere.

She punched a green button on the wall. "Ryder here. Orbit control needs your updated manifest before departure." Frowning down at her tablet, she added, "Also, I don't want to be rude, but I have another six ships waiting. Can you send a representative down?"

While she waited, she surveyed the ship's mural with a critical eye. On Mars, most visual art celebrated advancement of some kind. Art served a useful purpose, reminding everyone how hard work benefited the greater good. A new strain of life-sustaining wheat or a breakthrough in radiation shielding would spark an explosion of salutary works across Epiphany. Earth, though? They showed off their icy mountains, forests, and natural beauty. And what a bizarre brag that was from a planet that couldn't get its shit together.

Those glaciers had melted long ago.

Still, Earth art could be whimsical. Loretta especially liked the enormous red-petaled flowers on the side of Kacey's shuttle, the *Poppy Moon*. Granted, if Kacey had her way, her ship would have been covered in rave glitter and pink unicorns, but no doubt her employer would nix that plan.

Where was the damn crew? After several minutes with no reply, she pressed the green button again and added an extra measure of impatience to her voice. "Are you coming, or should I ask the harbormaster to push your departure out?"

A bored-sounding male voice replied. "Acknowledged. We'll send someone down in a sec."

Loretta thudded the toe of her boot into the hard ground and rolled her shoulders back. Kacey's job offer was stuck in her mind like a student's shiny new pulsar inside a sealed holster. As much as she wanted to unwrap it, it wasn't hers.

Laying beacons was important work. Without an interstellar relay network, staying in touch with distant outposts meant sending ships back and forth across the inky expanse like ancient mail carriers on horseback. That meant waiting dozens or even hundreds of sols for news.

Those doomed scientists on Selven Beta A might have been saved if Mars had been faster to send a rescue team. Even then, the corps wasn't outfitted for that kind of action. When colonization efforts began in earnest, Mars and Earth would need people like her. Helpers who didn't seek conflict, but who weren't afraid of it either.

As exciting as that sounded, those problems were still decades away. Via longstanding treaty, colonization wouldn't proceed until Earth and Mars agreed on terms. And good luck with *that*.

What Kacey had skimmed right past was the fact that humanity already knew what was 'out there.' Earth and Mars had jointly planted eighteen scientific outposts on other worlds, each within a hundred sols' journey of the Exchange, a unique, stable wormhole positioned within reach of Sol's system. And in fifteen years of breathless exploration, scientists had encountered — What? — hundreds of new species of plant life? Some weird amoebas in a stinky pond? Nothing intelligent. Zero survivable atmospheres outside the safety of a controlled environment. As harsh as Mars could be, and as difficult as their challenges were, humanity's view of the expanding frontier made home seem downright hospitable.

Did she want to see the universe? It probably wasn't worth it. To look into that terrifying emptiness, to risk it all to see with her own eyes a few alien bushes? *No thanks.* Yet despite that harsh reality, 20 billion humans gazed up at the stars, wishing for someplace better than the paradise they already had.

She upped her face shield's magnification, searching for signs of movement in the upper windows. When she saw nothing, she opened her shield and liberated a mini scope from her thigh pocket. Peering through it, she saw a flash of dark in the cockpit. The crew was still inside, taking their sweet ass time.

No one respected a remedial.

Out of sheer boredom, she inspected the shuttle bay with her distance scope, testing its limits. The frigid air stung her face, but it felt good to breathe non-recirculated oxygen for a few minutes. Stepping off the control platform, she took a closer look at the mural. Paint used for interplanetary craft had to be cured at extremely cold temperatures to avoid flaking, as at near-light speed, even motes of dust could be problematic. Why then did the painting of the mountain look... rough?

The shuttle's cargo doors were sealed, but the crew had left a side hatch open, probably to cycle out weeks of accumulated cooking smells and body odor. Crates were piled up inside, secured properly to the walls and floors with clamps. *Good.* Most shuttles used grav lock — high-tech magnets, basically, but clamps meant a power failure wouldn't send your gear flying across the hold to smash someone into red paste. When her scope ran past a green smear, her heart jerked.

That. Why was it familiar?

The visible range was near the end of her scope's capabilities, but if she held *very* still...

The cargo boxes were standard; six-sided crates made of hardened synthetics. A familiar icon printed on the side of several boxes sent a shock down her spine. Three concentric green circles, with a red dot in the middle.

You've got to be kidding me.

Corps investigators had found that exact same symbol printed on crates found with anti-charter propaganda. There was nothing illegal about the text, but the unsecured explosives were another matter. They'd been tucked along with the pamphlets in a storage space near Welling University, a hotbed of Free Mars activity. There had also been printed blueprints of Epiphany's life support systems. A cache of material for a crime that had thankfully been thwarted. Unfortunately, an extensive search had found no records of firms using the green target marker.

Yet there it was, right inside the *Steady as She Goes*.

Holy shit!

Her heart pounding with the thrill of discovery, Loretta snapped three quick pictures with her scope and shoved it in her pocket. Mindful that she might be observed, she slowly made her way over to the control platform. Slapping the green button with the side of her fist, she said, "Hey! I need to get to shuttle bay ten. I'll be back in half an hour. *Please*, be ready when I get back."

To her relief, the control panel accepted her arbitration code. Using it, she put a security lock on the upper shuttle bay doors to prevent orbit control from releasing the *Steady as She Goes* into atmo.

She activated her emergency line. "Harbormaster. This is arbiter Loretta Ryder in shuttle bay nine. I'm detaining *Steady as She Goes* in relationship with an ongoing priority-one investigation. Please send a security team to shuttle bay nine. Acknowledge."

"Stand by," a voice on the line replied.

Loretta grabbed her tablet and dialed Kacey. It looked like she was still with her ship. A dark grease smear marred her cheek.

"What's up, assface?" Kacey said cheerfully.

"Do you know this mark?"

Kacey squinted at the blurry photo of the cargo boxes. "Nope. Why?"

"How about the *Steady as She Goes*? She has an Earth crew, contracted through some outfit called Glaxa.

Her forehead furrowed. "What's this about?"

"Later! Just tell me."

Kacey made a face. "It's not like all pilots know each other. If you want, I can ask around. Maybe—" Her face went pale. "Lore. There's someone—"

Pain exploded as something hard and sharp slammed Loretta between the shoulder blades. Air whooshed out of her lungs as her belly hit the ground.

"Lore!" Kacey's voice screamed through the tablet.

A heavy boot landed on Loretta's back and pressed down, hard. She heard something heavy and metallic scrape the ground nearby. "Don't move. Give me the unlock code. *Now.*"

She heard her tablet skitter across the ground. The open edges of her face shield scraped the floor, making it impossible to lift her head or engage the face shield. A pair of shiny black boots stepped into her peripheral vision. Small ones.

A woman?

The boot on her back pressed down even harder. Sharp crackling pain shot down her body, making her eyes water.

"The code."

"Fuck you," she wheezed.

"Thanks," he chuckled, "but I'm in a committed

relationship." He sounded confident. Unbothered. Not at all concerned about the squad of well-trained ass kickers headed their way right now. Without warning, his companion pulled her boot back and kicked Loretta in the lower ribs.

She coughed, tasting blood.

"You can tell me," he said patiently, "or we can beat it out of you."

She let out a whimper. Her hands had been pressing futilely against the ground, trying to lift her body, but now she shot them out at her sides. "Fine! Okay. But I need to enter it myself. There's a—"

"You think I don't know how the system works?"

Another kick from Ms. Boots, this one higher, just beneath her armpit. White-hot stars exploded in Loretta's vision. Whoever this bitch was, she knew where a body's pressure points were.

They'd done this kind of thing before.

The boot on her back shifted slightly. The pressure on her back lessened. "Fine. We'll do this the hard way then."

"There are cameras everywhere, you stupid fuck."

Fabric rustled as he reached down for her. When the woman kicked again, she rolled. Not away, like she'd expected. Instead, she moved toward the offending foot and grabbed the shin, holding on for dear life, twisting to throw her off balance.

Something unzipped behind her. "Hold her," the man said.

Help was coming. She need only keep these two in the shuttle bay until the security team arrived. It wasn't like they could leave, not without punching their way through the upper doors and shredding their shuttle like tissue paper.

Ms. Boots swiveled. She stepped over Loretta, clamping her feet tightly against her sides. Loretta's roll had repositioned her, though, and she looked up, catching sight of her attacker's surprisingly pretty face. She had to be — what?

— about twenty-five? Her hab suit was a dull black without insignia. A long dirty-blonde braid dangled over her shoulder. Before Loretta could reach up and grab it, the woman dropped down, landing on her solar plexus with the full force of her weight.

"Oof!" Loretta lost her breath for a second time. She tried to twist her hips, but Ms. Boots had a powerful grip, and she was bearing down on her shoulders.

"She saw my face. We need to—"

"Hold on! I told you, she's—"

Something cold and hard pressed against Loretta's calf, where the man had crouched down behind his companion. She felt a prick of pain so small she hardly registered it. Immediately, her traitorous arms loosened, falling slack to her sides, and the woman's face blurred pleasantly into the grayish ceiling.

She had just enough of her wits left to notice when he pulled her helmet off. "Keep your mouth shut. Or we'll shut it for you. Permanently."

Her eyelids slid shut. They were heavy, but not half as heavy as the rest of her, which was pressing down, down, like her body might drop through the floor and into the untreated soil below.

"What are you..." she slurred.

The murmured conversation above her seemed to float away. Just before she lost consciousness, klaxons sounded as the shuttle bay's control system prepared to open the upper doors.

CHAPTER SIX

Pain flashed against her right cheekbone.

Her left.

Right.

Light exploded, slamming into Loretta's retinas like twin supernovae. Her heart shuddered. Lungs seized. She bolted upright, gasping. Chaos. Noise. Blurred walls whipping past; orange text in a long smear. Voices shouted furious in the distance. She tried to move, but her legs were strapped to a wide, black platform. Oily grit pressed into her palms. Something metal below her? A vibration she felt in her bones.

Familiar eyes caught her attention. Pink-edged eyelashes beating like hummingbird wings. A pink-lipsticked mouth moving in strange shapes without sound or sense. Small hands gripped her shoulders, tight enough to pinch.

Air rushed into her lungs, hot and moist. Scented with the faint grassy tinge of an industrial recycler. The maelstrom of senseless noise resolved into a single female voice.

"Lore! Breathe. For fucks' sake. *Breathe.* I pumped you full of stimulants, and you're way too busy to die. Do you hear me? Wake up! You have shit to do."

"Whaa?" Loretta's tongue felt twice its normal size. Her face burned like she'd lost a helmet seal in atmo. Her eyes watered. *That wasn't right.* Where *was* her helmet? She blinked rapidly, trying to clear her blurred vision.

Her mind offered fragments. Shards of memory that didn't quite fit together. Certain bits were clearer than others. *Right!* She'd been working, and there'd been a shuttle. An ugly one with a mountain on the side. Someone had jumped her! Her mind's eye showed her a pair of standard black boots. She wasn't sure why. That part felt fuzzier. Just out of reach.

Her ribs hurt like hell, all along her right side. Her lungs felt raw, as if they'd been scrubbed with sandpaper. She touched her stinging face. "Were you... slapping me?"

Kacey grinned like she'd won a sweepstakes. "There she is! Don't you remember? I picked you up off the ground and you started babbling about how we needed to catch those fuckers before they leave orbit."

"I did?" That didn't sound at all familiar.

"Yes! Shake it off. My slapping hand is tired and we need your brain if we're going to pull this off. Probably." She grabbed Loretta's hand and wrapped it around a thin metal rail to her right. "Hold tight. We're almost to my ship."

The platform beneath them jerked. Nausea arrived in a sickening wave, and the platform shifted again, almost tossing Loretta's upper body over the side. *The side?* She wiped her eyes with the back of her free hand and looked again. She and Kacey were riding on a flatbed cargo trover, the kind used to haul crates. Only there were no crates, and someone had cinched a wide yellow strap across her thighs in a kind of improvised seat belt. Loretta twisted around. Up front, where a qualified driver would usually sit, the big blond ox she'd seen moving cargo earlier was working the controls, looking down at them with visible confusion.

Straight ahead and closing fast, two dockworkers stood in mute horror as the vehicle sped at them like a boxy black bullet.

"Hold on!" Kacey flung herself on top of Loretta, pinning her to the trover bed. Loretta gripped the opposite rail just as the trover swung hard to the left, narrowly avoiding the men.

"What the hell, man!" one called.

"You're going to kill someone!"

Loretta winced. The dockworkers were tapping their com panels, calling for help. Further back, almost too far away to see and losing distance with every step, a squad of cadets in security gear were chasing after them, waving their arms and yelling. "Um. Kace."

"Yeah?" Kacey tugged the yellow strap across Loretta's legs to check it was secure.

"Where did you get this trover?"

"Borrowed it."

"Where's the harbor crew? And security? They're—"

"Sitting in their offices jerking off? Yeah, that's what I figure too. Are we gonna go get those bastards, or what?"

"They got away?" Loretta blinked. She moved her arms and legs carefully, checking for injuries. Her heart pounded like it wanted to leap out of her chest and her stomach was sloshing around like a barf-filled water balloon.

How had that shuttle gotten clearance for takeoff? She'd secured the upper doors. She was sure of it!

Kacey's mouth tightened. Her gaze swept around them in a wide arc, as if scanning for threats. "I don't know what they drugged you with, but they left you lying on the ground in there like a landed fish. For fucks' sake, Lore, they could have killed you! If I hadn't been nearby, only Sol knows how long you'd be laying in atmo while the bay recycled." She glanced over and cocked an eyebrow. "So I say we run them down, shove a firecracker up their ship's ugly ass, and bust them wide open like a Founders' Day Piñata."

Up front at the drive module, blondie turned, grinning at Kacey. He signaled something complicated with one hand.

Kacey laughed! "Theo says he's never driven a trover before. They're *really* fast."

When the trover swung wide and to the right, Loretta was ready, gripping the side rails tightly. The *Poppy Moon* stood in graceful splendor deep inside the shuttle bay, her long-stemmed flower mural a demure contrast to the fiery attitude of her pilot.

Loretta clutched her stomach as Kacey loosened the leg straps. Whatever her attackers had injected her with was at war with the stimulants coursing through her veins, and her innards were about to cry uncle. She leaned over the trover rail and squeezed her eyes shut. "Kace. I'm going to—"

Kacey's hands quickly smoothed Loretta's hair back as she lost her lunch next to the trover. Theo was already running toward the shuttle bay's control panel. He slammed a button with the side of his fist and the massive door began to slide down. Klaxons sounded in the gangway outside, followed by the automated safety message.

Emergency lockdown initiated. Stand back. Repeat. Stand back. Fire crews are on their way.

"Look," Kacey said into Loretta's ear. "By the time you cut through all your fucking red tape that shuttle will be gone. We can catch up with them if we leave now. Are you up for that? If you'd rather wait for your crew..."

My crew is back in forty-two beta, Loretta thought grimly. *Assuming they even want to see me, given the way I acted.*

Loretta looked up at the *Poppy Moon*. Her cockpit window was a crescent shape, points aimed down toward her engines. Shuttles weren't equipped with weapons, and it wasn't like they'd be allowed to attack even if they were armed. *Poppy* was about half the size of the *Steady as She Goes*, and perhaps more maneuverable, but no cargo shuttle was made for extended flight in atmo.

She hopped off the trover, dancing her feet to one side to avoid the pile of puke she'd left on the ground. Every cell in her body screamed *go*, but for what purpose? For once in her life, she needed to think more than one move ahead.

We can't just let them get away. They brought a frigging bomb into Epiphany! And if they try again… No. I'll regret it forever if I don't take this chance.

Besides, what are they going to do? Demote me?

Loretta nodded at Kacey. "Take me up. I want a better look at their ship, and a recording of their drive signature. Maybe the harbormaster could—"

Kacey was already in motion. "Theo! Can you buy us time while we go on a scouting mission? Pretty please?"

The interior shuttle bay doors closed with a hydraulic hiss, which was good, because moments later it seemed the calvary had arrived. Loretta heard their shouts outside, someone calling for assistance to open the bay. Theo signed something with a wry smile, and Kacey ran to meet him, standing on tiptoe to kiss his cheek. "You're the best. And can I borrow one of your new toys? It's for a good cause, I promise."

He shrugged agreeably, then lightly tapped the heels of his palms together. That's when Loretta noticed his meaty hands were encased in thin black gloves. They left his fingertips free.

She felt a start of surprise when he shot her a tiny smirk, and signed directly toward her, his thick fingers forming complex shapes with beautiful fluidity of motion. A strangely robotic voice came out of a small metal box worn at his hip.

"Good luck."

Loretta pounded up the loading ramp after Kacey. The rough metal grating thudded beneath her feet. From a distance, the interior of the shuttle looked like a forbidding, black vault, but inside, it was surprisingly spacious and light. The *Poppy Moon* was several stories tall, and her cargo hold was currently empty. Up ahead, a narrow ladder with grippy, textured rails shot straight up toward the cockpit. Instead of heading there, like Loretta expected, Kacey jogged across the scuffed metal floor toward a bulkhead in the rear of the hold. She pointed at a row of dented lockers near the ladder. "Grab an atmo suit, will ya? The one in number four should fit you."

"Why?"

Kacey didn't answer. She was too busy prying a panel off the bulkhead. As soon as she'd lifted it off, she disappeared inside the opening.

Loretta ran for the lockers and found what looked to be a standard atmo suit with helmet. She stripped her orange jumpsuit off and stepped into the new one, wrinkling her nose at the sudden scent of rancid ammonia. Whoever had worn this previously had been in dire need of a shower. Looking down, she noticed thick, rubbery patches on the suit's knees, elbows, and belly. The ones on the joints made it difficult to bend her limbs, but the helmet seal was solid. All green indicators across the display.

She took several deep breaths, tasting the standard mix of oxygen, nitrogen, and the faint tang of chemical purifiers.

Her attackers had taken her helmet. Had they hoped asphyxiation would kill her so they didn't have to do the deed themselves? Shuttle bay recycling times varied, but they had to know they were putting her life at risk. But if they'd wanted her dead, why not kill her while she'd been unconscious?

They were in a hurry. And they wanted my helmet cam footage before it synced with MarsNet.

Loretta shoved her crumpled orange suit in the locker and slid the crossbolt shut. Why couldn't she remember their faces? Whatever drug they'd dosed her with had left her with a pounding headache, and it was as if her synapses were firing in slow motion, refusing to put two and two together.

It was a man and a woman. That much I remember. And those shiny black boots.

"Loretta! Let's move!" Kacey's voice was as cheery as it was impatient.

Inside the bulkhead compartment Kacey stood next to a golden canister the size of a greenhouse water tank. It rested upright, like a pill inside a straw, and there were a pair of what looked like helicopter skis attached to one side.

Kacey opened a hatch — there was barely room to do it — and revealed two padded seats, one beneath the other, facing upward. Loretta peered up. Long rails ran alongside what had to be a... launch tube?

Loretta felt her eyes widen at the sight of the huge engine affixed to the underside of the tiny craft. The flanges were wider than the ship itself and filthy black. The casing had been welded smooth in several places where it looked like the metal had split apart. "What is that supposed to be? A skimmer? For fuck's sake, Kace! Do your bosses know about this? If they find out you turned a — a freaking *broom closet* into an unauthorized launch tube, they'll take your wings from you."

It was easier to stammer about procedure than it was to admit to the cold sweat that had just broken out all over her body. She'd been up into orbit twice. Once during a middle school field trip, and a second time for mandatory cadet training. Both times she'd learned the same lesson. No matter how brave you thought you were, sometimes your body said, "ha ha no thank you" and forced you to curl up into a ball until it was all over.

Kacey planted a gloved hand on the side of the craft and shot Loretta a sympathetic smirk. For once, she was wearing all her safety gear.

"Loretta, meet *Beetle. Beetle*, meet my good friend Lore. She's a nervous flyer, so let's be understanding, okay?"

"I am not a—" Loretta felt her mouth pinch. "This isn't about me. I'm just—" She was about to explain in no uncertain terms that she wouldn't be setting foot in that deathtrap when their coms beeped.

It was Theo's speakerbox, "We have visitors, boss."

"Liftoff in two minutes," Kacey replied. "We'll be as quick as we can."

"Affirmative." Just before the com cut off, a rapid-fire stream of guttural syllables came over the line.

Kacey gripped a strap inside *Beetle* and lifted herself into the pilot seat. "Was that Pennsylvania Dutch?" She barked a laugh. "That'll keep them on their toes."

"Theo's Deaf?" Loretta tried to remember her training module on integrated sign language. With the advent of audio-neurological reconstruction, ISL wasn't spoken on Mars. Theo might be from Earth, but still, as marsfaring crew, he would have been eligible for treatment the moment he signed his contract.

"No, Theo's hearing." Kacey flipped a series of manual switches above her console. Like everything else about her, *Beetle*'s instrumentation looked scavenged, in good condition, but a mishmash of shapes, sizes, and colors. "His vocal cords were damaged in an industrial accident on Luna. Buckle in and close the hatch, will you? I need to get us clearance."

"Is it safe?" Loretta's hand hesitated on the assist grip.

"No, Lore," Kacey glanced skyward as if praying for patience. "*Beetle* is a death trap and my grand plan is to kill us both. Because that's how I jazz."

Loretta pulled herself up into the navigator's seat and reached for the safety harness. Gravity had never felt so heavy, lying on her back and staring at the tiny circular opening at the end of the tube. She tossed her weight left and right. The seat didn't budge, and that was a comfort.

"I've been dreaming about you." Kacey's voice was a seductive purr. Her small hands ran over the panel in front of her, caressing the ship.

Loretta's mouth went dry when she looked down at where the navigator panel should be. Instead of a display showing instrumentation and position, there was an open, square bracket with drill holes around the outer edge. She picked up the wire harness dangling down through the opening. The end was a melted lump of plastic.

"Kacey? I'm not sure if—"

Her gloved index finger shot up in the air.

"What?" Loretta snapped. "Do you need to flirt with your damned ship some more?"

A weary-sounding female voice came over the com. "Oh, I see how it is. First, you leave Mars without saying goodbye. You go *weeks* without answering my vids. And did I say you could borrow my black vinyl pants? You can't just stroll into town, buy me dinner, steal my best outfit, and expect—"

"But I *really* missed you, babe," Kacey interrupted. "In fact, I was hoping we could have dinner tomorrow? I brought you a special present from San Diego."

After a pause, "How special?"

Kacey chuckled. "It'll blow your mind."

Kacey hopped in and out of beds as casually as a hummingbird flits between flowers, but this was the first time Loretta had heard her friend try to flirt. She sounded like a complete toon.

This isn't going to work.

"I *suppose* I could let you make it up to me," the woman said slowly.

Or maybe it will.

"Wonderful. And Lin, while I've got you on the line—"

"Here it comes."

"I need a hatch override in shuttle bay thirty."

"You know I'm not supposed to do that," Lin said sternly. "Let me prep your shuttle for cycling and—"

"Babe, we dropped a radiation panel. You know what my boss is like. If she finds out, I'll be up to my ass in paperwork, and the longer that takes, the less time I'll have for the most beautiful woman on Mars."

Loretta felt her mouth twitch.

"Any chance you can let me out?" Kacey teased. "It's just my maintenance skimmer. I don't even need it all the way open, baby. Just a few meters. I'll be quick. Promise."

Lin smothered a high-pitched giggle. "Sure. I give you an inch and you take the whole damn mile."

"I love it when you talk in imperial units," Kacey rasped into her mic. "So fucking hot."

Loretta punched Kacey's shoulder lightly from behind. She flung up a middle finger in response.

"Okay," Lin said. "Make it fast, okay? Just tap my feed when you're back so I can let you in."

"You're the best. I'll be thinking about you *all* night..."

Finally! Now we can-

Whatever thought had been germinating in Loretta's brain was left plastered on the shuttle bay floor as *Beetle's* engine roared to life and punched them into the sky. A hard white dot of light overhead flung wide to swallow them whole. The scream tearing its way out of Loretta's throat lodged uselessly in her sore lungs, and her atmo-abused skin stretched painfully thin.

No-please-no-no!

Kacey squealed! Her exuberance at the prospect of imminent death compressed into a skein of sound that wrapped around them both as *Beetle* shot out of the launch tube and spiraled up into the pinkish gray sky.

Loretta's gut became a dense, watery center that the rest of her flesh whipped around. Every child knew the human body was mostly water, but *feeling* it was something else. A wet, warm tide flooded her upper thighs.

This might be how it felt to die, but she couldn't be dead, because Kacey's whoops had dissolved into a girlish cackle, a broken glass sound of pure delight. Loretta cracked one eye open just in time to see the last of the clouds whip behind them and stars burst into view. Pinpoints in the darkness rushed toward them like fireworks.

Without warning, everything stilled. Loretta felt her body lighten, her stomach float queasily up toward her diaphragm. A lock of her hair, unmoored from its fellows during the mad rush to the shuttle, floated toward her eyes and was blown back by her suit's environmental controls.

Slowly, Kacey pivoted *Beetle*'s nose around.

Loretta's breath caught in her throat. She floated above her planet, but this was Mars as she'd never seen or imagined it before. She recognized the rough-hewn geography of the southern hemisphere, marked with ancient craters, and the faint icy crust at the northern pole. Yet at this distance, she could actually *see* the edge of the troposphere, the shimmering, ethereal shell of trapped gasses that would one day become a breathable atmosphere. Swirls of mother-of-pearl clouds moved slowly across the north, obscuring Epiphany and her outlying research stations.

Her heart shuddered, but not with fear this time.

Awe.

How impossible it seemed that this mass of rock and gas had held and nurtured everything she'd ever known, and everyone she'd ever loved. Her parents. Travis. Marcus. Risha. From a bare expanse of lifeless rock, her people had carved out not just an existence, but a miracle, proof that human life endured, even in a dark and unforgiving universe.

She blinked.

Also, Mars was really, *really* pretty.

"What a rush!" Kacey's arms floated up toward her instrument panel. Loretta was surprised to find she could move freely again as well. Her limbs felt like wet noodles, but her fingers flexed in front of her eyes, apparently unwounded.

Everything seemed intact.

"Are you okay back there? You didn't puke in your helmet, did you?"

"No, but I know why this suit smells like piss now."

A low-res vid of Kacey's sympathetic face appeared in the upper quadrant of Loretta's helmet display. "It happens to the best of us. Now, help me find those bastards."

CHAPTER SEVEN

Loretta upped the magnification on her face shield. It didn't help. Even though Kacey had pointed them away from the planet, and Sol's reflection was less, she only saw stars. "How am I supposed to find them? With my eyes?"

She waved the melted wire harness in the air.

"You could, but there's a—" Kacey paused. "Right. I forgot to put the new nav panel in. Don't worry about it. I caught a glimpse of the ship before they cold cocked you and I'm ninety percent sure those were Pinafore engines. Quality shit, if you can afford it. Top tier fuel efficiency. Luckily for us, that means they're running cooler than most." She clicked her tongue. "There can't be too many shuttles with that config and... Ha!"

"You found them? Already?"

"You're gonna love this." Kacey snorted. "They're in the departure lineup, waiting for clearance from orbit control. They knock you out, leave you for dead, but afterward, they get in line like good little Martian bootlickers. Amaze. I'm heading in for a closer look."

Kacey spun the ship in a spiral, three times to the left, one time to the right. Loretta gagged. Thankfully, there was nothing left in her stomach to throw up. "Do you have to do that?"

"Sorry, I keep forgetting you hate space."

"I never said—"

"You don't need to play stalwart soldier with me, sweetie. You know I love you, even when you're pissing yourself like a baby."

"I thought you said that happened to the best of us!"

"Yeah, well, I was trying to make you feel better."

Beetle's rear engine vibrated as she accelerated, but thankfully, the craft showed no signs of stress. Loretta sat in silence as Kacey worked the controls.

"Aha!" Kacey pounded her fist on her armrest. "Look at that, will ya? I have their drive signature. Huh. Looks like the signal's dirty."

"Dirty?"

Kacey tapped her com twice. "Theo. I'm sending you a transpo signal in the encrypted feed. Store it for me, will you?"

"Bylo by mi potěšením," the mechanical voice replied. Two clicks followed.

"Sir!" An exasperated masculine voice was barely audible in the background. "Your translation unit is malfunctioning. If you could just change. Yes, *chaaange* to English, we could communicate better. Here. Look at my mouth. *English.*"

Something clicked, and a long reply followed, this time in Japanese.

"Sir, he stole a trover. Perhaps if we take him in for questioning—" This speaker sounded younger, less sure of herself.

"The code *clearly* states that translation services are provided on demand prior to arrest except in cases of imminent bodily harm. Are you being harmed, cadet?"

"No sir."

"Then get someone down here who can fix that damn box!"

"Perhaps if we used our tablets—"

Kacey turned off the com. "Yikes. She sounds like a smart one. Let's not dawdle. And to answer your question, a dirty signal just means multiple waveforms combined into one output. It lets you spoof your sig if you need to swap identities without installing a secondary transponder. It's old tech. Not much used anymore. Well, not by anyone running a ship *that* fine."

"Fine? *Poppy* is way nicer."

"Sure, she's great, but looks aren't everything."

"Kacey, we can't just—"

"*Trust me.* We don't even have a transponder. They won't be able to see us. We're too small."

Red warning lights flashed overhead. An automated voice sounded through an overhead speaker. "Warning. Warning. Oxygen failure in thirty seconds. Twenty-nine. Twenty-eight..."

"Kacey!"

Kacey's small fist slammed the panel above her head. The blinking stopped. "See? We're spifferific. Just keep your pants on. And your helmet. Life support is... a work in progress."

Loretta caught sight of something small and reflective. Only it wasn't a reflection at all, but a pair of engines glowing softly in the darkness. As they got closer, she saw a familiar outline. The hawklike nose of the ship they were hunting.

"I'm taking us in," Kacey said, blowing out a breath that seemed to say that she too, wasn't immune to fear.

Not that she'd ever admit it.

The *Steady as She Goes* loomed large and black beneath *Beetle*. Zooming over the *Steady*'s flat, black underbelly, and closing the distance slowly, Loretta felt like a winged insect buzzing over the surface of a large, dark animal. The *Steady*'s signal lights illuminated her hull with a soft gray glow. Those lights would snap off just before she left formation, but Kacey had tapped into orbit control's feed, so there was little risk of being surprised.

When they returned to the docks, Loretta knew her superiors would want answers. Already she could imagine the shock and disapproval on their faces, and the dreary sequence of administrative reviews that would inevitably follow. She was prepared to defend her actions, even if it meant more punishment. But did Kacey understand what she was risking?

"Maybe we didn't think this through. If orbit control finds out you were up here in an unlicensed craft..."

Kacey had been glancing out the window, checking the evidence of her eyes against what she saw on her instrument panel. They'd nearly matched the shuttles speed, and now it hardly felt like they were moving at all. "Did I ever tell you about my first bicycle?" she asked.

"Is this really the time?"

"I was about six," Kacey continued unfazed, "And I found it in a dump not far from the place we'd been holing up. The bike was too big for me, and it was a rusted piece of crap with dented fenders, but after I cleaned it up, it was perfect. That summer, I rode my new bike up and down the old, abandoned highway as fast as my legs would take me. I loved feeling the wind blowing through my hair. And I've *always* had amazing hair."

"No argument there."

"Back then, it was long. Down to my butt."

"Okay, but what does this have to do with what we're—"

"And do you know what *never* happened?"

"What?"

"No one ever pulled me aside to ask for my license to ride a damn bicycle."

"Kacey—"

"Earth may be a shit sandwich on rye, but there's one thing they get that Mars can't seem to grasp. Sometimes, a bike is just a bike. Like *Beetle*." She patted the console. "Minimal life support. No fancy backup systems. She's just a bike! I made her because she makes me happy. *Relax*. We're out for a ride, and you're sitting on the handlebars."

"I'm not trying to be difficult. I'm just worried that—"

"Now, let me tell you about my *second* bike."

Loretta threw up her hands. "I can't wait."

"I'd been hearing my whole damn life how special your planet is. How advanced you all were. How enlightened. After I promised to be a good little Martian, my handlers offered to get me a toy as a reward. Whatever I wanted! I asked for a bicycle. Not a shitty Earth bike. A *Mars* bike. It had to be better, right? Because Mars has the best of everything."

She flipped a small silver switch to her left.

"Can you guess what they gave me? An *exercise* bike, bolted to the damn carpet. Here you go, little girl. Here's the toy you wanted! That's when I realized Mars was a scam. I wanted to feel the wind in my hair. But there's no wind on Mars. Just a bunch of people telling you how much better things are, even when they suck."

Loretta hesitated. Where was this sudden hostility coming from? She leaned forward. "Did I piss you off?"

"There's a whole damn universe out there, Lore! And people too. Real human beings trying to make things better for everyone. Yet here you stay, bolted to the damn carpet. Have you ever felt the wind in your hair? Can you even grasp what that means?"

So that's what this little tirade was about? The job offer? Loretta blew out her breath. "I told you I'd think about it."

"Sure you will." Kacey patted the console. "Anyway, *Beetle* is my coolest bike yet. She can fly, but that's not all."

Slowly, *Beetle*'s rails connected to the underside of the *Steady as She Goes*. A faint *thunk* vibrated through the craft and through Loretta's legs. "What was that?"

"*Beetle* has sticky feet! Isn't that great?" Kacey half-turned in the cramped space. Her eager smile flashed. She looked as proud as a momma cat with a litter full of freshly groomed kittens. "There's a box under your chair. Grab it, will you? There's a transmitter inside. Let's have ourselves a little fun before I take you back home."

Loretta wrested the container from its safety webbing beneath her seat and set it in her lap. The box was full of junky looking parts, circuit boards in a dozen shapes and a rainbow of colors. Small rounds of wire in several thicknesses. A sharp-looking pair of clippers. A crumpled protein drink pouch.

She shunted items aside, digging deeper.

Her fingers brushed something large and plastic. She pulled it out and stared. It was a semi-translucent pink unicorn horn, still in its original clamshell packaging. It was stubby, and there was a suction cup on one side. "Happy Unicorn Fun Time?" Loretta read off the box. "What's this?"

"Put that back. You're looking for a flat oval, about the width of your palm. It's a mid-range transmitter. Private frequency. *Poppy* can use it to map the *Steady's* trajectory after she breaks orbit."

Loretta found the transmitter stuck to the inside of the box. She handed it to Kacey. That's when the frequency they were monitoring came to life.

"Orbit control, this is *Steady as She Goes*. Requesting priority departure."

The feminine voice shook loose something in Loretta's memory, sending a waterfall of information tumbling down almost faster than she could process it. "That's her! The bitch who kicked the shit out of my ribs. Quick, call your friend. Maybe she can delay them until a security team gets here. Gah! Why didn't we think of that sooner? All we needed to do was—"

"No. I'm not getting Lin swept up in this. She already stuck her neck out for me once, and that's plenty. Besides, the moment these clowns know they're made, they'll make a run for it. And I'd prefer not to have *Beetle* ripped in half, thank you very much. Or my gloriously hot body, for that matter."

How to make Kacey understand? "But they're terrorists. They tried to blow up a university! We have to take the risk, Kace. If they get away—"

Kacey tapped something on her forearm panel.

"You're locking me out of the channel? What the hell?"

"Listen. I didn't come up here because of your mission, or the code, or anything like that. I'm up here because those assholes hurt my friend, and I want them to pay."

"Is that so." Kacey's voice had a wobble in it. She wasn't telling the whole story.

"Fine! I also figured maybe there will be a reward for catching them. And I don't mean a ceremony in my honor. None of that symbolic shit. I'm talking about transferrable credits, the kind I can turn into alcohol, fuel, and one of those structure-printed pleather dresses they sell at the new shop in thirty-two charlie." She grinned. "I digress. My point is, *yes*, we're going to get our revenge. And I'll help you. But we'll do it my way. The smart way."

"Because you're so much smarter than me." Loretta tried to keep the resentment out of her voice but couldn't quite manage. God, Kacey could be a pain in the ass sometimes.

"No, because you know fuck all about space, so that means I'm in charge so long as we're up here."

This was difficult to argue with. "Fine." Loretta crossed her arms. "What do you need me to do?"

"Give me the horn."

"What?"

"You heard me." She took the toy. "Now, *because I trust you*, I'll patch you into the radio. If something happens — and I'm *not saying it will* — I need you to improvise."

"How?"

"You do know the meaning of the word? Keep them distracted until I get back." She reached beneath her seat and pulled out another box. She shoved something in her side pocket, then clipped a small pulley to her waist on a D-ring. The other end, she clipped to a grab bar near her seat.

Loretta felt her heart lurch. "Wait! You're going outside? What if they get clearance? If they accelerate—"

Kacey pointed to a tiny switch above the pilot seat. "*Beetle*'s sticky feet release is right there. Ears sharp, and let's hope they don't get shifty."

"Shifty? Kace, I'm—"

Loretta's mouth snapped shut when orbit control replied, "*Steady as She Goes*, you'll need to wait your turn. Are you having an emergency? Assistance is available."

"No emergency," Ms. Boots said, hurriedly. "Slot us in when you can. Thanks, OC."

Someone's nervous, Loretta thought with grim satisfaction. *And it's not just me.*

"See?" Kacey said. "We're gonna be fine."

Loretta watched, stunned into silence, as Kacey army-crawled along the surface of the *Steady as She Goes* like she'd done this kind of thing a million times before. The tie-cable she'd clipped to her waist stretched out behind her, frighteningly thin and delicate. More a thread than a cable.

There were no visible handholds on this part of the hull, yet whatever those black, rubbery patches on her atmo suit were, they seemed to keep her knees, belly, and forearms affixed to the *Steady*'s hull.

Sticky feet indeed, Loretta mused. Even seeing it with her own eyes, it was hard to believe that Kacey had gone out into hard vacuum like there was nothing to it. That would have turned any normal person's nerves to jelly, but Kacey was crawling along like a toddler in pursuit of a cookie, humming cheerfully into the feed all the while.

For the first time, she considered the possibility that Kacey Holt might actually be a spacefaring badass.

"We're looking good," Kacey's voice was calm as could be. A faint hissing sound came over the line, then stopped. A moment later, it was back.

"Is that a leak?" Loretta upped her magnification, but all she could see was Kacey's hab-suited butt and the bottoms of her boots as she worked. She'd stopped near a partially shielded utility box.

"No leak. *There*. And over there. Oh, and we can't forget the *pièce de résistance*." Her breathing sped up. A moment of exertion. "Okay! I'm on my way back. Then we can — *Shit!*"

"What? What's going on?" Loretta couldn't see much. Kacey was still on the hull. She hadn't spun off into space. But she held a long, black stick in her hand.

An antenna?

"Cheap piece-of-trash Earth tech," Kacey spat. "If you're going to make your ship out of literal garbage why not push the whole damn thing into the sun and save us the indignity of having to look at it." Kacey tossed the antenna up and away. Planting both forearms down, she pivoted and crawled back toward *Beetle*. Faster this time. "Lore, I need you to stay calm."

Electricity shot up Loretta's spine and into her fingertips. "Why would I need to be calm?"

"Just because they *might* have noticed one of their signals go out, it doesn't mean they—"

"Unidentified craft. Identify yourself immediately."

"Oof! Someone's cranky." Kacey's too-casual tone was betrayed by the fact that her breaths were ragged, and her voice was heavy with fatigue. "Lore, remember when I said you might need to improvise?"

"I'm on it." Loretta activated the channel. "*Steady As She Goes*, this is orbital control security craft *Alpha Echo Three*. We received a report of anomalies in your drive signature. Prepare to be boarded."

"I said improvise, not make them shit their pants!"

Loretta changed frequencies. "I'm trying to distract them!"

"You suck at it."

"They won't dare take off now. They can't risk—"

"Oh. I get it. You're pissed!" Kacey's giggle came out of nowhere. "You want to make those bastards squirm. Honestly, Lore, I respect that."

"I'm just doing what you told me."

"Your capacity for self-denial astounds me. Can you not hear yourself? You want to kick their salty asses. You want payback!"

"*Alpha Echo Three*," Ms. Boots said, her voice cautious, "We're not reading your transponder. Requesting verification from the lead operator."

Loretta switched channels. "Acknowledged, *Steady as she Goes*. Please stand by." She glanced out the window. Kacey was less than a minute out. "See? They aren't going anywhere. I'm calling the harbormaster. They've probably got a security team en route already. They need to know these are the bastards that—"

Kacey's voice broke in, panicky. "Shut up! You're still on their frequency."

Loretta punched the button. "Fuck! Sorry. I'm sure they didn't—"

"Jesus! Why not give them our exact position, our names, and our favorite brand of whiskey while you're at it. Who taught you to use a radio?"

Her attitude was getting old, quick. "A radio? You call this patched-together contraption a radio? I'm surprised you didn't opt for two tin cans and a piece of yarn. Earth yarn, obviously, because everything that doesn't come from *your* home planet is a useless piece of—"

"Unidentified craft," Ms. Boots snapped. "You are impersonating a Martian official. Identify yourself immediately, or we'll have to notify—"

"Don't you dare answer them," Kacey said. "I'm almost there. We just need to lift off and—"

Loretta was done being told what to do. That carload of assholes in the big black bird were acting like they had the upper hand, but that was them trying to have it both ways, threatening her while pretending they had the laws and customs of Mars on their side.

They were stalling.

She switched to their frequency. "Bullshit."

"Excuse me?"

"I said, *bullshit.* You're not calling anyone. You attacked a member of the Diplomatic Corps today, and you think you can just walk away like nothing happened? I know exactly who and what you are. People so threatened by what Mars represents that when persuasion fails, you resort to violence. You honestly believe you can run your illegal cargo through our ports, attack our citizens, and we'll let that stand? Do the smart thing. Stand down. I guarantee you'll be treated fairly."

A fist pounded on the window. Loretta leaned forward to reach the latch. Her bruised ribs screamed as they brushed the hard edge of the pilot's seat.

Kacey flung herself into her chair, slammed the hatch down, and flipped *Beetle*'s disengage switch. Only after they were clear did she pull her safety harness on.

"Who are you?" Ms. Boots demanded.

"Oh, I think you know," Loretta said. "And one way or another, we'll continue this conversation. Soon."

The woman's voice dropped to a furious whisper. "Listen, you little shit. I don't think you know who you're dealing with."

"Tell me then. Who am I dealing with, exactly?" When they didn't immediately reply, she added. "Yeah. That's what I thought. Not just criminals. Cowards too. You should have killed me while you had the chance."

She delighted in the silence that followed. Damn if it didn't feel good to hear them twisting in the wind! Until a face-to-face reunion could be arranged, it would have to do.

Hopefully Theo's tracker would get them what they needed.

The *Steady*'s signal lights were turning off, one section at a time, but *Beetle* had already lifted away.

Kacey pointed to her left. "Look!" She rolled the craft for a better view. "Quick! I left them a present."

Loretta squinted. Just before the last of the lights turned off, she saw it. A neon pink unicorn spray-painted on the *Steady*'s hull. The creature stood on its hind legs, holding up a hoof in a rude gesture. Something small and pink wiggled down near the creature's groin.

Happy Unicorn Fun Time.

Laughter burst from Loretta's lungs. "Has anyone ever told you what a freak you are?"

Beetle pivoted again, aiming for the planet below. Her engine vibrated as they picked up speed.

"All the time," Kacey said, a smile in her voice. "By the way, I hope you appreciate what this little adventure is gonna cost me."

"Don't worry. I'll tell the harbormaster that the whole thing was my idea."

"Oh, I don't care about *that*. But you owe me a shopping trip. Now I need to buy Lin another present. And trust me when I say she's impossible to shop for."

They were halfway home when a thought occurred to Loretta. She reached up and tapped Kacey's shoulder. "I never said we should chase them, did I?"

"Sure you did."

"Out loud?"

"I know what's in your heart, Lore. Even when you're too chickenshit to admit it to yourself."

CHAPTER EIGHT

Marcus Wells bent forward and sniffed the plant resting on the shelf in front of him. The reddish, lily-like bloom gave off a faint scent of rotting meat, or at least, that's what the text beneath the planter box claimed. He found the aroma unusual, organic and faintly coppery, with an undertone of something that sent up a faint warning flare in his belly. An echo of an ancient survival instinct preserved deep within the genes of *Homo sapiens*.

Sunlight filtered prettily through the gold-tinted dome overhead, scattering the most advantageous wavelengths of light over the residents of greenhouse eighty-two. On the far side of the densely packed acre, near the entrance, a gaggle of eager schoolchildren had gathered around a large and feathery mangrove palm, listening to a lecture from a junior botanist.

Tamatha Clark's dry voice slithered into Marcus's ear from behind. "You'd think the botanists would have bred that foul stench out of them by now."

Her disapproval hung in the air, faint yet somehow less subtle than the bug-enticing intoxicants of the *Helicodiceros muscivorus*. No doubt the estimable Tamatha Clark would have preferred to convene inside council offices, where they'd be surrounded by an army of fussing assistants and the subtle luxuries accorded to a person of rank, like the endless supply of pu-ehr tea she favored.

Marcus knew better.

Certain matters were best handled outside the rooms of government, lest a taint of corruption seep into the hallowed halls themselves. Tamatha, for all her experience, still saw politics as the art of moving people around on civilization's chessboard, always seeking victory over whatever enemy was the loudest or most fashionable, regardless of the long-term view.

"These specimens are controls," he replied, stepping aside to give her a better look. "Besides, they're beautiful in their own way. Imagine all the genetic variants that must have competed and died out to create this lady." He smiled down at it. "No perfect conditions. No being coddled by curated sunlight or carefully titrated nutrient mixes. Raw evolution is unforgiving." His fingertip grazed the plant, noting it's plump smoothness. "She's a survivor. Like us."

"I see you're feeling philosophical today."

Her tone was light, but her gaze swept warily around the garden. They were well out of earshot of the students and their minders. Tamatha's fear was grounded in the future, not in the moment upon which they stood. Even the color of her stylish silk pantsuit — sage green — might have been chosen to help her blend into the background.

Clever as a fox and twice as jumpy. I wonder what she wants from me this time?

He guided her further into the maze of pathways, toward the distant edge of the dome. "You said you wanted to chat?"

He gestured at an empty bench. Outside, through the blurry, double windows of a nearby airlock, a trover rested next to a supply shed. Whoever had parked it had neglected to cover it against the threat of sandstorm damage.

Tamatha wouldn't sit. Instead, she brushed dirt off a shelf with her palms, fussing like an inept housekeeper, scattering precious soil on the floor. "I wanted to say I'm sorry about Loretta. We all know how important she is to you."

"And you think I'm angry?"

She met his gaze then. "You'd be within your rights. How is she holding up?"

His smile sought to soothe her. "Oh, she's a bit embarrassed. But she's rising to the occasion."

"With your help, no doubt." She shot him a wry smirk in response. "I've always wondered why you took a special interest in that girl. Did you suspect that she knew more than she was letting on? Or was it guilt?"

She must be feeling bold indeed, to ask him *that* question. She knew his personal history as well as anyone else on the council, and it was only natural that she'd filled in a few gaps on her own.

Tamatha Clarke had many talents, but courage wasn't one of them. That's why she was feinting, needling him about what she knew, hinting instead of striking true.

"Oh, I was friends with her father, once upon a time. I figured it was the least I could do, keeping an eye on his kid. He would have done the same thing for Travis, had our positions been reversed."

"I do find it difficult to imagine," she said mildly. "Marcus Wells, champion of the Martian cause, breaking bread with a traitorous thunderhead like Tom Ryder." Quickly, she shoved her hands in the pockets of her outer tunic, as if tucking her snide comments away for safekeeping. "Although I suppose we were all young once. It's easier to be swept up by rhetoric when your reasoning skills have yet to be fully formed. As you probably know, the prefrontal cortex isn't—"

"Risha isn't speaking to me," Marcus interrupted, losing patience with her nervous chatter. "She thinks we threw Lore under the bus."

Tamatha frowned. "We knew someone would need to be tossed, so to speak. Unfortunately for your girl, she handed us the perfect opportunity."

She was right about that. Anti-charter sentiment had been rising alarmingly fast in recent months and Loretta's behavior at the shooting range had created a perfect media moment. Her righteous anger in the field had rallied the pro-charter base, most of whom believed that the Martian government needed to take a harder line on uncivilized behavior. At the same time, the Ombuds' swift punishment had been a soothing balm for the moderates and fence sitters.

Politically, it had been a win-win. And personally? Well, Loretta had always been a fighter. She'd emerge stronger, after she'd had time to think matters through. Young people were like young plants. You could guide their growth if you were patient, but push too hard or too fast, and they were liable to snap.

Still, there were trials ahead for both Loretta and his son. Once you'd shaped a young life to the extent possible, there came a moment to step back and let them succeed or fail. Travis, he sometimes worried over.

He had a lot of Bianca in him.

"I played my part, you understand," Tamatha said, wringing her hands, "but I took no pleasure in it."

Marcus hadn't missed the flash of surprise on Captain Hamid's face when he'd glanced at his tablet during the hearing. The man was competent enough but as imaginative as a block of printed composite. Someone had encouraged him to goad Loretta, right before he'd pushed her against the wall.

Is that what this meeting is about? Feeding her starving ego? I've met cats with more self-discipline.

His winning smile landed on her like a spotlight. "I take it we have you to thank for Captain Hamid's sudden stroke of brilliance?"

Tamatha beamed up at him, her eyes crinkling with pleasure.

May fate burn me down if I ever become that weak.

It was human nature to crave recognition, to want everyone to see how you'd laid your own brick on the road to victory. Still, the councilwoman's neediness was the behavior of a child, not that of a fully formed adult. Certainly he expected more from those dedicated to the Martian cause.

Yet we must work with what we have.

Marcus looped his arm through hers and strolled forward along the path in the manner of old friends enjoying the day. "You know, if the founders hadn't been so sentimental, we wouldn't be in this mess at all. I'm sure a hundred years sounds like forever when you're standing at the starting line. Yet here we are, watching our government collapse before our eyes. All for one line buried in the preamble."

"The Martian charter will stand in force for one-hundred years, after which a vote of all citizens will determine if it shall continue," Tamatha recited. "Imagine that. The founders were wise enough to create a sage governing body, but in a sheer act of lunacy they threw it all away for the sake of... what? Novelty? The council should have issued a ruling years ago, declaring the preamble null and void."

"Accepting the vote was the safest option. Otherwise we'd risk sparking a revolution. Then where would we be?"

She conceded the point with an irritated flick of her hand. "Still, I'm sorry it had to be *her*. Loretta is..."

"Exactly where she needs to be. Tomorrow, we'll have a fresh set of polling numbers, and we'll see how much the dial has moved."

Her mouth pinched into a small, tense circle. "Don't blow sunshine up my robes, old friend. I can see the truth simmering behind those eyes of yours. The winds are against us and we're almost out of time. Our careful campaigning hasn't saved Epiphany from ruin, and the average citizen is more interested in feeling powerful than in stewarding the future for their own descendants.

"Can you believe they want to reconstitute the council via popular vote?" Her mouth twisted into a snarl. "By all means, let's determine the fate of civilization on a fucking popularity contest." When she paused at a flowering bush, she seemed visibly shaken. Her pale finger skimmed one of the soft white petals, barely touching it. "I suppose we're finished. That is, unless you have a plump white rabbit to pull out of your hat?"

He understood that she didn't actually want to know the answer to that question. She hoped to push him toward action. It might have been insulting — the notion that he needed her anxious prodding — but he understood her intent. On the important things, they were in accord with one another. Tamatha Clarke might do her best work when surrounded by stronger souls, but she had a talent for the softer maneuvers, and thus they were best left in her capable hands.

Still, he'd heard the tremor in her voice. The fear, burbling beneath the surface like water in an underground stream. She wanted to push him, yes, but beneath the maneuvering, there was a deeper need.

She wanted someone to tell her it would all be okay.

Managing other people's emotions was the cost of progress and peace. He'd built his political career on that notion, and as much as he wearied of bolstering up his lessers, it was essential work.

"I started Travis on the Gharison papers," he said, enjoying the sudden tension in Tamatha's posture when he shifted subjects. A fight-or-flight response? Another echo, he mused, of the animal nature they shared.

"Good. And Loretta?"

"Not yet. Travis leads from his head. And Lore…"

"Pure ovarian fortitude." Tamatha chuckled. "Guts and instinct. That can be good or bad, depending." Her expression brightened. "Shall I ask my eldest to speak with Travis? Sasha's a bit further along, and he may want someone closer to his age to discuss things with."

"That's very kind of you."

For a moment, her guile seemed to slip, revealing the unhappy woman beneath the mask. "Sometimes I worry, old friend."

Comfort it is.

"We'll get through the vote. Trust me on that."

"Not only that. I'm afraid that…" She glanced away, unwilling to finish the thought.

He plucked a forbidden flower off the bush in front of them and tucked it into her lapel. He stilled her objection by pressing his index finger against her dry lips. "I need you to remember that we're doing Mars a service." He lowered his hand and rested it lightly on her shoulder. Two soft pats. *There there.* "And if our duty is a struggle? That's good, because moments like this should weigh on our hearts. These aren't normal times, Tam. It's only natural to wish for a gentler path forward."

Her hand went to the blossom. She twirled it in her

fingers before slipping it into her pocket out of sight. With a tiny smile, she murmured, "You've always had a way with words. I wonder if they'll be a comfort when they throw us in Hellas for treason."

Before he could answer, his tablet chimed. It was the harbormaster herself. "Sir," she blurted, "we have a security issue I'd like your guidance on. Can you join me in my office?"

Her tone seemed to say *right now*, so he nodded curtly. "I'm on my way."

He slid the tablet back into his pocket and looked up to see Tamatha watching him with naked amusement in her pale, gray-blue eyes. Even now, with disaster at the gates, she couldn't resist a little slash of the claws.

"Oh my. Did one of your rabbits escape?"

CHAPTER NINE

Late that night, as the service crew traded empty bottles for full ones behind the long blue counter of the Helios Bar, Loretta leaned her elbows on a damp table and flipped through the photos she'd been snapping all evening. Earlier, the club had been packed. Patrons had stood elbow to elbow at the counter, offering good-natured jibes to the bartender as he poured with a generous hand. Now, she could hear herself think.

Someone had turned off the synth-kiln beat pulsing through the speakers, and the big, dim room felt oddly hollow without the bass vibrating the dance floor, competing with the swells of raucous conversation and sudden bursts of laughter.

They'd had a good time.

She archived the selfie she'd taken of herself and Travis. Her, tucked beneath his muscular arm, both of them laughing at some joke she couldn't remember. There was only one snap of Theo. Kacey had cajoled him into staying for a beer or two, but he'd left quickly, signing something Loretta hadn't understood. She swiped one more time, finding her photo of Kacey and Lin in the midst of a tickle fight in their corner booth. Kacey's face was beet red from the effort of joyful resistance.

With a tap, she sent a copy to Kacey. A memento of good times enjoyed among friends, and — she hoped — a reminder that Mars wasn't all bad. They'd gotten off easy given the sheer number of code violations they'd stacked up during their little adventure. Kacey hadn't even been cited for their unsanctioned flight, instead receiving a speeding ticket for the launch and a reminder to register her maintenance scow before the next inspection.

No doubt the evidence they'd offered had garnered sympathy with investigators. That, and the sight of the chief councilor barging his way into the room to demand appropriate representation for his adopted daughter and her friends. Marcus liked to play the stiff-lipped dignitary, but beneath that facade, she knew he cared deeply about everyone he'd gathered under his wings. Only after he'd ensured she was in good hands had he departed with a curt nod, leaving the harbor crew to continue their questioning.

Bizarrely, the harbormaster had never received her request to lock down the *Steady*'s shuttle bay. Somehow, her attackers had diverted the call and spoofed the response. How was that even possible? The investigators were looking into it. And now, thanks to Kacey and Theo, they had footage of the ship, recordings of the drive signature, and even voiceprints from the chat she'd had with Ms. Boots over short-range com. Those terrorists might run, and surely they'd try to hide — possibly behind a distant moon where their signal wouldn't be picked up by listener beacons. Even so, they'd never be able to return to Mars undetected.

The only fly in the punchbowl was Kacey's insistence that they not tell authorities about the transmitter she'd planted on the *Steady's* hull. Something about gray market tech? The worry in her voice had been palpable, so despite knowing better, Loretta had agreed to hold that detail back for now. Until *Poppy's* computer was done analyzing the data, there was nothing to report anyway.

She saved my ass today, dragging me out of that shuttle bay. Keeping one little secret is the least I can do.

"Shall we call it a night?" Travis stifled a yawn and pointed at the back corner booth, where Lin and Kacey were making out, oblivious to the world around them. Kacey's fingers were buried into the thicket of Lin's shiny black hair. "I think they've forgotten we're here."

Loretta felt her own yawn building. She let it out, tilting her face away to spare him the worst of her beer breath, then pulled him closer, wincing as pain shot out from her abused ribs in a hundred spiky directions. "I don't think they'll mind if we sneak out. Besides, I'm wiped. How about you?"

His fingertip ran up her bare arm, sending shivers down her spine. "Not entirely. Shall we go back to your place?"

She leaned over and kissed the back of his smooth hand. The numbers on his watch made her sit up straighter. *Ouch!* It would be a while before she could move fast without pain. "Did you realize it's tomorrow? You have work. *Fuck.* I have work! In like, two hours. And I'm already swimming in the shit for abandoning my shift today. I mean — yesterday."

He plucked her tablet out of her hand and punched something in. "There. You're taking a sick day. Captain's orders."

"I don't need—"

"Slow your roll, mighty Thor." He rubbed her upper back, gently as to not aggravate her injuries. "You've had quite the day, eh? After a thorough ass kicking and a space chase in what was basically a chair strapped to a salvage booster," he shook his head disbelievingly, "you sat through three hours of grilling with investigators, and then, instead of resting up like a mere mortal, you let Kacey drag you straight here for — what was it, again?"

"Laser disco." She blinked sleepily. "And I rested! I took a long nap after the medics patched me up. And to be clear, I did not get my ass kicked. My ass is fine. It's *perfect*." Spinning around to prove this true, she felt a wave of nausea and almost tumbled off her seat.

"And how many beers did you have before I got here?"

"Twenty-seven."

He gave her his best you're-not-funny look. It was too cute! Everything about Travis Wells was precious. His nose. Those pretty brown eyes of his. The way he was always worrying about her for no good reason.

Did she tell him often enough how much she adored him? Probably not. But that was something easily mended.

She kissed his perfect nose. "*You* are my favorite person on the planet. No. In the solar system! Speaking of which..." She gripped his firm bicep and squeezed. "Hmm. I agree. Yes. Very nice. You should come over and help me rest. Have you ever heard of Happy Unicorn Fun Time?"

His mouth twitched. "I can't say I have."

Her finger waved in the air. "I'm not entirely sure how it works. But I'm guessing one of us would have to be the unicorn. And the other one..." She frowned. "Or maybe we're both unicorns? I'd ask Kacey, but she's got her hands full."

"Perhaps another time," he replied, laughing a little. "Come on. I'll walk you home." He glanced over at Kacey and Lin, who were about to round third base in front of everyone.

"Hey!" He called out. "Don't make me get the hose, you two."

Kacey looked up, grinning. "Spoilsport!"

Loretta waved goodbye. Grabbing Travis's chin, she turned his face toward hers. "Stop ogling the ladies."

"I was doing no such thing." He grinned, then looked her

up and down with a critical eye. "Although, on second thought, I should let you sleep. No offense, babe, but you look like you went ten rounds with a jackhammer, and you're being extra silly. Sleep first. Fun later. Okay?"

"Yes sir." She saluted him.

"Very funny."

Loretta touched her swollen cheek. Most of her bruises were below her neck, but it would take a week or more for her atmo-abused skin to heal. She probably looked like an overripe tomato, but everyone had been too nice to say anything about it.

My friends are the best friends.

She nodded reluctantly. "Okay. But I'll walk myself home. If you come along, one thing's gonna lead to another, and I won't get any sleep at all. But I'm glad you came out with us tonight. I missed you."

"You see me every day."

"So?"

His shy smile was the best thing she'd ever seen. Better than the sight of that ridiculous pink unicorn. Even better than hearing Ms. Boots panic, when she realized she'd been made.

"I'll check on you later," he said, letting his hand slip from hers. "But do me a favor, will you? The next time you think it's a good idea to go chasing after rogue spacecraft, let the professionals handle it. You could have died up there."

Loretta stood. Aside from a rather pleasant, full-body buzz, she felt steady. Firm on her feet. "Indeed. The next time I'm jumped by terrorists, I promise to call you for a professional consultation."

"I'm serious."

"So am I." She leaned in close for one more kiss and spoke low. "Kacey had my back today. She was... kind of amazing. But don't worry. Next time, we'll see them coming."

It was a nice night for a walk. Sunrise was still a few hours away, and she had the wide pedestrian corridor to herself. She passed the arched entrance to the transit hub without slowing. It was about five kilometers to her hab, and a walk would loosen up her stiff muscles. The body had a tendency to clench up around an injury, and her side was covered in bruises. There were no broken bones, thankfully. The drugs the medics had given her were incredible, but there was only so much they could do.

Despite her nap and the long night out, she still felt wired, buzzing with the energy of their narrow escape. The *Steady* had shot into orbit less than thirty seconds after *Beetle* lifted off her hull. If they'd still been attached...

Maybe it was better not to think about the what ifs.

Unfortunately, Kacey's tablet feed hadn't captured any usable footage of her attackers. Just a man's blurred fist, his shoulder, and a glimpse of his short, dark hair. The harbormaster's office had all crew manifests on file, including ID photos, but the looks the investigators had traded made her wonder if something had happened to that data. Thankfully, *Beetle* had recorded the crew's voiceprints along with their engine signature.

They hacked the system somehow. It won't matter in the long run, though. Voices can be spoofed over a com, or even deleted if you've got a wiz on your side, but the minute they walk into a shuttle bay and their voiceprints hit MarsNet, we'll know who they are.

It wasn't enough, but it was more than they would have had without Kacey's help. Regardless of her motives, she'd made a difference today. Everyone was a little bit safer now.

I hope she realizes that.

She smirked at the memory of Kacey hollering and whooping as they'd blasted up into orbit. *Beetle* was one hell of a bicycle! As much as she hated the sensation of launching, and as much as she never, *ever*, wanted to do it again, she had to admit there were *some* good things about space travel. Like that view...

She'd never understood art — not really — but outside, in the natural world, there was a kind of beauty that could make you feel like you were being blown apart and put back together again. Put back correctly, this time. Perhaps it was impossible to love something fully until you'd stepped away from it, seen it entire, unspoiled by the bias of your own expectations.

Beauty *and* truth, wrapped up together.

She chuckled at her strange flight of fancy. *Maybe I am buzzed.* Soft LED lights illuminated the rounded white ceiling above her, casting a soft glow onto the gray carpet beneath her soft-soled boots. So far, she'd passed the entrance to an office complex, a smattering of food depositories, and a primary school.

None of it looked familiar.

Pausing at the nearest hub pickup point, she checked the map. She'd diverted south and missed the turnoff toward her hab. Perhaps a ride home was in order. While she waited for the next pedestrian shuttle, she opened her inbox, something she'd been avoiding ever since her public humiliation.

Oof.

Her tablet glowed red with hundreds of missed messages. Some were notes of support from friends and clients in forty-two beta. There were dozens of nastygrams, all but two sent through anonymizing relays. She binned the insults and activated her work filter. Halfway down the list, she saw several messages in a row from Amparo Phan.

Loretta, one of my research assistants wants to transfer. Will you come see me?

Loretta, I've become aware of a serious contractual breach and I need your guidance. Come by my office immediately.

Loretta, did you get my previous messages? Come by my hab tonight if you get this.

She snorted softly. Amparo was a food sciences rock star, and she knew it. Still, she didn't usually send interoffice mail. More often she'd send one of her flunkies, or just grab the closest arbiter when one walked by, regardless of where they were headed or what important work they had going on.

Despite all that, she could be a pleasure to work with, if only because she kept her bullshit to a minimum and expected her juniors to do the same. Her team specialized in potato protein synthesis.

That might not sound sexy to an outsider, but forty-two beta was a prestige district, popular among scientists and laypeople alike, in part because it held one of the most profitable research pods in Epiphany. Starvation had been an ever-present threat during the early colonization period, and now, the highly nutritious, space-efficient crops designed by Martian scientists were highly sought after on Earth and Luna.

The messages had kept on coming, even after she'd been demoted. Amparo hadn't mentioned her public disgrace, either because she didn't care, or — more likely — because she was so wrapped up in her own work that she hadn't even noticed.

Loretta bunched the messages for forwarding to her replacement. Before she hit transmit, her tablet asked if she wanted to add one more message to the bunch.

Huh.

Unlike the others, this message had been fully encrypted and sent privately to Loretta's non-work designator. The subject line read: **Please Call Me Immediately**

She really had a bug up her butt about something. I wonder who pissed her off?

The application crashed when she tried to open the message. When she looked for it a second time, it was missing. Perhaps Amparo had recalled it? The metadata must have been stuck in her tablet's buffer.

A soft chime signaled the arrival of the next passenger shuttle. When the doors slid open, Loretta stepped inside the rounded cube and moved to the control panel. After a moment's hesitation, she spoke.

"Forty-two beta. Food sciences lab, level three."

Amparo often worked all hours of the night. A brief chat about the chain of command was in order, and if she wasn't there, a personal note might get the director off her back. Captain Nancy was more than capable of handling whatever was bothering their resident potato goddess, but sometimes, when it came to touchy egos, face-to-face was best.

It shouldn't take long.

Loretta stifled a yawn and did some mental math to keep herself awake while the shuttle zoomed forward along the magnetized track. *Two thousand, nine-hundred, eighty-six hours of remedial service to go.*

CHAPTER TEN

Loretta let herself into the Food Sciences building and turned left down a narrow hallway. The windowed panels showed empty labs to her left and right, they were full of long white tables holding sensitive equipment. In the dimness of the early morning, the only light came from small LEDs embedded beneath the upper cabinets; they cast a bluish-white glare on the pristine countertops and reflected along the edges of the darkened display screens. Every three meters or so, head-high greenhouse units held shelves of sprouting plants. Every tiny cup of soil nurtured a precious experiment, offering hopes of better nutrients, stronger disease resistance, or improved taste. The grow units were shielded in transparent plastic, their contents rendered blurry to outside view by a thick layer of condensation.

It's awfully dark in here.

She flashed her wrist console against the lock at the end of the hall. The angry beep she got in response sounded like a pissed off child's toy. She input her backup code on the numerical pad near the handle and was rewarded with the suction-smooch sound of the door seal releasing.

So much for security. Her captain's credentials had been stripped, but the backup codes were probably held in a different database. She'd fix it later.

Inside the potato synthesis lab, the lights didn't respond to her command. Not so much as a flicker. The whirring of the environmental controls was a comforting sound, proof that not everything had broken down, but why wouldn't the damn lights come on? Come to think of it, the display screens were usually illuminated, even when the stations weren't in use.

Yet every screen in the room was dark.

Something squeaked in the distance. Possibly the sound of a foot on hard flooring.

"Director Phan? Are you here? I got your messages." A familiar green ceramic mug caught the corner of Loretta's eye. Amparo always kept it close. Her oldest son had made it at school when he was younger, and while it had clearly been shaped by inexperienced hands, he'd carefully incised the image of a potato leaf in the clay before glazing and firing it.

She moved closer. The director's display screen had been smashed. Splinters of clear composite littered the countertop. The keyboard was on the ground, a few keycaps splayed across the floor like small, dark stones.

Her muscles tensed and she swung her head around, seeking movement. But there was nothing.

I don't like this.

Two of the greenhouse stacks were dark, their support systems turned off. Weeks of effort ruined. Her gut roiled.

I like this even less.

She stepped over the mess, moving quickly and quietly to the office suites in back. A body lay on the ground, blocking the hallway. She saw the legs first, chubby, splayed out slightly. One of the woman's shoes had been knocked off, and her sock had some sort of pattern on it. Amparo Phan's black, shoulder-length hair splashed against the hard white tiles. She looked almost like a child in a planetarium, staring rapt at the ceiling.

Only her ribs didn't rise and fall.

Loretta dashed forward, dropping to her knees next to Amparo. She set her tablet on the ground and activated voice control. "Emergency services!"

She felt for a pulse over the carotid artery. There was none, but Amparo's skin felt warm. There was still time. Her mind whirled, searching for the checklist she'd been drilled on. Twice a year, the same training, the same lesson. Muscle memory. It was right there, beneath the surface.

No pulse. Warm. Non-responsive.

The faint smell of soil and liquid fertilizer reminded her she was in a laboratory. Right. Potential contamination risk. The botanists worked with chemicals. Substances. Loretta snatched up her tablet on the way to the emergency pod affixed to one wall.

"Emergency services, respond! This is arbiter Loretta Rider. We have an acute medical emergency in forty-two beta. Food sciences. Third floor. Respond!"

After ripping open the cover of the pod, she quickly donned a pair of gloves and a portable hood respirator. She snatched the first aid kit and hurried back.

Her tablet was still blank. She tapped it twice, using her free hand to adjust Amparo's head back, clearing her airway.

No signal.

What the fuck did it mean, no signal? This was science central, not an expedition tent in the frigging outback.

No pulse. No breathing. No help coming. She could run for help, and help wasn't far, but with respiration stopped, every second counted.

Scooping a rescue breather over Amparo's chin and nose and affixing the pump unit above her sternum she applied downward pressure and activated the kit. The *thwock-thwock* of the breather began immediately. What else? She pulled up her hands, saw a long streak of blood on her forearm.

She pulled up the lower edge of Amparo's sweater, looking for a wound. That's when she saw the telltale mark of a pulsar blast. Only there was a shockingly deep cavity in the center, where the wound had seared clear through her skin.

What the hell?

The bloody opening was surrounded by the familiar red corona left by a pulsar's energy discharge. Blood was everywhere, soaking Amparo's clothing, but it didn't seem to be flowing.

The rescue breather chugged valiantly, but instead of the mechanical rise and fall of the chest she hoped to see, a sign of blood-rich oxygen being forced through the body and into the brain, she heard only a faint hiss.

The little machine beeped twice and began spitting out a recorded message.

No life.

No life.

Tearing off her respirator, she screamed for help as loud as she could. One hand was wrapped around Amparo's. The other she used to try to cajole her useless tablet into action.

No signal.

She threw the useless thing against the wall, where it shattered. After calling for help again, she shook Amparo's shoulders, then checked the rescue breather to make sure air was flowing. Her hands kept working, checking. Pull off her own mask and shout for help. Breathe deep. Shout again, this time loud enough to tear her throat.

"Help! I need help in here!"

All she could think of was Amparo's snot-nosed kids. Those irritating, scrappy little boys who'd run around the lab like they owned the place, getting into everything. They'd gotten older. Taller. But they'd never stopped opening cabinets. Asking what things were for. Peering into the greenhouse units. Driving Amparo's assistants nuts.

No signal.

No life.

Yelling for help still, she grabbed a pair of metal shears from the first aid kit and slammed them into the cabinets, making a racket. Finally, someone shouted in the distance. They were coming. *Help* was coming. Footsteps thudded in the hall. Ripping into the kit once more, Loretta tried to apply pads from the portable defibrillator to Amparo's chest, to shock the heart. Sensing no arrhythmia, the machine refused to fire.

No life.

By the time the medics pushed their way into the room, even the rescue breather had given up. Loretta let the medics move her away. She felt Amparo's limp hand slip out of hers.

Fuck. She burst into tears and slid down the wall, wrapping her arms around herself. Sometime later, as the medical team zipped the body into a sterile sleeve in respectful silence, one of the medics helped her to her feet and drove her home.

CHAPTER ELEVEN

Travis opened the oven door and peered inside. The scents of garlic, onion, and rosemary hit his nose like a delicious missile, but the transitory pleasure did little to lift his spirits. Chicken fat sizzled quietly at the bottom of the big glass pan. Just a few more minutes for the protein to brown. He washed and chopped vegetables, pushing down the blade with more force than necessary. Thin slices of carrot fell away from the knife, ovals of yellow, orange, and purple. Loretta had given him this recipe ages ago, one of hundreds she'd found in her mother's old cookbook. He'd hoped that a home-cooked meal might lift her spirits, but she'd begged off, insisting that she wasn't fit for company.

She's sitting alone in her hab, feeling like trash, and she won't even let me take care of her. It was selfish to be disappointed, he supposed, but he couldn't help it. He hated it when she locked him out, but she claimed she wanted to be alone.

I'd drop off the food if I thought she'd even answer her door. The last time I pushed, she accused me of making things all about me. And hell, maybe I am. It just sucks not to be... needed.

The knife slipped, and he looked down, startled by the red

line of pain across his left index finger. Blood welled up and dripped onto the cutting board. Sticking his finger in his mouth, he set the knife down and went in search of a bandage.

I bet she'd let Kacey in. The antiseptic spray he found in the cabinet smothered the pain in his finger, but the sick, jealous feeling in his belly wasn't so easily banished.

Every time Kacey comes back to Epiphany, Loretta's personality changes. Kacey loves to run her mouth, and Lore laps up everything she says because they've been friends for so long. Worse, she doesn't even realize she's doing it.

He wrapped the bandage around his finger, pressing to activate the coagulant.

Fortunately, it sounded like Kacey's next job would be a long one. Placing com beacons was tedious, dangerous work. Her crew was headed out into interstellar space. Absent Kacey's influence, Loretta would be freer to focus on what mattered. Her career and her family. She needed to recover from the painful backward steps she'd taken, and he was ready to help her do it.

We're good together. She knows that. I've been afraid to leave Dad alone, but I think he'd understand if I moved out. He only wants us to be happy.

Back in the kitchen, he cleaned up, gave the veggies a thorough rinse, and tossed them in a big bowl along with olive oil, salt, and lemon juice. A moment later, he heard his father's voice calling from the front door.

"It smells great in here! What's the occasion?"

Travis carried the salad into the living room and set it on the table near the sofa. "Loretta didn't want company, so I figured you and I could have dinner. Maybe catch a vid later? It's been a while since we had a guys' night."

Marcus squeezed Travis's shoulder as he walked by. "Sounds great. I've been stuck in security council meetings all day and I could use a break. Let me get out of these work clothes and I'll join you."

Before long, they were seated side by side in front of the entertainment display. Marcus flipped to a basketball game and turned the volume low. "Are you okay? You seem quiet."

"Loretta's upset. You know, about what happened to Dr. Phan. We all are."

Marcus rubbed his eyes. "Everywhere I went today, people came up to me, asking how something like this could happen here." He looked pained. "Dr. Phan dedicated her life to the people of *two* worlds, feeding the hungry, and serving as a role model to our younger scientists. I promised them we'd bring her killer to justice. But that's a strange word, isn't it?"

Travis glanced over. "What do you mean?"

"Justice. The balancing of the scales." He set his plate down, the meal untouched. "It's a complex concept in the best of times, but when a life is taken? There is nothing that will bring our loved ones back, no comfort that can erase the harm done. After I spoke with Director Phan's husband, all I could think about was that we've lost one of our own. Someone precious. The pain will be with us for a long time. But I was asking about *you*, kiddo."

It was difficult to know what to say. His father was a good listener, yet he didn't appreciate indulgence in the lesser emotions. Self-pity disgusted him.

Tonight though, there was something about his father's tone that invited confession. Losing Director Phan had affected him deeply; that much was clear. And here he was, trying to connect, to reach out.

"I'm just feeling sorry for myself," Travis admitted. "I

went to see Loretta and she damn near threw me out. She was a wreck. It's like she feels personally responsible for what happened. But the minute I tried to talk her down from that, she got all prickly. She won't listen to reason. She—"

"She's reliving what happened to her parents."

"What?"

"Rebound trauma, they call it. Director Phan's oldest son is about the same age Loretta was when her parents died. Loretta may not realize it, but she sees herself in those children. And remember, forty-two beta was her responsibility."

"Not anymore. Not since—"

Marcus's chuckle surprised him into silence.

"Son, don't you believe for *one second* that Lore stopped feeling responsible for her people just because of a demotion. That's not who she is."

"I suppose not. I just wish..." He felt his father's gaze on him, his keen mind weighing every word like they were precious metals, determining their worth in a calculus only he himself understood. "She doesn't need to go through this alone."

Marcus squeezed his shoulder and bent down slightly to look into his eyes. "You've got a good heart. And I'm proud of you."

Warmth spread through Travis's chest. He sat up straighter, smiling for the first time since he'd come home from work. His father didn't believe in unearned praise, so he knew he could trust it.

They ate for a while, chatting about Travis's recent arbitrations, glancing up at the basketball game whenever the roar of the crowd snagged their attention. In the comfortable interlude between dinner and dessert, Travis broached a new subject.

"If you have time, I was hoping we could talk."

"What about?"

"I finished reading the Gharison papers."

"Ah." Marcus smiled and stretched his arms back along the couch pillows. "I was wondering when you'd be ready to discuss them. Tell me, what was your first impression?"

"I felt... disgusted, I guess? Confused too."

"That's not uncommon. But can you tell me why?"

It felt so strange to have his father's undivided attention, to be the source of that curiosity in his eye. *He actually cares what I think, doesn't he?*

Travis laid out his thoughts neatly, as he'd been taught to do. "Well, growing up, I was taught that the First Thirty colonists were, heroic figures I guess. They were scientists and engineers. They suffered enormous hardships to give humanity its first foothold on Mars."

"And is that not true?"

"At a high level, I suppose." Travis's hands tightened in his lap. The personal journals of Nathan Gharison had been drafted by hand in old-Earth style, and some of the language had been difficult to decipher. Altogether, his journals had chronicled the first ten years of the Martian founding. Some pieces he recognized from modules in primary school. The digging of the first tunnels, and early successes and failures in stabilizing the food and oxygen supplies. Those stories were all there. Only there were sections he'd never seen before, stories he'd never so much heard a whisper of. During the first half of the third year, Gharison described a brutal power struggle between him and his wife, and another couple, the Richardsons.

In the end, Nathan Gharison had killed them.

"He murdered his friends in cold blood." As Travis said the words aloud, he felt a deep unease in his body. This discussion felt *wrong*. Not just the facts, but their utterance.

"In cold blood," Marcus said slowly. "That's an interesting turn of phrase. Taken right from a crime serial, I might say. You found his actions cold-blooded?"

"He straight up murdered the Richardsons! Poisoned them and set it up to look like a suicide. I don't see how anyone with a functioning soul could do something like that, Dad. And he's supposed to be one of our heroes. It was horrible."

"It was indeed. No sane person would ever want to do something so drastic, so violent. Especially to a friend, a colleague you'd been working with, side-by-side." Marcus shifted his position on the sofa. "The Gharison papers make for unpleasant reading, but there's a reason I granted you access. Tell me, if Nathan Gharison were here with us, in this room, how do you think he'd justify his actions?"

Travis felt his mouth tighten. "He said it plainly in his journal, didn't he? The Richardsons wanted to leave the tunnels and build habitats aboveground. They believed the colony was ready, and it sounds like they were pretty persuasive, too. The wheels were already in motion for the move. Everyone thought the Gharisons were being pessimistic."

"Would the move aboveground have worked?"

"No. I remember that part from school. The panels they manufactured were flawed. They had excellent temperature control, but radiation would have poisoned everyone within a year. The colony would have died." Surprise pricked at him. He recognized the look in his father's eye. "Hold on. You *agree with* what he did? That's insane!"

Marcus's mouth curled with distaste. "Hyperbole won't help us, son. Remember, this is an intellectual exercise. No one is being harmed by our conversation."

"Sorry. It's just... so fucked up."

"On that, we agree." A faint smile touched Marcus's lips.

"Where did these papers even come from?"

"Thirty years ago, during an expansion dig, we found a cache of documents and tools that had once belonged to Gharison. We suspect he hid them away in the outback sometime after the first expansion. Of course, by that time, the colony was ready to move aboveground. Their science was solid."

"And Gharison became our first Chief Councilor." Travis leaned back into the softness of the cushions. "Did the other colonists know?"

"There's no evidence he ever told a soul, not even his wife." Marcus sipped his wine. "So, let us summarize the unpleasant truth we've been dancing around. Gharison was a murderer. He also saved Epiphany from destruction and saved twenty-eight lives, including his own. What does that make him?"

Travis rolled the question around in his mind. No answer seemed satisfactory, but his father was waiting.

"I don't know."

"A good answer, son. An honest one. No one expects you to process this all at once. Now, you said you felt disgusted and confused about what you'd read. We covered the first part." He shot Travis a wry smile. "Why were you confused?"

Travis felt his tight shoulder muscles release. This subject, at least, was easier to broach. "Here's what I don't get. Why didn't we learn this stuff in school? Everyone knows Nathan Gharison, the biologist. The Green Thumb. Our first arbiter. I've read our history. All the original sources. Or at least—"

"You thought you had. It's a fair question." Marcus looked thoughtful. "Every civilization has strengths and weaknesses, son. Often, the strengths are forged in crisis, those terrible moments when life and death battle for supremacy."

"Like the year the First Thirty almost starved."

"Yes. Mars is home to humanity's best biologists, not because we're innately gifted in that subject, but because our need for survival guided our focus."

"That makes sense."

"We live in a bubble, son. Our domes protect us from the harsh environment and our scientists protect us from starvation. But who protects us from the worst of our own nature? From our irrationality? From our species' tendency toward violence, or the other side of that coin, our selfish sentimentality?"

Travis listened, trying to grasp the meaning behind his father's words. Human beings had evolved from a base animal nature. To counter outmoded evolutionary instincts, wisdom was best developed within the embrace of a well-ordered community. Every arbiter had been taught those facts. Yet Marcus seemed to be hinting at something else, something too slippery to hold on to.

"I'm sorry, Dad. I'm trying to follow you here, but—"

His father's good-natured smile wrapped around him like a warm hug. "You're doing *fine*, son. One step at a time. Listen. There's a good reason the council restricts access to certain documents. We wouldn't give a pulsar to an impulsive child, would we? Information can be every bit as dangerous to a mind ill-prepared to receive it. We *must* be responsible."

A thread of anxiety wove its way through Travis's gut and pulled itself taught. "I... suppose that makes sense. But if that's true, why did you ask me to keep this from Loretta?"

Marcus shrugged as if the answer were obvious. "She isn't ready. You are."

That's... flattering. Usually, he thinks she can do no wrong.

Still, he didn't agree. "I don't see how that's true. Besides, I hate keeping secrets from her."

"You won't have to keep them forever. Lore lacks your maturity, but she's on the same path. In time, we can all discuss these matters together. For now, this will be a good exercise. In showing you can follow orders, you'll prove not just to me, but to the entire council that you can be trusted with privileged information. Agreed?"

"Of course."

"Good. Then I'd say you're ready for the next lesson, and trust me, it's a doozy."

Travis laughed at the playful phrasing, so unlike his father.

"I have a question for you to chew on." Marcus raised an inquisitive eyebrow and placed his palms together. "Can Epiphany survive without men like Nathan Gharison?"

"Back then, you mean? That was a different time. He—"

Marcus shook his head emphatically. "No. Not 'back then', son. Now."

CHAPTER TWELVE

Amparo Phan's celebration of life was a strangely beautiful affair. Her friends had cleared the center of her favorite greenhouse, the one with a rare, pink-tinted dome that cast a soft golden light on everything below. Dainty shadows fluttered on the smooth tile floor. Yesterday, volunteers had strung potato blossoms made of paper on long silvery threads, and now, their rounded blooms fluttered gently overhead.

Everyone in forty-two beta had been invited to write a message to Amparo's family on a blossom. When Loretta's turn had come, she'd found herself unable to form a single sentence. The pencil in her hand was a useless thing. There were no words for what she'd seen in the lab. No comfort in repeating well-worn platitudes or expressing sympathy.

Amparo was dead.

She could have prevented it, but she hadn't.

Amparo Phan's friends and family took turns speaking at an impromptu podium that was nothing more than a simple stack of crates, the sturdy kind used for transporting soil. Bright light from above cast shapes and shadows onto the hair and shoulders of the audience.

The mood in the room shifted, rising and falling like an ocean wave, carrying the hearts of the people with it. Loretta felt herself adrift on that wave, lost in her grief, yet somehow buoyed by those around her. Strangers and friends. Laughter at a funny story. Tears running down the face of Amparo's assistant, Henry McCormack, wiped hastily away by his freckled hand. Loretta saw her own grief reflected in the lines of Travis's face. His hand felt heavy and warm in hers, his fist knotted tightly. She understood his anger. The overwhelming desire to repair what had been torn asunder. How bizarre and wrong it was to be grieving someone so young, so vital. Death came to everyone, even in Epiphany, the most advanced civilization humankind had ever built.

But not like *this.*

Never like this.

Loretta's attention drifted to the people seated around the margins of the gathering. Plants had been pushed against the walls, densely packed, forming a thick green ring that surrounded the assembly like a hedge. The room was full to overflowing, not because of who Amparo was or how she'd lived, but because of the way she'd died. Everyone was on edge. Mars's first murder in seventy years, and it had happened right here, in forty-two beta.

If I'd still been on duty.

Loretta tightened her jaw...

If I'd checked my messages sooner...

An arrow of grief struck Loretta dead-center and smoldered in her chest.

She'd spotted dozens of ombuds — only a few were familiar — and several journalists from the evening newsfeeds. Notables from all over Epiphany were in attendance. Even a university president or two. Every single member of the council.

People died. Usually of old age, and occasionally via accident or disease, but no one should die in fear and terror.

It was pointless. Cruel. All week she'd been plagued by nightmares, images of Amparo's final moments, her pain, the slow-dawning realization that she would never, ever, see her family again.

It wasn't fair.

No.

It was fucking unacceptable.

Rumors were already swirling about the identity of the midnight killer, as the feeds were calling the person responsible. Loretta squeezed Travis's hand, craving the comfort of his touch. His arm slid over her shoulders and she shot him a grateful smile. Already, anti-charter zines blamed the corps itself for Amparo's murder. Some in Free Mars had seized on the fact that pulsars could only be legally owned by members of the corps. Somehow, this was evidence the government must be responsible.

Accusations without evidence. Insinuation without fact. An anxious fever was spreading through the city, blighting minds and inflaming old grievances. And in just five days, every Martian citizen of voting age would be called upon to vote their conscience. Defeat seemed inevitable. Epiphany was changing and she couldn't stop it; already, she felt the bedrock upon which she'd built her life shifting beneath her feet.

Marcus wasn't saying much, but he didn't have to. She saw all that he felt in the way that he carried himself, she understood the crushing weight of the responsibility he bore.

What matters is that we continue to take care of one another, she reminded herself. *It's scary, not knowing what the future will be. But Epiphany is my home and these people are my family, and we'll figure it out, together.*

Circumstances that cannot be changed must be accepted. Marcus had taught her that, but it was a lesson she'd never wanted to learn. Wasn't acceptance the same thing as defeat? Didn't it mean that you'd stopped fighting for what you believed in? It felt too much like surrender, and yet... change was an unavoidable part of life.

The coming weeks would be hard on everyone, her family included. If the corps was dissolved and replaced with something different, what would they do? What role could they play? She didn't know but perhaps that was the hard thing about change.

The not knowing.

She bit her lip. What was that saying they had on Earth? *Right. The people have spoken.*

After the eulogies were complete, Loretta stood and stretched her sore legs. Up front, by the podium, Amparo's husband and sons were quickly surrounded by a phalanx of friends and family. She smiled up at Travis and let go of his hand. "Excuse me for a moment."

She'd expected to wait for her turn to pay her respects, but to her surprise, the crowd parted to let her in immediately.

"It's Loretta," someone murmured.

Like his late wife, Vivian Phan was of Asian and European descent. He had a slight frame and a rather pointed chin, and he'd pulled his dark hair into a distinguished-looking bundle at the nape of his neck. The man looked utterly exhausted.

Diego, the older boy, was keeping his little brother entertained by sharing videos on his tablet. All the while, a rosy-cheeked woman — an aunt, maybe? — watched over them like a hen guarding her chicks.

Vivian beckoned her closer. "Loretta. Hi. I was hoping you'd come."

Someone pushed a chair over. As she sat down, she noted the way the Phan family's inner circle had faced outward, talking to one another at full volume, protecting those inside from the media circus that surrounded them.

Loretta hesitated. There was so much she wanted to say but her tongue felt fat and stupid in her mouth. Even in her own mind, it all felt like excuses.

"Mr. Phan, I..."

"I wanted to thank you. The medics told me how hard you fought to save my wife." He shot her a tiny smile. "Amparo liked you. Did you know that? She told me you'd go far in life."

"That's a big compliment, coming from her."

He smiled at the insinuation. "I know exactly what you mean. Amparo, well, she could be..."

"Intense," Loretta offered.

"Yes. She never did a single thing halfway. And neither does your father, by the way. He's been on the phone with us every day since it happened. He tells me his investigators are getting closer to the truth."

She'd wondered about that. Marcus had been close-lipped on the subject and too busy to spend much time with them. Officially, the murder investigation had belonged to the arbitration team at forty-two beta, but she understood why Nancy accepted the harbormaster's offer to take point. Nancy was solid, but she was barely one week into her captaincy. Taking on Mars's first murder investigation in living memory was one hell of an ask.

Especially with the entire planet watching.

Loretta tugged her uniform jacket down, smoothing the blue-gray fabric. After laboring at the docks, it felt strange to have something so tight-fitting on her body. Fortunately, she no longer looked like an angry tomato.

For the first time since her demotion, she felt like herself. The uniform helped, probably. And even without a Captain's insignia on her shoulders, she could still make a difference.

She needed to.

"I know they'll find the person responsible," she said, knowing it was true. "I'd stopped by the lab that morning because Amparo had been trying to reach me. Something about a contract breach? It made me wonder if she was having problems at work. Did she mention anything to you?"

No doubt the investigators would have asked all these questions already. Still, she couldn't be sure. She'd sent them her full report. They'd thanked her for it.

Since then, nothing.

Vivian looked down at his hands for a long moment. When he looked up, he seemed hesitant. "I want to answer your question, Loretta, but honestly, I'm not sure if I should."

"I don't understand."

He glanced up. The woman standing guard nearby had a strong familial resemblance to Amparo. The same stocky body. That rounded face with a skeptical, piercing gaze. "Molly, take the boys to get something to drink, will you? I'll join you in a minute."

After they'd moved away, he leaned in close, speaking quietly enough that the music and chatter could drown out their voices. "Amparo trusted you. That means I can too, right?"

"Of course. What's all this about?"

He looked pained. "Amparo was upset about something the week before she died. At first, I thought she was frustrated with her experiments. That happens sometimes. But it was more than that. She was *angry*. I confronted her about the way she was acting, and she said she saw something at work."

"What did she see?"

"She refused to say. I kept asking, and she kept insisting it was safer if I didn't know. I won't lie — I was worried she might be having some sort of mental health crisis. It wasn't like her to jump at shadows. But I don't think she was imagining things. She was scared. Pissed off. And she wanted to talk to you, specifically."

Loretta's gut tightened. "Do you know why me?"

He shook his head. "No. But she was searching for something, night after night, sitting on the couch with her tablet, running queries on the net."

"And you told the investigators about this, correct."

He winced. "Not exactly."

"But—"

"Look." He moved closer, lowering his voice to the faintest of whispers. "Amparo was freaking out, keeping secrets from me, which was *not* like her, and the next thing I knew, five security officers showed up at my hab before work, saying they needed to take me and my boys into protective custody." An angry blush covered his cheeks. "They kept asking me why someone would target my wife. And they acted like..."

"What?"

"Like she'd brought it on herself." His expression darkened. "They wouldn't let me call my arbiter, Loretta. They kept me in that room and hammered me for hours. I didn't even know where they'd taken my kids! By the time they told me about Amparo..." He struggled to keep his composure. "I just need to understand what happened."

Loretta's hands tightened in her lap. The harbormaster's investigators weren't a part of the corps, and for a good reason. Their mission was planetary security from external threats. They even maintained a small gunship fleet for defense. They weren't military, exactly, for Mars had no need of one, but still, they weren't exactly known for their tact.

"They never should have treated you that way. I am so sorry."

"Listen. I don't want trouble. But for whatever reason, Amparo was afraid of running what she saw up the chain. I don't know who I'm supposed to trust right now."

She nodded once. "Thank you, for trusting me. I'll see what I can find out. And it's possible the investigators are already all over this."

"Maybe." His mouth tugged down. "If my wife were here, she'd tell you to be careful. So do that, for her, okay?"

It wasn't hard to imagine Amparo's earnest dark eyes, her forceful voice issuing that instruction. The part where she'd been afraid? That was more difficult to visualize.

"I promise." Suddenly, it was no longer difficult to know what to say. "We'll bring your wife's killer to justice. I swear it. And no matter what, I'm here for you and your family. From here on out, no matter what you need, you call me, okay?"

Without waiting for a reply, she slipped her tablet into her hand and tipped it toward his, transmitting her private designator.

CHAPTER THIRTEEN

"It sounds like someone killed her to shut her up." Kacey tossed a bolt to Theo, who caught it in one hand. He glanced at Loretta and nodded as if to emphasize Kacey's point.

"But what did she see?" Loretta sat cross-legged on the floor inside *Poppy*'s cargo bay, watching Kacey and Theo inspect and replace sections of the shuttle's radiation shielding. "She worked in a food sciences lab. It's all plants and test tubes. Nothing worth killing over."

Theo placed one hand crosswise atop the other, palms down, fingers up the upper hand bent. He made a C-shape and swirled it around. Loretta concentrated, but she felt a surge of frustration as she lost the thread. She'd memorized the ISL alphabet and a few dozen basic signs — it seemed the polite thing to do — but Theo's hands were so fast and her knowledge so limited that it was impossible to follow his meaning.

He must have seen her scowl because he activated his speaker box before repeating himself. "What about the director's web searches? What was she looking for?"

Loretta signed, *Sorry, Theo*. "I'm not annoyed with *you*. I just wish I could learn sign language faster."

Theo never used the speakerbox when he was hanging

out with Kacey. He didn't seem to like the device very much, although Loretta wasn't sure why. Didn't it make his life easier? Someday, when they knew each other better, she'd ask him about it.

"Don't worry about it," his speakerbox sounded. He shot her a shy smile as he lowered his hands.

"All personal communication on MarsNet is encrypted," she explained. "Messages, searches, reading, entertainment choices. Cam feeds too, unless you've released yours to your employer during work hours. Guaranteed privacy, in your hab and on the net is written right into the charter. If a wiz is clever, they *might* be able to delete someone's data, even make educated guesses about which blocks contain what information, but you're sure as hell not cracking encryption."

Loretta hesitated. She wanted to ask Kacey, again, if they'd gotten any hits from the transmitter she'd affixed to the *Steady*'s hull. The last she'd heard, *Poppy*'s computer had been unable to pull any data from the shuttle's trajectory. It was as if the *Steady as She Goes* had disappeared from orbit without a trace. Or more likely, the makeshift transmitter had failed.

When they know something, they'll tell me. I won't win any points by rubbing her nose in the fact that it didn't work.

According to Marcus, the harbormaster's team had sent bounty packets to docking facilities on Earth and Luna. Anyone providing accurate information leading to the retrieval of the *Steady* and the arrest of her crew would be entitled to a full Martian homestead, meaning a family-sized habitat, citizenship, and a suitable work contract for every adult. A prize so valuable that money literally couldn't buy it.

One way or another, her attackers would be caught. Still,

it would have been nice to bring them in personally, if only to make up for some of the harm she'd done to the corps. And she could have given the prize to someone deserving. Someone who loved Mars enough to make it their home.

Kacey pointed at a red metal toolbox on the ground. "Bring me a twenty millimeter, will you?"

Now that their deliveries were complete, Kacey and Theo were taking advantage of their shore leave to prepare *Poppy* for her next assignment. Apparently that meant tearing the shuttle apart and replacing any pieces that didn't meet Kacey's exacting standards.

"Have you questioned the scientist's coworkers?" Kacey asked.

"I'm not a captain anymore, remember? And I couldn't go butting my way into that investigation even if I was. Not officially."

"You can't make an omelet without cracking a few heads." Most of Kacey's attention was fixed on her task. When she'd fixed the new panel in place, she spun around. "And who cares about being official? You're just a human being, asking questions because your coworker's husband asked you to. Anyway, it's not like you need to be all obvious. Be sneaky! Like me."

Theo's faint wheeze sounded suspiciously like laughter.

"One time," Theo's speakerbox sounded as he signed rapidly with both hands, "Kacey snuck onto another ship because she'd skipped dinner and—"

Kacey became a pinkish blur, sprinting toward Theo. Her tackle failed when she bounced off his chest like a kitten who'd splatted against a sliding glass door. Kacey rolled as she hit the ground and popped right back up, light on her toes like a boxer. Theo's hands were still in motion, but his speakerbox had gone silent.

"Hey!" Loretta plucked a bolt out of the toolbox and pitched it at Kacey's rear end. "Don't turn his equipment off. That's rude. Not to mention a violation of—"

Kacey turned, her hands on her hips, speaking in the doofiest tone possible. "A violation of his rights under section suck-my-butt, subsection no-one-cares, part A of the confederacy of bitches, subsection twelve of—"

Loretta and Theo were both laughing now.

"Okay, I *may* have had that coming," Loretta admitted. She glanced at Theo, who only seemed amused by Kacey's antics. He shrugged, apparently unwilling to take sides.

Theo might be the largest human being she'd ever met, muscled like a human tank and capable of breaking either of them in half, but he was, above all, a mellow guy and more inclined to laugh things off than take offense.

It was no wonder he and Kacey were friends.

"Like I was *saying*," Kacey said, "before Theo so rudely interrupted with stories that do *not* require repeating, I bet someone saw something. Luckily, you know these people. And bizarrely enough, they seem to like you."

"Ha ha."

"So go talk to them! Just don't wear a sign that says," Kacey swiveled her hips and held both hands up in the air, "I'm unraveling a conspiracy, ask me how!"

Loretta glanced at Theo. "It's not just me, right? She acts this way at work, too?"

Theo tapped his ear like he couldn't hear, then shrugged.

Very funny, Loretta signed, delighting at the way Theo's eyes lit up in response. She'd memorized that one just that morning, suspecting it might come in handy.

The corps taught that peace was only possible when you spoke a person's language. Usually that wasn't meant literally, but still, the axiom seemed to hold.

Also, it felt good to see the big guy smile.

"Sure," Kacey said, continuing her little tirade. "No conspiracy here! This is business as usual. That's why you're out here talking to us instead of running this through proper channels." Kacey finished turning the bolt she was working on, then set her heavy wrench on the ground, shaking her arm out. "Not that I mind, to be clear. I'm glad you're finally thinking for yourself. Up there," she pointed skyward, "that's what we need."

She'd been touched that Kacey had invited her along, and after seeing what her friend was capable of up there, it was hard not to feel flattered too. Maybe, in an alternate universe, it would have worked out. A universe where her duties and heart weren't already spoken for.

"What was that?" Kacey came storming over. "That look! I can see the wheels turning."

There was no reason not to admit it. "I suppose I was imagining what it could be like. To go up into space with you. Captain Kacey and her friends, having adventures."

Theo's speakerbox sounded, this time in a booming voice straight out of a movie trailer. "Three heroes. One epic adventure. Sneaking onto ships to steal the best snacks. Looking for love. Proving that there's still a thread of hope in a dark and violent universe."

Kacey snorted a laugh. "Hope? Now *that's* hilarious."

Loretta put two and two together. "Wait. You broke into a ship to steal snacks? What are you, five years old?"

Kacey pointed at Theo. "Turncoat! Bastard! I'm gonna—" She sprinted right for his position, her arms stretched out. He covered his speakerbox with one big hand and twisted left and right, dodging her grip. With his free hand, he signed furiously.

"Did she tell you about the time she—"

"Noooooo!" Kacey screamed, drowning out the speaker.

Laughing so hard that tears sprang from her eyes, Loretta

bent forward, clutching her sore ribs. When she looked up, Kacey seemed oddly subdued. Turning away, Kacey grabbed handful of washers out of their container and placed them over her fingers like gaudy, oversized rings. "We'd have a good time, you know."

"I know, Kace. And a part of me wants to go. Truly. But—"

Kacey held up both hands. "Stop, will you? I don't want to hear it. We don't leave for another four days. That's plenty of time to deal with your emotional baggage and pack your shit."

"It's just that—"

Kacey made a face. "Hey! If you're gonna break my heart, do it later okay? I need to prep my ship, and you've got people to talk to."

That's when Theo tried to break the tension by playing the theme song of a popular murder mystery program over his speaker.

They laughed together, and if their merriment felt forced, Loretta knew it was only because they'd soon be parted. For all her bravery and bluster, Kacey wore her heart on her sleeve.

I'm breaking her heart?

Kacey was laying it on extra thick this time. Loretta picked up the heavy box of bolts and carried it closer to Kacey's position. She slung her arms over her friend's skinny shoulders and squeezed.

"We'll always be friends. Even if I can't go with you, it doesn't change a damn thing."

Kacey and Theo's next assignment might be long, but the rhythm of their lives would remain the same. Kacey would disappear for a while to work, and then she'd return, full of stories about where she'd been. It would be nice to have more time, but all you could do was make the most of what you had.

Distance didn't matter. Not really.

Kacey shrugged Loretta's arms off, reaching for her wrench, refusing eye contact. "I know. And it's not like I need you to come. Anyway, I should get back to work."

That was as obvious a dismissal as Loretta had ever heard, so she told them she'd see them later. Kacey had been right about one thing. If someone had killed Amparo Phan because of what she'd seen, it implied there was some sort of a cover up underway. And if Vivian Phan hadn't told the investigators that his wife had 'seen something' at work, they might remain ignorant of what had truly happened.

Be careful, he'd said. Part of her wanted to go straight to the harbormaster, to lay every fact out at the feet of those authorized to handle it. Yet that would also be a betrayal of sorts, a violation of the trust he'd placed in her.

Also, Amparo Phan was no fool. She wouldn't have kept her concerns secret without an extraordinarily good reason.

She bit her lip. It wouldn't hurt to gather more information, if only to uncover whatever it was that Amparo Phan had been upset about before she'd been killed. And as soon as she knew what that thing was, she'd go straight to Marcus.

He'd know what to do.

CHAPTER FOURTEEN

Travis Wells set his coffee mug down and activated the display above his desk. A small velvet box rested atop his inbox. He picked it up, rubbing his thumb across the soft surface. It opened with a soft click.

The box contained a full set of captain's insignia, only the pins were of a style not used in more than fifty years. The traditional red, black, and yellow gemstones had been replaced with ordinary red rock from the outback, sanded but rough to the touch. The V-shaped casings were made of cheap composite instead of polished titanium, another small nod to the materials that had been available on Epiphany at the time of the founding.

A tiny card tucked into the lid of the jewel case explained that the insignia was a gift from the council and to be worn at the centennial celebration.

He closed the box and slipped it into his messenger bag to take home. Already, work crews were hanging new art in Epiphany's central plaza in advance of the centennial. The evening news feeds had been temporarily canceled in favor of educational programs reminding citizens of the many sacrifices and victories that had carried Epiphany to this moment.

Just last night, Marcus had invited him to give a speech on

behalf of his district, and there was much to do to prepare. Travis smiled at the thought. He'd never attended a party with a third of a million people before! Word was that even some dignitaries from Earth would attend. There were so many people that his father wanted him to meet. Some would be involved in negotiating a new colonization treaty, with massive implications for future expansion.

It was an exciting time.

And perhaps a party was just the thing to lift everyone's mood a little. And as solemn and sad as Dr. Phan's funeral had been, participating had been a good thing for Loretta. She'd been feeling terrible about what happened, even though it was in no way her fault. Now, she was back in uniform, splitting her time between forty-two beta and her remedial service hours. The fire was back in her eye, and for the first time since her day at the hearing, she seemed to be moving forward again.

Travis skimmed through the pile of requests that had accumulated overnight. To his right, through the viewport that overlooked the vast manufacturing floor of twenty-six charlie. Technicians swarmed down the lines like ants, dutifully checking readouts from the printers, performing quality checks on the dazzling array of goods produced in Epiphany's largest and most sophisticated production facility.

Once upon a time, nearly all of Epiphany's non-essential goods had been manufactured off-world. Understandably, the earliest craftspeople had focused on the means of survival. Entertainments had taken second place to manufacturing hab suits, paneling, and agricultural equipment. Now, thanks to decades of planning and diligent sourcing of rare materials, Epiphany was nearly self-sustaining.

Someone cleared their throat behind him. "Captain? I'm sorry to bother you."

It was Rashida Zane, his newest arbiter. He noted that she still wore her dark hair like a cadet on inspection day, knotted high above her collar, strands combed so smooth and tight that they tugged at the delicate skin of her temples.

"You're never a bother," he replied. "What do you need?"

She frowned down at her tablet. "I'm afraid we have another report of missing materials. Last time, it was streng composites. This time a pallet of small chipboards has gone missing."

"And you're concerned there's a pattern."

She nodded. "I found an incident report from last fall. We had a spate of disappearances, but they turned out to be accounting errors. Everything checked out after an audit. This time, I went straight to the warehouse. The supply coordinator showed me where the pallets should have been. But the berths were empty."

"Let me see." He held up his tablet and waited while she swiped the documentation over. "Hmm. These are low-value parts. Maybe the thief didn't think we'd notice the shrinkage. What are the chipboards used for?"

Rashida scrolled through information on her tablet. "General purpose chipboards... used in hab appliances, children's toys and," she paused.

"Yes?"

Her hazel eyes met his. "They're used in pulsars, sir. The newer models, anyway. Previously they used the XWR-90 chipboard, but the updated software requires—" She broke off at the sight of his expectant look. He'd coached her on keeping her reports succinct. "Sorry, Captain."

"No worries. You're doing great." In a year or so, he'd lose Arbiter Zane to another district, one better suited for her excellent memory and detail-oriented mind. Until then, he'd be happy to train her. Such was the duty of any district captain.

"So," he continued. "you've noticed something suspicious. What's your next move? Are you familiar with audit procedures?"

"I am, sir. But here's the thing, I asked to review footage of the warehouse, and I included supporting documentation, just like you taught me. But it bounced right back."

"What do you mean, it "bounced"?"

"See for yourself."

She handed her tablet over. Instead of the standard acceptance or rejection, there was a single line of text in the response.

REQUEST DENIED. DATA ACCESS CODE 84-59A-SEC0

"That's strange," he murmured. The data requisitions team denied requests from time to time, and when they did so, they always quoted the relevant portion of the charter. Sometimes, an arbiter hadn't included adequate documentation. Other times, the data needed to be partially scrubbed to maintain the privacy of non-interested parties. But this string of letters and numbers? It was new.

He captured a copy of the reply before handing the tablet back. "Tell you what. I'll run this up the chain and see what I can find out. Maybe they're upgrading the system and we hit the server mid-upgrade. But send me your documentation, will you?"

"Thanks, boss." Her smile faltered. "The theft... You don't think it's related to what happened to Director Phan, do you? If those chipboards can be used to make our pulsars..."

Ah, that explained why she'd seemed so concerned. "Honestly, I doubt it. It's far more likely someone's trying to make counterfeit Foogies."

Rashida's giggle reminded Travis just how young she was. The perfectly pressed uniform and her serious demeanor were in some sense, a front. Young arbiters wanted to be taken seriously, and he couldn't blame them for that.

It wasn't so long ago that he'd been playing the same game, fighting for the respect of his captain among a dozen peers who all wanted the same placement he did.

"Those stupid talking shoes?" Rashida grinned. "Have you ever heard a primary school class stomping down the hall in those things? They sound like a herd of farm animals. I feel for their teachers." Her hand drifted up to her pinned hair, perhaps to loosen the tension, but she lowered her arm when she caught him watching. "So, what should I do in the meantime? Focus on my other open cases?"

He felt a flutter of amusement at her half-hidden disappointment. "I see that look in your eye! You want to keep chasing this mystery, footage or no. Am I right?"

"Maybe." She smiled a little. "I know we have more important cases. But I've got a feeling about this one. The tech who showed me where the pallets should be? He wasn't there this morning. His supe moved him to another warehouse."

"And you suspect... what, exactly?"

She held up a hand. "Nope! I am not ready to use the S word. Our people are solid. And they get the benefit of the doubt, always."

He raised an eyebrow. "But...

"*But*, after what happened to Director Phan, we need to keep our eyes open. They never found who planted those explosives over near Welling University, remember?" She glanced out the viewport, taking in the view of the manufacturing lines down below. "I've been thinking, if I were a terrorist looking for raw materials, our district would be mighty attractive. Think about it. The chem labs have way more security than us, and hospitals are another option, but they're staffed 669 sols per year, with full overnight coverage." She sighed. "Also, there *might* be one more reason I want to chase this down..."

"What's that?"

She held up her tablet and made a face "Wallace keeps messaging me about his living conditions, and the busier I am the easier it is to put him off."

Travis knew what she meant. Ed Wallace oversaw a small but important program producing high-energy lasers, and historically, directors in their district had been allocated larger and more luxurious habitats than other residents. Even with the current housing shortage, Wallace was convinced that his spacious yet ordinary hab was a personal insult, demeaning not only his work, but his reputation in the scientific community.

Do assholes even realize they're assholes? Or do they know and not care? Somehow they left that question out in Moral Philosophy 201.

"I'll swing by and have a chat with him."

She tapped her tablet his direction. A fresh bunch of angry messages landed at the top of his inbox like a steaming pile of manure. "You are the *best* captain ever."

"I'll trust you to remember that come peer review time." He glanced down at the denial message from the data requisitions team, one more time. The error code was strange, but he could have sworn he'd seen the designation SEC0 somewhere before. If only he could place it.

Rashida was waiting to be dismissed, and Travis caught a glimpse of one of the manufacturing supes waiting impatiently in the hallway outside. "I'll let you get back to what you were doing, Zane. Keep up the good work."

Travis affixed his best professional smile and waved his lurking visitor inside. "Come on in, Stu, and close the door."

Henry McCormack was deep in conversation with his team when Loretta arrived at the food sciences lab. A dozen white-jacketed scientists had formed a half-circle in front of him. They nodded along as he issued instructions in that calm, clear voice of his. Henry's reddish-brown hair curled at the nape of his neck. Seeing him standing there, his shoulders squared, gesturing as he described out the work of the day — it was almost as if he'd absorbed some of Amparo Phan's intensity. Loretta watched from the doorway as Henry's gaze went from person to person, silently checking in, ensuring they'd understood what he wanted.

Only after the researchers had scattered, heading to their individual workstations, did Loretta approach. Before she could even react, Henry reached out and snagged her in a quick hug, pounding her back twice before releasing her. "Welcome back," he said with a small smile. "Nancy said you'd be rejoining us, but I wasn't expecting you so soon."

A gentle warmth spread through Loretta's chest, and she smiled back at him. Henry wasn't much of a hugger, but there had been a lot of that going around lately. "Captain says I can split my time. I'll be working mornings at the docks, but I'll be here in the afternoons." She shifted her weight from one foot to the other. "Officially, I don't start for a few days, but—"

"But it feels good to keep busy." Henry's hands crept down his lanyard, toward his ID badge. "At least, that's what I keep telling myself. That, and I know Amparo would be pissed if we didn't keep things moving along." Loretta followed Henry's eyes as they swept across the lab, checking on his team before landing on an object at Amparo's workstation. Someone had tucked a bloom of hothouse flowers into her green coffee mug, and the delicate greenery spiraled over the side, almost touching the pristine laboratory table. The broken display had been taken away, and there was a new one in its place.

"Long after you and I are a memory," Loretta recited, "the work of Mars will continue. Layer upon layer, we add to what came before, building a future we can scarcely imagine."

Henry lifted an eyebrow. "Nathan Gharison?"

She tapped her skull with an index finger. "They made us memorize his speeches at the academy. Oh, and before I forget, congratulations on the promotion. There's no one better suited to lead this project than you. You know that, right?"

Henry's ears turned faintly pink. "Nothing's official yet."

"Nancy says it's a done deal. Amparo would be proud to see you taking her place. You always were her favorite. That's why she was so tough on you."

"I can still hear her, talking to me. Yelling at me to check the nutrient mixes or telling me not to rely on sensors because the damn things always lie." He glanced up, his eyes bright. "Can I show you something?"

"Please do."

He led her to a small grow unit full of potato sprouts. She recognized the branching leaf structure, the darker green spreading from center to edge.

"This here is Amparo's gift to us. We spent three *years* testing and retesting new genetic lines, earning failure after failure. So many times I believed we'd taken the wrong path. Yet Amparo kept pushing, and here we are."

Loretta bent forward and peered into the grow unit. To her eyes, the sprouts were unremarkable. "What am I looking at?"

"You're looking at the future. We've achieved *eighteen* percent increase in protein synthesis with high palatability.

Best of all, these little geniuses can thrive in a low nitrogen environment. We can't plant them outside today, but if those smug bastards in eight alpha keep up their current pace with terraforming advancements? Loretta, we'll see outdoor agriculture in our lifetime. Can you imagine it?"

Henry's enthusiasm was infectious. "That's... beyond anything I'd been taught to expect." Her finger traced the text on the grow unit's outer display. *Solanum Amparos.* "You named it for her?"

"She'd have hated that, but since she's no longer here to object..." An echo of grief flashed across his ruddy face. "We all played a role, but the breakthrough was hers. Did you know her ancestors were farmers? They lived in Spain during the heat famine."

Loretta hadn't known, but the story didn't surprise her. All told, four billion people had died in less than forty years as Earth had grappled with runaway climate change. Even now, post-stabilization, every family carried memories of how they were touched by humanity's greatest calamity.

"At the time, the large industrial farms were stubborn. They kept producing water-intensive crops even as resources dried up. But small family farms in the Spanish countryside formed collectives, crossbreeding and sourcing plants from more arid regions around the world. Hundreds of thousands of lives were saved, including Amparo's ancestors. And she carried their stories here, to our lab." He tapped the grow unit with an affectionate hand. "She knew we'd find what we needed, and she was right."

Loretta tried to remember what she'd been taught back in school. "But what about temperature variation?"

Henry waved one hand dismissively. "These little beasts are as hardy as fuck. And anyway, you should see what the rock jocks can do with a few thousand liters of—" He shook his head. "I always forget you're not a scientist."

"That's *very* kind of you to say, Director McCormack. And congratulations on the breakthrough. Keep this up and future schoolchildren will see your face in their biology textbooks. Has the education department asked you to pose for an etching yet?" Tilting her head left and right, she teased, "Maybe you should grow a beard? You'd look even more distinguished."

Henry's eyes crinkled with mirth. "Yes, please take me down a peg when my ego threatens to burst. Now, why do I have the feeling that there's something you need to ask me?"

She tipped her chin toward his office door. "Because you've always been a perceptive guy. Can I borrow you? It's about Amparo."

Inside his office, Henry opaqued his inner office window but didn't sit. He leaned against his messy desk and crossed his arms in front of his waist. "Please tell me they've caught her killer. It's not like we're quavering in our boots here, and we've upped security, but..."

"They're working on it. Whoever broke in managed to cut the power and access to MarsNet. That's not easy to do. But we will bring them to justice."

"Justice." Henry glowered. "I know we're supposed to be too enlightened to throw people in a deep dank hole until the end of time, but I have to say—"

She understood his anger, had seen it simmering beneath the surface when they'd spoken outside. "Henry, I don't think—"

He held up a hand. "Look. I understand the scientific consensus. I understand that violence doesn't counter violence. We've got thousands of years of history to back that up. But when I think about—" He took a shaky breath. "When I realize this monster was standing *here*, in our lab, that they *took* her from us, when I think about the ways she suffered, I—"

"Henry." She touched his shoulder.

He rubbed his eyes. "I'm sorry. I know I shouldn't say these things out loud. I just figured you, of all people, might understand."

"I do. More than you know. We feel what we feel." She put her hand on her chest where her own grief still burned. "What matters though is what we do. And to find out what happened to Amparo, I need your help. Off the record this time."

That caught his attention. "I thought the harbormaster is investigating."

"She is. And I'll circle back with her team. But I need to know what Amparo was wrapped up in before she was killed. Did she seem upset? Was she behaving any differently?"

He nodded. "Yes."

"Tell me."

He blew out his breath. "Amparo was always intense, but you learned never to take it personally. When she was impatient or snappish, there was a reason. And she *always* came back and apologized if she'd been too harsh. That was her in a nutshell. She'd rush around, barking orders, hardly noticing that she'd terrorized the latest batch of interns, but the moment things slowed down and we'd solved whatever the problem was, she'd touch base, soothing hurt feelings, letting everyone know how much she appreciated them."

That tracked with Loretta's experience, so she nodded. "You're saying she was like Dr. Jekyll and Mr. Hyde?"

His mouth quirked up on one side. "Oh, she was never that bad. It was more like she forgot how to say please and thank you when she was in the thick of things."

"But this time was different."

"Yes. Not only was she biting people's heads off, but she was also distracted, not paying attention to her own experiments. Twice, we lost samples because she forgot to pull the trays in time. And that's never happened in the twenty years I've worked with her. It was strange enough that I wondered if she and Viv were having problems."

"Did you try to find out?"

"I did. She told me she was worried about the experiment, which was basically a non-answer, since we worry about every experiment. And she apologized. After that... she was holed up in her office, working on her computer, alone. I wondered if something I'd said had scared her off. I was her assistant, yes, but it wasn't like she couldn't talk to me."

"You told the investigators this?"

"They never asked. They only wanted to know if she'd received any threats. Then they took her computer away for analysis."

"When did it start, her change in demeanor?"

He pulled up a calendar on his tablet. "It was near sol 650. I remember because she'd just returned from a field expedition and she left me in charge while she was gone."

"What kind of expedition?"

He hesitated. "You probably know that rock and soil composition vary significantly across the Martian surface."

"I did not, but it makes sense."

"Usually we create mixes here in the lab, approximating conditions found in the outback. But for our latest round of tests the director wanted bona fides from several regions, especially those currently undergoing terraform experiments.

"Because the atmosphere is locally richer, and maybe it influences the soil makeup."

"Exactly." He seemed pleased that she'd understood. "When we conduct our first test plantings outside, that's where we'll start. Amparo talked the geologists into taking her out in a skimmer to gather the first batch of samples."

"Do you have a list of the locations she visited? And who was with her at the time?"

"Sure. Do you think that's relevant?"

Even if Henry would believe a fib, she didn't feel right about offering one. The work of an arbiter was difficult under the best of circumstances, and without trust, it became nigh impossible. Maybe once or twice you could get away with a lie, but only a fool dealt in short-term wins.

"I'm chasing a theory," she admitted. "I can't say more. Is that okay?"

"It is." He moved to his workstation. "I'll send you her survey plan. It reveals our preferred planting areas, so I'll ask you to keep this to yourself unless absolutely necessary."

"Agreed. Did anyone else go on the expedition with her?"

"Just the pilot. I've got his name right here."

CHAPTER FIFTEEN

Loretta followed the windowless pedestrian path, enjoying gravity's tug as she descended the gradual slope. The Geological Sciences Institute was five levels beneath the Martian surface, deep in the undercity, and probably there was a joke in there, something about getting the geologists ever closer to their objects of fascination.

She paused at an interpretive display embedded in one wall where clear paneling showcased a section of bare rock beyond the human-built structure. The rock's surface had been smoothed to show faint striations, each layer labeled clearly for the benefit of curious visitors. Accompanying text explained that the first human settlers on Mars had tunneled deep underground to mitigate the impact of radiation on their fragile human bodies. They'd understood that even under the best conditions, living on the 'red planet' would shorten their lifespans.

As a child, she'd been gobsmacked by that grim bit of trivia. The founders understood they'd be giving up decades of their own lives. They'd left friends and family behind, all for a risk that might never pay off. Setting off on their small ship without fanfare, the founders had trusted their experimental solar sails to carry them across the expanse to their new home.

Later, as Loretta bent her own trajectory toward a life of service, she'd come to understand their choice, at least a little. Everything and everyone would die in the end. Nothing was forever, not even the stars. Sol would go supernova in the fullness of time, yet with enough stubbornness and smarts, her species might have a fighting chance.

If a person was lucky, they'd live a life that mattered, surrounded by people they cared about. And becoming a part of something bigger than oneself was a way to preserve that gift of life for future generations.

The First Thirty had understood that. So did she.

The path curved to the right. Up ahead, near the Geology Institute entrance, someone had posted dozens of drawings, children's artwork from a recent school visit. Loretta smiled, the pictures calling to mind blurry memories of her own childhood field trips, the clatter of her classmates' shoes as they'd sprinted down the pathways. Teachers shouting from behind, demanding they behave.

Her mother had loved taking her students out for field trip days. She insisted that her kids were better behaved for a whole week afterward, because young people weren't meant to be cooped up inside a classroom from morning till dusk.

But that had been a long time ago.

A stone-faced arbiter checked Loretta's ID at the entrance and directed her down a long, featureless hallway. Nothing about this "geology lab" fit her mental picture of what a laboratory should be. There was no plant-smell, for one thing. No visible experiments or sleek, windowed rooms. She wandered through a maze of hallways and unmarked doors, finally locating the spot she was looking for.

Inside the conference room there was a biggish table and five well-worn chairs. The air smelled like stale coffee, and a wrap-around wall display showed a slideshow of geologists in action. Figures in heavy-duty hab suits bent over collecting samples in one photo. A beaten-up trover caked in yellowish dust rested near a silvery expedition tent in another. A cheesy public relations photo showed three men and four women standing proudly next to a portable lab unit, a new one, given the shine of the metal and a lack of pitting on the struts.

"Arbiter Ryder?" The man who'd just let himself into the room was about thirty, with a round, dimpled face and eager blue eyes. "I'm Dr. Terrance Egan. I understand you wanted to meet with me?"

She held out a hand for him to shake. "Loretta, please. Thanks for seeing me on such short notice."

He invited her to sit and poured two cups of coffee from a communal dispenser at the far end of the room. She sipped hers, pleased to find it fresh and hot.

"Thanks," she said. "I had an early start today and I could use a pick-me-up."

"You said you wanted to discuss Director Phan?" He sipped his coffee then set it down, wrapping his meaty fingers around the mug. "We were horrified by what happened, of course. Is the corps concerned that there could be another attack?"

"No, nothing like that," she said soothingly. "I'm here because I'm deconstructing Director Phan's movements, trying to understand what she did and who she spoke with in the weeks leading up to her death."

"Interesting! You believe it was a targeted attack?" Egan leaned forward, pushing his coffee mug aside. "I spoke to one of the investigators, and they seemed to be operating under the assumption that she was in the wrong place at the wrong time. They thought she might have interrupted a burglary; someone trying to steal valuable research samples."

She caught the hint of skepticism in his voice. "But you don't buy it."

"I don't know what to think. But it's not like Epiphany is full of free-roving criminals. We haven't had a death like this in…"

"Seventy years," she prompted.

He nodded. "The fellow I spoke to wasn't in a sharing mood. I'd have loved to hear the data supporting their hypothesis, but when I asked, they stared at me like I was being weird."

"Curiosity is a scientific imperative, no?"

"That it is." He picked up his mug and took a sip.

"Speaking of data, I'm hoping you can provide some. I understand Director Phan went on a geological expedition before she died. To gather soil samples."

"Indeed she did. I flew her out there myself."

"You're a geologist and a pilot? That's impressive."

Egan shrugged modestly. "It was more of a compromise, really. I wanted to be a shuttle pilot when I was young, but my parents felt a scientific career would be more appropriate. That's when I hatched my scheme. I talked them into paying for ten hours of flight lessons for every semester I completed on the honor roll."

"So now you get the best of both worlds."

"Exactly!" His expression brightened. "And you can imagine how Director Borden jumped at the chance to hire a researcher who could fly our skimmer. They even let me design my own kit, with a bucket attachment and a portable digger. It's—" He dropped his hands, which had been about ready to sketch out the shape of his ship in the air. "Sorry about that. I'm rambling. What else can I help you with?"

"Did anything unusual happen during your flight?"

"No."

"Did Dr. Phan seem upset?"

Egan frowned, thinking hard. "Nothing like that comes to mind. Of course, not everyone is comfortable flying, and I could tell she wasn't used to being outside in a hab suit, but she was a real trooper." He tapped his tablet and brought up a geologic map of the Martian surface. With a swipe, he sent the images to the wall display. Three yellow dots glowed on the flattened-out topography. "We made three stops and retrieved about five kilos of material at each site. She dug up some small samples manually and we tested them in our port-a-lab, then my portable digger did the rest."

His map was a mess of wavy lines and symbols. "Do you have satellite images of those regions?" Loretta asked.

"I sure do." A few more taps, and he'd pulled up photographic images. There was nothing interesting, at least not to her untrained eye.

"Is there anything particularly noteworthy about those regions?"

"Well, every soil composition is unique and interesting. Here, in the west," He pointed at one image, "we have what used to be a river delta, back before Mars lost her original atmosphere. The organics there created a different mix of..."

Loretta nodded along, letting him spool out information, only half her mind on the specifics. Whatever Amparo had "seen at work," it seemed unlikely to have occurred during her expedition. That meant she needed to return to the lab, to find the 'contract breach' Amparo had been so upset about. Henry hadn't known what it was, but one of the other scientists might.

"I'm boring you, aren't I?" Egan seemed faintly amused.

"Not your fault, doc. I did fine in school, but science was never my forte. I've always been better at reading people than data."

"Well," he shot her an encouraging smile, "we need all kinds of talents to make the world go round. But let me bottom line it for you, as my bosses like to say. Terraforming isn't just some dream for the future — it's already underway."

She'd heard that line before. "At the academy they taught us that we could last three or four minutes in atmo, depending on temps. Longer maybe, if we're within reach of a panic shed."

Egan nodded. "That's about right. We've only been terraforming for twenty years, and there's still a lot we need to sort out. Temperature extremes are coming down faster than we'd expected, but a breathable atmo is still a ways off. At this point, our biggest limitation isn't knowledge, but the availability of raw materials for atmospheric reconstruction. But Mars is generous, geologically speaking, and I believe we'll find what we need."

Loretta smiled at his optimism. "I'm always glad to learn a bit more about what our scientists are up to." She pulled up her notes from earlier, to jot down a summary of what she'd heard. Later, after she'd spoken to everyone, she'd review everything, looking for insights she'd missed.

Her eye landed on something Henry had mentioned.

"Huh."

"What is it?"

"Probably nothing important," she said. "It's just that Director Phan's notes say that she visited four sites on her expedition. The other one was," she flipped her tablet around and showed him. "Somewhere near those coordinates."

Terrance Egan stared at her tablet for a long moment. His face had gone slack. "That's odd."

"Odd because you didn't go?"

Egan's smile was quick. It lashed out and grabbed her. As he exhaled, his shoulders dropped. Then he renewed his eye contact with the deliberate caution of someone measuring drops out of a pipette.

"We had a full day with just the three stops. She did mention she hoped to make another trip, though."

Controlled respiration. Attention heightened. Either he's anxious about what I'll say next, or he's gearing up to kick my ass.

She'd furrowed her forehead without realizing it. Rolling with it, she stretched her arms out and sighed. "Well, I have to say I'm disappointed."

Egan's eyes widened slightly but his arms didn't tense.

Anxiety it is.

"It's just that I've been hoping I'd find my smoking gun," she said, laughing a little. "Some clue that would put us on the trail of whoever killed Dr. Phan. And what do I find everywhere I go? Scientists, doing their damn jobs."

Egan's relief was palpable.

"I don't suppose Dr. Phan said where she was headed after you returned to base?"

"She said she was off to have dinner with her boys." His gaze met hers, less hesitantly this time, but his voice wavered. "Family is so important, don't you think?"

She'd been a fool not to understand earlier.

Fear. That's what she was sensing. Not the nimble dance of someone hiding the truth, but the desperate squirm of a man doing his best not to say too much. She'd heard that same tremor in Vivian Phan's voice at his wife's funeral.

Be careful, he'd said.

"You have kids?"

"Just one. Our daughter, Melodie." This time, his voice was soft, almost pleading.

An icy finger ran up Loretta's spine.

"How about you?" he asked, his voice strained.

"No kids yet. But I'd like to have them, someday." She kept her voice light, hoping he'd understand. "Amparo has two boys. A husband. Friends. She was a brilliant botanist too. They deserve the truth."

He glanced down at his coffee cup. "Absolutely. I wish I could help, but..."

"I know." She tucked her tablet under her arm and lifted her chin, then took a big swig of the coffee from the cup he'd provided. "Thanks for the chat, Doc, and good luck with the... rocks, I guess."

She'd meant it to be a joke, and he'd chuckled just like she'd hoped he would. He seemed relieved that she hadn't pressed the topic further.

Only he'd already given her more than he'd realized. It was best to let everyone assume she'd left this room empty-handed, at least until she better understood what was going on.

Something was scaring these scientists. Frightening them so badly that they were afraid not only for themselves, but for their families. First Amparo Phan. Now Terrance Egan. And it might have something to do with that fourth survey stop. *What in the hell was going on?*

Loretta returned to her hab and set it to privacy mode. She needed to think, so she stripped off her uniform and stepped inside the shower, turning the water as hot as it would go and letting the bubbly water slough off some of the tension she'd been carrying all afternoon.

Her first impulse had been to go directly to Marcus and tell him what she'd learned. She was halfway to council chambers when she realized that she was being an idiot. She'd told Egan that she was looking for a smoking gun, and that wasn't far from the truth. If she went to Marcus with vague worries about frightened scientists, and no useful evidence, what could he even do?

She closed her eyes and leaned into the spray. Her long auburn hair rippled heavy down her bare back, warm and thick in the water.

There might be an innocent explanation for what she'd seen today. The harbormaster's investigators were apparently a bunch of assholes. What if they'd warned Egan not to talk?

So he talked about his kid. And he seemed upset when I asked him about the fourth survey site. So what?

As much as she hated to admit it, even to herself, this wouldn't be the first time she'd let her suspicions run amok. Back when her parents died, she'd refused to believe it was an accident. She'd spent years looking for "the real reason" why a trover could explode without warning. And her court-mandated therapist had a lot to say about that.

Ms. Ryder's fear of losing her loved ones manifests as severe anxiety with hyper-vigilance as her primary coping mechanism. When her sense of safety is threatened, she may become inappropriately aggressive.

She'd scoffed at that report. Yet hadn't there been a slippery bit of truth in it? All her life, she'd felt an invisible threat over her shoulder, some dark-looming danger too nebulous to name. She'd lived with the bone-deep knowledge that at any moment her entire world could go to shit. And she'd coped by being *ready*. Prepared to defend the people she cared about.

Someone needed to be.

But what if that obnoxious therapist had been right? And all the ombuds too, acting like she was seeing danger where none existed. Was she out chasing ghosts? Was she using her job as a crutch for her damaged psyche? And what if Amparo's death was just what it seemed to be, a sad crime, perpetuated by someone who'd shattered seventy years of peace for reasons no sane person could ever understand?

Pivoting, she let the hot water run over her face, embracing the heat and the sting of it.

No one asked me to solve this problem.

She turned off the water, stepped out of the shower, and dried off. After wrapping herself in a fluffy robe, she went into her bedroom and opened a private terminal, pulling up satellite maps of the planet. With quick fingers she input the coordinates for the fourth expedition stop, the one that hadn't been on Dr. Egan's map.

What was it that Tamatha Clarke had said at her hearing?

Truth is a patient thing.

She snorted at the thought. *Truth may be patient, but I'm not.*

The image quality was fairly poor, but when she zoomed in, it was possible to see the faint outline of an ancient crater, an unremarkable geologic feature. Panning left and right, her eye snagged on a detail.

The image was much lower resolution than the photos of the areas surrounding it. After perusing the helpful wiki provided by the imaging team, she figured out how to inspect the image files themselves.

The satellite capture of the fourth survey site was fifteen years older than the other images in the database. That might explain the slight blurriness. She squinted at small, dark shapes on the western crater rim. They might have been panic sheds, but that seemed unlikely given the location. A few spare oxygen packs wouldn't do much good that far from civilization.

But there was more than one way to look at this problem. She logged into the corps' personnel safety system and pulled up a planetary map. After drawing a geofence loop around the missing survey site, she input the date of Amparo's soil gathering expedition.

"Let's see who's telling the truth here," she muttered.

Positional tracking was mandatory for any journey outside the safety of Epiphany proper, and records were retained for one Martian year. After a moment, the response to her query flashed on the screen.

REQUEST DENIED. DATA ACCESS CODE 84-59A-SEC0

What in the hell did that mean? Drumming her fingers on her desk, she leaned back in her chair. A few moments later, she called Henry McCormack.

"Hey Loretta." Henry was in motion. She could see the golden-hued dome overhead and the hint of chub beneath his chin.

"Quick question. How many soil samples did Amparo bring back from her expedition?"

"Four crates worth. About five kilos each."

"One from each stop."

"Yes. Why do you ask?"

Four crates. Four locations. Dr. Egan had indeed been lying his lying face off.

Fuck.

"Let me guess. Still chasing that theory?" Henry smiled at her through the screen.

"Something like that. Thanks. I gotta run."

"Hey! Are you coming to the centennial kickoff?"

She blinked twice. Given all that had happened, attending a party was the last thing on her mind. "I'm not sure."

"Well, our whole team will be there, and that means you should be there too," Henry said, giving her a rather stern look. "I'll save you a seat, Arbiter Ryder."

"See you soon."

CHAPTER SIXTEEN

"Captain Wells?"

Travis looked up from his half-eaten lunch to see a stranger standing in his office doorway. The guy's posture and bearing screamed "private security" but there was no corporate sigil on his jacket. He was on the young side for someone working in the private sector, perhaps twenty years old, with dark blond hair and hazel eyes. He wore a charcoal gray uniform with red piping on the seams.

"Guilty as charged," Travis replied. "What can I do for you?"

"Actually, the better question is, how can I help you?" He stuck out his hand. "My name is Sam Rathburn and I supervise the data requisitions team. I understand you ran across one of our error messages."

It took Travis a second to tear his mind away from the report he'd been working on just moments before. "Yes. One of my arbiters did, actually. I told her you were probably in the middle of a system upgrade. Do you have the data we asked for?"

"Something even better." Sam's grin was enthusiastic, almost childlike. "But I'll need you to come with me."

Travis's stomach growled in protest. He'd been working his way through a stack of appeals all morning, and he'd hardly had time to use the restroom. "Can I finish my lunch first?"

"Nope! I'm afraid we're on a very tight schedule. But trust me, you're going to want to see this."

Sam peppered him with mundane questions about twenty-six charlie as they headed for the nearest hub pickup point. If it wasn't for the guy's upbeat attitude he might have seemed nervous, but perhaps he had energy to burn. Data requisitions was a low-level support team concerned with upholding personal privacy rights. They provided access to shared data where legally permitted and educated the public on their rights and responsibilities.

It was necessary work. It also sounded horrifically, almost apocalyptically dull.

Travis moved toward the shuttle doors inside the transit hub, but Sam beckoned him back. "Hang on a sec, will you?"

There were six other pedestrians waiting; only after they'd boarded a shuttle and departed did Sam tap his pocket tablet against a control pad near the emergency exit. The door popped open, and he stepped inside.

"There's a shortcut."

"But—"

"Hurry! I'd rather not take the long way around."

Was sneaking through the tunnels what passed for excitement in data requisitions? Travis slipped inside and let the door shut behind him.

"It's right up here." Sam pointed up the narrow hallway. Green dashes showed the way toward an emergency assembly point on the level below, but instead of following that path, Sam turned left down a hallway and pressed his palm flat against a biometric reader next to an unmarked door.

Sam held the door open for him. "Welcome to data requisitions."

Travis looked up and around. The room felt large and chilly, although the dark gray walls and dim lighting made it difficult to take in the contours of the space. A massive display shone high on one wall, like a half-height theater screen that started at head level.

Six curved rows of workstations faced forward in classroom style, pointed at the enormous display. Several dozen workers sat at those desks, typing away or scrolling through what looked like video footage, manipulating rollerball interfaces to move the images forward or back. On the big screen, dozens of video feeds formed a quilt-like panopticon.

Travis blinked up at the screen. On one feed, he saw the seating area outside the council chambers where his father worked, every seat full of petitioners awaiting their hearing, ombuds striding past in their flowing gray robes. In another feed, a well-known reporter from the evening newsfeed adjusted her collar while she read her script off a tablet, preparing for her segment. College students ate lunch in a busy cafeteria. Schoolchildren were playing tag during their recreation period. A foursome of cadets chatted and laughed as they walked to their next assignment.

"This is..."

Sam grinned. "Impressive, right?"

"You're reviewing data requests?"

"No, those are our live feeds." He guided Travis over to a desk in the front row. The pretty, dark-haired woman seated there looked up with a smile. She looked to be about seventeen — the entire team seemed to be comprised of young adults — and she wore the same style of uniform as Sam.

"Hey boss."

"Ames, this is Travis Wells. Tell him what you're doing."

"Sure thing." She sat up a tad straighter in her chair. "I'm on a three-hour watch right now. We used to do six-hour shifts, but the human mind can only stay alert for so long." She gestured to the wall display. "Up there, we can monitor a wide range of feeds, and if there's an obvious disturbance, say, a fist fight or raised voices, our system will flag it for us."

Travis felt his jaw clench. There were so many questions he desperately needed to ask, but at the same time, he didn't want her to stop talking.

"My job is to monitor for any security incidents before they become serious," Ames continued. "Here's a good example." She pointed up at the large screen, then pulled up a copy of that feed on her personal display. It showed a man standing in a hallway outside a closed door. Text at the lower edge of her screen read, *Welling University #75*.

She popped her earpiece out and held it out on the palm of her hand. "Go ahead. Have a listen."

Travis tucked the device in his ear. Immediately, he heard the student mutter something, probably into his tablet.

"The Prof isn't here, Billy. You want to meet? We can talk about—"

Travis jerked the earpiece out. "Why am I listening to this? I have no right."

Ames glanced at Sam for guidance.

His expression was sympathetic. "Don't worry. Everything we do is perfectly legal, and there will be plenty of time to discuss the specifics. For now, let's finish your tour. Ames, show him the rest of it."

She nodded. "Right. This is why the human touch is important. Our system can flag loud voices, movement patterns, even signs of stress, but it's not great at the subtle stuff like body language. We know Welling is a hotbed of Free Mars activity, and I noticed this guy was lurking, so I may as well clear him."

"Clear him of what? He's just standing outside his professor's office."

"Sure. That's probably all this is." Ames smiled encouragingly. "So, anyway, I opened a channel, and let's say that was inconclusive. But no worries; I have one more trick up my sleeve." She tapped her terminal and brought up what looked like a mind map diagram. "I can access his tablet here," she tapped a tiny drawing of a tablet at the center of her screen, "and examine any active metadata."

She pointed. "See? I've got the student's name, and the name of the person he's calling. Looks like he's talking to his girlfriend. And there are no flags by either of their names."

Travis leaned closer. There was another icon on the screen; this one looked like a padlock superimposed over a square. "What's that?"

She tapped again, and it brought up a long list of names, designators, and subject lines.

Those are private messages.

This time, he took care to keep his tone neutral. When his father learned about this place, he was going to hit the roof. "But isn't that encrypted communication?"

"Indeed," Sam said, "all message traffic is encrypted. That's central to the charter, and we respect the law. All we're doing is glimpsing the metadata. Every message has a header and a designator address. Basic information about what's being delivered, absent the content. Those details are used for routing, and we can use them to assess patterns." He reached down and tapped the symbol again, closing the window. "But there's nothing to be concerned about here. Mr. Callahan might be lurking outside his professor's office, but he's no threat."

Travis felt his gut tighten. "And if you thought he was?"

"In that case, I'd make a formal request, asking for permission to monitor him more closely." Sam held up a hand as if staving off objections. "Now, those requests are rare. We only use that level of scrutiny in cases of suspected imminent threat. Usually," he gestured up at the massive overhead display, "this is more than enough to meet our needs. We believe in using a light touch."

Travis was thinking fast. He'd visited data requisitions once or twice, and the place he'd been to had looked nothing like this. Either something had changed, or this entire program had been hidden from public view.

If people knew about this, they'd be furious. And rightly so.

Sam thanked his employee and guided Travis toward a small office in the back of the facility. "I can tell you're surprised by what you've seen here today." The office was well-appointed, with new furniture, fresh plants in large pots, and excessively plush chairs that looked straight out of council chambers. "Perhaps you're even dismayed. But I promise you, the work we do saves lives."

Travis sat in the chair he was offered. It looked like it had just rolled off the factory line. "How long have you been in operation?"

"Eighteen months. Your father recruited me personally, and after he explained what the council was hoping to achieve, I knew I wanted to help. He charged me with hiring only the most trustworthy people to take on this great responsibility, and I'm proud to say I've succeeded. We have an incredible team here."

My father.

He wasn't about to embarrass himself by saying those words out loud, but from the look Sam was giving him, he saw that his ignorance was no secret at all. Swallowing the sudden bitterness in his mouth, he added, "And the security code my arbiter saw?"

Sam winced. "We've had to tighten access to some of our systems recently and unfortunately, our wiz wasn't up to the task. We had some data leakage. Thankfully, your father said it was time to orient you anyway, so there was no harm done."

"Orient me? To what?"

"Until now, I've been reporting directly to your father. While it's been an honor to work with him, we're both hoping that you'll agree to become our new director. We need someone who understands the current system to lead us through the next few years, during the transition."

It was impossible not to feel like an idiot. He'd been thrust into a conversation with no context, and worse, Sam knew it. He'd been polite from the start, almost deferential, but there was a touch of pity in his eyes, as much as he tried to conceal it.

Dad trusted this guy with his secrets, but he never told me a thing. Sam's too nice to say so out loud, but we both know it's true.

"What transition are you referring to?" Travis asked.

"That topic's way above my pay grade. Thankfully, there's someone better suited to talk you through it." He glanced at his watch. "He should be joining us any moment."

As if the words had summoned him, Marcus walked through the door, looking entirely pleased with himself.

"And that's my cue," Sam said. "Come find me later, after you've been briefed."

Travis waited for the click of the office door. Marcus had taken the seat Sam had vacated. Now he slung one ankle over his opposite knee, waiting patiently for Travis to make the first move.

He expects me to be angry. I can already see him sizing me up, getting ready to explain why he's right and I'm wrong. Mastering himself, Travis limited his outward reaction to a mild frown.

"You kept this from me."

"I did." Marcus didn't flinch.

"Are you going to tell me why?"

Marcus shifted in his seat. He picked idly at the closure of his polished brown shoe. When he looked up, it was with a certain wariness.

"I guess I've been waiting for you to grow up."

What a load of shit that was. "For fuck's sake, Dad! I'm twenty-six years old. And more than that, I have done everything you've ever asked of me. Top of my graduating class. Promoted to my captaincy with full honors. I'm damn good at my job, and I've never done *anything* to—"

"You're right." Marcus held up his hands. "Son, you are entirely correct. My one regret is not bringing you into my confidence sooner. The error was mine. Please believe me when I say I've been looking forward to this day for a very long time."

"What day is that? The day when I learn you've been spying on everyone behind their backs? And violating the charter you swore to uphold? What gives you the right?"

"I've been waiting for you to become this." He leaned forward and touched Travis's chest. "The man I've always known you could be. Passionate. Committed. Ready to serve the greater good."

"I don't understand."

"Then allow me to explain. Do you remember that night at dinner when I said I'd taken the wrong lesson from your mothers' death?"

Of course he did. It had stung, learning that his father had felt he'd had nothing left to live for. Because, wasn't *he* worth living for? Only, his father's depression hadn't been anyone's fault. He'd been suffering.

He hadn't meant to be cruel.

"I do. You said Greg Qual helped you."

"Back when Greg was elected chief councilor, Epiphany was spiraling toward crisis. As our population grew so did our problems. Crime. Random acts of violence. And for the first time, there were coordinated efforts to tear down our system of government."

"The same kind of problems Earth has."

"Precisely. We'd traveled far, and we'd built a gleaming city at the base of an ancient volcano, but it turns out we were every bit as flawed as our ancestors. The council was faced with a choice. We could follow in Earth's footsteps, either allowing our worst impulses to run amok in the name of freedom, or clamping down hard, spending precious resources on prisons and popularity contests instead of schools and research facilities. Greg knew that either path would be catastrophic to our larger purpose."

"You're talking about the Martian promise."

Marcus's smile radiated out like Sol's warmth. "Yes! Epiphany isn't merely a city on another world. It never has been. Our home is a promise to all of humanity. We're here to be an example, living proof that our species can overcome the mistakes of our past. We are explorers. Builders! Achievers. Our story has only just begun."

Travis nodded. His father was speaking to hopes that everyone on Epiphany shared, the ideals they'd been taught since they were children.

"Civilization is a fragile thing," Marcus said, the lightness in his voice fading fast. "There will always be threats. Some come from outside, a meteor strike, for example. Those we know how to deal with. More often the danger comes from our own nature. Violence can be like a disease, destroying us from within." Marcus gestured at the closed door, toward the facility beyond it. "Qual proposed the creation of an immune system of sorts. A way to zap away dangerous cells before they can threaten the body as a whole."

"But isn't that what the corps does?"

"Most of the time, yes. But in cases of existential threat, we need a stronger medicine than our peacekeepers can offer. And most importantly, we must spare our people the pain that comes with our most agonizing decisions."

"Why?"

Marcus leaned closer and reached for Travis's hand. He clasped it, warm and safe.

"When your mom died, I nearly lost my mind. At first, I was furious at Earth for allowing those violent protests to go on unchecked. I was even angry at *her*. I told myself that if she hadn't been so idealistic, so eager to help strangers, she might still be alive."

Marcus's voice was tinged with an old bitterness, but only for a moment.

"But here's the thing, kiddo. Your mom's essential goodness? That's what made me fall in love with her. It's also what made her such an excellent physician and mother. Wishing her kindness away, her tender heart, that would be madness itself."

"So you set all this up, because..."

"Epiphany *needs* idealists like your mother. People who believe in humanity's ability to overcome our worst instincts and do what is right, not just for ourselves, but for those who will come after."

"But what does that have to do with—"

"Listen. Because this is important. As keepers of the promise, it's our responsibility to create a safe place for good people to flourish. For their idealism and honor to grow unhindered. And when our way of life is at risk? When someone comes charging into *our* paradise, threatening everything we built? We must mitigate that threat, swiftly and discreetly. *That* is the council's purpose. The terrible responsibility people like you and I must carry."

"So people like Mom can do their work in peace."

"Exactly. I won't lie, Trav. What the council does — the compromises we make — sometimes, they keep me up at night. I'd love to live in a world where gentleness and reason are enough to keep our people safe. Until that reality exists, we'll do what we must. Always for the greater good."

Travis sat quietly, letting all that he'd heard percolate through his body like precious water through soil. For once, his father didn't try to hurry him along. He merely sat, listening, as if he'd be content to wait forever.

A potted plant with splendiferous green leaves shimmied gently in an air current atop the desk. Travis reached out and ran his fingertip up a stem from soil to leaf, considering all that had gone into its existence. Martians had taken a lifeless world and restored it, at least to an extent. There had been one feat of science after another. Yet it was the people of Epiphany that he'd always been the most proud of. They'd built a peaceful society, resolving to live in alignment with the common good. All his life he'd believed that there had been no murder. No crime beyond petty thievery and an occasional drunken fistfight.

It had seemed so incredible, because it was.

The truth hurt sometimes, didn't it? Loretta liked to say that, when she got news she didn't like, or when a client she admired lost their case. She'd say, *The truth hurts, but I'd rather you give it to me straight.*

He smiled at the memory. Most people were nothing like Loretta Ryder. If they were, Epiphany would be an even better place than it was. They might not need arbiters at all. But his father was right. Epiphany was changing. Already, the city was bursting at the seams. There was even talk of the need for a second settlement, for more homes and labs, so more citizens could be granted the privilege of having children.

"I'm glad you told me," Travis said, finally.

"Thank you for hearing me out," Marcus's eyes crinkled when he smiled. "I've been asking a lot of you lately. But only because I know you're ready to step up. Now, about the director position. This office is yours, when you're ready. I figured you'd want some time to wrap up matters at—"

"Hang on. One step at a time, okay? I'm still wrapping my head around this. Also, why me? I'm sure there are others who—"

"No." Marcus was adamant. "There's no one better qualified to be the council's eyes and ears. You know how to lead and inspire others. And you've proven you can be trusted with sensitive information. We can finally work side by side. Assuming that's what you want?"

Travis wasn't ready to answer. Not while there were so many questions clogging his mind. He began with the one that seemed the most important, the only thing that might justify what he'd seen. "Sam said what you do here saves lives?"

"That it does."

Travis pushed himself to his feet. "Show me."

CHAPTER SEVENTEEN

Late that evening, in the comfortable darkness of her habitat, Loretta gently untangled her sweaty legs from Travis's and rolled onto her side. Earlier, they'd eaten a meal together in silence as Sol sank beneath the horizon, wrapped up in their own thoughts. As the sky darkened, Deimos had risen like a bright white star, somehow fiercer than his twin Phobos despite their difference in size. Named for the sons of the Greek god Ares, the moons were said to represent panic and terror. Yet all they did was circle the planet, traveling along an orbit that they hadn't chosen and couldn't change. Perhaps that's where their fear was supposed to come from, that terrible inevitability?

She ran a hand along her bare belly. *I suppose it's good that I'm a woman and not a moon.*

Falling into bed together had been a relief. Lovemaking was its own language, complete with a grammar of motion; punctuated breaths, fast and slow. Her hands, buried in Travis's hair couldn't tap nervously on her thigh. Her mouth, pressed against his, had no secrets left to utter. All that she was and all that she felt had been laid bare. There were no secrets held inside her like painful little knots of string, tugging at every tender nerve. No uncertainties to wrestle with. No guilt and no mistakes. But now, with her head resting comfortably on the warmth of Travis's chest, the thoughts she'd dismissed earlier came rushing into the forefront of her mind.

If I tell him what I'm worried about, he'll want me to go straight to Marcus.

Right there was her problem. She was accustomed to building up her arguments, point by point, laying out what the correct course of action should be. Standing on that solid foundation, even beneath the cool-eyed discernment of the ombuds, speaking from the heart had always come easily. Because the ultimate decision was out of her hands, her only duty was to help her superiors see the light of truth.

But here? Now? There was no light to see by. No hard-edged facts she could point to. Nothing concrete.

She had a frightened geologist in one hand and the grieving family of Amparo Phan in the other. A fourth box of soil from a survey expedition that had only gone to three places. The vaguest hint of a cover up, all wrapped up in an investigation that had never been rightly hers to begin with.

If I go to Marcus now, he'd be right to laugh me out of the room.

Only that wasn't fair either. Wasn't Marcus the one who'd always told her to trust her gut? To ask the questions no one else was willing to?

Her brain said yes. Her gut said no. What harm would it do to wait until those organs were in alignment?

Travis's fingertips trailed down her arm. "What's going on in that head of yours?"

"I keep thinking about Amparo. It's just... I can't make sense of what happened."

"I talked to my dad earlier today. He says they're really close to naming their suspect. In fact, I expect there will be an announcement soon."

She lifted up, propped herself on one elbow. "That's great news! Isn't it?"

He'd sounded glum a moment before. Now he smiled. "Yeah. I suppose you're right. You didn't hear that from me, by the way. The council is keeping this one locked up tight. Everyone's afraid of getting it wrong."

"Understandable."

"How long until Kacey heads out?"

She didn't mind the abrupt change of subject. If they were that close to finding Amparo's killer, perhaps the investigators already knew everything she did. If not, she could present additional information for the trial.

Thank Sol. It was being handled.

"Just a few more days," she answered, tearing her mind away from tomorrow's problems. "She actually invited me to go with her. To join her and Theo on their next contract."

He chuckled, a rumbly sound low in his chest that reminded her of a purring cat. "I'm trying to imagine you in space. Remember that time you barfed on the trover during exercises?"

"Hey!" She crab-walked her hand across his body, then gripped his wrist, pinning him. "I have a delicate stomach! Don't judge me."

"What did you tell her?" Travis sounded so anxious that she let his wrist go, pulling back so he could see her expression.

"I told her no. She was only asking to be polite. You know how boring she thinks our lives are."

"Polite is not a word I'd use to describe Kacey," Travis countered. "Do you know she said I look like a human turnip?" He gestured down his torso. "I work *very* hard to stay this fit. Most people like broad shoulders on a guy. But to Kacey? I'm just Travis, the human turnip, and not good enough for her best friend Loretta."

Loretta hid her smile. Travis's triangular upper body and lush thicket of dark hair up top *could* be seen in the light of a certain vegetable. He didn't understand that teasing was how Kacey invited people into her circle.

And at least she was trying.

"Don't take it personally," she said. "I love Kacey to death, but she's never had a filter. Every thought in her brain comes stampeding out her mouth. You should consider it a compliment. She doesn't hold back with you because you're one of us."

He shrugged. "If you say so. Anyway, it sounds like her next contract will be a long one. You should spend some time with her while you can."

"Yeah." She flattened herself out on the bed and tugged the covers over her body. "I stopped by her hab earlier, but she wasn't in. I think she's avoiding me."

"She's probably out with Lin."

"Maybe." Loretta tried to push her doubts to one side. "Sometimes, she takes things so personally. Our therapist – the one Kacey and I went to when we were younger — she said kids like us have to grow up too fast. Do you think that's true?"

"Kids like who?"

"Kids who lost a parent. Do you ever feel that way?"

"Nope. I've always been like this. Mature beyond my years." His cocky grin faltered. "Why?"

"It's just... When Kacey invited me to go flying, it got me thinking. Can you imagine what it must feel like, to be up there? I thought about you and me, packing our bags, heading up into the great unknown."

He lifted an eyebrow. "Well, that would be quite the career pivot."

"I don't need a pivot. It's more like — You and I are on this road, right? And it leads to a good destination. But lately, it's like I can see everything laid out in front of us. We move in together, maybe have some kids, get old and wise and boring..."

He kissed the back of her hand. "You will never be boring."

"You know what I mean. Doesn't it ever bother you that we've got everything figured out?" She shivered despite the warmth of the covers. "Sometimes I wish we could take off. Disappear. Start over somewhere else."

"Like a couple of wacky kids in an Earth movie, running away from home."

"Exactly! You and me against the world."

"Now you're talking like one of those lunatic colonists. But we could take a vacation if you're feeling antsy. Maybe a shuttle cruise."

She snorted. "Shuttle cruises are boring."

"It wouldn't be if we're together." He stretched, his toes pointing toward the wall. "You're *sure* you weren't tempted to go with Kacey?"

"Not at all," she fibbed, feeling a tiny flash of guilt as soon as she spoke the words. Travis was acting insecure and she didn't want to feed those feelings. "I know where my home is. Speaking of which, I had *another* thought today."

"More than one? Holy shit."

She grabbed one of his pillows and yanked it away, smirking when his head lightly banged against the headboard. "I'm trying to be serious, for once."

"Apologies. Please continue."

"At some point, I figure we'll want to move in together."

"At some point." He was playing it cool, but she loved the sight of his quick smile, the way he scooted a tiny bit closer.

"And I'm the one with a big hab all to myself. Living here makes sense. But if I let you move in, you'll learn all my secrets."

"I already know you're gassy, sweetheart."

"Shut up!" She laughed. "*Also*, I'll have to learn how to share my space."

He covered his mouth with one hand. "The horror! Two people living in a three-bedroom habitat. How will we survive?"

"It's a process! That's all I'm saying." She reached out and ran her hand along his jaw. "Let's start with something simple. Can you keep a secret?"

"Is it a sexy secret?"

"No."

He pretended to roll away. "Never mind then."

"Travis!"

He sat up straighter and folded his hands in his lap. "Yes. I will keep your secrets, Loretta Ryder. Please proceed."

She rolled her eyes at his mock prissiness. "Stay put." She slipped on a dressing gown and went to her closet, returning with a storage crate. She sat cross-legged on the bed and unfolded the lid. From the top, she pulled out a soft pink teddy bear, a faded pair of red slippers, and a cheerful yellow blanket made out of real wool yarn.

"That stuff looks old."

"These things belonged to my mom." She shook the blanket over Travis's legs. "She made this, when she was a girl. Her grandmother taught her how."

He ran his hand appreciatively over the intricate stitches. "This is beautiful. Dad and I don't have any family mementos from Earth. My great-grandparents were laborers and they arrived at the docks with the clothes on their back. Or so my dad likes to say when he wants to brag about how far we've come."

There was a rectangular wooden box at the bottom of the crate. She lifted it out and set it in her lap with the brass latch facing him.

His eyes went wide as she opened the lid.

Travis jerked back as if the box's contents might bite him. "Lore! You *cannot* have that."

"You're familiar with regulation 859?"

His forehead furrowed. "Museum law?"

"Indeed. This is a bona fide historical artifact, held in a private collection."

"You're talking about the family heirloom exception. But..."

"Pick it up. It's not loaded."

She turned the box so they could both see inside. Nestled in a form-fitting insert lined with dark purple silk, an antique Colt revolver gleamed beneath the dim bedroom lights. The blue-black carbon steel surface had been polished to a near-mirror finish, and the textured handle looked like wood, although it was made of something stronger. The narrow barrel looked ridiculously long, terminating with a notch up top that served as a sight marker. The trigger was a delicate metal half-moon, surrounded by a sturdy finger guard made of the same material.

Above it, tucked securely in an indentation, was a single bullet, its outer casing darkened with age.

Travis hadn't moved, so she reached for the weapon, looping her fingers around the handle, lifting it carefully, keeping the muzzle pointed away from them. With her free hand, she pulled the cylinder to one side, revealing six small chambers.

"The projectiles go in there." Showing off a little, she flipped the cylinder back into place with one clean twist of her wrist. "Revolvers were designed for reloading on horseback. You use one hand for loading ammunition, the other keeps hold of the grip. Can you imagine firing this on the back of a moving animal?" She pivoted her hand, admiring how even dim light reflected off the metal, marveling in the sheer heft of the thing. "It's a beautiful piece of machinery. No electronics at all! It runs on pure physics, like an antique watch."

"But it's so..." he seemed to be struggling to find a polite word, "primitive. What else do you have stored away? A Civil War cannon shoved in the back of your pantry?"

She tucked the gun back in the box. "Sadly, no."

"I take it there's no stun mode."

"Not unless you count using it as a club. They called that pistol-whipping."

"Yuck." His nose crinkled. "I cannot believe you keep that thing in your bedroom closet. And in the same box as Teddy?" He clasped the bear protectively to his bare chest, relinquishing it reluctantly when she held out her hands.

She put the gun away and stacked the soft goods on top of it. "The gun belonged to my great-grandmother. She was a peacekeeper, back during the Fall. One of the best in the Pacific Northwest. I grew up on stories about Grandma Helen and The Word."

"Your gun has a name?"

"My mom said it started as a family joke. Apparently great-grandma Helen always had to have the last word. At some point, the name stuck."

"She liked to be in charge, eh? I imagine carrying a literal death machine on her hip didn't hurt."

"Probably not," Loretta conceded. "Like you say, pulsars are better. Safer, for sure. And I never need to worry about ammunition."

"Have you fired it?"

She hesitated. Owning a family heirloom wasn't against the code, but her illicit trips to the firing range almost certainly had been. Still, she'd meant what she'd said earlier. If they were going to be partners, she wanted him to know everything. Not only her strengths, but her imperfections too, every stubborn inch of who she was and who she hoped to become. "Once or twice."

"How did you even get—" He held up his hands. "Actually, never mind. I don't want to know the details."

She set the crate on the floor next to the bed. "So. Now you know my deep dark secret, Mr. Wells. Have I scared you away?"

He stroked his chin. "It sounds like the salient fact here is that my hot girlfriend comes from a long line of ass kickers."

She laughed. "More or less."

"Then I suppose it's good we're on the same team."

She leaned forward and kissed the tip of his nose. "Always."

"Well, I know your deep dark secret," he teased. "Does that mean I need to tell you mine?"

He looked worried, but he didn't need to be. She loved him, didn't she? And she wasn't going anywhere. She tackled him back onto the bed, pushing his shoulders down, laughing. "Hey, let's not take *all* the mystery out of our relationship. One step at a time, right?"

He ran his fingers through her long hair from crown to tail, spreading the long strands over her shoulders. For a moment, he looked past her, his thoughts a million miles away, but his smile returned when he focused on her. "You know I love you, right?"

"I do."

She thought he would kiss her then. Instead, he pulled her down, wrapping his arms around her, holding her close, murmuring into her ear.

"Good. Then all is right with the world."

CHAPTER EIGHTEEN

Loretta woke at the sound of someone knocking on her hab's front door. She yawned and swung her legs over the side of the bed, touching her bare feet to the cold floor. Her visitor hadn't used the chime, and the knocks were soft, if insistent.

It had to be Kacey, on her way home after a long night with Lin at the club. Maybe that meant she was finally ready to talk, to put her hurt feelings aside long enough for them to hug and reconnect before her long journey. Or possibly she was feeling beer brave and ready to have it out.

You never knew with her.

Loretta slipped on a robe and activated her hab's nightlight. Travis was still sacked out, his arms splayed out on the mattress as if he'd splatted onto the bed from a great height like a cartoon character.

She opened the door and found herself looking into the muddy brown eyes of Ginny Westmoreland, the harbormaster. Westmoreland had one of those faces that managed to look pissed off even when she wasn't, but Loretta felt a second start of surprise when she got a better look at her. Westmoreland's mouth twisted bitterly. Her dark glower seemed to say that she'd rather be anywhere else. Fear sliced through Loretta's gut, hot and swift like a sword.

Why was the most senior officer in the docklands at her door in the middle of the night?

"Harbormaster," Loretta stammered, pulling her robe tighter. "To what do I owe the pleasure? I mean — Is everything—"

"I need you to come with me."

Loretta felt her hand tighten automatically against the edge of her doorframe. She hadn't forgotten what this woman's team had done to Vivian Phan. In open defiance of every right accorded a Martian citizen, they'd hauled him into an interrogation room and denied him representation. Westmoreland must believe her rank and status meant she could do whatever she liked.

She was wrong about that.

Still, there was no reason to deny the woman's request out of hand. Not until she knew what it was about.

"Very well." Loretta kept her voice mild. "Where are you taking me?"

The harbormaster's mouth tightened and her flinty eyes seemed to say *none of your damn business*, but she said, "Councilor Wells has requested that you join us for a meeting. It's a matter of some urgency."

Marcus wanted to see her? He'd chosen an odd messenger, but she detected no deception in Ginny Westmoreland's expression. Every emotion seemed written on her face, backed up in triplicate and placed in plain view.

She doesn't want to be here.

"I'll get dressed. Would you like to come in and wait?"

"Are you alone?"

"My boyfriend is sleeping inside. Why?"

"Tell no one where you're going. Do you understand?" Westmoreland spat her words like projectiles.

For fuck's sake, Major. You haven't even told me where you're taking me.

Loretta kept her face impassive. "If he wakes up, I'll say I was called into work. My shift at the docks starts soon anyway. Is that acceptable?"

Finally, she caught a glimmer of something like respect in the woman's eye. Or was it relief? Either way, she seemed to have dialed her hostility down a notch. "It is."

"Then I'll be quick."

About twenty minutes later, Loretta was relieved to learn the harbormaster had spoken the truth. Together, they'd taken a private shuttle to the docklands, and after a short ride on a trover, Westmoreland had ushered her into a small conference room in a distant wing of the facility.

Marcus was waiting there.

"Thanks, Ginny." Marcus looked up from his tablet, his tone weary, a sheen of sweat on his forehead. He looked like he'd been wearing the same clothes for days. "I appreciate everything your team has done, and you have my word, the council won't forget your accomplishments."

Westmoreland's ugly scowl was back. "Sir, like I said before, we'd be happy to—"

"You've made your position perfectly clear." Marcus tucked the tablet into a soft-sided messenger bag on the table.

"Councilor Wells—" Her posture stiffened, almost like she was a first-year cadet and not the woman currently running the most sophisticated logistical operation on Mars. "I..."

Marcus stood. His chair scraped the floor as he shoved it back and out of his way. "You are dismissed, Major." His tone was deadly calm, but his gaze was pure fury. "I'll call you when and if I need you. Until then, either do your damn job or I'll find someone who can."

An ugly blush crept up Westmoreland's neck. Loretta

froze, averting her gaze. She'd never heard Marcus speak so harshly, and she suspected, neither had the harbormaster. That he'd done so in front of a junior-ranking person was an extra layer of humiliation.

What in the hell was going on?

Westmoreland rattled off a terse apology and took off, not quite slamming the door in her wake. Marcus rubbed his eyes and sat back down. When he glanced up again, he looked like a man who'd been shaken awake from a bad dream.

"Are... Are you okay?" she asked.

"I'm sorry you had to see that." He gestured that she should sit across from him. "It's been a long couple of days, and I'm afraid I'm not at my best. Please, forgive me."

"I guess we've all been on edge lately. What do you need? Is this about what happened to Dr. Phan?"

"Yes." His mouth was a grim line. "Ginny's team is a rather blunt instrument but they served their purpose. We now know who's responsible for the director's death."

"Who?" She didn't feel like sitting. She crossed her arms and waited, one foot propped against the wall.

"Our adversary was clever. He used a wiz to blot out most of the evidence, but thanks to a brilliant young woman over in data requisitions we were able to retrieve much of what had been deleted." He opened his bag and pulled out a stack of data tablets. They were edged with blue and white markings, meaning they were for council eyes only. "But we've been able to place him at the scene of the crime. He's the one who deactivated the security systems in forty-two beta. His pulsar fired the fatal blast. We've also connected him to the explosives found at Welling University earlier this year. Welling is his assigned district, so it was probably a simple matter to bypass their security."

"*His* pulsar? And his district? You're saying it was..." She bit away the end of her sentence, not wanting the taste of it in her mouth.

"Yes. Amparo Phan was killed by one of our own arbiters. His name is Darren McManus, and for the last three years he's been a rising star in the Free Mars movement."

Time stood still. Darren McManus? The name triggered a burst of memories, only none of them fit with the violent scene she'd come upon in the food sciences lab.

Darren wasn't just one of their own. He was the quiet, self-effacing man she'd gotten to know in her weapons proficiency class. He was a crack shot who never showed off, even when he could have. Generous with his knowledge and patient with the greenest cadets, Darren had talked about his wife Alicia and their long wait for a birthing license. In the end, they'd been surprised with twins. Double the effort and quadruple the fun, he'd joked, pulling up photos on his tablet to show the cadets.

Darren had been the one with the presence of mind to take Tina Brown's pulsar away from her. He'd so obviously been horrified by what she'd done.

"I know him," she said quietly. "He's... I don't believe he'd hurt anyone."

She felt Marcus's hand on her shoulder. He'd stood and now he was maneuvering her into a chair. "Trust me. I know exactly how you feel. This isn't a conclusion we came to lightly."

"But why? Why did he kill her?"

"There's still a great deal we don't understand. But Darren has been a leader in the Free Mars movement for some time, and—"

"You keep saying that, but—"

"You didn't know?" Marcus frowned to himself. "I

suppose there's no reason why you should have. Oh, there are sympathizers, even within our own ranks. And there's nothing illegal about holding an opinion, as disappointing as their disloyalty may be."

"Even if that's true, what does that have to do with Dr. Phan?"

"Our leading theory is that leaders of Free Mars were growing concerned that the vote wouldn't go their way. Director Phan was scheduled to give a keynote in favor of charter ratification at the centennial celebration. She was a passionate and persuasive speaker. Perhaps by silencing her, and by throwing suspicion on our entire organization in the process, they felt they could sway public opinion." He sighed. "He may have been right about that. We've seen a sharp rise in anti-charter sentiment these last few weeks. Ever since—"

She wouldn't let him soft-pedal it. "Ever since I fucked up."

Marcus swallowed. "For now, it's important that we take him into custody before he can hurt anyone else. That's where you come in."

"Me?"

"You know the man. And I believe he trusts you." Marcus leaned forward now, his gaze burning into hers. "You can convince him to come in peacefully. I'd like you to ask him to meet you near Hellas. We can have a security team waiting there. I have little doubt that he'll lie to you — spinning some story about how none of this is his fault. You need to be prepared for that. He's a desperate man, and desperation can drive a person to madness."

Loretta looked down at her hands. They looked small and pale against the scuffed white table. The cramped room stank of anxious sweat and takeout food. Was Marcus right? Could she bring Darren in peacefully? Somehow, he'd modified his pulsar to burn clear through Amparo's torso, leaving a deep gouge that had perforated her organs and killed her. Either that or he'd set the thing to *punish* and held it steady for — how long? — minutes? She'd never seen a wound like that before.

"I'd like to see the evidence."

"Of course. I've got it here for you to review. And there's one more thing, kiddo. I'd planned to make this announcement during the centennial celebration, but it seems we may as well make things official now, given that you're going to need these."

He opened the messenger bag and retrieved what looked like a small velvet jewelry case. He opened it, facing her.

She blinked down at the three small gemstones signifying a district leader's rank. "Captain's insignia? I don't understand." She looked up to see his proud smile shining down upon her as if this were a happy moment instead of a frightening one.

Her mouth went dry.

"Director Phan's murder has exposed a dangerous flaw in our systems," Marcus said. "For too long, we've labored under the belief that our principles alone are enough to keep us safe. It's like you said during the hearing. We must be better prepared. Not only for the rhythms and routines of an ordinary day, but to defend ourselves against *any* threat that might destroy our community."

When she was little, Loretta had loved spinning herself around in her mother's desk chair until she'd felt too dizzy to stand. She'd hop out of the chair and tried her hardest to walk a straight line across the room, planting each foot with purpose, willing herself not to fall. After she'd grown up, the same trick had only left her feeling sick.

Her gut roiled, churning up acid.

As much as she wanted those stones back on her collar, and as much as she'd feared — deep down — that she'd never, ever be trusted with a commission again, the speed at which this was all unfolding left her feeling dizzy.

"You agree with me?" she managed to ask.

"Yes. Moreover, so does the council. We're creating an internal affairs unit, a small cadre of trusted arbiters dedicated to identifying and neutralizing threats within the citizen body. And we'd like you to lead it."

"But my service hours..."

"Will be served concurrently with your duty time. We can't have our best people suiting up orange and moving cargo. Not now. Not with so much at stake."

It was hard to know what to say. She sat mute as he pinned the insignia on her collar. At last, she found her words. "Thank you, for placing your trust in me. I won't let you down."

"I know you won't, Lore. That's why you're here." He tapped the tablets into a pile and unlocked them with his security code. "If we're throwing a lot at you, it's because we know you're ready. Once we put the vote behind us, we'll be even freer to focus on bigger and better things. The future can be ours, but we can't just sit back and wait. We need to create that future, intentionally, with the full force of our wisdom and strength."

Marcus sounded excited. Hopeful. As much as she wanted to feel that way too, she couldn't. Not right now. Not even with her rank restored and her prospects brightened. There would be no pleasure in the task ahead, no joy to be had in finding justice if it meant yet another family would be ripped apart. First the Phans. Now the McManuses. It hurt to think of it.

"Nothing about this feels right," she murmured.

The naked shock on Marcus's face took her by surprise.

His eyes sprang open wide. His mouth opened soundlessly before snapping shut. He leaned forward and spoke, openly curious. "I agree we need to do this right. But Loretta, what does that mean to you?"

It was such a "Marcus question" that she couldn't help but smile. "I'm thinking about Darren's wife and kids. What this arrest will mean for them. I heard how the harbormaster's team treated the Phans, and I won't be a part of anything like that. No more bullying. No more threats. We do this right. The Martian way."

Why did he look so terribly sad? No doubt he was thinking of Amparo and her family. Marcus knew very well how it felt to know your partner was never coming home again.

His worried expression made her wonder if he regretted choosing her for this mission. Maybe he thought she was too young or too immature to handle it. Well, if that was the case, she'd reward his trust by doing her duty well.

"It'll be okay," she said, offering him an encouraging smile. "I've got this." She reached for the tablets. "First, I want to look at the evidence you've gathered, to better understand how he thinks. I need a plan that minimizes the chance of any more violence. And I have to move fast, before he tries anything else."

"That's my girl," Marcus murmured.

She would have bristled at those words if they'd come from anyone else, but hearing the tenderness in Marcus's voice, they only served to warm her from the inside out. This was the moment she'd long been preparing herself for. At last, she was back on the path she'd been destined to follow.

It was time to get justice for Amparo Phan.

CHAPTER NINETEEN

The corridors were quiet and largely deserted as she made her way from the transit hub to the residential tower where Darren and his family lived. She took the elevator up to the fifteenth floor and paused in the hallway outside the McManus habitat, standing back as to remain off camera.

Before she'd left the docklands, Marcus had offered her a six-person security detail, a run of the harbormaster's armory, anything she might want or need. In the end, she'd decided to proceed as she'd been taught. There was only one thing that worked when emotions were running high. You had to show up, look the person in the eye, and start up a conversation.

A trapped person might panic. A desperate individual sometimes made poor decisions or even put other people at risk. Yet on Epiphany, there was literally nowhere to run. She'd asked Marcus to station his security teams near the docklands to prevent an off-world escape, an unlikely but not impossible move for a hunted man — and then she'd headed out alone.

She took a breath and stepped up to the door, her finger hovering over the chime. It all felt so surreal, trying to square the Darren she'd known with the man she'd seen in the videos Marcus had shown her. First, he'd shown him giving a fiery speech to students at Welling, railing against the council and the corps itself. As horrifying as it had been to hear those words coming out of an arbiter's mouth, that alone hadn't been suggestive of a crime.

Only motive.

But data requisitions had recovered a vid — glitching due to missing data packets yet fairly complete — and it showed Darren bypassing security at the food sciences lab shortly before Amparo had been killed. A detailed forensic analysis of Darren's pulsar records showed that they'd been carefully scrubbed and renewed with false data. The worst part had been a series of images taken by a security camera at Welling. They showed Darren and Amparo arguing. Darren's normally placid expression had been twisted with anger. Amparo had looked so frightened! Even without audio...

It killed her that she'd been so wrong about the guy. Up until just a few hours ago, she would have trusted Darren to have her back, without any hesitation.

But maybe her instincts weren't as good as she thought they were. She pressed the chime and waited.

Alicia McManus opened the door, her shoulders back and her head held high. Defiance sparked in her pale blue-gray eyes. She was in her mid-forties, like her husband, with stylishly blue hair highlighted in silver.

"What do you want?"

Loretta kept her voice low. "I want to come inside and talk to your husband."

"We're busy."

Loretta shoved her foot forward, blocking the door before it could close. "If you don't let me in, they'll send someone else. Please?"

Alicia's gaze went right over Loretta's shoulder, sweeping down the hallway behind her. "Give me your pulsar, then."

"I didn't bring it."

She didn't seem to believe her, so Loretta stepped back and slowly spun, lightly patting the thigh holster on her slacks, showing her that it was empty. Loretta had never seen a negotiation improved by the addition of a firearm, and she had no reason to believe Darren would hurt her.

Of course, Amparo had probably thought the same thing.

"Tell him I'm here to talk," she said. "He knows me."

She kept her posture loose and nonthreatening. Finally, Alicia stepped back to admit her. "You can come in. But my kids are eating breakfast. Let's keep things... civil."

"I'd like that too."

The McManus hab was about the size of her own. There was a biggish, comfortable living area full of squashy furniture and an attached kitchen with counter-level seating. A hallway led back to the sleeping quarters.

Loretta followed Alicia's gesture to a corner of the living room. She waited while Alicia activated a display surface in the kitchen to keep the kids entertained. Nearby, a coffee table was loaded with children's art projects and borrowed data tablets from the central media library. Loretta felt herself smile at the sight of Alicia and Darren's twin girls chatting at the counter between mouthfuls of scrambled eggs, their short legs swinging above the crossbars of their chairs. They were about seven years old, with the same unruly brown hair as their father.

"I've been asked to bring Darren in for questioning," she said, when Alicia joined her.

"Whatever they're accusing him of, he didn't do it." Alicia folded her arms as if the matter were settled.

Whatever they... She didn't know what this was about, did she? Of course she believed her husband hadn't done anything wrong. But she already knew something was up or she wouldn't have been so defensive.

"That may be," Loretta said calmly. "But I need Darren to turn himself in. We have some questions about—"

"About what?" Alicia flared. "The fact that he's spoken out about the charter? The fact that people trust and believe him? The council might *wish* they could outlaw dissent, but they can't. The charter explicitly allows the free expression of ideas. You can't silence him just because—"

"Hold on. You think this is about his speeches at the university?"

Alicia dropped her hands to her side. "What else would it be?"

"We have questions about his relationship with Amparo Phan." As soon as she spoke the words, she knew they'd been a mistake. Alicia stepped back, horrified.

"I want you *out* of my house. Now."

"I promise, we only want to—"

She grabbed Loretta's sleeve and dragged her deeper into the hab, back toward the bedrooms. She dropped her voice to a whisper. "He told me the council would try something to discredit him. But this?" She rubbed her eyes. "I should have listened to him. We should have gotten the girls off-world while we could. Shit!"

The childish patter in the other room dropped away. One of the girls whispered, "Mommy said a swear."

Alicia looked like she was about to cry. She stood up straighter and tried to pull herself together. "Sorry, girls! Finish your breakfast, okay?"

"Will you walk us to school today? Mrs. Anderson said—"

"You're not going to school today," she snapped.

In unison, "Why?"

"We'll discuss it after our visitor leaves."

"I need to speak to Darren," Loretta reiterated. "Is he here?"

Public security cams had shown Darren headed home the prior evening, and he hadn't been seen leaving the area. But as an arbiter he'd know where the safety cameras were. How to avoid them.

"He's not."

Westmoreland's team would have pushed their way deeper into the hab. They'd have tossed the bedrooms, making sure the man wasn't hiding in a closet or behind a piece of furniture. But Alicia was telling the truth. Besides, Darren didn't strike her as the kind of person to hide under a bed. He wouldn't use his family like a shield. Maybe she hadn't known him as well as she'd thought, but she knew that much.

"Where did he go?"

"To work."

"I checked. He's not there."

Alicia shrugged, feigning indifference. "Then I don't know what to tell you."

Loretta stood silently until Alicia made eye contact. "Then tell me how to *help* him."

"You're not on his side. Don't pretend that you are."

"My only goal here is to bring him in. And if you like, I'll stay at his side until his representative arrives. Why don't you call your arbitration office to get the ball rolling? We can do that right now."

It was hard not to think of Amparo lying on the ground, to relive the horror of finding that horrible wound in her belly. Telling Alicia what her husband had done wouldn't help.

She'd never believe it.

Yet even in the most difficult moments, an arbiter's duty was to find common ground. To form agreements even out of the tiniest scrap of shared territory.

"I won't let anyone violate his rights," Loretta added. "But if he runs…" She grimaced. "Let's just say I'm not a fan of how the harbormaster has been handling their investigation up until now. I'd much rather bring him in myself."

Marcus had wanted her to have Darren meet her at the arbitration center closest to Hellas Detention Facility. She'd nixed that idea because Darren wasn't a moron. Also, why trust someone to treat you fairly when they'd been lying to you from the very start?

She was gratified to see Alicia's body language had lost some of its stiffness.

"Will you talk to him?" Alicia asked.

"What do you mean?"

"Exactly what I said." She crossed her arms over her waist. "Are you going to haul Darren off immediately, or are you actually going to stop and listen to what he has to say?"

"I'm not sure who the interviewers will be," Loretta began, but Alicia cut her off.

"That's not good enough. Darren isn't your enemy. He's corps, just like you. And when you throttled that idiot — Cadet Brown — he said you'd just made a mistake. Some of the others, they wanted to use that story to bolster our cause. To show the brutality of the corps. Darren didn't like that."

"I'll hear him out," Loretta said. "I promise."

Listening was never too steep a price to pay for peace.

"Good." Alicia seemed to be thinking hard. "Also, I'm going to give you access to our hab's private feed. Every single byte we have stored in memory. That should be a months' worth of video, at least. Darren likes storing clips of our girls for the family album."

Loretta felt a start of surprise. "Why would you do that?"

"Because maybe then you'll see we're not what you think we are. Go ahead. Listen in on our private conversations. Watch my girls brushing their teeth. Hell, listen to me sing in the shower! You'll see that Darren did *nothing* wrong."

"Did he know Amparo Phan?"

Alicia didn't like that question. Shifting her weight from one foot to the other, she let her gaze drop to one side. "He talked to her a few times. Ask him to tell you about it. I wasn't there."

Sensing the door was finally open, Loretta pressed her advantage. "Where is he?"

"I'm not sure," Alicia sighed. "He said he was going to work. But I can give you a list of places he might be." She grabbed a piece of scrap paper off the coffee table and wrote a list on it. After folding the paper with one hand, she stepped forward and tucked it directly into Loretta's jacket pocket. "There. You should check those places. But before you go, I actually have something of yours. You should take it with you."

This bit of news was so surprising that Loretta's hand stilled atop her pocket. "You do? What?"

"Here." She opened a drawer in a small cabinet and took out a large white envelope. "Darren was supposed to give this to you when he was taking your class, but we kept forgetting about it."

Loretta opened the envelope and slid the contents out. It was a single piece of paper with a ragged edge. The page was thick and yellowed with age. Someone had spilled something on the outer edge. She felt a flash of shock when she realized what she was looking at.

"This is from my mother's cookbook."

"A recipe for Triple Chocolate Cake, to be precise." Alicia smiled at Loretta's surprise. "Your mother loaned it to me forever ago. We were always trying to recreate old Earth recipes with local ingredients. Usually with horrid results, at least when it came to baked goods. Martian flour is more nutritious, but it doesn't rise the same way."

"I didn't know you two were friends."

Alicia reached out, smoothed back a lock of Loretta's hair that had escaped from her braid, an unexpectedly tender gesture. Stunned, Loretta thought back, trying to find an image of Alicia's face among the blurry memories of her childhood. Back before the accident. There had been lots of people in and out of the family habitat. Ensconced in her bedroom, reading or doing homework or chatting with her schoolmates, she'd heard the laughter of grown-ups in the other room, and the sound of good-natured arguments among friends.

But that had been such a long time ago.

"You look a lot like Selena," Alicia said. "Darren and I tried to visit you, afterward, but your therapist felt it was best not to overwhelm you with too many authority figures." She glanced toward the kitchen. Her daughters had gone suspiciously quiet. "After a while, it just felt like you were too far away. But you seemed happy. And you deserved to be."

Alicia's expression tightened. She touched the yellowed edge of the recipe. "See? Right there is the good stuff. Your mom really wanted it to work out, but we never could quite crack it. Maybe you'll have better luck than we did."

"Thank you." Loretta wasn't sure what else to say. She'd terrified this woman and then she'd pissed her off. Now she was offering up an old memory like a gift.

"You're very welcome," Alicia said. Then, in a much sterner voice, one that seemed more steel than air, she added, "You can repay me by not throwing my husband to the fucking wolves."

"Mooooom!" her daughters yelled in unison.

In a quieter tone, she added, "Please, don't hurt him."

"I would never do that. I swear."

She tucked the envelope under her arm and departed. Outside the hab, she half expected to see one of the harbormaster's security teams waiting, either watching her progress or hoping to tell the council they'd chosen the wrong woman for the job.

But there was no one there. Just a quiet residential corridor and the faint sound of conversation to the north.

Inside her hab, Loretta started a pot of coffee to brew. Travis had left a handwritten note next to her favorite mug, atop the counter.

Babe,

Sorry I missed you this morning. Dad asked me to help him with preparations for the centennial celebration after work. You're welcome to join but I told him you and Kacey might have plans. Dinner tomorrow? Your place? I'll bring my great-grandfather's trebuchet. And dessert.

Love you,

T

With a smile, she folded the note and slid it beneath her reading tablet. Then she sat at the counter to review what Alicia had given her. The list wasn't terribly promising. Alicia had jotted down the location of Darren's arbitration office at Welling University, almost a dozen restaurants, and several public gathering areas, including a library popular with parents of young children.

At the bottom of the page, Alicia had drawn a cake and underlined it three times with heavy strokes of her pen.

That was weird. *I'm trying to arrest her husband and she took time to draw, what? A doodle?*

She couldn't discount the possibility that Darren's wife was sending her on a wild goose chase, hoping to distract her long enough for her husband to escape through the docklands. If Darren had gone to work or to a restaurant the public feeds would have spotted him, and she'd checked the feeds before she'd left. Habitat towers weren't monitored, as they were considered private spaces, but it was difficult to travel from district to district without passing through a public square or a transit hub at some point.

Where would I go, if I was trying to hide?

Emergency access passageways led to well-stocked bubble pods that contained hab suits, food and water, medical supplies, and other life essentials. A pod would make a good place to hole up for a while, if — let's say — you believed you were about to be arrested for murder.

But even then, what was his end game? Hiding forever? Stealing a research tent and hiding in the outback until the portable survival units ran out?

It made no sense.

Neither did it make sense for Alicia to lie to her. Well, perhaps it did, but Alicia hadn't been lying. At least not after she'd promised to hear Darren out.

There'd been something in the woman's tone, a pointed focus in her eyes when she'd handed over the envelope.

Alicia wants me to hear his side of things. And that can't happen if I don't find him.

Loretta rubbed her face. At the burbling of the coffee pot, she went over and poured herself a cup. It was too hot to drink, so she grabbed the archival box where she kept her mother's cookbook and set it on the countertop. Then she slid the cake recipe out of the envelope.

The page was definitely from her mother's cookbook, but why had it been ripped clean out of the binding? Why hadn't she sent a digital copy, or even loaned her friend the whole book?

The photo of the cake had darkened with age, but she saw there were three wax candles sticking up from the top, surrounded in wreaths of chocolate frosting.

There had been three candles on Alicia's doodle, too. And she'd drawn three lines beneath the little sketch.

The recipe felt oddly heavy, and whatever mess someone had spilled along the side was browned with oxidation. Loretta absentmindedly touched the edge, wondering if she might clean it somehow. The page was dog-eared in the corner. Not just folded. Split in half?

Both halves of the dog-eared triangles were smooth. This wasn't just a single piece of paper, but two, carefully pressed together.

A tiny thrill ran up Loretta's arm and pinged her brain. Was that what this was? Some sort of hidden message?

Loretta rummaged around in her junk drawer until she found her father's old penknife. Carefully sliding the small blade into the opening between the dog-eared triangles, she shimmied the sharp edge down the outer edge of the doubled paper. Old glue fell away in dirty amber shards. She brushed the mess off the counter onto the floor and carefully pulled the sheets apart.

Her heart did a tiny leap inside her chest when she saw the familiar handwriting, carefully rounded print with those tiny ornamental swoops along the upper corners of the capital Bs and Ds.

An old memory flickered to life. A warm afternoon. She and her mom sitting cross-legged at the coffee table, playing together. Loretta came up with silly stories, and her mother had drawn the characters out on the page. Cats with black-rimmed glasses. Rabbits wearing tuxedos. A castle on a tall hill above a windy purple ocean. Her mother had labeled each picture, sounding out the letters before handing over her pen so Loretta could try.

This was Selena Ryder's handwriting.

The left page was a diagram showing a labyrinthine maze of tunnels and small rooms. Stars, hearts, and tiny cat heads marked various points, although the meanings of the symbols were unclear. At the center, a larger, circular room was nested inside layers of curved hallways. The further out the passages went, the squarer and more regular they became, almost like an old-fashioned English garden.

The facing page contained mostly text. Beneath a header of hand-drawn molecular diagrams, she found a list of names and notations, about twenty entries in all.

Danielle Halvor, 2B

Lian Zane, 5C

Edgar Landry, 2B

Stefan Patroklos, 5A

None of the names sounded at all familiar. It wasn't until she snapped an image of the map and asked MarsNet for a pattern match that she realized what Alicia had been trying to tell her.

CHAPTER TWENTY

One hundred years prior, The First Thirty had landed on a planet unprepared to sustain human life. Knowing what awaited them on the red planet, the founders had constructed their habitat in advance of their arrival. It had taken over a decade to deliver and test their primitive life support systems and another three Martian years for the automated diggers to tunnel a habitat deep beneath the Martian surface.

Now, those tunnels were abandoned. Every so often a documentary crew would work their way through a mountain of red tape to secure permits allowing them to pick through the detritus Epiphany's museum curators had left behind. More often, the first habitat was a tempting (and forbidden) escape for teenagers looking for privacy or cheap thrills. A few times, smugglers had been caught moving illicit cargo down below, hoping to avoid scrutiny. An attempt had been made to seal the whole area off, but after a few accidental deaths from asphyxiation or rockfall, the council had given up, stationing cameras in the periphery, posting warning signs, and sending an occasional security crew through to discourage any permanent settlement.

After descending a series of ladders to the safest known entry point, Loretta stepped around a small rockslide and headed deep into the first habitat. Her nose crinkled at the stink of chlorine-scented air. The raw rock walls shed regolith, finely compacted rock tinged red with iron oxides. It smelled foul and was dangerous to breathe in large quantities. The First Thirty had embedded thousands of small green plants in the walls, not only to help feed themselves but to stave off the madness they feared might plague them while living entirely underground. Those plants were gone now, and the tunnels were smothered in shadow, lit only by low-power LEDs set into the walls at long intervals. The original floor coverings had either rotted away or been scavenged, and it felt strange to be walking over hard rock in her soft indoor boots. She ran one hand over the tunnel wall, feeling the grit and sharp points left by those early diggers.

She rubbed her fingers together. They were coated in brownish-red dust.

Luxury accommodations, these were not.

She didn't bother to hide her approach. If Darren intended to stay hidden in this maze of tunnels and rooms it would take a large and dedicated search party to find him. There was no shortage of places to hide.

"Darren?" she called out. "It's Loretta Ryder."

Her footfalls echoed ahead of her as the angle of the pathway deepened. Consulting the map on her tablet, she saw a right turn ahead that should lead toward the room that had served as a crew area for the First Thirty. Recent security sweeps had verified that the space was still intact. Her tablet's status bar blinked red.

No signal. Offline mode only.

MarsNet hadn't kept these areas linked up to the network. Why would they? Darren had chosen his hiding spot well.

She turned right. Up ahead, on the ground, she spotted a

portable lantern and something that looked like an insulated tote. The lantern cast a circle of blue light on the wall next to it. Definite signs of life. But were those things Darren's, or did they belong to someone else?

Her fingers brushed her pulsar, still safely in its holster. There were no cameras in this part of the settlement and no one to call if something went awry. She doubted that Darren would kill her — what good would it do him? — but if there were smugglers down here, she wasn't about to take any chances.

"Darren? I spoke to your wife. She asked me to hear you out, and I promised her I would."

"Hi Loretta."

His voice was right behind her. She stopped the scream threatening to tear its way out of her throat and held her arms out at her sides. Turning slowly, willing herself to be calm, she saw him standing in a shallow alcove, half-hidden in the darkness. Darren didn't look fearful, or insane, or ready to start a fight. If anything, the guy looked faintly embarrassed.

"Sorry about this." He lifted his pulsar and fired.

When she came to, her arms shivered in the cold. The ground was hard beneath her body, but someone had placed something soft under her head and neck. It did nothing for her splitting headache. Her eyes fluttered open. She was not in her bedroom, or in her habitat.

Darkness enveloped her like a shroud. The air stank like rotten cleaning chemicals.

Darren.

Jerking upright to a sitting position, she grabbed for her pulsar only to find the magnetic holster empty. That's when she saw a bit of folded fabric on the ground next to her. It was her uniform jacket. Her eyes must have been adjusting to the darkness because a shape moved nearby, some ten feet away. The contours of a man.

Darren had stunned her and taken her gun away.

"Sorry for scaring you," Darren said quietly. "There's a small tracker embedded in your jacket, near the cuff. I'm pretty sure they don't work down here, but I'm not taking any chances."

"Sure. And sandworms haunt the Cassini Crater." Marcus hadn't mentioned that Darren was suffering from paranoia, but now she had to wonder. It might explain why he'd been acting so out of character. Either way, she still had a job to do.

She reached for her jacket, wincing as sparks of pain shot down her torso and into her lower back. She'd landed on her still-healing ribs. Her hand went to the discharge burn just below her clavicle. Darren had hit her where all arbiters were taught to aim during a stun maneuver, off-center and high, minimizing the chance of an adverse cardiac reaction.

It stung. Fortunately, the pain only served to piss her off, and she needed that energy right now.

"Go ahead. Check your jacket."

She caught a faint glint of something smooth in his hand. Her pulsar? She couldn't tell. He was far enough away that he could easily shoot her again if she tried to nab him. He'd lay her out flat before she'd gotten to her feet.

I need to distract him. Then I can make my move.

Humoring him, she ran her hand along her uniform coat. There was a small tear near the right wrist cuff. Inside, she touched a thin, flat strand of flexible composite. It felt like a relay bus, only smaller, like those used inside hab suits to control life support. The wires had been cut cleanly in half. "I don't know what this is," she admitted. "But you didn't need to shoot me."

Every hab suit came with an emergency positioning system. That made sense, given the dangers of being outside in atmo. She'd never heard of a tracker being placed in standard clothing, but she also didn't see why it mattered.

Unless you were a murderer running from the law.

"I'm not happy about it either," Darren replied. "Alicia filled me in on what you told her."

"You two have a way of communicating?"

Darren had turned off his lantern, but the faint LED illumination in the passage behind him gave her a sense of his shape, even the bend of his nose and the outline of his thick eyebrows. His posture had tightened when she'd mentioned his wife.

"I don't actually care about that," she corrected. "Here's what matters: The harbormaster has been investigating Amparo Phan's murder, and we've gathered some evidence that worries us."

That was an exceedingly polite way to put it, she thought.

"I viewed that evidence this morning. And now I'm here to bring you in for questioning." She stood slowly, bracing herself against the rough stone wall.

"So what did I do, Loretta?" Darren got to his feet, shadowing her stance, staying mobile.

I'm probably faster than he is. But he's bigger, with more muscle. I need to keep him talking.

"You know what you've done. As for your defense, you can—"

"Indulge me. Tell me what they showed you before they tasked you with hunting me down."

If he wanted her to feel sorry for him, he'd have to work harder. Protocol discouraged arbiters from getting into extended back-and-forth with citizens under arrest, but she'd promised Alicia she'd listen. That, and Darren had all the weapons.

For now.

"Well, first they showed me your speeches."

"What did you think?" His mouth twitched. "I've never been much of a public speaker, but I think I did okay. Also, that thing they say about imagining your audience naked? Surprisingly ineffective."

If he was trying to get her to lower her guard, it wouldn't work. "Here's what I'd love to know. If you have such a low opinion of what we do, why did you join the corps at all?"

"Ah. You didn't actually listen." Darren sounded almost disappointed. "What else did you see?"

"I saw you breaking into the lab."

"Did you?" He sounded faintly amused at the notion. "What else?"

"I saw you threaten Amparo."

"Well, that's fascinating, because it never happened. How did I threaten her exactly?" He tried to keep his voice nonchalant but failed. Anxiety plucked his syllables like guitar strings, sending out waves of emotion.

Only she needed him distracted, not afraid. Fear made people do stupid things.

"You were yelling at her in the photos. She was super upset. And—" Her tongue stilled. He was right. She didn't know what words he'd spoken to Amparo, only that he'd been angry, and that she'd been terrified. Yet it didn't matter. She hadn't come here to hold a one-woman hearing or to render final judgment in the darkness of the tunnels beneath the city. "Look. I'm not saying I know everything that happened. But you're a suspect in her murder, and that means you need to come in. Tell the ombuds your side of the story. At your hearing—"

"I'm never going to get a hearing." Darren rubbed his

eyes. The dust was getting to him too. She should have bolted forward, grasping the advantage, but the sudden defeat in his voice had surprised her. She'd seen his shoulders slump, a sign of hope leaving the body.

He actually believes what he's saying.

"You're wrong," she said.

"I'm surprised that Marcus sent you. Normally he prefers to let his private army do his dirty work. But now he's looped you into this mess. Maybe he's not as smart as I thought. Either that, or he thinks you're too wrapped up in your loyalty to him to see what's right in front of you." He let out a long breath. "I guess we'll find out, won't we?"

Marcus didn't have a private army. Probably Darren meant the harbor crew, but even then, he was twisting the truth. Marcus hadn't wanted to go outside the corps, but there had been a conflict of interest. A pulsar had been used! An organization couldn't ethically investigate itself.

She almost argued her point, but the memory of Alicia's plea stilled her. With a sigh, she added, "I promised your wife I'd hear you out. And I'm here, aren't I? You claim that I can't see what's in front of me. You'll need to be more specific."

He was quiet for a long moment, framing his arguments. Finally, he asked, "Do you have a warrant for my arrest?"

She'd been expecting another Free Mars rant, more vitriol about how the council was too powerful for its own good. Maybe even a fervent denial that he'd done anything wrong when he'd threatened Amparo. Instead, his question had come out of nowhere, a verbal right hook that stung more than she wanted to admit.

"I don't," she said slowly. "But my orders came from the council directly. They said this was—"

"Let me guess. An urgent security matter."

Her mouth snapped shut. It's true, Marcus had used that phrase. The charter allowed for a certain amount of leeway in urgent security matters. Surely a literal *murder* fit that description.

"You were demoted, Loretta. We all saw it. And you know that low-level arbiters don't conduct arrests. You know the process. We never move without a warrant. And when one is issued, we always travel in teams of two. Where's your secondary?"

"I—"

"Who restored your rank?"

"Marcus said—" She broke off as the implication hit her. Did Darren actually believe she'd been bribed into going after him? Her face burned. She felt her fists clench at her side. She didn't give a shit about the rank! She only wanted to do the right thing.

"Listen." His tone was sympathetic now. "I don't agree with how harshly you were treated by the ombuds. But don't you find any of this strange? What did the council offer you in exchange for my unwarranted arrest? Did they offer you your old job back? I bet they appealed to your love of Mars. Anyone who's ever met you understands how much you care about our people. Just like I do."

"That's not..." Her defense evaporated on her lips. He was twisting what had happened, trying to dirty up what she'd been sent here to do. It was sick! She felt...

Oh Sol.

Only Darren wasn't finished. He kept on talking in that calm, clear voice of his. "I'd bet that no one from forty-two beta even knows what you've been asked to do. At least tell me which ombudsperson authorized my arrest. And why were you called up in the middle of the night?"

His questions landed like punches thrown straight from the hip; only her iron will prevented her from flinching.

Marcus had warned her that Darren would spin a story. Was that what this was? Even a green cadet understood that dishonest people sometimes used honest arguments to achieve their aims. Marcus had wanted her to move swiftly, to bring Darren directly to Hellas where he could be contained. If Darren was telling the truth — it might explain why Marcus had been so insistent on that plan.

Still, he'd backed off, hadn't he? Marcus hadn't forced her to do anything.

Marcus would never do what Darren was accusing him of.

Were these lies or delusions? Did it matter which?

She'd caught the tiny spark of hope in Darren's voice, and the thread of desperation running through it. Dangerous or no, he was being sincere. He believed what he was saying, every bit as much as Marcus had believed the words he'd spoken to her.

"Uh. They—" she stammered. "It's just that the council didn't want anyone to panic."

"Listen to yourself. Do you remember what we were taught? What you told our cadets? We follow the code, yes, but always in full view of the public. You're being manipulated. They took your rank, and then they offered to give it back, but only if you play ball, right? Who acts like that?"

Acid churned in her belly, corrosive and nauseating. She wanted to fly at the man, to scream at him, to give him the biggest ass kicking of his life, if only to prove with her fists what she needed to be true.

Mastering herself with effort, she spat, "But why? Why would the council do this?"

Darren looked at her for a long moment before answering. "What's happening the day after tomorrow isn't a vote, Lore. It's a coup. One the council doesn't intend me to survive."

"But that's stupid! Why you? You're not important. You're just—"

"The council can't afford to lose. The charter allows a *one time* vote for a new constitution. If the council retains power over Epiphany, they'll keep it, forever. A new constitution means new rules, but that's not their biggest fear. A new government would take a good, hard look at how we do things around here. It will be impossible for them to hide their crimes. Already, it's a struggle."

He was talking nonsense. She told him so.

"There's a facility to the northeast, not far from the Lyot crater. It's coded as a top-secret research and development lab, but in reality, it's a prison."

"Bullshit."

"It's called Facility Zeta. They claim it's a re-education program, but what it amounts to is unsanctioned kidnapping and torture of Martian citizens. That's where the council sends anyone who refuses to toe the line. And it's where they'll send me, assuming they let me live."

Loretta felt as if the ground beneath her feet had dropped three inches. The Lyot crater was just a few dozen clicks from Amparo Phan's fourth survey spot. The location that Terrance Egan had sworn they'd never visited. All despite a fourth box of soil sitting inside Henry McCormack's laboratory.

It fit.

On expedition, had Amparo run across a secret, one so dangerous that the council had decided to silence her forever?

She shook her head. "The council could never keep a secret that big. People would figure it out. And what about the prisoners? You say this is happening right under our noses, yet not a single person has spoken up?"

"Many have tried. Those that weren't dismissed as crackpots had a tendency to disappear. Then, thirteen years ago, a group of activists tried to launch a rescue. They planned to bring the prisoners back to Epiphany, where they could tell their stories and shine a light on what was really happening at Zeta. Only the mission failed. That's where—" Darren stopped, blew out his breath. "Well, you know. Ten people died, including your parents. Only a few of us escaped scrutiny, and most were put under heavy surveillance. We've been rebuilding ever since. We even tried to get our own people assigned to Zeta to gather proof, but—"

"Wait. You're saying my parents were involved in this."

Darren's expression darkened. "I'm saying that the council murdered your parents, along with eight other people, all to keep their dirty secret thirteen years ago. And when Director Phan learned the truth, they killed her too."

She stared at him. Dust motes hung in the air between them, frozen in time.

Loretta backed up step by step, putting herself flush against the wall. If she'd been able, she would have pushed right through the rock's surface, sprinting away as fast as her legs could take her. Merciless, Darren kept talking, unspooling information like a hellish red thread that threatened to strangle her.

It *hurt*.

"Marcus is clever," he said. "He plucks his team directly out of diplomat training, just a few at a time, ensuring that he can control them from the very start of their careers. And he's got the Harbormaster in his pocket."

Darren's jacket was filthy with regolith. His bloodshot eyes were watchful, wary, as if he expected an assault at any moment. Yet he spoke clearly and calmly, as if they had all the time in the world.

They didn't.

"If all this is true, why not tell people? You could make some sort of announcement."

"And the good citizens of Epiphany would just believe us?" Darren flared, his eyes flashing. "Because we say so? The Martian promise is a seductive idea, but it's based on the notion that we are somehow superior to every other civilization that's ever existed. Think about that! No murders in seventy years? Loretta, there are almost three hundred thousand people living in Epiphany. We're not beyond crime. We haven't cured corruption. We're not gods. There are only a few differences between Mars and Earth. Our settlement is small. Our people are wealthy. And we have a secret facility where we throw away our trash."

"People aren't trash!"

"Then we agree." He sounded relieved. "We agree! Look, I'm not asking you to betray your family. But you can't let this lie—"

"Then what about Amparo? You argued with her. I saw it!"

"Dr. Phan saw something she wasn't supposed to during her expedition. She was on the ClearNet asking questions that were going to put her in the council's crosshairs. I pulled her aside, tried to explain to her what was really going on, and—"

"She didn't believe you." Loretta hadn't meant to speak, but the words slipped out.

"No. Just like you, she told me I'd lost my mind." He

leaned against the wall and rubbed his arms against the cold. "But I received a message from her the night she died. She wanted me to meet her at the lab. When I arrived, she was already dead."

Loretta bit her tongue. She'd been about to ask why he didn't call for help. Why he didn't come forward afterward. But she understood what he'd feared. Perhaps that had been the plan, all along. To put him there, at the scene of the crime.

"I couldn't raise emergency services, but I heard you coming up the hall." He winced. "So I ran. I'm not proud of that. I knew I couldn't explain why I was there without getting into what I'd told her. And then..." He shrugged.

"I need to talk to Marcus." She straightened up. Her fingers buttoned up her uniform jacket. She smoothed over the torn spot on her cuff, her eyes stinging. "You should stay here. Stay out of sight until I get back. I'll go to him, and we'll talk, and he'll—"

"Loretta."

His pity cut like a knife. "*Fuck* you, Darren. Fuck you for telling me this, and fuck you for..." Her breath hitched. "For making me feel like..." She blinked to clear her eyes. Breathed deep to cycle the gritty air through her lungs. Her voice lowered to a whisper, "How dare you try to make me believe..."

He stepped forward, moving slow.

This is it. Right here. I can take his pulsar. It's right there at his hip. I can take it, and I can put him in an arm lock, and I can...

Her weapon glinted in his hand. Darren was handing it to her, grip out, a terrible sympathy in his eye. "Loretta, this vote is more important than most people know. It's our last chance to dissolve the council without bloodshed. And I didn't kill Amparo Phan. I think you know that."

She took the pulsar. Holstered it. Forced herself to stand

still until the throat-clawing horror subsided. Thirteen years ago, lost in grief, she'd pushed so many memories away. But Tom Ryder — her first father — he'd had a way of calming her down when she was afraid. Even when she'd messed up so badly she believed there was no hope of making things right. He'd knelt down, putting his head on the same level as hers, always treating her as if she were capable of understanding grown-up things. He'd taught her that what was broken could be put back together again, but only if she was brave.

Truth is truth, he liked to say. *It would be wrong to look away.*

"Okay," she said.

Darren's eyes widened. "You mean—"

"I *mean*, I'm not taking you in until we get this sorted out. That's all I can promise right now."

A small explosion sounded in the distance. The floor shook and a rancid cloud of regolith filled the air. Loretta held her sleeve up, breathing through the thick gray fabric, her eyes squeezed shut. When she opened them again, she saw Darren turned away, listening intently. His hand went to his trouser pocket. "They're coming from the south. You need to get out of here before they figure out we've talked." He pointed. "Take the eastmost path and loop around to the north. There's a narrow gap through a rockfall, but the passage beyond it is secure. You can climb to the upper levels there."

"Who is coming?"

He grimaced. "The harbormaster's people, I expect. They probably got tired of waiting, and they may have tracked you on the feeds. They've got eyes everywhere in the city proper. Hidden cams in the recycler vents. Loretta, I need a favor. You have to get my wife and kids off-world."

She may as well have asked him to fly them to Phobos on her back. "Even if I was willing, I can't—"

"Your pilot friend can get it done. I've heard she has contacts, ways to help people disappear. *Please.* If they can't find me, they'll use my family to get to me. I know you may not believe everything I'm saying but—"

The whites of his eyes flashed in the darkness. His fear was more convincing than words could ever be. "I'll try. But what about you?"

"I have to stay, to help protect the vote. We're trying to rally as many people as we can, to remind everyone that democracy doesn't have to mean losing the best parts of who we are. And we're making headway. The council wouldn't be taking these risks if they believed they were going to win." He shot her a rueful look. "I *am* sorry, Lore. I hoped you'd never have to join this fight."

He peered down the tunnel, listening, ready to bolt. She saw it in the tenseness of his shoulders, and in the way he'd grounded his feet like a runner at the starting line.

He glanced back and whispered. "There's a cache of untracked hab suits near the exit. Dress up orange and opaque your helmet. You never saw me, understand? Move!"

Something small and dark glinted in his hand. He ran, disappearing into the deeper darkness beyond. A moment later, the ground shook, and a wall of rubble fell between them.

CHAPTER TWENTY-ONE

The hab suits were right where Darren had said they'd be. Loretta stepped into one and sealed it, ignoring the way her uniform jacket bunched up at the shoulders. She reached for a metal rung on the escape ladder and climbed. Her mind ran in small, panicked circles but her body knew what to do. The rhythm of the climb worked to steady her, to bring her pulse back to normal. One grip. One footfall. The feel of textured metal beneath her boot. She focused on the smooth motion of lifting herself up, to the next rung, and the one beyond it. She opaqued her face shield and swung to the left, landing lightly on the platform at ground level.

Her underarms felt moist. Grit from the tunnels below still coated her fingers beneath her black work gloves. She pushed through the utility door and headed right, toward the docklands.

Kacey and Theo were kicked back in their shuttle bay, relaxing atop a thick blanket. Punkfeld music pulsed from Theo's speakerbox, dispensing a relentless, grimy beat. Theo was flat on his back with his head propped up on a cloth tool bag, dozing. Open takeout boxes from a bunch of different restaurants were scattered around them in various states of demolishment. Kacey sat cross-legged next to him, her chin propped in her hands, watching media on her tablet. She looked up when Loretta approached.

Kacey gestured at the remains of their impromptu picnic. "Sorry. We probably aren't supposed to eat in here. But we have *tons* of leftovers. Want a bite? I won't tell if you don't." She picked up a greasy paper bag and shook it. "We have cookies! Good ones. My favorite is the lemon ice. Here, take the whole lot. I'm sure you and your friends could use a—"

Loretta opened her face shield.

Kacey dropped the cookie bag. "Oh! It's you. Why didn't you say something?"

"Can we talk?" Loretta swallowed. She'd meant to sound casual, but her voice came out half-strangled, as if every syllable had needed to work its way through an obstacle course on the way out.

Kacey jumped up on her feet and came in for a rib-cracking hug. She jerked back when Loretta winced. "Sorry! I'm sorry. I'm aware that I've been a bitch lately. I know you have a life here. Travis is a good guy, and you love him. I was just being—" She broke off, her eyes narrowing. "Are you okay?"

Loretta felt her face do something complicated. She'd spent her long climb trying to find some fatal flaw in Darren's story but she'd come up empty. He'd seemed so sincere, and what he'd said fit neatly with the mystery of Amparo Phan's fourth survey stop. He wasn't wrong about the breach in protocol, either, including the lack of a posted warrant. It had seemed okay, in the heat of the moment, but now?

And those chemical diagrams in the cake recipe... the computer said they were for explosives. I should have asked Darren what that meant.

She blinked.

And Marcus... He fought for me when I wanted to investigate my parents' death! And it wasn't like he was happy about sending me after Darren. Maybe the harbormaster has been feeding him lies? All I know is that there's something rotten here.

Something horrid.

Kacey snapped her fingers in front of Loretta's face. "Hey! Are you with me? Is it Travis? Is he okay?"

"He's fine." *Sol. If Marcus is in the thick of this... It's going to kill Trav. It's going to break his fucking heart.*

She kept her face forward, mindful of the public feed cameras aimed at *Poppy Moon* and her crew.

And Kacey. Darren said Kacey had ways of helping people disappear?

His story was madness. Yet everything he'd said had a stink of truth to it. Only, how could Darren know more about her best friend than she did?

Kacey frowned. She seemed to be making her mind up about something. Her finger poked Loretta in the chest. "Stay right here. Don't move." She skipped away a few steps and kicked the bottom of Theo's right boot. When his eyes opened, she said, "Hey, big boy. I could use some exercise to burn this food off. Dance party?"

After a flash of shock almost too quick to capture, a slow smile spread over his rugged features. He turned off the music and reactivated his speakerbox.

"You know I love dancing."

Kacey shoved a take-out box into Loretta's gloved hands. "Make yourself useful, will ya? Carry this into our shuttle." She reached down and pressed the suit's wrist control to close and opaque Loretta's face shield. To Theo, she spoke more loudly than was necessary. "This one's gonna help us finish loading."

It took Loretta a moment to realize that Kacey was keeping up the fiction that she was just another remedial helping out at the docks. She picked up a few more boxes and carried them into the shuttle's open cargo door.

Inside *Poppy Moon*, Kacey held down a button at the control panel to close the shuttle's exterior door. With nimble fingers, she input a nine-digit code into the keypad. A moment later, party music blasted through the ship loud enough to make the floor paneling vibrate beneath Loretta's feet. At the highest point of the cargo hold, a tiny disco ball popped out of an overhead hatch and began to rotate, scattering colored light on the walls and floor.

Loretta stared. It might have been hilarious, if she wasn't so full of dread. She'd come here because she didn't want to be alone, not because she though there was anything her friends could do. Telling Travis had to be her next move, but what could she even say? He wouldn't believe her.

Hell, she didn't want to believe what she'd heard, either.

Kacey and Theo were donning their hab suits. Theo's was navy blue with orange visibility panels, and Kacey wore her habitual pink with silver glitter accents. After a moment of private conversation with one another, they approached, forming a huddle with Loretta in the middle. Kacey grabbed her wrist console in surprisingly gentle hands and quickly connected her into *Poppy*'s encrypted feed.

"What the hell, Lore? Did someone hurt you? You look hurt. And I don't just mean physically. Do I need to kick someone's ass?"

Loretta felt Kacey's small hand land on her shoulder, squeezing softly, giving her a tiny shake.

Theo bent into her field of view, his broad forehead creased with worry. He signed, *Are you okay? Can we help?*

The last of her finely-honed control abandoned her; tears streamed hot and angry down her cheeks. She was the world's biggest fool. Either she'd just been co-opted into the very conspiracy she'd been trying to unravel, and she'd become a traitor to the cause, or Darren was right and everything she'd been taught was a lie.

Lies upon lies, all shattering like glass beneath her feet.

Where was she supposed to stand, now?

Theo held up a finger, then opened her face shield. He took a large, clean handkerchief out of a cargo pocket and wiped her face before closing her helmet again. He shot her a sad smile, then signed something she didn't understand.

Kacey translated. "Just tell us. It'll be okay. I promise."

So she told them. Everything she'd learned. All the things she feared. Talking helped. By the time she was done, she knew what her next move would be.

"I need to find facility Zeta," she said, feeling a bit steadier now. "Either it's just a secret R&D operation and Darren is an extremely persuasive sociopath, or—"

"Or Daddy Dearest has been locking his critics up where they can't cause trouble." Kacey shot Theo a tense look. "I hate to say it, Lore, but that tracks with what we've been hearing."

"What are you talking about? Oh! And before I forget, what's up with this rumor that you're smuggling people off-world? That's insane. You'd never be able to—" She broke off at the sight of Kacey's tiny smirk.

"I haven't told you everything about my life. But to answer your first question, we've heard stories of people forced off-world by the Martian government. It goes like this: a citizen and their entire family are invited to Earth for a symposium or whatever, but when they try to return home, they find their credentials have been revoked. Other times, people just disappear."

"And you think the council is responsible? You have no proof! Why would they—"

Kacey held up her hands. "Don't shoot the messenger! I have zero interest in the local political bullshit. I'm just telling you what people whisper when there are no arbiters around to listen. You think your parents were mixed up in this mess? Those names you found inside that recipe card - who were they?"

"Mostly people who left Mars a long time ago. And a few who died."

"Like, they were murdered?"

"No! They were sick, or they died of old age. But most of them weren't dead. They relocated to Earth or Luna."

Theo signed something.

"You think they were prisoners?" Kacey nodded. "That tracks. Lore, if your parents wanted to break people out, maybe they kept a list of who was there. What rooms they were in. You know, spy shit."

"My parents weren't like that."

"But the molecular diagrams in your mom's cookbook were for an explosive," Kacey reminded her. "Officially, your parents died in an explosion, right? A trover collision? I wonder if it was the same substance."

Loretta felt her hands tighten at her sides. "You're saying they blew *themselves* up?"

"No, but your mom taught chemistry. And you said it was a cake recipe? There's this ancient Earth manual, The Anarchist's Cookbook. Maybe your mom and Alicia McManus weren't actually trying to make dessert. Maybe they were cooking up a bomb."

Theo signed something.

"I agree," Kacey grinned. "Totally badass."

"So, assuming this isn't a madman's fantasy," Loretta began.

"Which is isn't." Kacey cocked one eyebrow.

"Maybe my parents tried to blow up the facility to create

an escape path? Or even a diversion." Loretta spoke slowly, then shook her head. This flight of fancy was getting out of hand. "But... my parents weren't terrorists! They were boring and normal, and they bickered over what serials to watch. I mean — I loved them very much, but there was nothing like that going on. Hell! They were..."

Kacey touched her shoulder. "Hon, if your source is right, your parents were trying to free people from hell. To get them out, so they could tell their stories. That's not terrorism. That's fucking heroic."

"I'm sure every terrorist thinks they're a hero. But that's not the point. The point is, I know who my parents were. They weren't the heroic type."

"Then why did your mom hide a bomb recipe inside the family cookbook?"

Loretta looked at Theo for support, but he seemed to agree with Kacey. She sighed. "Maybe you're right; maybe you're not. But until I see this place with my own eyes, I won't know what to believe. I'll take a trover, and gear up, and—"

Kacey scoffed. "My glorious shapely ass you're going by yourself! I'll fly you. We'll take *Beetle*."

"You don't understand. I need to get inside. That means breaking and entering a secure government facility. They'll have records. And I can gather evidence of what's really happening. It'll be dangerous, but—"

"You want to know if your parents are locked up in there," Kacey said.

Loretta felt her chest tighten. "That would be... a very stupid thing to hope for."

Kacey's grin was pure wickedness. "Hope *is* often stupid.

We're in agreement on that point. But, given the circumstances, I will fly you out to the secret prison facility that definitely exists so you can sneak around and gather evidence that Marcus Wells has been a very naughty boy."

"I'll just load up a trover. If Darren was right..."

"That'll take too long. You'd need to refuel somewhere and there's no guarantee you won't break down en route. You're the least sneaky person I know, and you'll probably get caught within an hour."

"I can be sneaky!"

Kacey didn't even respond to that. "We'll take my bike! *Beetle*'s sensors will come in handy. They'll never see us coming. You can't do this alone, Lore. You need me."

Loretta wanted to argue some more, but Kacey rudely muted her microphone, cutting her out of the conversation. Now, she was rolling her shoulders back, jiving with the music echoing throughout the ship. She shimmied her skinny butt, stepping from side to side.

Theo responded by flinging out his beefy arms and doing a little dance of his own. He worked his shoulders up and down like pistons, then moonwalked back a few steps, shooting Loretta a wink.

Despite how insane they both looked, and despite how patently stupid this plan was, Loretta couldn't help but laugh.

We could end up in Hellas for what we're about to do, or worse. And these two want to have a frigging dance party.

At the sound of Loretta's snort-laugh, Kacey reauthorized her mic access. She clapped her hands together and pointed at Theo.

"Theo, sweetie, it sounds like we need an extraction. One adult and two littles. Lore, how tall are Darren's kids?"

Loretta put her hand at ribcage level.

Theo nodded and removed a bulkhead panel, lifting the massive thing off the wall one-handed. From a compartment, he pulled out several large cargo crates, flattened and ready for assembly.

"They'll have eyes on them," Kacey warned him. "And we may need to leave early. You understand? Let's make sure all our chickens have come home to roost."

Yes, he signed. Pointing from Kacey to Loretta, he added, *Be careful. Don't die.*

Kacey turned back to Loretta, hands on her hips, her toe still tapping to the music. "What gear do we need? Keep in mind that *Beetle* can't carry much."

"Well, I'll want vids," Loretta said. "Something not connected to MarsNet."

Kacey rolled her eyes as if the request were beneath her. "What else?"

Loretta felt for her pulsar; it was buried deep inside her hab suit, in the holster of her uniform slacks. Unfortunately, there was no guarantee her weapon would function outside Epiphany proper. Every pulsar was connected to MarsNet or an authorized travel module, like the one the corps had installed at the shooting range.

"I need to get something from my hab."

"Give Theo a list. And your access code. He'll take care of it while he's out making deliveries. Right, babe?"

Theo nodded. He'd already assembled the crates. Inside one, he affixed something that looked like a portable rescue breather to an interior wall. He smiled at Loretta's surprise, then shrugged as if it were no big deal.

F-U-N P-A-R-T, he finger-spelled.

"This is the fun part, huh?"

He nodded emphatically, then pointed to his chest.

S-N-E-A-K-Y

She felt her heart lift at his eagerness, but the rumble of fear in her belly was stronger.

Be careful, she signed back, repeating his words from earlier. *Please, don't die.*

CHAPTER TWENTY-TWO

Loretta and Kacey flew fast and low through the outback. Skimming over the Martian surface, *Beetle* traveled in a wide arc, curving away from the city to avoid surveillance. Loretta watched the horizon and tried to relax into the unfamiliar sensations. Skimming wasn't half as bad as launching into orbit, but it felt strange to be zooming so close to the ground. Whenever she glanced at the blurred soil beneath them, her gut felt swimmy. Behind them, Epiphany was shrinking in the distance. The city's outer districts looked like a cluster of bubbles, pastel-hued and delicate enough to pop with a careless finger.

Kacey hummed to herself as she flew. Her small fingers rested comfortably atop the dash, and she seemed perfectly content. Loretta remained silent, not wanting to break her friend's reverie. It wasn't hard to imagine a much younger Kacey flying down an abandoned freeway on her bicycle, her long hair flying back in the wind and her high-pitched giggle echoing across the remains of old Chicago. Out in front of her, the brightly colored roofs of the suburban slum where she'd been born must have looked like an endless ocean of corrugated metal and tent-fabric, but Kacey had never fallen victim to despair. Instead, she'd cobbled together a measure of joy, even in something as small as a bike frame and a pair of wheels.

She still refused to talk about how she ended up a stowaway on that ship, or where the scars on her legs had come from. How did she keep dancing in the face of all that she'd seen?

I wish I had one tenth her resilience. If I did, maybe I wouldn't be so scared right now.

Loretta glanced down at the newly installed nav screen. *Beetle* was a small yellow dot flowing smoothly along the path Kacey had programmed into the computer. A bumpy-looking topography map outlined features of the Martian surface in their vicinity. They were headed to the coordinates of Amparo Phan's fourth survey stop, not far from Lyot Crater. From there, they'd navigate by feel, relying upon *Beetle*'s sensors to find Facility Zeta.

Assuming it existed.

"You're awfully quiet," Kacey said.

Loretta shrugged before realizing Kacey couldn't see the gesture. The low-res vids in their helmet displays showed facial expressions, but nothing below the neck. "I guess I don't know what to say."

"I'm sorry I didn't tell you everything about my job."

"It doesn't matter." She'd meant it, but Kacey continued as if she'd never spoken.

"It's not that I don't trust you. I do. But you shouldn't have to keep my secrets. That's not fair."

"I take it you're not a cargo pilot?"

Kacey smirked. "Damn straight I'm a cargo pilot! Best you've ever seen. But I work for myself, more or less, not one of the corporates. And sometimes..." She raised an eyebrow.

"Sometimes, you help people disappear." Theo hadn't missed a beat when Kacey asked him to pick up Darren's family. "You're a smuggler."

"Hey. The only difference between hauling and smuggling is how other people feel about what you're carrying. And I never carry — ahem, special cargo — that didn't specifically ask for my help." She aimed a smug look through her feed. "In commerce *and* in the bedroom, consent is what matters."

Loretta held back her retort. It must have slipped right past Kacey's high-minded ideals that a local government might wish to *consent* to what moved through their ports.

But none of that mattered right now.

"Do you think we'll find a prison?" Loretta asked.

"If so, they won't call it that. Re-education camps are a thing where I come from, although getting caught running one is a good way to get strung up by an angry mob. Ever since Earth became less..."

"Civilized?" Loretta suggested.

"Less organized, I was going to say, ordinary people have been more willing to take matters into their own hands. But people still get away with a lot of heinous shit. Prison masters said they were running work camps or factories. It plays better in the press."

"Darren said it was kidnapping and torture."

"Well, most prisons are all about torture," Kacey said quietly.

"That's not true."

"Isn't it? You take a human being and cut them out of society. Separate them from their family. Take away their clothes, their access to information, anything that might connect them to their identity. Then, give them a number instead of a name." Her unhappy sigh crackled across the feed. "For the record, I don't *want* to find a prison out here. For all our fuck ups, I thought Mars had gotten this part right."

"Hellas is okay. I've been there. No one's tortured. They have therapy. Classes. Lots of time with family and friends. Even Marcus did a stint there for assault."

"We have rehab facilities on Earth too. Commit a rich person crime and you'll be put in a comfortable if socially embarrassing facility to receive your official slap on the wrist. Ooh la la."

Kacey's superior attitude was getting old. "So are you pissed that people are punished too much, or not enough?"

"I guess I believe if punishment is what you're after, you're already doing it wrong."

Loretta sat with that thought as Kacey piloted *Beetle* up a steep slope. On the other side, they followed a jagged path between two mountains. When they reached the top of an icy crest Kacey pointed to something tall and black nestled into an eerily flat, almost featureless area below. "Well, isn't *that* interesting!"

"That can't be..."

Kacey flipped a switch. "Sensors confirm it."

The *Steady as She Goes* stood in dusty isolation atop a scarred, circular launchpad like a chess piece abandoned in a vast desert. Only the shuttle looked somewhat different than she had before. The big mural was still there, with its frosty mountain and evergreen forest. Up top, her big hawklike nose still looked menacing. But her lateral profile looked... thinner? And no one would miss the two enormous guns mounted to her body, one on either side where before there had been wing-like protrusions.

"Kacey, is it just me, or—"

"That's a Martian gunship all right." Kacey settled *Beetle* onto her skids, choosing a spot shadowed by a cliff where Sol's light wouldn't reflect off her golden hull.

Kacey slammed her fist lightly against the dash. "Arg! Those damn Pinafore engines! I should have known those fuckers had funding." She held up a finger and traced around the outline of the shuttle. "That's smart, actually. Way easier than building a ship from scratch. First, you'd manufacture hull plating to cover up the guns. Then you'd modify the cockpit a bit. That mural is just a false flag. Literally. That picture just screams Earth, doesn't it?"

"I did note the shitty craftmanship."

Kacey flicked a cool glance her way. "Those two who jumped you — What do you wanna bet they were working for the harbormaster this whole time? The Matri — I mean — *Poppy's* sensors never picked up a signal outside atmo because the *Steady* never broke orbit. She probably swung around the back of the planet and landed right here."

"But why did they go to the docklands at all?"

Kacey shrugged. "Beats me."

"They took my helmet so my feeds wouldn't sync with MarsNet, but they probably didn't have to hack the docklands database, did they?" Loretta blew out her breath. "There never were any terrorists. The harbormaster's goons planted that evidence to throw more suspicion at Free Mars. And those crates we found..."

"Sweetie, I know it's hard for you to pound this particular nail through that beautiful head of yours, but you've been *working* for the dang terrorists. I mean, you almost iced a father of two this morning because Marcus told you to."

"No! I didn't! I mean... Fuck! Look, I get what you're saying. But those guys," she pointed toward the shuttle, "they are *not* corps! Don't you dare paint us all with the same fucking—"

"I know! I hear you. I just needed to be clear about which side we're on. So, we found a Martian gunship, sitting on a launch pad in the middle of nowhere. But where's the crew? Did they park the thing and trover off? It's a ghost town out there."

Loretta peered out across the landscape. A facility would have entrances. Structures. Something! There wasn't so much as a trover track in the rocky soil surrounding the ship.

"Can you tell if there are people in there?"

Kacey flipped through several screens on her nav panel. "I'm not reading any anomalous temperature signatures. Not even near the engines. I'd say it's been here for a while."

"Can you scan the surrounding area?"

"Sure. I've got a cave mapper here and a few rad sensors that might pick up solar reflection if it's strong enough. They come in handy when you need a place to hi — Holy shit! Will ya look at them tacos!"

Kacey sent her visual to the rear nav screen. The *Steady's* landing pad sat dead-center atop a massive underground structure at least ten levels deep. The image wasn't high resolution, but it was possible to make out the shapes of rooms and passageways.

Images flicked across the nav panel. Kacey was capturing snapshots, taking different angles, examining the deeper depths. The upper two levels looked like office space, with many small rooms laid together. There were four large, multi-level chambers tucked deep inside the honeycomb-like facility. If only they could see more than a simple outline of the walls!

Kacey switched to vid view and zoomed in on the *Steady*, snapping closeups. "This is good! Anyone with half a brain will see that these so-called terrorists are actually harbor crew, flying a modified ship. Now we can—"

Loretta already knew where Kacey was heading. "I'm still going inside."

"Don't be reckless. We have what you wanted. Footage of the gunship, and scans of the facility. You can take this to your people and—"

"If Darren is right, they're holding Martian citizens down there. And we can't just—"

"What's your plan? Bulldoze our way in, with no backup, to bust them out? Even if you managed, it's not like they're going to fit inside *Beetle*. She's not a fucking clown car. You need to come back with a bigger ship. More guns. Lots and lots of people. Possibly some missiles."

Kacey was afraid. And who wouldn't be? She was one hell of a pilot, and she had a knack for talking her way out of a jam, but she'd never been comfortable with physical confrontation. She'd flunked basic self-defense during her brief stint in the corps, and she'd never even learned to fire a pulsar.

"I know I can't bust people out." Loretta blew out her breath. "But I need to show Epiphany what's really happening here."

"We've got what we need."

"Not even close. We found a ship parked in the outback. And images of some underground building. You think that Marcus," she winced, "I mean — that *they* can't explain this away? If this is a prison, we need to show actual human faces to prove the lies. Everyone needs to understand what's been taken from us. What's been hidden out here, all this time."

"We don't know how many guards are in there."

Loretta felt for her weapons. The Word was far heavier than her pulsar, but she'd brought both. With luck, she wouldn't need either.

"How close can you get me to the *Steady*?"

Kacey's hand inched toward the throttle, sneaky-like.

Loretta reached up and unlatched the hatch. She pushed it open, and the sweltering heat of the day rushed in, oppressive even through their hab suits. *Beetle* might not have full life support, but she did have temperature control.

Kacey tried to pull the hatch back down. "Be reasonable."

Loretta planted a palm against the glass, not pushing, but not letting go either. "If you won't fly me there, I'll walk."

"Then how will you get back, dingus?" Kacey snapped. "Did you factor that into your suicide plan?"

"I guess I'll just need to," Loretta held up air quotes, "borrow a trover. And you're right. You're not trained for this, so you're not coming. Just get me as close as you can, then wait with *Beetle*."

With a groan, Kacey closed and locked the hatch. "Fine. Whatever. Suicide plan it is. But if you're going, I'm coming with."

"No. If I don't come back out within the hour—"

"Right. Like I'd *abandon* you here. If we're going to be stupid, we'll be stupid together. Besides, if everything goes tits up, I want the scary chick with all the guns standing between me and the bad guys."

"I'm not scary."

"Have you seen you?" Kacey paged through the images she'd captured with *Beetle's* sensors. "Hold on. I bet there's a back entrance. They need some way to get people in and out, and I'd rather not bust down the front door."

"But I have a better idea," Loretta said.

"Well?"

"If I tell you, you won't want to do it."

Kacey groaned. "We're busting down the door, aren't we?"

"We'll be fine."

"Says who?"

"Says me."

"Because you get to make all the decisions?"

Loretta felt her mouth quirk up. "Yes."

"Why?"

"Because you know fuck all about dealing with a highly trained security force, so that means I'm in charge."

There was a long pause, during which it was difficult not to feel smug. Kacey was the bossiest person she'd ever met, but there were times to lead, and then there were times to shut the fuck up and follow.

Was she capable of the latter?

"Theo will be extremely upset if we get murdered," Kacey muttered, tossing her head.

"I'd never want to upset Theo."

Kacey's hands moved to her controls. "Okay, then. What's the plan?"

CHAPTER TWENTY-THREE

Loretta watched as Kacey shoved handfuls of rags into her tool bag. The cloth contraption was the size of a small duffel with a crossbody strap for whipping it around from back to belly in one smooth motion. Unfortunately, the contents jangled as she moved. She zipped the thing closed and wiggled around, jumping from one foot to the other. Apparently satisfied, she turned back to *Beetle*, running her small, gloved hand along the side of the skimmer as if she were an anxious pet in need of soothing.

Sol was a fiery white dot burning high in the Martian sky, but hopefully the stone outcropping they were nestled behind would protect the skimmer from view. That is, unless someone flew directly over her...

Loretta shoved the thought away like a cat swiping an offending object off a table. The time for second-guessing was past. You managed what risks you could, and then you took your shot.

That was life.

Before they'd left *Poppy*, they'd swapped their brightly colored hab suits for sets in a muted gray, and they'd done their best to further camouflage their approach by rubbing the fabric with palmfuls of reddish-yellow dust from the Martian surface. Close up, they merely looked filthy, but at least now there was a chance they wouldn't be picked up by routine surveillance. Two solid-colored blobs would be far more conspicuous on camera than a couple dusty shapes, which might very well be rocks.

Loretta pointed at a large stone some thirty meters ahead, directly between them and the launchpad. It was the last object big enough to hide behind, and from there, they'd be crossing a flat, featureless expanse. "After we hit that point, we'll move to a crawling stalk, bellies on the ground. Keep your face shield down and try not to move in a straight line. We'll take small breaks every couple minutes."

Kacey had scrubbed off her makeup, but a few stray bits of glitter still sparkled on her cheek. Without her dramatic dark eyeliner and careful contouring, her wide cheekbones gave her a babyish look, making her seem far younger than she was. A warrior without her armor.

She lifted her chin. "I can keep up."

"I know. But if they have any automated surveillance out here, we can fool the sensors if we stop and start. Think sandstorms. The gusts aren't steady, they rise and fall."

This here was the weakest part of her plan. If they were spotted on their approach the guards inside would raise defenses before they'd even had a chance to breach the perimeter. Kacey hadn't found external cameras on her scans, but that didn't mean they didn't exist.

"Let's move," Loretta said. "You go first, and I'll watch your back."

Kacey, being small, practically disappeared into the sandy haze ahead. The wind was low and steady, nothing approaching a storm but enough to send a hiss over the audio feed when swaths of gravel hit the side of their helmets.

Loretta's ribs ached as she dropped behind the rock, pressing her belly to the ground, shifting to a frog-crawl. Were they leaving tracks in the dust? It was impossible to say without looking back, and there was no benefit to doing so.

She heard Kacey's slow breathing over the feed. They rested, then moved, and rested again. Facing downward, keeping a low profile, Loretta didn't see the *Steady* so much as she felt its presence looming over them. She glanced up mid-way to check her position, and nearly panicked when she saw no sign of Kacey.

There was only dust, and haze, and a small boulder with a scattering of fist-sized rocks around it. At least, that's what she thought until the boulder flattened. A small dusty appendage reached out and scooped up a few of the rocks. The presence of the smaller stones had sold the illusion better than she'd imagined possible.

That's our Kacey, she thought with a measure of pride.

Sweat rolled down her sides and pooled near her belly as she continued the crawl. After what felt like hours, but which was probably no more than forty minutes of careful movement, they met up at the edge of the landing pad. Kacey was crouched low, fiddling with her wrist control. Text scrolled down a tiny panel on the back of her gloved hand. She grunted her approval. "Still no signs of life. You can try that hatch to your left."

The hatch opened, and after a short climb, they were inside the claustrophobic black vault of the *Steady as She Goes*. Compared to *Poppy*, the central cargo hold was enormous, but the ship was packed with hard-sided crates. Most were secured with grav lock, but others had been piled high in tower-like stacks that looked ready to topple at the slightest nudge. Loretta took point, using her helmet light to find pathways on the ground, pulling in her arms to avoid the walls of the carelessly constructed maze.

Mid-ship, they climbed the ladder up to the crew level. Loretta swung off the ladder and paused on the flatway, holding up a finger. Silence pressed into her ears like thick, sweaty fingers. Despite their cautious approach, every footfall sounded like the pounding of a drum, and if there was anyone on board, they would likely be up here.

She felt a surge of glee when she saw a small plaque on a door ahead and to the left. The *Steady's* crew were nothing if not organized, and with a bit of luck, well...

With luck, there nothing she and Kacey couldn't do.

Kacey squirmed like a toddler in her stolen uniform. The black cap was slightly too big for her petite head, but they'd managed to stuff her pink mohawk inside it. She flung herself down on a hard bench that ran the length of the locker room and tugged at her boot laces.

"I look like a toon."

Loretta tugged her own jacket down. Harbor crew uniforms weren't too different from those worn by corps, although the black fabric was thicker and kind of scratchy, designed more for durability than comfort. "You look fine."

"And why are you so perky? Do you get off on slithering through dirt like a garter snake?"

"Snakes garden on Earth? Huh! I must have missed that lesson in terrestrial biology."

"Not *gardener* snakes. Gart—"

"I know! I'm just yanking your chain. And if I'm happy, it's because I figured I'd have to jump a few people to get our disguises. I'm a big fan of not getting punched in the face."

"The day is still young."

Loretta shook her head. "I know you like to shit talk to blow off steam. But once we're inside..."

"Yeah, yeah. I'll dust off the old stick of obedience and jam it where the sun don't shine."

Kacey picked up the empty cargo box she'd 'borrowed' and set it atop a portable wheelie. "I've mapped our ingress route, and marked some places where we might find what we're looking for, but they're only educated guesses."

Loretta put their hab suits and Kacey's tool bag inside the crate and covered their gear with items she'd scrounged from the crew lockers. "Hopefully we'll leave the same way we came in, but if not, I want our suits within arms' reach. If we get separated, grab yours and look for an airlock."

Loretta slipped The Word into her thigh holster. Her great-grandmother's revolver was quite a bit longer than a pulsar, not to mention significantly heavier. She felt the weight of it pulling down, testing the fabric. So long as no one took too close of a look at the grip she'd be okay.

She held her pulsar out to Kacey, butt forward.

"Take this."

She may as well have offered a palmful of excrement. Kacey's nose crinkled. "No thank you. Those things freak me out."

"You don't have to use it. Just carry it. Everyone inside is going to have one."

Kacey tossed her head. "Peer pressure won't work on me. I've seen *all* the public safety vids."

Loretta aimed the pulsar at a distant bulkhead. "I set it to stun. See? Point, wait for the dot, then release. Gives them a little jolt and knocks them out. It is *so* much easier than flying."

"Says you."

"Please? I'll feel better if you can defend yourself."

"We have a deal. You're the scary chick with the weapons. I'm here for moral support. And being sneaky. And delivering cargo." She gripped the wheelie's upper handle. "See? I can push shit around with the best of them. Let's go before I—"

Something clanged outside the locker room. Footsteps thudded in the hallway outside. Kacey blanched and made for one of the empty lockers, obviously intending to shove herself inside. Exasperated, Loretta yanked her backward, ignoring her yelp of protest. "Attention, Cadet," she snapped. "Remember? Ready for inspection?"

Kacey had been a part of the cadet wing, however briefly. Loretta pushed her chin slightly up with her index finger. "Let me handle this," she murmured.

They were both standing at attention when a crewman stepped inside the locker room. He was in his mid-twenties and wearing lieutenant's insignia. He glowered at them as if anticipating an ass-kicking was in the offing. "What do you two think you're doing?"

Loretta felt the smooth barrel of her pulsar in her hand. *Shit.* She could have holstered it if her slacks weren't already stuffed full of cold carbon steel. She shifted the pulsar to her left hand and dropped her right arm to her side. She stepped closer to Kacey, hoping to block the view.

Out of the corner of her eye, she saw that Kacey trying to appear stoic. Unfortunately, the best she'd managed was to look utterly constipated, as if the sheer force of bottling up what she wanted to say was causing her physical pain.

Relationships in the corps tended to be quite cordial, even during training, but the harbormaster preferred a more confrontational style.

Perhaps she could use that.

"We're tracking down a missing delivery," Loretta said, maintaining her bearing but letting a hint of irritation creep into her voice. "This one," she flicked her eyes toward Kacey, "was taking her sweet ass time." She winced. "Sorry, sir."

"Hold on, there." He stepped forward, closing the distance between them. His square jaw might have been handsome if it wasn't for the piggy little eyes set into his face like marbles, roving over her pinned-up hair as if eager to find fault. "Why do you have that?"

"Why do I have what, sir?" She spoke in the clipped, overly formal voice she'd heard the harbor crew use in the docks. It sounded ridiculous, but when in Rome...

He pointed to her pulsar. "*That.* Why are you bringing a dip weapon onto my launchpad?"

A *dip* weapon? She had no idea what he was talking about, and she was about to stammer that she'd found it laying on the ground when Kacey's derisive snort cut through the air. "I told you it wasn't worth it."

Kacey glanced at the lieutenant, waiting for permission to continue. At his brusque nod, she added, "We were at the docklands, and overheard them talking shit about how we can't stand up to *their* standards. The one in charge left her pulsar sitting around where anyone might grab it, so, we took it from her. Figured she could explain to her supe why she couldn't even keep track of her own weapon."

The lieutenant looked faintly amused by this explanation. *Thank Sol.*

Loretta winced. "I apologize. I know it's against protocol. It's just..." she swallowed, "they piss me off, sir."

"Understandable." he said. "But that's a stolen weapon, and it could be tracked back to our position. You're lucky it was me who caught you and not the colonel."

Loretta took care to look abashed.

"What are you transporting?" he asked, holding his hand out for the pulsar.

Loretta handed it over. "Um, it's—"

"They didn't say," Kacey said. "Just that if we didn't find it, we'd spend the rest of the day wishing we'd never been born."

The lieutenant actually chuckled at that. "Where are you headed?"

Kacey didn't answer. They had a map, kind of, but the sensor-generated images were rough, and nothing was labeled. Loretta thought back to the list from her mother's recipe. There had been names and notations. It was worth a shot.

"Five charlie," Loretta blurted.

"Is that so?" He glanced at her with a new kind of appraisal. "Well, you'd better get going, Cadet?"

"McNamara," Kacey answered. "And this is Henderson."

"Ah." His tone was less sharp now. "You must know Klaus McNamara, then?"

Kacey smiled at the question. "Klaus? I've met him a time or two, but he's no relation."

He nodded, apparently satisfied. "On the double, cadets. Let's keep the lines open."

Only after they'd passed through the *Steady* and traveled out the connecting tunnel to the facility below, did Loretta release the breath she'd been holding. Kacey inclined her head to the right, pushing the cart down a side hallway before they dead-ended at a security station. While Loretta kept a lookout, Kacey used a portable scanner to find the utility crawlspace she'd found during their impromptu planning session aboard *Beetle*. Pulling the bulkhead panel off was quick work, and before long they were inside a dark passage not much wider than their wheelie. The ground was littered with utility boxes and thick cabling.

Kacey pulled the bulkhead panel closed, then clipped a portable flashlight to the brim of her cap. The air smelled faintly of metallic composites and life support exhaust.

"You still suck at improvising," she teased.

"McNamara? Where did you even get that from?"

"The surnames McNamara, Henderson, and Smalls are overrepresented in Epiphany. Their grandparents must have boinked like horny little bunnies before population controls were put in."

"And?"

"When pretending to be someone you're not, pick a common name, but not an obvious one, like Brown."

She grasped the heavy end of the wheelie and lifted, leaving the handle side for Kacey, who had less upper body strength. She backed up deeper into the passage, stepping over cable bundles and metal boxes, trying not to trip or make noise.

"That's smart. But what's a dip?" She realized the answer as soon as she asked the question. "Oh. Diplomatic Corps. That's what you all call us."

"Only when you deserve it."

The air was thin and dusty. Visibility was poor. They paused twice to rest. Kacey consulted her map at each turn. At a T-intersection, she set her side of the wheelie down with a groan. "See that seam here? There's a hallway on the other side. Help me find the media fiber bundle. I want to see what kind of system they have."

A short way down the wall, Kacey found a junction box that interested her. A short time later she'd clipped a complex set of wires into various points in the cabling. Text scrolled down her glove display, and she snorted.

"You're not going to believe this."

"Tell me."

"These toons managed to hide a whole-ass *building*

underground without anyone knowing, but then they planted a launchpad on top like a freaking "You are Here" sticker. And, on top of that, they're using twenty-year old tech for their security system? A child could bypass this!"

"I seriously doubt that."

She smirked. "Well, I could have. Anyway, I'll go into the admin panel and tell it there's a critical software update. By the time it finishes scanning and rebooting itself, we'll be long gone."

"Seriously?"

"Well, it'll buy us half an hour, anyway. We'll still need to watch out for human security but—"

"Where did you learn all this stuff?"

"You have your job; I have mine. Anyway, you can thank me by not playing the hero when we get inside. We get your proof, and then we're gone, right? *That*'s the deal."

"Agreed."

All was well until they tried to get out of the utility crawlspace. Along the wall seam, where a standard bulkhead panel should have been, there was a door sealed with a heavy-duty padlock, the kind used in atmo where delicate electronics tended to fail. Kacey lifted the bulky metal piece, scowling. "I don't know how to pick these. Do you?"

"You said you could fry the locks."

"I figured this place would use standard tech or better. But they probably had crates of old shit in a basement somewhere and decided to put it all to good use pissing me off."

Loretta pulled The Word from her holster and aimed it down at the padlock. "Don't look. There could be shrapnel."

"Where did you get that thing?" Kacey hissed. "Cowgirls R Us?" She dropped to a crouch, hands over her ears.

Loretta hesitated, then pressed her ear to the wall. She heard nothing. No footsteps. No voices. Looking away with a wince, she fired.

The crack of metal on metal was as loud as she'd feared, but she'd aimed down and there was no damage to the door. The padlock had deformed, splitting along the bolt end. With some eager wiggling she managed to pull it apart. She hoisted her gun and pushed the door open with the ball of her foot.

"Let's move."

They stood at the midpoint of a long hallway. Facility Zeta was bright and light with white walls and cream-colored carpet. It looked less like a secret prison facility than a receiving area for visiting dignitaries. Even the art on the walls seemed chosen to impress, a collection of abstract paintings depicting colorful planets, some with rings, others accompanied by pearlescent moons. One showed a binary system, two stars orbiting in tight formation.

Kacey snatched the small flashlight off her cap and stuck it in her pocket. From another pocket, she pulled several mini cams the size of large buttons. She stuck them on the crate at waist level, placing them in the front and on both sides. She held out a button cam for Loretta to take.

"Come on, Henderson, let's make our delivery." Loretta followed as Kacey led her down the hallway, to the right, and past a row of unmarked doors. A chill ran up Loretta's spine when two women in lab coats approached from the opposite end of the hall. They were chattering about their weekend plans. Neither wore name tags, nor did they seem terribly interested in the 'cadets' passing them by.

Loretta's heart, which had been thudding like a fist on a sheet of metal, slowed as the strangers continued walking.

"Look," she murmured.

Up ahead, a large window overlooked something on the left side of the hallway. Bright light passed through the glass, casting an illuminated square on the opposite wall. Loretta stepped past Kacey, taking point. They slowed as they reached the overlook.

The room was both wide and deep, extending at least four floors below them. On the lowest level, two dozen workers in white jumpsuits were bent over a manufacturing line, inspecting components as they exited an automated assembling process.

It was a factory. One not too dissimilar from the place where Travis worked. The workers wore blue caps over their hair, and gloves to protect their hands. The space below was bright and spotlessly clean.

For a moment, she felt weak with relief. Maybe this was a research and development facility after all. Perhaps Darren had been lying about Amparo, or this whole thing was some terrible misunderstanding. She affixed the button cam to her cap and stepped forward to get a closer look.

A uniformed crewman moved past the window, close enough that she could see the closely trimmed hair beneath the back of his cap and the crisp fold of his jacket collar. Instinctively, she jerked back. He was standing on some type of balcony rim that ran all the way around the room below. She carefully peered down and around, spotting four armed guards watching the manufacturing floor. Only their weapons weren't like any pulsar she'd ever seen. They were long, like the rifles she'd seen on old military footage from Earth. Instead of keeping them safely holstered, the guards carried their weapons openly, pointing them at the workers below.

The guard had walked right past her, oblivious to the two 'cadets' gawking at their operation from above. Down on the manufacturing floor, a worker had paused to shake out his arms. A supervisor came over — perhaps to suggest he take a break — the thought crossed her mind — but instead, the supervisor gave the guy a small shove. As the worker turned to move back to the line, she saw a four-digit number on the back of his jumpsuit.

Heat crept up Loretta's body, rising from her belly like magma in a volcano, threatening to overflow. Darren had been right. So had Kacey. And even though she'd known Darren was telling the truth, deep down in her bones, it was impossible to accept.

Things like this didn't happen. Not on Mars.

Take their name and give them a number. Isn't that what Kacey had said? It was one thing to hear those stories, to understand that humanity had been capable of terrible things, once upon a time. It was another thing to see it with her own eyes. These people had been imprisoned without trial. They'd been denied the rights they were entitled to. Violated. Also, why were the workers—

Prisoners. Call them what they are. Those guards aren't here to protect them, and the supervisors aren't going to give them breaks when they're tired.

The prisoners were decades older than her, for the most part. She saw it in the softer shapes of their bodies, and in the snatches of untreated hair knotted below the bright blue caps they wore.

And as for the way they moved, shoulders hunched like animals expecting a beating...

Her hand reached for her pulsar and encountered the hard, heavy grip of The Word. She let her fingers run across its textured surface. How long had those people been trapped here, living underground?

How long could hope survive, when you knew help wasn't coming?

Kacey touched her shoulder. "Keep walking," she said, her voice tight. "We need to finish the job."

Reluctantly, Loretta stepped forward. Kacey was right; their work was only half-finished. They had footage, and now they needed names to match the numbers on those jumpsuits.

"Just one more stop, right?"

Loretta nodded, not trusting herself to speak. Every muscle in her body was coiled like a tight metal spring. She wanted nothing more than to bust a hole in that damned window and show those heavily armed cowards what being a servant of the people actually meant. Not pointing guns at frightened old men and women to make them work harder for you. Not shoving people around when they were in pain. Certainly it didn't mean *pretending* that you were on the side of truth and light.

How could they betray their own people? Like it was nothing. Like this was just another day at the office.

No matter the truth of things, she and Kacey were only two people, surrounded by enemies, and she had a single antique weapon on her hip. A sustained confrontation would mean death.

Justice... Well, you could hold it off for a while. But not forever. And there was more than one way to win a fight.

She shot Kacey what she hoped was a reassuring look. "Yeah. Just one more stop."

CHAPTER TWENTY-FOUR

Three times, Kacey stopped near a closed door and pulled out her portable sensor array. Each time, she shook her head no. They were en route to a fourth site when muffled conversation filtered down the hallway. This was a large group, and they sounded eager. Their footsteps were swift. Fortunately, there was a restroom nearby. They ran for it and made it just in time. Loretta put her back against the door and waited. The gaggle passed by, and relief flowed down her limbs like cool water. She couldn't quite capture their words, but they didn't sound like they were on the hunt.

"Our luck won't hold forever," she said, opening the door once the coast was clear. "We need to find their server room. Hell, even a terminal would do."

"In a server room, I can make a direct link. Without authorization, a terminal won't help." After the last close call Kacey's face had gone sweaty and pale. Anyone who looked at her would know she didn't belong.

It was a problem.

"I can get us authorization."

"You can? Why didn't you say so?"

They paused at a room further down the hallway. Kacey aimed her palm-sized device at the door. After a moment, she scowled and shook her head.

"No terminal?" Loretta whispered.

"It's probably a terminal," Kacey mouthed. "But there's someone in there." She reached for the wheelie.

"How many?"

Kacey held up one finger, then two. She shrugged. Her eyes went wide after taking a closer look at Loretta's expression. "No!"

"Yes."

The longer they spent skulking around in the halls the more likely they'd get caught. Kacey had said the security system reboot would take thirty minutes. They'd been inside at least that long.

It was now or never.

Loretta shot Kacey a tiny smile, ignoring the emphatic shake of her head. "Wait one minute, then follow me inside."

The door opened easily. The room was small but it did indeed contain two terminals, large, C-shaped workstations with display screens embedded into custom electronics panels. One station was occupied, and the woman sitting there – a corporal, by her insignia - didn't even turn around.

"Tim? I thought you were done for the day."

An electric surge of excitement shot through Loretta's body, running from the bones of her feet to her arms and shoulders. She'd had a long, shitty, miserable day, but this would be easy.

Simple.

Thank Sol for that.

With an explosive leap, she surged forward and clamped one arm around the woman's slender neck, yanking her back and away from the terminal. Her other arm encircled her adversary's upper arms, pulling them away from the controls. As soon as she had the corporal 'hugged,' she hurled them both backward with maximum force.

They hit the ground together.

Her torso screamed a protest as the chair back landed on top of her, pinned down by sixty-three kilos of enemy bulk.

Oof. I'm gonna feel that in the morning.

Ignoring the urge to cry out in pain and triumph, she tightened her hold on the woman's neck, choking her out. For good measure, she took her other arm and punched the woman, hard, upward into her solar plexus.

She grunted in surprise as she lost her air. After a brief struggle, she went limp.

Kacey was staring, open-mouthed in the doorway, apparently too stunned to move.

"Close the door, will you?"

"Did you... Is she dead?"

"Please," she scoffed. "She's going to come to in a minute. Quick, help me tie her to this chair. Shit! I should have thought to bring—"

Kacey was already unspooling a long length of rope from inside the crate. She grinned at Loretta's surprise. "I move stuff for a living, babe. You never leave home without twine, tape, and snacks."

When their prisoner woke, she immediately began to struggle. Fortunately, the tape covering her mouth held firm and so did Kacey's knotwork. After a moment, she stilled. Her pale brown eyes narrowed at the sight of Kacey, who'd taken off her hat and freed her pink mohawk. It lay in a soft waterfall over her shaved head. Kacey was celebrating their victory by noisily eating a bag of crunchy snacks she'd brought along, chewing with her mouth open.

Was it meant to be a subtle form of intimidation? Either that or Kacey seemed determined to annoy the woman to death. The corporal didn't seem frightened so much as she seemed pissed off.

Frightened people were easier to control than angry ones. Then again, as a member of 'team prison camp' the woman probably already knew that.

Loretta swiped the corporal's ID card against the pad at the workstation. Back home, terminal access required a card and some sort of biometric verification. A thumb print or an eye scan. Voiceprints on occasion. But here, instead of a demand for biometrics, the terminal demanded a twelve-digit passcode.

This was a problem. Much like the rest of the systems in Zeta, the technology was old. Probably half the shit here had been repurposed from Epiphany, a smart way to avoid raising red flags during construction.

To get the prisoner list, they'd need the corporal's cooperation, one way or another.

Loretta picked up the ID badge. "Corporal Beckley? I apologize for taking such extreme measures. If you cooperate, you'll face no further harm."

Kacey balled up her snack packet and tossed it at the woman's face. It bounced lightly off her forehead and landed on the carpet. She glanced at the terminal, then caught Loretta's eye. "She's not going to cooperate. Let's plank the little idiot and find someone else."

Corporal Beckley's eyes widened. She scooted back until her chair almost toppled.

Loretta turned away to hide her surprise. Kacey sounded downright bored, the consummate heartless criminal eager to get the job done. Her commitment to the bit was impressive.

I guess I'm the good cop this time.

Loretta casually rested one hand on the lower edge of the workstation. "Corporal, I need your access code to download a prisoner list. Do that for us, and we'll be on our way."

The furious grunts from the corporal's taped-up mouth

might not have been intelligible, but they made her intentions clear. She was — what — about twenty years old? Frightened, but determined not to show it. Brimming with bluster and bravado.

Kacey jumped up, binned her snack wrapper, and sat on the corporal's lap. She flung one arm over her shoulders like they were best buds, ignoring her attempts to squirm away.

"Look," she said. You're probably wondering how you got here. Life comes at you fast, too fast, and the next thing you know, two beautiful badasses have handed your ass to you on a silver platter. It's rough."

Muffled profanity followed, surprisingly clear despite the pink packing tape covering her mouth.

Kacey patted her on the shoulder. "One moment, you're a cadet, shiny and new and full of determination to suck ass all the way to the top! Then some bigwig pulls you aside, says you're one of the chosen elite, pats you on the head and gives you a cookie." Kacey pinched the corporal's cheek like a doting grandma. "What? No touching? Anyway, the next thing you know you're a drone trapped inside a soulless authoritarian regime. And I mean — Hey! We've all been there." She smirked at Loretta, "Right, babe?"

Loretta held back a snort by sheer force of will.

"All I mean is," Kacey pushed the wall with her foot, spinning both of them in the chair, "it's never too late to change. It's never too late to take a good, *hard* look in the mirror and say: You know what? I don't *like* secret prison camps. I don't want to lie to my family about what I really do for a living. I don't *enjoy* being a cog in a fucked up machine that eats truth and shits oppression. So I think I'll stop. Like, right now."

The corporal didn't seem convinced. With a disappointed sigh, Kacey dismounted the chair and stepped around behind her, clamping hands on her shoulders, holding her still.

Then, she pantomimed picking up a gun and shooting the woman in the head.

Loretta's stomach dropped. What in the hell was Kacey thinking? She would *not* shoot an unarmed prisoner in the head. She wasn't going to hurt anyone unless she had literally no other choice! Moreover, how would that even help?

Kacey made a 'come on' motion and pantomimed shooting the gun again. She twisted her index and middle finger together and stuck her hand behind her back. She placed one hand against her forehead, palm out, and pantomimed laughter, wiping her eyes.

Had she cracked under the stress? Was this one of her ill-timed jokes? How Theo dealt with this insanity, day in and day out, she'd never understand. Kacey was off the rails! And Theo, he was...

Well, Theo had taught her a thing or two.

Keeping her face impassive, Loretta moved her right hand to the grip of her gun. That got the corporal's attention! With her left hand, she signed, *What?*

Kacey slapped her forehead. She fingerspelled, P-R-E-T-E-N-D. Then the pantomimed shooting the corporal in the head.

Loretta's face burned. Maybe she did suck at improvising?

She unholstered The Word and pointed it directly at the corporal's forehead. As she slowly pulled the hammer back with her thumb, rotating a bullet into the chamber, a loud metallic click sounded. The corporal squeaked, her eyes as wide as saucers.

"You can help us," Loretta said, her voice deadly calm, "or we'll find someone more cooperative. We don't have time for games."

"Remember fifth grade science class?" Kacey's voice was bright, playful. She skipped around the chair and crouched down in front of the corporal's pale face. "The watermelon drop? They still do that, don't they?"

After a moment, she nodded.

"Good! Kids need to see science to understand it. It was like a rite of passage, calculating the amount of gravitational force needed to break a watermelon. We tried it inside, and outside, and then in the gee simulator. Do you remember that, Henderson?"

Loretta nodded.

"Mostly," Kacey said, "I remember the way the watermelon exploded when we finally figured it out. Not just a small crack either! It was a big, wet boom with red stuff everywhere." She flung her arms up in the air and wiggled her fingers. "Boom! I had squishy bits of watermelon on my face, and in my hair, and it was all over the walls..."

She crouched down next to the corporal and pointed at the revolver. "See that? It's an Earth weapon. A really old one. You'd think it just makes holes, like a spear or something, but it's far more interesting. When the metal projectile splits your skull, it deforms under the pressure and turns your brains into a pink, soupy mess. But does the skull explode?" She bounced up and down on the balls of her feet. "I fucking love applied science!" She held up a hand and took several steps away, toward the exit. "But this time, I don't want to get any of the pink stuff in my mouth."

Loretta kept her expression blank and adjusted her position, looking straight down the sight. The corporal was wiggling again, trying to break free. She screamed something behind her taped mouth.

"I really hoped she'd help us," Kacey said sadly.

Corporal Beckley's head bobbed up and down! She shouted some more.

Loretta slowly lowered her arm. Kacey sounded stern when she said, "Now, I'm going to take off the tape. If anything other than that access code comes out of her mouth..."

Loretta raised the gun again.

"Forty-nine alpha echo eighty-six delta zeta..." She spoke so fast that Kacey had her repeat it, slow enough to type.

"We're in," Loretta said, feeling weak with relief as the terminal bloomed to life, revealing a complex series of menus.

Crew member files were right up front, along with links to payroll reports. They'd infiltrated the human resources department, but thankfully the prisoner manifest wasn't hard to find. She glanced at Kacey.

"Explode her head like a watermelon? For fuck's sake! Who in the hell are you and what did you do with—"

"Nope!" Kacey had just finished re-taping the corporal's mouth. "We stay in character until *after* the curtain drops." She patted the woman's shoulder. "You did good, kid. Didn't even piss your pants." She pointed at Loretta. "She did once, during a routine takeoff. See? There's no reason to feel bad. Want us to rough you up some more, so you don't get in trouble?"

"Get over here and help me, will you?"

Kacey sat at the terminal and started typing. "Hold on! I'm searching. Okay, prisoner index. Let's see..."

"Look for—"

"I'm checking! Hold your horses."

They scrolled through the file, twice. There was no sign of anyone named Ryder. Kacey looked up. "Sorry."

"I knew it was a long shot." Strangely, she felt relieved. How could you lose what you'd already lost? At least her parents hadn't been suffering all this time. "Does this terminal connect to MarsNet?"

Kacey scrolled through the menus with a quick manipulation of the rollerball. "Looks like."

"Save our offline copies, and then I want to transmit our files digitally as well. Can you do that? The media outlets will be able to track the packets back, see where it was sent from."

"I'm on it. Hand me those button cams. Look at our map and find us an escape route, will you?"

Kacey was quick, as promised. The corporal watched them warily from her chair, but she was still, making no attempt to escape. Smart. What was done was done. Kacey was stuffing her hair back into her uniform cap when Loretta spotted a bright white speck on her jacket. Was that lint? No, it was—

Before her conscious mind had a chance to react, she'd thrown herself bodily at Kacey, knocking her to the ground. Overhead, just behind where she'd been standing, something exploded. Loretta looked up. Someone had blown a melted crater the size of a fist into the electronics panel near the monitor. Acrid smoke poured out the hole, and the scent of burning wires and melted composites filled the air.

"What was—"

"Stay down!" She shoved Kacey's head toward the floor and hopped to her feet, crouching low behind one wing of the C-shaped workstation, drawing The Word into her right hand. She stepped to the side and caught a flash of blonde hair and eager green eyes as Ms. Boots executed a flawless roundhouse kick to her temple.

Seeing stars, Loretta reeled back. She fired blindly to give herself cover. The report was loud — too loud! — but the calvary was already here and it was too late to hide.

She ducked down to find cover. Kacey was on her belly, and she'd wormed her way beneath the terminal, but she was pinned between Loretta and the wall, and Ms. Boots was blocking the door. Loretta held out The Word, using the shiny metal as a mirror to capture a reflection. But there was only haze and a small a smear of black.

So much for that idea.

Kacey's wracking coughs shot a jolt of alarm up Loretta's spine. Smoke from the electrical fire poured out of the workstation and hazed the air. It was getting harder to breathe.

"Do you know what I hate?" Ms. Boots's voice gave her position away. Loretta shifted The Word to her left hand, keeping it at the ready.

"What's that?" she responded, springing up, aiming a kick at her adversary's gun hand. She carried the same long rifle as the guards they'd seen earlier, and it was a stupid weapon for close quarters combat. Ms. Boots dodged, giving her an opening to step inside her guard and aim an elbow strike at her smug mouth and chin. The blow glanced off with minimal damage, but Ms. Boots dropped the rifle.

Her adversary's feet moved into a fighting stance. "Nepotism."

The answer surprised Loretta enough that she hesitated. That gave Ms. Boots an opening to send a single sharp jab right at her nose. Pain exploded, and she tasted copper.

"Argh!" She shook her head, scattering blood drops everywhere. Her left arm swung in a wide arc, almost like a slap, but with The Word held securely in her hand she felt a satisfying crunch of metal on bone as it smashed into Ms. Boots' jaw.

Only that had hurt almost as much as the punch! The Word fell from her pain-numbed fingers and thumped onto the carpet.

Her enemy was bent over, trying to recover. Loretta

dropped on top of her, grabbing her wrist and bending it painfully back. "Nepotism? Fascinating. My parents are dead, actually, but at least I knew they loved me. Do yours know what a piece of shit you are?"

Ms. Boots twisted, did something complicated with her shoulder and broke free. Her leg swung up and crunched into the side of Loretta's knee. Squealing, she went down, clutching her abused joint. In the haze, she caught a glint of silver on the ground, a tiny sliver of hope shining through the acrid smoke.

The Word.

Scrabbling for it, she managed to hook her hand into the finger shield. She spun it toward the corner to where Kacey was still crouched down, helpless, coughing. "Take it! Get the corporal out of here before all the air is gone."

Staggering into a half-crouch, she saw her enemy's shape in the smoke. Taking a breath — as nasty as the air was, she needed the oxygen — she leapt over the right wing of the terminal and tackled her, pinning her to the ground. "Go now!"

Swearing as the woman sank her teeth into the skin of her forearm, Loretta used all her weight as leverage to pin the woman's shoulders to the floor. With a bigger-framed person like Travis, or — Sol forbid — Theo it wouldn't have worked, but Ms. Boots wasn't any stronger than she was. Already, that wound on her jaw was swelling up. She wasn't so confident now that the person she was wailing on wasn't being held down.

Had she really come here alone?

Yeah. The arrogance tracked.

"You're only alive because Marcus called us off," she spat,

coughing, her words slurring. "You think you won? You actually believed we couldn't have blown that stupid little toy ship off our hull? Well, maybe you had protection before. But now—"

Loretta aimed one more punch, this time at her temple. It had the desired effect of shutting her up.

In the distance, klaxons sounded. Kacey was suddenly there, at her shoulder, pulling her arm. "Come on! We need to go!" She pressed the revolver into Loretta's hand.

Coughing, struggling to see with red, burning eyes, she dragged Ms. Boots unconscious body out into the hallway where the air was clearer. Kacey had the wheelie ready to go. Pushing it, they ran for their lives.

CHAPTER TWENTY-FIVE

Travis picked up his coffee mug and strolled down the hallway and into the viewing room. Here, he could see his team, working at their terminals, monitoring Epiphany for threats. He had to give credit where it was due, Sam Rathburn had built one hell of a team. Yet he'd seemed almost relieved to hand over the reins.

"I'm not a political animal," Sam had said, "I'd just as soon focus on the work and leave council matters to someone better qualified."

The viewing room was dark and cool, quieter even than a reading room in the central library. Fingers pattered soundlessly over keyboards. Only the occasional clearing of someone's throat interrupted the silence.

Trisha Ames glanced up as he came close to her workstation. Her chipper nature overlaid a well-ordered mind and a deep passion for her work. Already, he'd come to rely upon her assessments. She'd been endlessly patient with his questions, and with his concerns, which she'd never seemed offended by.

She was a keeper.

"Need something, boss?" Trisha's display showed dense columns of header data, representing terabytes of dangerous material snagged in the MarsNet protection layer like fish caught in a tightly woven net. He'd been shocked to learn that seventy-five percent of unauthorized transfers came from Earth. It was incredible how much propaganda was flung at Epiphany on the daily, although apparently it had been happening for years. Not only malware, which could infect their systems, but an endless spate of conspiracy theories, faked vids, and crackpot publications. Even direct attacks on the council itself, often coded messages from criminals in exile.

Their enemies were relentless.

"I'm just stretching my legs," Travis said. "How goes the battle?"

"It's been a quiet shift so far. I'm analyzing how the crud gets packaged with safe materials. We're pretty sure that people don't always realize what they're transmitting. They're like... unwitting drug mules. But if we can figure out the sources..."

He saw what she was driving at. "Then we can pressure our friends on Earth to deal with it. If they want access to our science, the least they can do is respect our laws. Keep up the good work."

He watched the big display while he finished his coffee, noting how the vid feeds rotated on an irregular schedule. Rathburn had thought through every detail of this program, and what he'd come up with was marvelous. What couldn't be predicted, couldn't be worked around. The council's instructions were clear, and the threats against Martian unity were higher than they'd ever been.

He'd been heartened by what his father had shown him. They'd watched, side-by-side, as a man who'd been about to arrange an 'accident' for his wife's lover was quietly apprehended and moved to Facility Zeta without so much as a ripple of trauma in the lives of those around him. The messages they'd had him record for his family, and the swiftness of that action... It had all been so clean. So bloodless.

A terrible crime had been thwarted. A Martian family and their community were thriving, innocent of the anguish they might have been subject to. In recompense for his hard work, the would-be-murderer would be housed, kept safe, and would be treated to regular updates on the lives of his children.

The evidence had been gathered carefully, and reviewed by the council itself, in a private session. And his father was right about one thing, most people wouldn't approve of the steps they'd taken. Hell, he'd struggled with it too! Yet it was impossible to deny the results. Peace on Mars. Not only in the sense of freedom from violence, but in the larger ideal of a community working toward the common good. The citizens of Epiphany would be spared the horror of dealing with the monsters in their midst. They could live, and love, and grow. They could continue to reach for all that was good and right, to serve one another.

Yet his new responsibilities left him with one problem. Loretta.

In a way, she was the exact kind of person they were trying to protect. Loretta led from the heart, and she believed people were good, deep down, if only you gave them a chance.

Could she understand why he'd accepted this job? His father had seemed optimistic that she'd come around, but Travis already knew better.

Not everyone was cut out for this kind of responsibility.

His father hadn't figured it out yet, but he would in time. And as for him? Keeping this program secret from Loretta would be *his* sacrifice to the cause. Could he live with the woman he loved, marry her, have a family with her, even if she never shared the same burdens? Even if he knew that if she ever found out what he was doing, she'd hit the damn roof?

It was either that, or lose her.

He looked around the room with an inward sigh. The only trouble with a well-oiled team? They hardly needed him, and already, the days felt long. He was about to return to his office to make some calls when klaxons sounded overhead.

"Wells!" Rathburn stood up at his station. "We have a breach at Facility Zeta."

The big display flickered. Every head in the room lifted to look. Dread tugged at Travis's shoulders as he watched four new viewports open. One showed a smoke-filled hallway. Two crewmen were coughing badly, half-carrying a woman through the smoke. She'd been badly beaten, but she was conscious. Two vids showed the prisoner populations at work. If they'd noticed anything amiss it didn't show in their body language.

The fourth viewport was dark, but after a moment it came to life, showing what looked like a service hallway. Two figures stood near an airlock, donning hab suits.

He recognized Kacey's pink mohawk right away. Her pointed chin. She slung a bag over her shoulders and shifted her weight impatiently from one foot to the other. His heart leapt into his throat at the sight of Loretta's grim expression. She slipped her helmet on and said something. Kacey nodded in response and Loretta punched the release with the side of her fist. They sprinted through the opening and disappeared.

He was vaguely aware of someone shouting his name.

Loretta had broken into Zeta? But why? Even if she knew it existed...

Kacey Holt. She'd dragged Loretta into this mess. He'd been nothing but generous with that mouthy bitch, and this was how she repaid her friends?

He felt his jaw tighten. For once, Rathburn's easy smile had been wiped off his face. He looked... horrified. They all did. Everyone was staring, right at him, waiting for instructions.

"A breach," he confirmed. "What's the protocol?"

Rathburn looked relieved. "Any security incidents at Facility Zeta are to be reported to your father immediately. Do you want me to send a retrieval team?"

A retrieval team? Right. That's what they called the crews who secured threats for removal to Zeta. He'd seen the way those crews operated, and he wasn't about to let any of them get within a mile of Loretta. Not until he'd safely separated her from that Earth bitch. The one who'd ruined everything.

"Not until I get authorization." Travis straightened up. "Send support teams to bolster security and offer medical support. I want a summary of what you're seeing sent to my eyes only, every five minutes. Track them."

"But—" Rathburn looked pained.

"You heard me. Do it."

"Sir! I've got something else." Trisha Ames was waving him down. "Look."

He jogged to her workstation. At the center of her display, Loretta's smiling face — her current ID photo — was illuminated with a red circle. Around her photo an array of captured messages glowed red, snared in their net.

"She tried to send something from a Zeta terminal. It looks like vid files. And a prisoner manifest, I think."

The big display changed again. Now it showed a single blurry vid taken from a great distance. Loretta and Kacey were sprinting across the outback toward a rocky outcropping.

"Sir, we have The Steady berthed there. The ship is armed. We can—"

"No!" He wheeled toward Rathburn. "Do *not* fire on them. That's an order."

Rathburn grimaced. "We at least should notify the harbormaster that we have two hostiles incoming. They can—"

"Did you fucking hear me? I said no!" Travis hadn't meant to shout, but now everyone was staring at him again. Watching him like he'd lost his mind, or even worse, decided to side against those he'd sworn to protect.

"Sir?" Rathburn tried to keep his tone respectful, but no one could miss the hint of challenge in it.

"That's right. I want you to let their craft land, and then you are to *seal* the upper launch bay doors. Do *not* engage. Do not surround them. We'll handle this without starting a firefight in the middle of the damn docklands. Understood?"

He nodded. "We'll get it done."

"Good. I'll return with instructions."

CHAPTER TWENTY-SIX

Kacey bolted out of *Beetle* the moment they settled into the bottom of the launch tube. She pulled off her helmet but didn't bother to strip off her hab suit. Loretta paused long enough to change out of her disguise, slipping into her gray-blue uniform like it was a second skin. She holstered The Word, transferred to her pockets the remaining ammunition and the four precious data chips Kacey had loaded up just before the ambush.

Her sweaty fingers reached up and unpinned the captain's insignia.

It wasn't hers.

Beetle hadn't been pursued on the ride home, but Ms. Boots knew who she was, and that meant everyone else would too, once she regained consciousness. They'd left her and the corporal out in the hallway where rescue teams could find them. Marcus might be willing to kill to keep his secrets, but she'd never sink that low.

There was no more denying it. No more hoping for some explanation that would make what had happened okay.

Darren had told the truth.

Theo was just outside *Poppy*, sweeping an already clean shuttle bay floor. He looked tense. Kacey signed something too quick to follow and Theo nodded in response.

"Sounds like we're good to go," Kacey said.

Loretta looked up. The rubbery refuel lines were already looped on their massive spindle, ready for the next arrival, and the display board near the entrance showed five green circles, the docklands signal for *Cleared for Departure.*

Kacey said, "You're coming with us."

"Not until I speak to the council. Someone needs to get the word out about what's really been happening. And Travis—"

"You still don't get it, do you?" Kacey had been stony silent on the way back, never a good sign. Now, she seemed torn between tears and fury. "It's not *safe* for you here!"

Kacey was trying to protect her, but she didn't seem to understand what was truly at stake. Either that, or she didn't care. Kacey had never truly considered herself Martian. She had a more simplistic view of things. You protected your friends, and everyone else could fend for themselves.

And that was the main difference between them, wasn't it? When you only cared about those closest to you, it meant everyone without a protector would be left out in the cold.

Helping one another. Standing together. That's what civilization was for. That kind of shared commitment had kept Epiphany alive these last hundred years.

She wouldn't abandon her home. Her people. The community that had surrounded her and lifted her up in her darkest hour.

"I can't run away from this fight. Not now. Marcus needs to be stopped. And our people need to understand that they've been lied to. I know the truth, and now it's my duty to share it. The polls open tomorrow morning, and," she held up a data card, "they need to know what they're choosing."

Kacey grabbed her sleeve. "Listen to me. Marcus and his cronies will try to shut you up, and when they realize that's literally impossible, they *will* kill you. Please. Come with us, just for now. You can send your proof from orbit! There's an encrypted channel, one used by some of the activists. We can get the word out if that's what you need."

"But Darren is still here. And Travis! I'm not leaving until I know they're safe. Besides, Marcus would never hurt me. He fucked up. Big time. Maybe he thought he was doing the right thing. Still, someone needs to bring him in."

"I've always known you were naïve. But I never took you for stupid."

Theo had been trying to get their attention. He tried to grab Kacey's shoulder. She shrugged him off. "Get off me! She needs to hear this."

Eyes, he signed, looking at Loretta. *Danger.*

"You should go, Kace. We can talk when you get back from your assignment. By then—"

"We're not coming back." Kacey flung the words out like fists. "This time, when we leave, it's forever. Why do you think I've been trying so hard to recruit you? Your sunny personality? Your skill in zero gee? I'm trying to save you, you idiot!"

Her threat made zero sense. "But you'll lose your spot on the pilot roster. You love flying! If you give up your license—"

"Have you been paying attention? At all?" Kacey stepped forward, standing a hands' breadth away, speaking quietly. "Think about it. When we were kids, Earth and Mars, they were like this." She interlaced her fingers and held them up. "Yes, Mars was rich and snooty as fuck, and Earth was poor as shit, but there was..." She shook her arms in frustration. "Remember when we had Earth journalists here? All the school exchanges? Kids used to visit here all the time. We had — hell, we had frigging tour groups!"

"Yes, but after—"

"Yes, yes. We were told they were stealing our science, not

giving credit where credit was due, claiming our hard work for themselves. But *all* of them, Lore? Remember the college exchange programs? That guy, Lance? And the funny kid from Kenya who told us about his crazy aunt, the one who had a chain of nail salons? Why did they stop coming here?"

"I don't know," Loretta said slowly. "I heard the Earth programs ran out of funding. They couldn't afford—"

"Gah! You've seen the shit we import. I shipped a shuttle load of Foogies last year. All sorts of crappy bric-a-brac. You honestly think we couldn't afford to bring some college kids over if we wanted to?"

"I suppose we could, but—"

"Think! You've had wall-to-wall coverage of the vote for weeks. How many of the programs actually talk to the Free Mars advocates? I'm don't mean those analysts who tell us what to think. How many *actually talk to the people?*"

"I'm sure there have been a few..."

Kacey put her hands on her hips. "Do you see what I'm driving at here?"

"You're saying we've become more isolated."

"For fucks sake! This isn't some benign phase Epiphany is going through. That prison camp isn't a fluke. We're swimming in a frothy fucking pot of simmering authoritarianism and every year they crank up the flame. Every newscast, there's some new reason to fear Earth. Every year, some tiny freedom stripped away in the name of security. You've seen it. Hell, you've even been fighting it in your own way! You're just too damn afraid to call it what it is."

Loretta's hands tightened at her sides. How dare she call *her* afraid?

"So your answer is running away. Instead of staying and making things better, you're—"

"If you think you can turn this situation around with a

few pleasant words and an appeal to reason, you're fooling yourself. It's not just Marcus, Lore. It's the whole fucking system. And I don't know about you, but when this place goes full-tilt bananas, like it's about to, after Marcus and his council of ghouls have unlimited power, I don't intend to be here."

"You're wrong."

Kacey tossed her head. "I'm so not."

Loretta's eyes stung. This was infuriating! For once. For one time in her life couldn't Kacey listen to reason? *For once, couldn't she think of someone other than herself?*

"Then what?" she demanded. "You'll be out there in hard vacuum, on your little ship, planting com beacons until the end of time? That's your grand plan? Sit it out and see who's left standing? Leave everyone down here to suffer whatever consequences come their way, alone and unsupported?"

"You can't save the whole world, Lore."

"Watch me."

Kacey rolled her eyes. "There she is! Epiphany's greatest hero. Too busy being right and proper to save her own ass. Too busy being the perfect arbiter to—"

"What about Lin? You're just going to leave her here? And the rest of your friends? You like to pretend you don't care, but Mars isn't just a government. It's people, and—"

Kacey recoiled as if she'd been struck.

Shame flooded Loretta, burning away what was left of her frustration. *She asked Lin. Of course she did. She probably got down on her knees and begged. Just like she's doing right now, for me.*

She went to Kacey, pulling her into a hug, not letting her squirm away. "I'm sorry. I was being an asshole. And I *do* understand. Okay? I get it, and you're probably right, but I still need to do this."

Kacey stopped fighting. Her body shook with sobs, and her small arms wrapped around Loretta's waist, squeezing like she'd never let go.

Loretta blinked away her tears. She needed to move, and they needed to leave. Every second counted now. "Take care of yourself and Theo."

Kacey shoved her away the moment she loosened her arms, her face twisted with grief. "Fuck you."

"Yeah, I love you too."

She glanced at Theo as she turned away. "You keep her safe, okay?"

Without waiting for his answer, she headed for the throughway.

CHAPTER TWENTY-SEVEN

Loretta's heartbeat pulsed with every footstep. It was hard not to run, but the sight of an arbiter hauling ass down the throughway was only going to draw more attention. As she headed for the nearest transit hub, she forced herself to recite what she'd learned.

Marcus Wells is a dangerous man. He's been lying to me since the moment I met him. Citizens of Epiphany have been kidnapped, imprisoned, convicted without trial. He didn't accomplish these things alone. Amparo Phan learned about the conspiracy, and she was murdered before she could talk.

My parents fought him and lost.

Marcus loves me. I know he does.

Marcus Wells is a dangerous man...

Five remedials came out of a locker room and headed along the pedestrian path. She followed them into a shuttle, rolling her shoulders back to check on her injuries.

She was in decent shape, considering. The pain in her ribs had subsided to a sharp-edged ache, and if her eyes were still hot and itchy from the smoke, at least she could still see.

The only sound was the faint hum of the transpo system, low enough to blend into the silence like the faintest of white noise. Despite their opaqued face shields, she felt the silent scrutiny of the remedials surrounding her.

"One hell of a day, huh?" she said.

She heard a snort from the petite figure next to her. "Tell me about it. I spend all day moving crates, and what do I dream about at night? More crates!"

"How many hours do you have left?" The question came from a guy who'd collapsed onto one of the benches, his legs splayed wide.

"Thirty-two," the short woman said. Turning, she asked, "Hey, you're the one who beat up that cadet, right?"

Loretta winced. "Not my finest hour."

The remedial shrugged. "Seemed like she had it coming."

Loretta smiled at the commentary. "No, I'm pretty sure I flubbed that one. She was just a kid. She didn't deserve to be scared like that."

The short woman cleared her face shield, revealing her round face and big blue eyes. Her mouth quirked up as if she were amused by the entire situation. "Emily Johnson. Eighteen alpha. Thirty-three hours for possession of contraband." Her nose crinkled. "I imported cigars, from Paris. My Da — I mean, I have a friend who likes them."

Loretta felt herself smile. "Was it worth it?"

"Yes and no. My husband's pretty pissed. He's got a promotion coming up and he's terrified someone will find out there's a remedial in the family."

The tall guy behind her cleared his shield. He had deep brown skin and a rather impressive beard that brushed the lower edge of his helmet. "Cigs? Damn! Who's your supplier?"

Scattered laughter rang out through the shuttle.

"Do me a favor, will you?" Loretta asked.

Emily looked skeptical. "If you want to smoke, I swear, my days of infamy are over."

"Nothing like that. But be sure to vote tomorrow, okay? It's important. Tell your friends too."

"Vote for the charter, you mean," another remedial muttered.

These people deserved the truth. Wasn't that why she'd gone to Zeta to begin with? Unfortunately, until Marcus was in custody, no one was safe with the bombshell she carried.

"You should vote your conscience. And as for me, I'll be voting for you."

"For me." Emily looked puzzled.

"Yeah. For a new constitution. You should get a say in how we do things around here. Everyone should."

"Me?" She smirked. "The idiot who got caught smoking a jimmy behind the club?"

Loretta laughed a little. "Yes! Because I've never met a person who didn't fuck up sometimes. That includes the ombuds, and the council, by the way. Being... ordinary doesn't mean we don't deserve a voice." She blew her breath out. "Well, that's how I see it, anyway."

Before she could say more, the shuttle slid to a halt. She shot the remedials a wave and stepped out into the arched path that led to Epiphany's central plaza.

The city's largest golden dome soared above her, the diamond-shaped panels faintly outlined behind the canopies of enormous trees that the founders had planted. The walls had been decked out in long silken banners for the centennial celebration, each one with a message of hope for the future. The botany graduate students had outdone themselves; every available surface overflowed with flowers in a rainbow of colors. Citizens crisscrossed the massive public space, chatting and heading to their afternoon appointments.

Marcus Wells is a dangerous man. He's been lying to me since the moment I met him. He loves me. I know he does. That doesn't excuse what he's done.

It would be so easy to slip, to look into Marcus's eyes and let herself believe whatever he said. That's why she kept on reciting, building the wall of facts as high as she could, igniting a fiery perimeter around her broken heart.

If only she didn't have a thousand memories of a thousand dinners in Marcus's hab! She could still feel the swell of pride from the last time he'd laid his hand on her shoulder, and that overwhelming urge to do her best, not only for herself, but for him.

She'd wept over Amparo's body, laying on the cold floor of the lab. And she'd vowed to find the truth. But was it a truth anyone wanted?

He didn't stop loving me when I screwed up. And if he'll let me, I'll be there for him too. Even if he hates me. Travis and I, together. Every step of the way.

She scanned the area around her. She heard comfortable chatter. Placid footsteps in all directions. Cool, clean air brushed her bare face. An ornamental fountain churned and splashed near the empty stage where the speeches would be held tomorrow. A stage draped in the pastel blue and cream colors of the council, as if all were already decided.

Act now. Cry later.

At a public kiosk near a row of shopfronts, she tucked two of the data chips into separate envelopes, addressed them to journalists with reputations for fair dealing, and dropped them in the bin for pickup. Then she headed for twenty-six charlie.

Travis's shift didn't end for another hour. She knew he wouldn't want to believe a word of what she had to tell him. She tumbled one of the data chips in her hand. Was seeing the same thing as believing?

Not at first.

Travis would be furious. Defensive. Still, it was time. He deserved the truth, and he needed to know that she wasn't going anywhere. She'd make sure everyone understood he wasn't to blame for his father's mistakes.

To her relief, the clerk at the front desk recognized her and waived her in without comment.

So far, no sign of pursuers.

A junior arbiter was sitting at Travis's desk, looking like she'd made herself at home. Her dark hair was pulled up in a tight bun, and that detail triggered Loretta's memory. "You must be Rashida Zane. Travis told me all about you. He said you're going to be running this place one day."

"Well, that's an awfully nice thing to say," she pulled her hands away from her keyboard and put them in her lap. "What can I do for you?"

"I need to talk to Travis. Is he around?"

Zane began to speak but seemed to think twice about it. "Um..."

"I'm Loretta."

"Right! The girlfriend. It's nice to meet you, but Travis isn't here."

"Do you know where he went?"

"I assume he's over in data requisitions."

"When's he coming back?"

"As far as I know, he isn't. He transferred over; we're just waiting for the official paperwork. Do you want me to call him for you?"

Travis had transferred? Without telling her? That might explain the pitying look Zane was flashing her way.

Marcus. He must be circling his wagons. Much of his "evidence" against Darren had come from data requisitions, and he must have people there, underlings he trusted. No doubt he'd moved Travis where he could keep a close eye on him.

Loretta's hand dipped into her pocket. "Can you do me a big favor? Tell him I stopped by with the files he was looking for. I might not see him later, and this is time sensitive, so I'll leave this with you."

Arbiter Zane lifted an eyebrow. "You heard me when I said he doesn't work here anymore, right?"

Loretta nodded. "It's a private matter, but important and urgent. Will you ask him to pick it up, please?"

"Sure." Her tiny smile seemed to say that she wasn't about to ignore a request from an officer, no matter how strange. "I can do that for you."

Loretta offered her thanks and made for the exit. She'd reached the main thoroughfare and was halfway to the transit hub when she caught sight of two women in harbor crew uniforms coming up the path. Pivoting neatly on one heel, she turned around, heading the long way around the complex, her heart pounding.

Kacey, I hope you and Theo are long gone.

Westmoreland's people were patrolling the hallways, and that meant she needed to pick up her pace. Thankfully, there was little chance Travis was in any danger. At worst, he'd learn the news when everyone else did.

With time running out, she needed to recruit some muscle to her cause. Happily, she knew exactly where to find it.

Risha Shay's office was tucked into a quiet hallway between the physics and mathematics departments at Olympic Mons College. Unlike the administrative ombuds who oversaw hearings in each district, academic representatives like Risha resolved disputes within the university system. She was a busy, important woman, but getting her mentor's attention was the least of Loretta's worries at the moment.

She'd picked up a shadow.

Loretta moved through the quad, not bothering to stop and admire the ancient volcano beyond the blue-tinted dome. She'd caught the same stern male face slipping in and out of the crowd behind her ever since she'd entered university grounds. He was wearing street clothes, but he moved like a man in uniform, and he'd been pacing her, waiting for the right moment to make his move.

He had a good twenty kilos on her, and it wouldn't be a fair fight, when it came down to it. Then again, 'fair' had left orbit years ago, around the time her parents died.

Feigning indifference, she paused at the front desk just inside the arbitration office and said she had an appointment.

The clerk frowned slightly as she glanced at Risha's closed door. "I'm afraid that—"

Risha was in her office. Good.

Loretta cupped her hands and yelled. "Risha! It's Loretta. Join me for a bite, will you? I got us reservations at that new seafood place."

The clerk glared up through pink-edged eyelashes like she'd just violated every statute on the books, but Loretta didn't care about niceties. She stood in a small receiving area, and there was an emergency exit to her left, past the restrooms. If the guy hunting her came up from behind, she'd be in a fight or flee situation, and she'd prefer not to fight.

Not yet.

Marcus had been smart. Careful, from the very beginning. A less patient man might have moved against Free Mars with force. Instead, he'd carefully constructed a false narrative. No doubt he'd want to hold her up as an aggressor. A traitor. Anything she did in public could be used against her. That's why she smiled and tapped her foot instead of busting into Risha's office by force.

Her muscles coiled like tight springs, storing energy for what came next.

If Risha didn't answer...

She was about to break for the exit when Risha stepped out, grinning like she'd received amazing news. "Loretta! I am *starved.* You wouldn't believe the day I've had."

The clerk's pale blue-gray eyes surveyed Loretta with faint curiosity, perhaps wondering what had accorded this rumpled upstart such gracious treatment. Loretta tried to smooth her messy hair. It must have come loose from its habitual braid during the struggle earlier and she hadn't noticed. Her uniform looked like it had been tossed on the floor and generally abused.

How far the mighty have fallen.

"Sal, postpone my afternoon meetings, will you?"

"But—"

"Yes, yes. The Dean is about to explode with incandescent rage. Tell him I'll call him tomorrow with a plan that should solve his little problem once and for all. Only don't call his problem 'little'."

"I wasn't born yesterday," the clerk said, scoffing. "Enjoy your meal. I'll hold your messages."

Risha looped her arm through Loretta's, gave her forearm a small pat, and guided them forward. "Seafood, eh? Have you tried the new Peruvian place? They say it's—" Risha glowered at the grim-faced man who'd just stepped into their path. "*Excuse* me."

Loretta tightened her leg muscles. Her right foot stepped back slightly. Her gaze settled on the soft meat of his throat, right below his Adam's apple.

The stranger's pale eyes flicked from Loretta to Risha. He seemed to be considering his options. After the briefest hesitation, he stepped aside.

Loretta felt a surge of relief when he didn't pursue them.

Westmoreland wasn't willing to go after an ombud, and having Risha on her arm was the equivalent walking around in power armor, at least for now. It wasn't why she'd come, but she'd take every advantage she could get.

Now, Marcus would know where she was.

"You'd think people had never used a hallway before," Risha said lightly. "Come on. It's my treat. You can tell me how you've been holding up."

At the nearest transit hub Risha called a private shuttle. Once they were inside, she flashed her pass in front of the control panel. The ambient lights switched from white to green, signaling privacy.

Risha turned, her eyes flashing. "You want to tell me what the hell is going on? Marcus called me an hour ago. Said you'd disappeared while making an arrest and he was worried you'd been hurt. Now you come barging into my office, looking like you've been through hell, blathering about seafood, which you know I'm allergic to. What happened?"

"Can we go to your hab?"

"That bad, eh?" Her lips compressed. "I suppose we should then."

After they'd arrived at her habitat, Risha led Loretta into the kitchen. Her home was unusually large, as befit a senior ombud, and exquisitely decorated in a minimalist style. An artificial skylight streamed golden light onto a wooden island in the center of the living area. An impressive collection of leather-bound books weighed down the shelves in her living room.

"Sit." Risha pointed at a chair. The curved back was inlaid with white and blue tiles, painted in intricate geometric patterns. The splash of color stood out among the blondes and ash browns of the rest of her furniture. "I'll make tea."

"I don't want any."

"Well, I do. You talk, I'll brew."

She told Risha everything, as succinctly as she could manage. Her mentor's mouth hardened, but she nodded along, asking clarifying questions in a cool, even tone. All the while her hands were working, pouring, whisking.

Risha carried two small enamel cups over. The tea looked pale green and frothy. "Drink that. And I want you to eat something too. You're running on fumes right now and you don't even realize it."

"Did you hear a word I said?"

"Indeed I did."

"Are you going to help me or not?"

"You can always come to me, Loretta. Although I wish you'd done so sooner." She sipped her tea. "Those data chips. Where have you put them?"

"I left one for Travis. And I sent two to RedShift and NightLock."

"I see. You went to the press. Covering your bases."

Risha was outwardly calm, but Loretta could see the wheels turning in her mentor's mind. Ombuds were expected to be even-tempered; no one ever rose through the ranks without bearing that trademark equanimity. But would it kill her to speed things up a little?

"I need your help."

"What did you have in mind?"

"For now, I need you to convene an emergency meeting of the ombuds. I'm formally requesting a warrant for Marcus's arrest." She placed the final data chip on the countertop. "I'll answer as many questions as they want, but we need to act fast. The vote is tomorrow at noon, and Marcus is planning on blaming Free Mars for everything. He—"

"Loretta, do you know what a EULA is?"

The interruption was unexpected, but she knew it must be important, or else Risha wouldn't have cut her off. "No."

"It's a bit of obscure Earth history. You see, the First Thirty weren't just a group of scientists and farmers. They were extraordinarily wealthy, individuals with the means to set up a colony on Mars when most governments could only dream of doing so."

"We don't have time for a history lesson. We need to—"

"Humor me. It's relevant. Erin Richardson's grandfather owned two telecommunication businesses. Gharison's ancestors made their fortune in fossil fuels back before renewables became standard. Several of the others came from tech dynasties."

"Okay."

"Many businesses of that era relied upon a legal framework called the EULA, or End User License Agreement. It was a devious bit of legal maneuvering. To sum it up, a EULA was a contract, benefiting one party. A business could say, for example, if you want to use my product, you agree to my rules. If you want access to electricity in your home, you do things my way. If you need healthcare... Well, you get my point."

"So it was a shitty deal."

"Yes. But to keep an appearance of fairness, they set up a kind of shadow court, one not accountable to the citizenry. When disputes happened — and they did — decisions were made by a neutral third party. An arbitrator. Typically one hired by the corporation itself. EULAs were presented as an efficient and cost-saving alternative to a messy and expensive public legal system."

Loretta's gut twisted. Risha was gazing down into her tea as she spoke, talking quietly, as if she dreaded the very words coming out of her mouth.

But why?

"Our system is similar," Risha continued. "We work off of centralized control. The Martian Code is interpreted and enforced by people like you and me, those of us chosen as neutral facilitators of the peace." She loosened her hair from her neck. "Looking back, I wonder if the founders put in place a framework that they felt comfortable with. It's likely they believed that decentralized control was too messy. Too prone to errors. Or possibly," she sipped her tea, "Epiphany was founded by a bunch of power-hungry fucks who didn't like the idea of everyone else having a say."

An electric jolt ran up Loretta's spine. "Hold on. Are you a member of Free Mars?"

"Not at all. What I'm trying to tell you is that despite the pomp and circumstance we wrap ourselves in, the Martian Code isn't actually a body of laws. It's a EULA. Laws can... change. Laws are," she bit her lip. "they're little stabs in the dark! Messy compromises. Victories on a battlefield of competing ideas. The pendulum is always swinging in a democracy. One side is up, then the other side wins for a while. Sometimes, terrible outbreaks of violence occur. Mars isn't a democracy, and that pisses a lot of people off. Trust me, I get it."

"I couldn't care less about what some old, dead people believed a hundred years ago. Right this second, Darren is stuck down in those tunnels, and he's been accused of a crime he didn't commit, and Marcus—"

"Loretta, Darren is dead."

"No he's not." She spoke the words as if uttering them would make them true.

"It's been all over the feeds." Risha turned on her living room display. "Darren McManus murdered Amparo Phan. He was killed this afternoon while escaping capture."

Loretta's mouth went dry. They were showing one of Darren's speeches. He'd lifted one fist in the air. "We *cannot* allow our voices to go unheard. We *will* act—" But rather than continuing to the next part of his speech, his words about peaceful resistance, they switched to the footage of Darren breaking into the food sciences lab. The image froze, showing his face in deep concentration.

"Director Amparo Phan leaves behind a partner and two sons," the program host said, her expression mournful. "Now, with information about tomorrow's centennial celebrations, my cohost will—"

The display clicked off.

"I'm sorry." Risha reached out and lightly gripped Loretta's forearm. Her palm felt cool and smooth. "I hate what's happening. I truly do."

She'd been a fool not to see it coming. The exaggerated calmness as Risha had brewed the tea. Her utter lack of surprise at learning what Marcus was up to. "You hate it, but you're not going to help me."

"When I was a cadet," Risha said softly, "we spoke about the nature of the code. We debated it! With fierce passion on all sides of the issues. For more than *thirty years*, I worked within the system to advocate for better government. I believed that when the vote arrived, the people of Epiphany would be ready to trust in themselves, to take back the power that the founders had allocated us ombuds. And do you know what I learned?"

Loretta stood. "I actually don't care."

Risha's knowing smile pricked her like the blade of a knife. "Nonsense. You care very much. You remind me of myself when I was your age. So full of righteous fervor! So certain that you've got it all figured out." She sighed. "Loretta, you're special. But most people? They view self-determination as a messy inconvenience at best. They don't actually want to be in charge of their own lives. They want to wake up, eat a good breakfast and go about their day unbothered by the need to stand up for anything at all."

"That's bullshit. They're being lied to! They're not cowards, they're—"

"Uninformed? That's what you were going to say, right? Well, you'd be amazed how much injustice people will put up with when it costs them little. I know it's hard to accept. But in time—"

"Then you're the coward." Loretta reached for the data chip, only to see that it was gone. Her eyes narrowed. "You say you spent thirty years trying to stand up for what is right? Well, this is your moment, Risha! This is your goddamn chance! And you're just going to... what? Shrug? Roll over? You know Darren didn't kill anyone."

"I suppose we'll have to live with our part in that. But I'm not twenty anymore. My time to be a revolutionary is long past. Think it through. Why would you throw away what we have, when no one even cares?"

"You're wasting my time. I'm out of here." She turned, but Risha's voice grabbed at her from behind.

"Fifteen years. That's how long Zeta has been operational. Half the ombuds at the appellate level already know. It's over, Loretta. We lost this war long ago."

Loretta turned back, furious. Only the look in her eye didn't dissuade Risha at all.

"All that's left is for Marcus to put the bow on his greatest creation, his vision for Epiphany's next hundred years. He's been preparing you. Travis too. Although word is that Travis is already part of his inner circle. He's—"

"Shut up!" Somehow, she'd reached for her teacup without noticing. It hurled from her hand and burst on the face of the fridge, sending shards flying. She glanced at the clock. "How long until they come for me?"

Her eye went to the utility closet in Risha's living room, an unmarked door below her HomeBot unit.

"I didn't call anyone," Risha said. "And for what it's worth, if you need a representative at your surrender meeting, I'm willing to— What are you doing?"

Loretta had made her way into the living room. She ripped the utility door open. As she'd expected, Risha's hab suit was bagged up inside, along with a small backpack of evac supplies.

"I'm taking these."

"Why?"

Loretta unholstered The Word, flipped open the barrel, and loaded the chambers with fresh ammo from her pockets. Theo had delivered not only her gun, but every bullet she'd kept in her crate.

"I suppose you expect me to let them haul me off with a song in my heart. Is that right?"

"Don't be absurd. No one wants to see you imprisoned! I know you feel betrayed, and that's fair, but—"

Loretta flicked the chamber back into place and holstered The Word. "Don't use your arbitrator-foo on me. I'm not your cadet, and we're done here." She growled, deep in her chest. "Kacey warned me, but I wouldn't listen. It's not just Marcus, or even the council. It's the whole fucking system. People like you who stand by and let their friends," her voice hitched, "people like Darren, and my parents, and—"

"Lore..."

But Risha's anguish was nothing to her now, just the ghostly moan of a long-dead warrior. Who was this stranger wearing her mentor's face? How long ago had her spirit fled? She gave Risha a long look, then reached down to grab the gear.

"If you could give me a head start before you call Marcus, I'd consider it a kindness."

"How many people do you plan to shoot with that thing if I let you go?"

"I'm not the one murdering people."

"But-"

"Risha..." She rubbed her weary eyes. "Let me see the damn sky one more time before you throw me away."

CHAPTER TWENTY-EIGHT

Loretta heard the trover coming long before it arrived. Engine noise rumbled through the long canyon behind the shooting range and plumes of reddish dust curled up into the sky. She felt the ground vibrate beneath her boots as the trover came alongside the supply shed and parked.

She'd expected a squad, but it was a single pair of feet that landed on the ground. She heard him coming, the footfalls barely discernible beneath the sound of a low wind blowing. The wind picked up thin sheets of dust and flung them southward, toward the distant red cliffs.

She shook the small canister she'd set on a knee-high stone at her firing position. Aside from the six bullets in her revolver, a dozen or so remained, the last of her supply. Lifting her arm with one smooth motion, she squinted down the barrel, looking down the sight at a targeting stone she'd set up forty yards distant. After so much careful shooting, her shoulder felt like jelly. She relaxed into her firing stance before squeezing the trigger, releasing her breath in time with the pull. The pinkish targeting stone split with a crack that echoed across the range. The compressed gravel ball in the center began to fall apart, dropping chunks of rock onto the ground beneath the stand. She could see the small circular hole where the bullet had penetrated. She hadn't hit dead-center, but very close.

The Word dangled heavy in her hand. A revolver was imprecise compared to a pulsar, yet there was no delay at the trigger. The recoil had been the hardest part to manage. Too often, it felt like the gun wanted to jump right out of her hand, as if it had ideas of its own.

Her tongue moved over her chapped lips, tasting salt.

She heard him coming, that familiar cadence, moving in time with a heartbeat she knew almost as well as her own. She'd had a lot of time to think since she'd left the city. She'd taken one careful shot after another, and after expunging every last bit of hope and fear from her breast she'd been left with the unadorned truth.

Alone, there was little she could do to bend the arc of her world toward justice. All that was left was to choose how she'd react.

Taking her time, she completed the rest of her shots, emptying the weapon and splitting several more stones. Flipping the barrel outward so she could prove it was harmless, she turned around.

Travis's brown eyes met hers. He wore the same expression he had on their first date, back when they'd both been leery of ruining their newfound friendship. His "I hope I don't fuck this up" smile.

"Hi," he said.

She bent down and started reloading the revolver. "Hey. Do you want to try? It's harder than it looks, but—"

"Will you come home? Please?"

She wasn't surprised that Marcus had sent the one person

who might convince her to stand down. And she could only imagine what lies Travis had been fed. She'd considered a thousand things that he might say, but somehow, his soft plea hadn't been one of them.

She holstered her gun and crossed her arms in front of her waist. "Oh, I think I'll stay out here. Maybe set up a homestead, learn how to farm." She'd meant to sound flippant and brave, like Kacey, but her voice wavered.

Travis shot her a tiny smirk and closed the distance between them. He was so close that she could see his exhalation fog his face shield before the system cleared it. The skin around his eyes was puffy and red. Had he been crying? For her?

Then maybe there was still a chance.

His hands grasped hers, squeezing gently through their gloves. "Are you okay?"

He sounded so worried, so *Travis*, that she closed her eyes against the flood of tears welling up. "I'm really not."

"Dad said we should wait you out. That you'd have to come inside eventually." He gently kicked the oxygen packs resting near her feet. "Did you raid the panic sheds?"

"Every one on the way here. You should file a report. Make sure they're put back before someone has an actual emergency."

"Lore, I—"

"How long have you known?"

"Come back with me. We can talk. You've got to be exhausted, and—"

"How long?" She forced him to look at her.

He shrugged. "Dad and I have been talking about stuff, for a while, I guess. He's been getting me ready to help him run things. He wants us all to work together, to keep Epiphany safe."

"And you're okay with all this?" She tried to keep her voice light and this time she succeeded.

"Honestly? Not entirely. But I guess I can see the wisdom in it. It's our job to remove threats. To keep people safe."

Of course Marcus had played that angle! Hell, he probably viewed himself as the hero of the piece. "But Darren didn't kill Amparo," Loretta said gently, looking down at their clasped hands. "She was killed because she learned about Zeta. The council killed her to keep their secret."

Travis didn't flinch. She caught his flash of unease. Those guilty eyes.

He knew.

She dropped his hands and stepped back. He pursued her, gripping her upper arms. His mouth twisted.

"Sometimes, the strong need to do terrible things to protect the weak. Not because we want to. Not because it's right. But because it's what keeps civilization together."

Her chest burned like a gasoline fire. "You don't actually believe that."

"I do."

"Marcus—"

"He believes in you, you know. Even after all the trouble you caused. He says you're a warrior. And we need warriors just like we need ombuds. Won't you come home? Please? Let's get a good nights' sleep. In the morning, we'll talk. My dad will explain everything."

He shot her a small smile. His hands released her, sliding down her arms, grasping her hands once more. His brown eyes, flecked with gold, held the promise of what she wanted. A warm bed. Rest. If she'd just look at things in the correct way, she could set her burdens down.

What a relief that would be.

Loretta's eyes welled up and fiery tears spilled down her cheeks. When had Travis lost his way? The man she'd loved was already gone, wasn't he? He'd been chipped away at, eroded, transformed into something else.

And she hadn't even noticed.

"I'm so sorry, Trav."

"It's going to be okay." The relief in his voice made it clear that he'd misunderstood.

He thought he'd won her over.

If only gravity could pull her down, through the planet's crust and into what remained of that ancient, molten core. There, she could dissolve, casting aside this grief, this horror, the cruel tearing of her love for him being ripped out of her body.

Oh, Travis...

Forcing herself to stand still, refusing the impulse that demanded that she shove him away, that she scream and beg, she resolved to speak calmly, as she'd been taught to do when dealing with dangerous people.

"You misunderstand. Your father is a murderer. Even if he didn't pull the trigger himself, that's what he's chosen to become, to get what he wants. And if you believe that's okay..." She swallowed.

"It's not like that. My duty has to be to—"

Her tenuous calm shattered like glass. "Your duty is to what? To shitting on every principle we claim to uphold? You can't have it both ways, Trav. You can't build an enlightened society on a system of violence in the darkness." She advanced on him, pressing her advantage, feeling satisfaction at his wide-eyed surprise, at the way she'd shaken his confidence. "Wrap this shit sandwich in any sophistry you want, and it will *still* taste like shit. You know better than this!"

"But you haven't even heard our side! What happened to Dr. Phan is terrible. I know! But if Free Mars takes hold of Epiphany..."

He'd flinched when he'd said the doctor's name, and that gave her a slender thread of hope to grasp. He knew, in his heart, that what his father had done was wrong, but so far, he'd chosen not to face it. If she could help him remember who he was...

She placed a gloved hand along the curve of his face shield. Sol, he looked exhausted! Every bit as soul-weary as she herself felt.

"You're an honorable man, Travis. And I know how persuasive Marcus can be. Hell, he had me right where he wanted me, right up until the last minute! But you know this is wrong." She tapped his chest. "In here. You *have* to know. Truth is truth. We cannot look away! Stand with me. Please. Help me end this. Without bloodshed. We still have a chance. If we work together..."

Travis's heart sank as Loretta argued her case. She was furious. Heartbroken. Desperate to make him understand. Did she truly believe he hadn't wrestled with this? That he hadn't had his own dark night of the soul? His father had said it would be pointless to argue with Loretta while she was angry, and he'd been right.

"Dad shouldn't have brought you into this. This never should have been your burden."

Her eyes flashed. "Don't patronize me."

"We're not monsters, Lore! The council has done a lot of good. We can show you. And it's not like we go out of our way to hurt people."

"Sure, you just throw them in a hole in the ground and tell everyone they left voluntarily."

"Some do! Like Kacey and Theo. Everyone wanted to arrest them after that stunt you two pulled today." He saw the fear in her eyes, the sudden apprehension. "But I know how important she is to you, so we let her go."

It should have made her happy, or at least bought him the tiniest bit of grace, but instead, she looked utterly disgusted.

"You let Kacey leave because she's important to me? That's not justice! That's you doing me a favor because *you* happen to hold all the power. You're not a king, Travis, and neither is your father."

That wasn't what he'd meant, and she knew it.

"Think what you want, but believe it or not, it wasn't all about you and me. We're well aware that Kacey's been smuggling people off-world. But why would we force them to stay when it's better for everyone if they leave voluntarily? Maybe if Amparo and Darren had left instead of—"

"Stop." Loretta's expression hardened. She looked away. "Just... stop. You've made your choice, and I've made mine."

"Loretta—"

"No. My answer, is no. Forever."

She still had that ridiculous killing machine on her thigh. When she caught him looking at it, she burst out laughing. Not her usual rollicking, joyful laugh, but a brittle, furious sound that fuzzed the edges of her com signal.

"After everything I just said. Given all that you meant to me. You think I'd murder you in cold blood?"

She unholstered the gun and flung it at him. It landed on the ground in a puff of dust. "Leave me alone, Travis. I'm going to watch the sunset, and then you can do... whatever it is you came for. I'm not going to fight you."

She strode away, shutting off her com.

In cold blood. He'd used those same words to describe

Gharison's choice, back when he'd first learned of the hellish sacrifice that had saved Epiphany from ruin. His father had accused him of being hyperbolic, but later, he'd realized that the phrase had simply been... imprecise.

Gharison couldn't have killed the Richardsons in cold blood because he'd loved them, right up until the end. His journals made that much clear. He'd made his choice knowing that it would tear his heart in two even as he saved the colony from destruction.

Loretta was incapable of destroying Epiphany. Despite her convictions, and her passion, she was only one woman. The council's plan would move forward, and in the years to come, their civilization would thrive.

His father believed Loretta would eventually come around. But Travis knew her as only someone who'd been in love with her could. Her gifts and her faults formed the immutable essence of who she truly was, and there was no happy ending coming. He and his father could spend the rest of their lives trying to persuade Loretta that their way was virtuous, but it wouldn't matter. Either her heart would break in the act of submission and she'd become a shadow of the person she'd once been, or she'd waste the rest of her days locked away at Zeta, fighting an unwinnable battle, growing more desperate and bitter by the day.

He picked up her revolver and tipped the barrel out just like she'd shown him in her bedroom. He shook the small shiny bullets into his gloved hand until five rested in his palm. Honoring her wish for silence, he spent a half hour cleaning up the mess she'd left. The broken targeting stones he collected and put into a pile for later reclaiming. He collected the pilfered oxygen packs and stowed them in the trover. The bullets, he buried in the ground.

It would be wrong to put his beloved in a cage. To

separate her from the world she loved so much. She'd never leave Mars under her own power, he'd seen that much during her argument with Kacey in the shuttle bay, before he'd let that wretched little ship go.

He'd done that for her.

Just like he was doing this for her.

She sat on a boulder, looking out toward the distant cliffs. The last of Sol's rays framed her body in light, and for a moment, she shone. Heart pounding in his chest, he stepped alongside her and watched the tiny orb sink beneath the distant horizon.

He saw the soft curve of her reddish-brown braid through the side of her helmet. His fingers remembered the smooth skin of her cheek, the way her eyelashes brushed against his when they'd first kissed. He'd never forget the way she'd made him feel, how in the light of her eyes, he became the only person in the universe that mattered.

"Lore?" He touched her shoulder as he stepped closer, already pulling back the hammer.

At this distance, he couldn't miss.

CHAPTER TWENTY-NINE

Loretta's final day was drawing to a close. Even before Sol sank beneath the horizon, her bluish light glowed luminous above the distant cliffs.

If this was the last sunset she'd ever see, she was going to memorize every detail. The way the light seemed to brighten just before it dimmed at twilight. How the soft-edged hills looked darker and more foreboding as shadows settled into every crevice and curve. There would always be sunsets here, even if she wasn't here to see them.

And even when Sol was gone, after the entire system had blown away in the wake of supernovic progression, there would be other worlds, vistas that humanity had yet to see. Kacey was up there, right now, flying toward the unknown.

There's a whole damn universe out there, Lore! And people too. Real human beings trying to make things better for everyone.

She smiled at the memory. There were indeed people like Kacey and Theo, putting themselves on the line for strangers and friends. And hadn't she tried to make things better too? Even if she'd failed, that mattered. Just like her parents had mattered. And Darren. Amparo. Travis was getting it all wrong, but in his own way, even he was trying.

What does it say about me, that I can't even bring myself to hate him?

Travis must have finished his dithering, because he was walking up to her now. When he spoke her name, he sounded so full of regret, she knew it was time to leave.

It was a mistake to search for his eyes, to seek the meaning they held, the shape of his innermost thoughts. By the time she registered that he was aiming straight for her heart it was too late to move. The Word jumped in his gloved hand and screamed.

An iron fist punched her, hard, right in the belly. She grunted as she flew back, toppling off her stone seat, landing flat on her back. After a stunned moment of silence during which she only saw the darkening sky, pain radiated outward from her wound like slashes from knived fingers. She cried out. Her gloved hand came up, stained with dark blood.

Sol. It *hurt!*

She forced a breath. Her lungs still worked, although every movement hurt and her body felt strange. It was as if all her abdominal muscles had been yanked to one side. Her strength was gone. She tried to roll and failed, her arms scrabbling around for The Word. If she got her hands on it...

WARNING. WARNING. LIFE SUPPORT SYSTEM DAMAGED.

Travis stepped into view, looking down at her. He still had the gun in his hand and his face was pale. "I'm sorry. I couldn't—"

"I'm going to tear you in half." That wasn't what she'd intended to say, but it's what came rushing out of her mouth. Revenge was of far less concern than putting pressure on the hole he'd torn through her body or figuring out how much air she had. Yet somehow, vengeance bubbled right up to top of her priority list.

Getting gutshot had that effect.

Travis held up The Word and showed her the empty chambers before dropping it on the ground in the dirt next to her. "We'll tell everyone it was an accident. No one will ever know you lost your way. You'll be remembered as a hero. A true daughter of Mars. I swear it."

WARNING. WARNING. LIFE SUPPORT SYSTEM DAMAGED.

Her hab suit was spitting air. Already, the oxygen supply dials were moving from green to orange. It wasn't the helmet seal. The bullet must have torn through the tubing. Either that or the oxygen pack itself was damaged. Whimpering at the pain, she felt behind herself. The bullet must have exited her body and blown straight through, because the back of her suit was partially shredded. With sticky fingers coated in dirt, she found both ends of the oxygen tube.

Thank Sol. She reached into her deep side pocket for the patch kit. Rolling on her belly, she almost passed out. Travis had already turned away, too weak to watch what he'd wrought. The bastard was walking back to the trover, sniffling.

That pussy-ass bitch. Weeping and wailing his way back home to daddy as if he didn't leave me here on the ground to bleed out. When I get up, I'm going to...

BLOOD PRESSURE FALLING. MEDICAL DISPATCH REQUESTED. ETA
FORTY-TWO MINUTES.

"Coward," she whispered. "You couldn't even..." Fury sharpened her senses, made it easier to focus, but she needed to save her air. The dials had gone from orange to red, and she'd never seen that before. With effort, she unwrapped the sticky patch from her kit and stuck it lightly to her outer pinkie. She pinched the tubing ends together behind her back, holding them tightly as she wrapped the patch around them.

Please, let this work.

A chime sounded! One of the blinking lights in her helmet feed went solid.

LOW OXYGEN WARNING. FOUR MINUTES OF LIFE SUPPORT REMAINING. LOW OXYGEN WARNING. THREE MINUTES OF—

BLOOD PRESSURE FALLING. MEDICAL DISPATCH REQUESTED. ETA FORTY MINUTES.

Travis knew she wouldn't last that long. And as for why he'd turned his back on her, well, that's because he was a moron. She forced herself up on her hands and knees, panting with the effort. Her middle felt wet and hot and cold at the same time. With a grunt she reached for The Word. In her breast pocket, she felt for the antique bullet she'd tucked away. Her grandmother Helen's bullet, the one her family had kept safe all these years. A memento of a peacekeeper fighting a different war.

She slipped it into the chamber with trembling hands and closed the barrel. It took every bit of strength she could muster to stagger to her feet, to shove aside the blackness that threatened to overwhelm her, to drag her into oblivion. Pushing every bit of rage and grief she'd been holding down through her muscles, into her legs, she stepped forward. She pushed hard, forcing her legs to run, ignoring the numbness spreading through her limbs. Travis's lumbering form was closer now, and he must have turned off his audio because he didn't turn. The spare oxygen packs she'd laid out earlier were nowhere in sight. That left only one option. She'd be damned before she'd die out here, gasping like a fish. Her arm raised. Her eye narrowed. She felt the silver line of truth that ran from her heart, down her arm, and right into her trigger finger.

She fired.

He dropped to the ground like a stone.

Collapsing almost on top of his prone body, she fought unconsciousness with tooth and nail. She rolled him over, saw the last traces of sense flickering in his eyes. A bloody red rose had opened up on the front of his hab suit, right over his heart.

"You..." Travis murmured weakly.

LOW OXYGEN WARNING. ZERO MINUTES OF LIFE SUPPORT REMAINING. LOW OXYGEN WARNING. ZERO MINUTES OF—

I would have fought for you, she thought. *I would have taken on the world at your side. But you threw it all away.*

Her lungs screamed for air.

Opening both their face shields simultaneously, she bent down and put her mouth over his in a final kiss. Pressing down, pinching his nose, she drew every last bit of oxygen from his lungs into hers. Slamming her shield shut against the cold, she reached for his oxygen pack, unclipped it, and snapped it into her secondary port.

Precious air hissed into her helmet. She gulped it down, feeling sensation return to her limbs. Weeping, she stood, heading for the trover...

Her legs collapsed before she'd made it a single step. She struggled, but there was no strength left in her body. Her abdomen felt slick with blood. The trover! The trover was...

BLOOD PRESSURE CRITICAL. MEDICAL DISPATCH REQUESTED. ETA THIRTY-FOUR MINUTES.

The trover was too far away.

She managed to roll onto her back. Above, the sky had gone dark. Constellations bloomed. Something glimmered gold in the corner of her eye. A meteor?

Dust blew across her helmet, hazing her view.

Have you ever felt the wind in your hair, Lore? Do you even know what that means?

Kacey was right. There was so much she didn't understand. But she needed to. She wanted to feel the wind, even just once.

Her arms felt like heavy iron bars as she reached for her helmet seal. With a press of her fingers, she released it. Air hissed out into the thin atmosphere as she pushed the helmet away.

She closed her eyes against the bitter cold. A slow, soft breath flowed out from her lungs. The Martian wind blew over her face, swift and strong; it carried her to the red rock cliffs standing guard on the horizon.

CHAPTER THIRTY

For a long time, she floated. There was no name for the black wind that carried her along from star to star, but she knew it had lifted her off the hard ground, that it had wept, whispering her name. Later had come a deeper dark and a longer drifting, this time closer to the surface, where she heard animals chittering and soft voices and the deep caw of a raven. When Loretta finally woke, she felt a sharp pain in the deep crook of her right elbow. She reached for the thing that had bitten her, to tear away whatever creature had sunk its teeth into her tender flesh, only her arms wouldn't move.

Everything hurt. Her body felt like it had been tumble dried on high and driven over a few times by a trover.

A body? *Her body.* She had one of those.

When she remembered who she was, her eyes opened. "Travis! I need to—"

She felt a big hand pressing down gently on her shoulder, holding her onto the bed. A hulking shadow shifted at her side, like a monster in the semi dark. The thing's shoulders were enormous, almost like a forklift come to life. She'd been dreaming that she died and perhaps she was dreaming still.

It had to be.

She blinked up at the high ceiling. Dark metal formed a shadowy box in which she was held prisoner, held down against her will. She wiggled her toes. They felt real. So did the padded bed, and the soft pillow beneath her head.

She saw hands. Big, meaty-looking hands with nimble fingers dancing at her bedside like they were trying to tell a story. Her head felt like it was stuffed with cotton wool, but those shapes almost made sense. His blond hair, she dimly recognized. That smile was too big to ignore, much like the man himself.

Theo. Not a monster at all, just an unreasonably large man sitting guard at the side of her bed.

She spoke his name.

He kept signing something. A word she knew, over and over.

Safe, he signed. *Safe.*

It took her a while to shake off whatever sedative they'd pumped into the IV in her arm. Her belly felt numb. Too numb! Like it wasn't there at all. She wiggled her toes again and felt relieved that they still worked. Theo released her left arm from the strap holding it down, but every motion felt strange, as if her entire body were lightheaded. Her hand went down and felt the blanket covering her body. Her mother's blanket. The one she'd kept in her closet.

"Did... Did I die?"

His reproachful look seemed to say that yes, she had either died or come very close to it.

"Travis? Is he..."

Theo shook his head. *Sorry*, he signed.

Only she'd known that, before she'd forgotten. When she'd taken aim, she hadn't missed. She touched her face, and the skin felt tight, not raw. The wound in her belly was well-wrapped and not leaking. She felt like she'd been asleep for a very long time.

Travis was dead.

"How long?" she croaked.

Theo held up eight fingers.

She struggled to sit up, but it wasn't happening. Not with all the straps crisscrossing the bed. "What happened to Epiphany? Did the feeds report what we found? Did they—"

Theo held up a finger, then inclined his head toward the doorway. Chilly air pricked at her free arm, and an off-brand MedStar knockoff unit beeped cheerfully next to the bed. Was she in a hospital? Her eyes widened when she noticed that someone had pinned the tail of her braid to her shirt. Small bits of Theo's short hair were... floating! Her arm didn't seem to want to stay put where it belonged.

"This is zero gee?"

Before Theo could answer, Kacey's voice boomed through the closed door.

"I told you; we're giving up the contract. Tell Jakob he can have the gig; we've got all the paperwork ready. We'll just take our regular finder's fee."

"No!" The woman who answered sounded ready to go to war. "Do you realize how hard it was to get that job? Without it, we won't be able to refuel or restock. And thanks to your stray kitten in there, it's not like we'll be welcome at any port with—"

Something thumped against a wall. Possibly a body. "This isn't a negotiation. Tell Jakob—"

"Just because you're our pilot it doesn't mean that—"

"It's just money. We can always find more. Loretta is—"

"She's an arbiter. A fucking bootlicker. And you expect us to—"

"I expect you to do the job I hired you for."

"I did. That's the problem."

Kacey wasn't having it. "Have you ever lost your entire planet, asswipe? Not just your family, and your friends, and your job, but your whole fucking world? Can you even appreciate what that means?"

This time, there was no reply.

"Loretta stays. We're turning down the coms job. If you don't like that, well... I don't much care. You can hitch a ride back to that crappy Boba shop where I found you."

The door slid open and Kacey came through, her heavy boots clomping against the floor, her pink mohawk styled into stiff, triangular spikes. "Can you believe her? What a—" Her face lit up at the sight of them. "Lore! You're awake! Are you okay? That's a stupid question. Are you in any pain? Theo, why is she still tied down?"

"Where are we?"

"You're on *The Matriarch*." Kacey rubbed her hand along the patchy gray wall like she was stroking a kitten.

Now that Theo had turned the lights up, Loretta saw how enormous the room was. They could have fit ten bunks inside, easy.

"What happened to *Poppy*?"

"Oh, she's in the shuttle bay down below."

"And *The Matriarch* is..."

"She's our home. You didn't think we actually live in that little shuttle, did you? There's a lot that I need to explain, but it can wait until you're feeling better."

"You rescued me?"

"Duh. As soon as we got our people transferred I came back to pick you up. Theo slapped a tracker on your gun, just in case."

Loretta glanced at Theo. He seemed enormously pleased with himself.

"We had a run in with one of the Harbormaster's ships," Kacey continued, "but thankfully they're as slow as they are stupid. But we were damn lucky I had a friend in orbit who owed me a favor. Their ship has a full med bay, but even then, it was touch and go. I'm..." Her lips compressed. "I'm so sorry about Travis. I didn't see much, but.,.."

Grief swelled, hot and acidic, a wave that might drown her if she turned toward it. "I'm not ready... I can't."

"We get it. Oh! Before I forget, Theo picked up your crate, like you asked, but he also grabbed your mail before we left. And we found something interesting."

Kacey retrieved a small box from the locker near the door. The container was about the size of four shoeboxes and marked as biological material. Notations on the side showed that it had been delivered to the wrong address, then rerouted.

Loretta opened the box. Inside she found a twelve pack of potato seedlings, carefully packaged. This wasn't an expensive temperature-controlled box like those used in the lab, but a much simpler model, the kind used to transport low-value plants to nurseries and habitats. But she recognized the six-digit experiment code printed on the seedling pack.

She ran her finger along the delicate green leaves. *Hardy as fuck*, Henry McCormack had called them. And he'd been right, because the plants didn't look any worse for wear despite their long journey.

"*Solanum Amparos*," she murmured, handing the box to Theo. "In the right hands, these seedlings could be worth as much as this ship. We should take good care of them."

"There was a data chip buried in the soil," Kacey said. "It's a video file, with your name on it." She tapped it against her tablet, scooted her way onto the bed, and propped the screen on her lap where they could all see it.

The vid was low quality, probably taken on a handheld tablet. At first, it only showed a couch and a worktable, an impromptu office set up in a darkened living room lit by a single lamp. A woman with a pleasantly round face sat in front of the camera, stroking her black hair nervously. She seemed determined. Focused.

"My name is Amparo Phan, and I'm the director of food sciences. When the council asked me to speak on the importance of scientific discovery for Epiphany's centennial celebration, I felt honored to be part of this important event. We all know that Epiphany wouldn't exist without the courage and hard work of all those who came before us. Today, I need you to find your own courage. To stand with me, and others, as we hold fast to the promise we've made to one another.

"Recently, during an expedition to the Lyot Crater basin to gather soil samples, I saw a man outside, running for his life. He was being chased by three members of the harbor crew, and they carried weapons I'd never seen before. While I watched, they shot and killed him."

Amparo took a deep breath.

"When I reported what I'd seen to the authorities, three different ombuds tried to convince me I'd misunderstood. But after speaking to my colleagues, and in exploring historical records for that area, I found something shocking. A secret detention facility, developed and run outside the law, authorized by the Council itself. Since then, I've discovered..."

Loretta felt Kacey's head rest against her shoulder. Theo's hand cupped her knee. They watched until the end.

Kacey picked up the data chip. "She was going to go public during the centennial celebration. During her speech. While the whole planet was watching."

B-R-A-V-E, Theo signed.

Loretta's heart hurt. "Yeah. She was." She took a deep breath. "Kacey—"

"Epiphany renewed the charter," Kacey said, her words tumbling out in a rush. "Seventy-two percent voted in favor. Marcus is blaming you for Travis's death."

It was hard to argue with that.

"He says that you and Darren conspired to kidnap Travis. That you planned to hold him hostage, to force cancellation of the charter. Just another Free Mars conspiracy."

"Do people believe him?"

"I don't know. But two days ago, the council put a bounty on your head. The largest in Martian history. You understand what that means, right? You can't go back; not right now."

Kacey was too kind to say the rest of it. After what she'd done to Travis, she'd never be able to return to Epiphany. Not now. Not ever. If she tried, she'd be condemning anyone who helped her.

Marcus had won.

She looked down at her hands. Turned them over to see the faint lines etched in her palms. They spread out like the delicate veins inside a leaf. Like roads on a map that led nowhere.

Kacey exchanged an unreadable look with Theo. She tapped her tablet and a panel slid up one wall, revealing a window the size of two dinner trays. Beyond it, the vast darkness of space seemed to swallow everything. There were no planets in view. Only a handful of stars.

"We're running," Loretta said. "Because of me."

"Don't think of it like that. It's just, so long as you're figuring out your next move, you may as well fly with us for a while."

"I cost you your job."

Kacey scoffed. "Com beacons? Let's face it. The money sounded good, but we would have been bored out of our minds. I've got a lead on something way more exciting. Word is there's a bunch of colonists looking for a ride to the Selven Beta system. It's a long haul, and we can't take the most direct route, so it may get interesting. We could use extra security in case anyone gets shifty. Are you up for that?"

Loretta nodded. It was the least she could do, to repay them for saving her life. Hell, they'd burned every last bridge they'd had in helping her learn the truth.

For all the good it had done.

Kacey held up the data chip. "I'll send this through all channels we have access to. Who knows? Maybe someone will—"

"Don't." Loretta held out her hand for the chip. Her fingers closed around it when Kacey dropped it into her palm. "I'm done getting people killed."

Theo winced.

"Lore—" Kacey began.

The pity in their eyes was too much to bear. She turned over in bed, facing the wall. When the flood came, Theo pulled the blanket higher, draping it over her shoulders. He turned off the light and settled back into his chair.

A door slid open behind her. "No one's alone on this ship," Kacey said softly.

Outside the window, the stars burned cold.

LORETTA AND HER FRIENDS WILL RETURN IN THE HARD WAY HOME

A NOTE FROM CHERI

Thanks for reading *Outlaw Justice.* I hope you had fun with it! I'm so pleased that you've met Loretta, Kacey, and Theo, and I'm looking forward to seeing where their story takes us.

My heartfelt thanks go to you, for reading my books, and to my friends and family for their support. My husband Patrick helped me develop the character of Marcus Wells and untangle the complexities of Martian politics, and the hardworking scribblers at the South Seattle Writers Group cheered me on from the very first chapter. And thanks to my talented beta readers, many of my author mistakes were shoved in an airlock and spaced well before this book landed in your hand. I'm grateful to Miraz Jordan, Beverly Roland, Ezra Wu, Alex Washoe, and Nicholas Marriott for their help preparing this book for publication.

PS: If you leave a review for Outlaw Justice you'll make an author (me) very happy. Thank you!

Let's Stay in Touch

Sign up for my list to receive a free starter library. Visit **cheribaker.com** to get started.

More from this Series

For a complete list of books in The First Guardian series, check out **books.cheribaker.com/Guardian**

FIND YOUR NEXT SERIES

Do you love snarky sleuths, office mysteries, and workplace drama? You'll enjoy the **Kat Voyzey Mysteries**.

If you prefer cozy mysteries that celebrate friendship and fun, check out the **Butterfly Island Mysteries**.

Ready for a vacation in your imagination? Set sail for cozy crime with the **Ellie Tappet Mysteries**.

How about a world of corporate espionage and betrayal? Meet Jessica Warne in the **Emerald City Spies Trilogy**.

Excited for more Space Opera? See what's available and what's coming next to **The First Guardian Series**.

MORE FROM CHERI BAKER

The Kat Voyzey Mysteries

Involuntary Turnover
Orientation to Murder
Death by Team Building
Cutting the Track

The Ellie Tappet Cruise Ship Mysteries

The Case of the Missing Finger
The Case of the Karaoke Killer
The Case of the Floating Funeral
The Case of the Lady in the Luggage
The Case of the Red Phantom
The Case of the Fond Farewell

Emerald City Spies

The Assistant
Power Play
Hostile Takeover

The Butterfly Island Mysteries

A View to Die For
Death at Dagger Cove
Shadow of a Doubt

The First Guardian

Outlaw Justice
The Hard Way Home

ABOUT THE AUTHOR

Hey there. My name is Cheri, and I'm a writer from Seattle, Washington.

I've been a book lover my entire life, and for many years writing was my hobby, something I did on the weekends or in the early morning before work. My first novel, *Involuntary Turnover*, was loosely based on my experiences working in human resources. Not the murder part; just the setting! It took me ten years to write my first two novels, working around the demands of a busy job, but eventually I traded my business suits for jeans and began writing full time. Now, I'm lucky enough to have wonderful readers all around the globe.

When I'm not writing I spend my time reading, hanging out with my husband, watching terrible monster movies, drinking coffee, having movie nights with friends, playing Dungeons and Dragons, walking through the city, and thinking up twisty murder plots. Rainy weather makes me happy, and so does the fact that you read one of my books! Thanks so much for supporting my work.